Bonus Novella!
For your enjoyment, we've added in this vo
Fanning the Flames, a Girls' Night Out story by Vi

Praise for the novels of *USA TODAY*
bestselling author

VICTORIA DAHL

"Wonderfully unconventional and deliciously sultry...among
[Dahl's] hottest to date."
—RT Book Reviews on *Looking for Trouble*

"Dahl brings her signature potent blend of heated eroticism
and emotional punch to another Jackson Hole cowboy story, to
great success."
—Kirkus Reviews on *So Tough to Tame*

"*So Tough to Tame* was a delicious, funny, warm-hearted read...
Obviously I highly recommend this book. It's like a comfort
read with a dose of sass and smarts; it's just about perfect."
—Smart Bitches, Trashy Books

"Dahl adds her signature hot sex scenes and quirky characters
to this lively mix of romance in the high country."
—Booklist on *Too Hot to Handle*

"Victoria Dahl never fails to bring the heat."
ws on *Too Hot to Handle*

"H   omance star Dahl
de   romance."
                                      Close Enough to Touch

"T   ws* on *Good Girls Don't*

"A l   out a woman many of us can relate
to."
—Salon.com on *Crazy for Love*

"[A] hands-down winner, a sensual story filled with memorable
characters."

"Sassy an
joyride of

Also available from
Victoria Dahl
and HQN Books

Jackson: Girls' Night Out series
Looking for Trouble
Fanning the Flames (ebook)

Jackson series
So Tough to Tame
Too Hot to Handle
"Too Fast to Fall" (*Be Mine* anthology)
Strong Enough to Love (ebook)
Close Enough to Touch

Donovan Brothers Brewery series
Real Men Will
Bad Boys Do
Good Girls Don't
"Just One Taste" (*The Guy Next Door* anthology)

Tumble Creek series
The Wicked West (ebook)
Lead Me On
Start Me Up
Talk Me Down

Crazy for Love
"Midnight Assignment" (*Midnight Kiss* anthology)

VICTORIA DAHL

FLIRTING
WITH
DISASTER
&
FANNING
THE
FLAMES

HQN™

Recycling programs for this product may not exist in your area.

ISBN-13: 978-0-373-77911-6

Flirting with Disaster
Copyright © 2015 by Victoria Dahl

Fanning the Flames
Copyright © 2014 by Victoria Dahl

All rights reserved. Except for use in any review, the reproduction or utilization of this work in whole or in part in any form by any electronic, mechanical or other means, now known or hereinafter invented, including xerography, photocopying and recording, or in any information storage or retrieval system, is forbidden without the written permission of the publisher, HQN Books, 225 Duncan Mill Road, Don Mills, Ontario M3B 3K9, Canada.

This is a work of fiction. Names, characters, places and incidents are either the product of the author's imagination or are used fictitiously, and any resemblance to actual persons, living or dead, business establishments, events or locales is entirely coincidental.

This edition published by arrangement with Harlequin Books S.A.

For questions and comments about the quality of this book, please contact us at CustomerService@Harlequin.com.

® and ™ are trademarks of Harlequin Enterprises Limited or its corporate affiliates. Trademarks indicated with ® are registered in the United States Patent and Trademark Office, the Canadian Intellectual Property Office and in other countries.

www.HQNBooks.com

Printed in U.S.A.

CONTENTS

This book is for everyone who's had to start over.

FLIRTING
WITH
DISASTER

CHAPTER ONE

Isabelle West edged her SUV up the steep driveway and winced as she heard a grocery bag tip over. She tried to identify the dull rolling sound that followed. Probably the cantaloupe. But maybe just a can of soup. It'd be a little surprise for her when she opened the hatch and saw what sprang out and tumbled through the snow toward the trees.

She was getting tired of that particular surprise and promised herself she'd order the cargo net as soon as she got inside. She'd been meaning to do it for…maybe two years now. But today she'd remember. She was trying to teach herself to be proactive. Or at least to manage the small things that every other adult seemed to have no problem with.

As she rounded the last curve of the drive and spied her little cabin, she wrinkled her nose. Not because of the cabin. She loved that. It was perfect for her in every way with its dark log walls and big windows and front porch. What made her wince was the sight of the manual garage door past the haze of snow sifting from the sky, a reminder that she'd also been meaning to call about getting a garage-door opener installed. That one had been on her mental to-do list for at least four years. Definitely not five.

"I'll do that, too," she said to herself as she pulled close to the garage door and tugged up the hood of her coat. "As a matter of fact…" She dug her phone from her pocket and held down the button. "Phone, remind me to order a cargo net and call a garage guy."

The phone beeped and said, "I'm sorry—I didn't catch that."

Gritting her teeth, Isabelle hit the button again. "Remind me to buy a cargo net and call the garage guy."

"I'm sorry—did you need me to find a mechanic?"

"Fuck you," Isabelle growled. She ducked out of her car, thankful that the giant, wet flakes of this morning had given way to the dry Wyoming snow she was more used to. The snow sounded like sand as it bounced off her jacket and slid to the ground.

She wrenched up the garage door and got back to her car without getting wet at all. But she couldn't say the same about her cantaloupe. As soon as she opened the gate of her SUV, it rolled past her outstretched hand and straight into a snowbank.

"Fuck you, too," she said to the cantaloupe, then felt immediately guilty. It took her only a minute to rescue the melon and dust off as much snow as she could. It hadn't really caused that much trouble. It took a lot more time to repack the bag that had tipped over and haul it inside.

Next time, she'd remember to put the boxes of art supplies she'd picked up from the post office into the back; then she'd have room to store the groceries on the floor of her backseat, where they'd be less likely to—

"Art supplies!" she gasped and rushed back out to the truck to haul in the boxes of goodies.

She grinned as she set the first box on the kitchen table and slit the tape to reveal the treasures inside. She'd been out of yellow ocher for three days now, and even though she hadn't needed it, the lack had hovered at the back of her mind like a foreshadowing of tragedy to come. She snatched up the tube and breathed a sigh of relief. Disaster averted. She was whole again.

After unpacking the box and carefully laying out each precious item on the kitchen table, she retrieved the other two boxes from the backseat and went through the same routine. She beamed at the sight of the bounty spread over the table. Seven more tubes of color, a new studio light to get her through the winter, a dozen pre-stretched canvases and her favorite brush conditioner that smelled like something close to sandalwood. It made the task of looking after her brushes almost soothing. Discovering it last year had been a treat.

Satisfied with her unveiling of the goods, she made five trips to the room she used as her studio, shelving the paints she didn't need yet and getting the new lamp set up at her current workstation. She played with the LED settings for a while, still dubious about the idea that she could get good color temperatures, but the settings seemed sufficient. Nice, even.

"Hmm." Isabelle crossed her arms and stared at the unfinished painting, trying to decide if the daylight setting was pure enough. There weren't new technological advancements in the world of oil painting very often, so she'd be happy if she could get excited about this one. Still, she'd have to work under the light for a couple of hours and see how it felt.

During the summer, she wouldn't need it much at all. This room was meant to be the great room of the cabin, and windows climbed up the two-story wall to the peak of the roof. The windows faced south, and during the summer, she had good light here for nearly twelve hours of every day. But during the winter, there were only a few decent hours of sunlight, and that was assuming the sky was clear.

As a matter of fact… She glanced out, hoping to spot an approaching break in the clouds, but it was solid white out there. A good time to try the lamp, then. It was almost two, so she should force herself to grab lunch first, but then she'd have hours to work.

Her thoughts were interrupted by the heavy slide of fur against her ankle. "Hey, Bear," she said to the cat, surprised by his affection. He was an ornery twenty-pound stray who'd wandered into her cabin three years before, and he didn't cuddle often.

He meowed loudly for attention, but when she leaned down to scratch his chin, he sidestepped and eyed her scornfully. "I suppose you just want food?" she asked. She'd run out of wet food yesterday, which was why—

"The groceries!" she gasped, but her heart barely managed a quick leap before she calmed it down. The bags in the SUV were fine. It was cold enough that she could leave them overnight and not lose anything. Except bananas, maybe. Those weren't as hardy as people thought, not in the cold. If it were summer, though… Yeah. She'd lost hundreds of dollars of food that way over the years. But this time the only bag in danger was the one on her kitchen counter.

She rushed to the kitchen and unpacked that bag, happy to find that, aside from that damp cantaloupe, everything else was perfect. She shoved a frozen meal into the microwave, opened a can of food for Bear and went to haul in the rest of the bags. Half an hour later, she was organized, full of chicken piccata and happily planted in front of her canvas, adding a glistening highlight to a long stretch of a man's triceps.

Glancing from the canvas to a spread of photos hung

on a board next to it, she nodded. "Perfect." Her eyes swept down the triceps muscle to the hard knot of elbow beneath it. What a beautiful line.

Her attention twitched for a moment, and Isabelle glared at the gleam of the light on wet paint, but then she shook off the random irritation and dipped her brush in white again. Just the tiniest drag of paint, just—

Her hand jerked, nearly touching the canvas before she pulled back. "What the hell?" she snapped as she finally registered that a sound had interrupted her. A loud sound. The staccato knock of some stranger come to screw up her workday.

She wanted to ignore it. It definitely wasn't Jill, her neighbor and the only person who dropped by unannounced. Jill didn't knock like that. She rarely knocked at all, because she knew Isabelle wouldn't hear it. But it could be one of Isabelle's other friends. Lauren. Or maybe even Sophie, who was supposed to be back in town soon.

Had Isabelle forgotten another meetup? It was possible. She vaguely remembered Lauren mentioning something about a new girl they might be able to bring into their little group of friends since Sophie was usually on the road these days.

Isabelle set down the brush, wiped her hands on a rag and decided she'd have to answer the door, just in case.

Whoever it was knocked one more time, just as Isabelle reached for the door. She yanked it open, ready to apologize to Lauren, but it wasn't Lauren. Or Sophie. Or any other girlfriend. It was a man, taller than she was, snow dusting his short, dark hair and drifting in on the breeze as she frowned.

"Sorry to disturb you, Ms....?"

Really? He was going to start this off by asking for

her name? "Yes?" she responded, tempted to close the door on his face and march right back to her studio. Whatever he was selling, she didn't want it.

His gaze sharpened a bit, but his chin dipped in acknowledgment, and he reached into the pocket of the nondescript navy blue parka he wore. "I'm Deputy US Marshal Tom Duncan."

Her hand tightened on the doorknob, and something went wrong with her ears. His lips kept moving, but she couldn't hear the words. Then he paused, watching her as if waiting for a response.

Isabelle cleared her throat, hoping the noise would force her ears back into working condition. "I'm sorry," she said with more calm than she could believe. "I wasn't paying attention. Who are you?"

His brow tightened with irritation. "I'm Deputy Marshal Tom Duncan."

"I got that part," she bit out, her veins too flooded with fight-or-flight to keep her voice even now.

"I'm in the neighborhood as part of a protection detail, and—"

"This isn't a neighborhood," she interrupted, angry that he couldn't come up with a better excuse. Did he think she was an idiot?

"All right," he said carefully, his jaw clenching around the words. She'd made him mad. Good. She hoped he was cold, too. Because he was ruining more than her day. He was ruining something much larger than that.

He tried again. "I'm in the immediate area with a protection team, and I wanted to make contact with each of the residents. First—"

"What immediate area?" She glanced pointedly toward the one other house on her road, knowing damn well that Jill didn't need the sort of protection a US marshal provided. This was ridiculous. Why was he even pretending?

"Ma'am," he snapped, the word crisp with impatience. "We're on Judge Anthony Chandler's property. I understand that he may not live on your road, but his residence is only a half mile through those trees. I'm informing you and all of your neighbors in case you see anyone from the marshal service near your property or on the road. If you see anyone you don't recognize, please give me a call."

He held out a card, and Isabelle glanced at it. She didn't take it. "You want me to call you."

"Yes. If it's one of my people, I'll confirm that. However, if it's not one of my people, then it could be the fugitive who's threatened Judge Chandler's life." He held up a creased photo of an unremarkable-looking white man in his forties.

Isabelle finally took the card and examined it as she spoke. "Someone threatened Judge Chandler, so I should expect a team of marshals hanging around my property. That's what you're telling me?"

"Yes." His gaze drifted past her shoulder, looking into her house. "Are you the only one living here at this time?"

"That's not your concern."

His eyes snapped back to her. "It's very important for your safety and for ours that we be aware of any unusual activity. Trespassers, items missing from your home or property, even trash you might find on a trail. Have you seen anything unusual?"

Isabelle gave him a flat look. "Just you."

His jaw tightened again. It was a nice jaw. A nice face altogether, lean and angled and just starting to show his age around his eyes. Too bad he was a liar.

"The man who threatened the judge is a survivalist, the brother of Ephraim Stevenson, whose trial begins on Monday. I'm advising you to be aware. And please notify any other residents of your home to do the same."

She held his gaze for a long moment, trying to give nothing away while still conveying that she knew this story was bullshit. That he wasn't fooling her. That she wasn't scared.

But she was.

"Sure, Marshal," she finally said, forcing a patently pleasant smile. "I'm happy to cooperate with any reasonable law-enforcement requests. But I'd appreciate it if you stayed off my property. If I need your help, I'll let you know."

She stepped back and closed the door. Hard. The defiance dropped from her shoulders. She covered her eyes with one shaking hand. For a moment, there was silence outside. Then she heard the crunch of his boots on her snowy porch steps. Isabelle leaned her back against the door and slowly slid down until she hit the floor.

They'd found her.

The ax had always been hanging over her, waiting to drop. In this day and age, you could never truly disappear. Not for good. But she'd tried.

For a girl like her, it hadn't been easy. She'd been sheltered. Twenty-two years old, but still a child in important ways. Always taken care of, always protected.

Still, she'd managed to hide for fourteen years. She'd moved several times, assumed a new identity, built a successful career. But they'd found her.

So why hadn't Deputy Marshal Tom Duncan arrested her immediately?

Surprised to find her eyes were blurry with tears, Isabelle wiped the wetness from her face and pushed up to her feet. She slipped over to the front window and carefully peeked outside.

The only sign of him was the set of footprints that led up to her porch and the set leading back down to her drive. There wasn't quite enough fresh snow that she could track his prints down her driveway, but he hadn't sneaked off into the deep snow at the side of her house. He was gone. Which didn't make sense.

She wasn't a dangerous criminal. She hadn't even been a criminal at all until she'd purchased fake IDs and changed her identity. If he'd come here to arrest her for that, he would've just arrested her. He didn't need to retreat to assemble a backup team or call SWAT. A set of handcuffs would've done the trick. Even one of those plastic zip ties would've incapacitated her.

So they weren't here to make a simple arrest. There was only one explanation. Her father must be back in the country, and they assumed he'd be in contact with Isabelle. They were going to watch and wait.

"Asshole," she muttered as she closed the curtains and locked her door. She hadn't bothered with that kind of thing in years. She'd finally felt safe from the world up here in the mountains outside Jackson, Wyoming. What the hell was she going to do now?

She stood in her entry for a moment with no clue what her next move was. She couldn't run again. She didn't want to. This was her life. Her *real* life. The world she'd chosen for herself.

She wouldn't run.

Fuzzy with shock, she headed back to her studio, feeling like a toy that was slowly winding down.

Did that guy really think she'd fall for such a flimsy story? She'd been around cops all her life. A protection detail was a protection detail; they didn't canvass neighborhoods asking who you were hiding in your house.

Her head buzzed with the noise of a thousand memories as she stopped before her easel and took up the brush. She held it poised above the line she'd painted earlier, but the color wasn't alive anymore. It wasn't good. She looked at the photos again, trying to absorb the life captured there, but when she looked back to the canvas, her mind gave her nothing. Nothing except Chicago and her parents and her old home and friends and *Patrick*.

She set the brush down and switched off the lamp. She wouldn't be able to work this evening. And she wouldn't be able to relax. That was the reason she'd started this new life in the first place. For peace and quiet and *forgetting*. And now he'd blown it up with a casually dropped bomb. Deputy Marshal Tom Duncan, asshole extraordinaire.

Heading toward her tiny living room and the ancient laptop she kept there, Isabelle pulled his card from the pocket of her jeans and shot it a nasty look. She'd find out exactly who he was and what he wanted, and she'd figure out if there was any way to make it better. And then she'd get back to painting.

TOM STOPPED AT the end of the snowy driveway and glanced back toward the cabin. He could barely see it from here. Just the highest point of the roof, the sharp corner dark against the gray clouds and blurred by falling snow. But her house number was posted here on the road, likely only because it was required by law. The woman didn't seem the type to welcome unfamiliar visitors. Certainly not the kind with badges.

Still, her reaction wasn't necessarily unusual in Wyoming. Plenty of good people around here were raised to distrust the federal government. That didn't mean they were doing anything wrong. They were just private. And maybe that was exactly what she was, too.

But Tom's mind buzzed with warning. He'd find out who she was, at least. See if she had a past. Or a warrant.

He typed her address into his phone to reference later, then tucked it away so it wouldn't get wet as he walked through the snow to the next house a few hundred yards down the road.

She'd looked harmless enough. In her thirties, maybe, dark haired and serious, though her skin had been streaked with the occasional swipe of color on her fingers and wrists. An artist, he assumed. Eccentric. So maybe she was only growing pot in her basement.

He glanced back again. From this spot in the road he could see her dark front window. She wasn't watching him leave, at least. Still, Tom was too curious to wait until later to find out more about her, so he pulled his radio out and transmitted her address to the local sheriff's office for identification. It took only a moment for his radio to squawk back.

"Tax records show that property belongs to Isabelle West. Purchased in 2006."

Tom made note of that on his phone as he headed up the next driveway. This cabin sat a little closer to the road, and lights blazed from every window, despite that it was only 4:00 p.m. The afternoon was dreary enough to need it, but the rooms behind Isabelle West had been dark.

Further research would have to wait until he was at his computer, but he couldn't stop himself from looking toward her place again, noting that from this cabin's front porch, he could see the steps that led up to the other cabin and part of its driveway. He watched for one moment then raised his hand and knocked.

"Be right there!" a woman called, her footsteps quickly moving closer. The door nearly flew open.

Her greeting was a marked contrast to what he'd received from Isabelle West. This woman was a little older. Fifty, or maybe a bit older than that, as the black twists of her hair were streaked with gray. Her wide smile grew wider as she looked him up and down. "Hello!"

"Ma'am," he said, flipping out his badge, "I'm Deputy US Marshal Tom Duncan. Sorry to bother you, but I'm giving everyone in the area a heads-up that we're on protective detail in—"

"Oh! Is this about Judge Chandler? That poor man. I read about it in the paper. You're no bother at all, you fine thing. Come on in out of the cold."

"Ma'am, I—"

"Don't *ma'am* me. Have I gotten that old, or are you just past charming? Nothing wrong with calling a woman *miss*. Or *ms.*, if you're going to quote me. I don't want my feminist card revoked. I've worked too damn hard."

Tom blinked several times and followed her into her house and all the way through to a kitchen where the aroma of roasting meat overwhelmed him. Cast-iron pans hung from the ceiling along with dried braids of garlic and herbs that he'd never be able to name. Whatever they were, they smelled damn good.

"I have the perfect tea to warm you up, Tom." She paused and turned purposefully toward him. "I'm Jill Washington."

He shook her outstretched hand. "A pleasure to meet you, Ms. Washington."

She flashed a smile at that, then got back to work making tea. Tom didn't particularly like tea—he was a black-coffee kind of guy—but he'd do everything possible to keep her friendly. If he needed an ally in this non-neighborhood, she was clearly the prime candidate.

"I'm getting snow on your floor," he said, reaching to take his boots off, but she shook her head.

"That's why they're stone. Hard on the back, but they absorb all manner of sins. Your boots are fine, so say what you came here to say." She bustled around her kitchen as she spoke, getting cups and saucers and a tiny pitcher of cream.

As he took a seat, Tom gave her the same speech he'd given Isabelle West, though with a very different result. Jill was all concerned expressions and sympathetic tutting as he explained why he needed community support. The judge's home was isolated, and the man refused to live in a hotel for the two weeks the trial was expected to last. "Everyone around here knows each other. You know better than I who belongs here and who doesn't."

"Well, it'll be easy to spot strangers here on Spinster Row."

He frowned as he accepted the cup of tea and waved off the cream. "Thank you. Spinster Row?"

She laughed, the sound natural and well used. "A joke. It's just Isabelle and me on this part of the road. She's unattached, and my relationship is complicated, starting with the fact that my girlfriend has been stationed in Guantánamo for two years and doesn't seem inclined to come visit. But that's more than you asked."

But not more than he wanted to know. "I met Ms. West a few minutes ago. An artist of some kind?"

"A painter."

Maybe she really was a free-spirited libertarian who didn't like government types. "So it's just you two up here? No kids or live-in companions I should know about?"

"It's just us. I guess I shouldn't tell a stranger that, even if he is a cop, but everyone else around here knows."

"I promise I wouldn't ask if I didn't need the information," he assured her. "I live alone myself. I understand the safety issues."

She laughed heartily at his wink.

"And what do you do for a living, Ms. Washington?"

"I'm a chef. Or I used to be, I suppose. Now I write cookbooks and while away my days here in my little place. It's just me and the elk and a deep freezer full of test recipes. Oh! I've got just the thing for you. Beef Stroganoff. You look like a red-meat kind of boy, and you're probably living off pizza on a job like this. Where are you from?" She hurried to the freezer and pulled out a paper-wrapped packet.

Tom knew the polite thing would be to say no, and he really wasn't supposed to accept gifts, but his stomach tightened at the thought of giving up a good meal. He was sleeping on a cot in the judge's basement, and despite it being a rather luxurious basement, it wasn't home.

He gratefully took the frozen meal. "Thank you. That's very generous. I'm over in Cheyenne."

"Are you single? Four hundred and fifty miles might be considered long distance in most states, but here in Wyoming, Cheyenne's practically within dating range of Jackson. I'm not asking for myself, of course." She looked purposefully in the direction of Isabelle West's house.

Tom smiled, hoping to charm her into giving up a little information about her neighbor. "Ms. West didn't seem inclined to find out more about me."

"Oh, God, that's just Isabelle. If she was working when you knocked on her door, you're lucky she didn't throw her brush at you."

Not exactly a recommendation for dating, but Tom didn't mention that. "She did seem a bit antisocial."

"Don't let her fool you. She's a lot of fun, but she does value her alone time. Like most people up here, really."

"But not you?"

She laughed again, shaking her head. "I can talk to anyone. For *hours*."

"Well, I'm afraid I have to move on before the sun sets."

"Fine, but stop by for dinner tomorrow. You protect me from that crazy Stevenson man, and I'll feed you. Deal?"

He stood and shook her hand. "Deal." He'd take her up on dinner in case he had more questions about Isabelle West. And because it was only day two, and he was already sick of pizza. And his team.

There were only five of them here, and his second-in-command was staying at a hotel across from the courthouse. They had a temporary office at the courthouse, but they were using the judge's place as a base, so Tom had decided it was best for operations if he stayed on site. Good for operations, maybe, but not good for his mood. At least the room he was sleeping in had a door, and there was a kitchenette in the larger open area of the basement. He could microwave his beef Stroganoff and close his door while he looked into the mystery of the grumpy artist down the road. She probably wasn't a threat, but he trusted his instincts enough to do a quick check.

But first he had two more miles of forest to check out and a few motion-sensitive cameras to test. Duty before mysterious artist. Or beef Stroganoff, unfortunately.

CHAPTER TWO

GOD, SHE HATED PEOPLE. Even living in a cabin in the Wyoming wilderness wasn't far enough away to be rid of them. Here they were, seeping into her house through seams and crevices, like slime. Or sludge. Or a trail of annoying ants.

Isabelle groaned and let her head fall back onto the office chair wedged into the corner of her small living room. Her neck hurt from hunching over the computer for too many hours. It wasn't a natural fit for her. The only things she used her laptop for were ordering supplies, shopping for books and looking at gorgeous men online.

But she'd spent last night and all of today clicking through link after link looking for a clue, any clue at all. She'd found nothing.

Marshal Tom Duncan was exactly who he said he was. No surprise there. And there were some articles about Judge Chandler and the security issues surrounding the trial of a survivalist who'd killed two state troopers. His brother had been involved in the shoot-out and hadn't been seen since, but he'd sent a threatening letter just a week ago.

So there was a case in town that involved the marshals. There was a possible reason for Tom Duncan to be here. But she still wasn't buying it. She knew how these people worked. He'd look into her life just for the fun of it. Just because he was in the neighborhood. And he wouldn't give a damn about what it would do to her.

She hadn't worked at all today. She'd stood in front of her current project, the biggest painting of the commission, and she'd done nothing but stare. Her hands had failed her. Her father was in her head again. Him and all the dangerous, lying men he'd brought into her world.

Now she was back at the computer, searching, searching. But there was nothing about her father there. Nothing but ancient newspaper articles and old court filings and everything she already knew. He'd thoroughly disappeared from the world. He hadn't been seen in fourteen years. If they were after her again, it wasn't because her father was back in the news.

So...what if Tom Duncan wasn't lying?

"Right," she huffed. They were always lying. All of them. She was vulnerable, so they'd play with her like a toy.

But there were such things as coincidences. There was a tiny possibility that a US marshal had shown up on her doorstep, and it had nothing to do with her father being a federal fugitive and Isabelle being an impostor. If that was true, she had to play it cool. Cautious and careful, but cool.

Isabelle stretched hard and pushed up from the chair. She'd found all she could online. Now she was chasing the same phantoms around and around. Tomorrow she'd paint even if she had to force it. But tonight she needed a shower. And a drink.

Forty-five minutes later, she twisted up her damp hair, shrugged on a thick coat and grabbed two bottles of wine. One for her and one for Jill. Tonight, Isabelle wasn't sharing.

It was almost full dark by the time she set off, but she

wasn't worried. On the off chance that a murderer was actually hanging around, his interest wasn't in Isabelle. The Stevenson family hated cops and judges, and a solitary woman with no family or connections wouldn't make very good leverage if he decided to take hostages.

She trudged through the snow toward the bright glow of Jill's house, not bothering to head for the road. The snow was deep here, but it was a straight shot, and she liked the lost feeling of wandering through the trees. The moon kept her company the whole way.

"I brought dinner," she called, holding up the bottles as Jill opened the door.

"Oh, and here I bothered making a pork roast."

"We can have that, too, if you want. It's up to you."

"Lush," Jill said, ushering her in and taking her coat. "I'm just glad there's someone around for me to eat with or I'd go crazy."

"I'd say the same about drinking," Isabelle said. She tugged off her boots with a sigh. "God, I've had a crappy day."

"The painting isn't going well?"

"I didn't paint one damn stroke today."

Jill opened the first bottle and poured two generous glasses. "Does that put you behind?"

"No, I was a little ahead of schedule. It just pisses me off." She glanced around the kitchen, noticing the loaves of herbed bread cooling on the counter. "Uh-oh. You're baking bread. A bad day for you, too?"

Jill arched a sour look over the tops of her reading glasses as she collapsed into the couch. Isabelle had never seen a couch in a kitchen before coming here, but Jill lived in this room, and it was big enough for the couch and the eight-person table that sat a few feet away.

She joined Jill and brought the rest of the wine for good measure.

"Well," Jill sighed, "we're officially seeing other people."

Isabelle gasped before she could stop herself. "You did it?"

"I issued the ultimatum, and Marguerite took me up on it, so I'm not sure if I did it or she did."

"Shit," Isabelle whispered, taking Jill's hand to give it a squeeze. "I'm sorry. So it's over?"

"I told her I needed additional company if I couldn't see her more than twice a year. I'm not saying it's over, but... She chose to spend her last week of leave on her own. So I guess I'll be seeing other women."

Isabelle gently clinked her glass against Jill's. "Back in the saddle?"

"If I still remember how to ride. Marguerite's last visit was eight months ago."

"You're probably better off than I am," Isabelle said drily.

"I don't want to hear that bullshit. I'm a black lesbian living in Wyoming. You get no sympathy from me."

Isabelle laughed until she snorted. "Okay, you've got me there. Then again, nobody's forcing you to live in Wyoming."

"No, but..." Jill waggled her eyebrows. "The flip side of that is I'm the only one around to fill the black-lesbian niche. Time to get back on the circuit."

"All right. You'll come out with me and Lauren for this week's girls' night out."

Jill shook her head. "No. I'm too old for that."

"Bullshit. You're fifty-five. You're hardly any older than I am."

Jill howled. "Are you kidding me? You're thirty-six.

Imagine how much you've learned since the age of sixteen, and then double that for wisdom. That's how close we are in age."

Isabelle rolled her eyes. "It feels a lot closer than that."

"Well, it's not. So next time you have a girls' night *in*, let me know."

"Come on," Isabelle pressed. "How will you meet anyone if you don't get out?"

"It's called *internet dating*. Maybe you've heard of it. I've spent more years picking up sexy young things at bars than you have. I'm done."

Isabelle gave in with a grumble. When Jill dug in her heels, that was the end of it. "Well, I'm sorry. I know last time Marguerite was here, you two were trying to work through it."

Jill waved a hand and got up to peek into the oven. "Enough about that. It's all I've been thinking about for months. And I've got the perfect new topic." She pulled the roast from the oven and smiled at Isabelle past the steam. "That hot US marshal who came by yesterday."

Isabelle groaned, then immediately wished she could take the sound back. It revealed too much. The man should mean nothing to her. She latched on to her only excuse. "He interrupted my work."

"Woman. No wonder you can't get laid. Did you see him?"

Isabelle frowned. Yes, she'd seen him. He'd been tall. Lean. With short, dark hair just turning a bit gray at the temples. And if she thought about it, he'd had a pretty great face. A strong nose and dark eyebrows over intense green eyes. And lips that looked soft to the touch against all that masculinity. "Hmm," she replied.

"Hmm, indeed. Aren't you always saying you wish you could get home delivery of someone like him?"

No. Not someone like him. Someone like him but in no way associated with law enforcement. "He was fine. Do you think his story was legit?"

"About the judge? Are you kidding me? It's been in the local paper all week. That man threatened to blow something up. You know the judge lives on the next road down the hill."

Isabelle shrugged. "I guess I haven't been reading the news."

Jill got plates from the cupboard, but Isabelle didn't get up to help. She knew from experience that Jill would only wave her away. Jill's work was her art. There were sauces to be smeared and rosemary sprigs to be placed just so.

"You haven't met the judge?" Jill asked.

"I don't think so. You know how I am."

"Hermit-y?" Jill tossed out.

Isabelle nodded. She wasn't ashamed of being a hermit. And she had damn good reason to avoid a federal judge.

"Well, his daughter is the one who writes that advice column. Do you know her?"

"*Dear Veronica?* Really? She seems damn cool, but I've never met her. Have—?" Her words were cut off by the doorbell.

Jill disappeared into the front room. For a moment, Isabelle had a hopeful thought that maybe Jill's girlfriend had dropped everything and flown in to try to make things work. But no. The military wasn't that big on romantic gestures, even for a lieutenant colonel.

Then the door opened, and Isabelle heard a man's voice. *His* voice. She jumped up and stared at the kitchen doorway in alarm. If she stayed hidden, she didn't have anything to worry about. He couldn't know she was here. Unless he'd followed her tracks through the snow. But what did he *want*?

She crept closer to the doorway, carefully keeping behind the wall. There was a living room and a short hallway between her and the front door, but his voice was deep, and she heard it rumbling as he spoke to Jill. Just a follow-up visit, hopefully. If this was really all about the judge, then—

The door closed, and Jill's footsteps started back toward the kitchen. But she wasn't alone. There were two sets of footsteps, one heavier than the other. Isabelle froze, her brain taking too long to respond to the change in situation, and she'd only just realized she should sneak back toward the couch when Jill stepped in. And he followed.

Jill's chin jerked back in shock as she caught sight of Isabelle and did a double take. Tom Duncan's nice dark eyebrows rose at the way she was huddled against the wall.

Isabelle stared up at him as she realized she'd pressed herself into a corner between the kitchen countertop and the doorway. It looked as if she'd been doing exactly what she had been. Hiding and eavesdropping. Damn it. She glared in defense at the man's questioning look.

Jill cleared her throat. "Look who decided to join us. I told him yesterday that he could stop by for dinner. Tom, you remember Isabelle."

"Ms. West," he said.

"I didn't tell you my name," she responded. Jill glared at her, but she ignored it.

His surprised eyebrows finally dropped, and he nodded. "It's my job to find out these sorts of things."

"Just out of innocent curiosity?" Isabelle countered.

"No, it's more about protecting the target. What if you were the cousin of the defendant?"

"Hmm."

"I told him your name," Jill said. "Regardless, he's staying for dinner."

He finally smiled, transforming his face from hard to handsome, but the look was all for Jill. "I really hope your offer was genuine, but I guess I'm here even if it wasn't."

"Of course it was genuine! Don't pay any attention to Isabelle. She's in the middle of a project. She'd much rather deal with her two-dimensional people."

Isabelle didn't deny it. "They're simple," she said. "Real people are way more trouble."

Jill hurried back to her task. "But we're much more fun, aren't we?"

"Some of you."

"It doesn't matter. There's no paint here, so you're not being interrupted. Now," Jill tossed over her shoulder, "pour Marshal Duncan a glass of wine."

"I'd better not," he said. "I'm not on duty right now, but I'm still the supervisor in charge. And it's just Tom, please. Eating the neighbor's food isn't part of my official duties. Speaking of... That Stroganoff was delicious. The whole damn house was jealous. Pardon my language."

Jill roared with laughter at that. "Please. I expect fouler language than that before this bottle of wine is gone."

"Okay," Isabelle volunteered, filling her glass again. "I'll get to work on that."

"All right, but bring the wine to the table."

Isabelle did as she was told, but when she got to the

table, she noticed that there were only two settings. She shot a resentful look at Tom, but he'd been invited and Isabelle hadn't, so she didn't bare her teeth at him before she grabbed another place setting from the sideboard. She even poured him a glass of water just before Jill brought all the plates to the table, one balanced on her forearm with ease.

"Let's eat!"

Tom pulled out Jill's chair, but Isabelle plopped into hers before he could get to her. That was when she noticed the streak of yellow paint down her shirt. Damn it. She didn't normally care, but she didn't want to feel at a disadvantage around this man. Plus, her supply of unstained shirts was dwindling. She had to start remembering to wear an apron. Or maybe a smock. Like a kindergartner.

She touched her mouth, hoping she hadn't accidentally nibbled on a brush earlier when she'd been trying to find the will to paint. She glanced up at Tom and found him watching her fingers. His eyes rose to meet hers before she looked quickly at her plate.

"Wow," he said a moment later. "This is good. Really good. I can't say I've ever enjoyed cabbage before, but... wow."

"Wait till you try the pork," Isabelle said while Jill grinned across the table at him.

He popped a piece of meat into his mouth and closed his eyes, giving Isabelle the chance to study him for a quick moment. Shit. He really did have a nice face. And despite her current hatred of all law enforcement, she'd had her attraction to the men in that field hard-wired into her from an early age.

His firm jaw bunched and flexed as he chewed, and when he opened his eyes, they were dark with pleasure.

"You know what? Maybe I will have a glass of wine. If there's any left? This meal deserves a toast."

"Tom," Jill said as she leaped up to open the second bottle, "you're my new favorite person. Why don't you just move in here and I'll feed you every day."

"Don't tempt me, because I might."

Isabelle watched them grin at each other as Jill poured him a glass. All right. So, Jill liked him. But Jill liked almost everyone. She was terrible at being a hermit. In the summertime, she sometimes offered lemonade to hikers when they passed by. If any hikers had the nerve to show up at Isabelle's door, she told them to use the hose for water.

"To new friends," Tom said, tapping his glass to Jill's. Isabelle hesitated a moment, but when he reached forward, she tapped his glass before taking a healthy gulp of wine.

"So where are you from, Isabelle?"

The wine soured in her throat as she swallowed hard. It might raise his suspicions if she spewed it all over the table at such a seemingly innocent question. Instead of choking, she cleared her throat. "Washington State," she said.

"I thought I heard an accent."

Her heart beat harder, but she shrugged. "My parents were from Cincinnati. I must've picked it up from them." Okay, a Cincinnati accent wasn't quite the same as Chicago, but her accent was subtle enough at this point. She waited to see if he'd press harder, but he didn't.

"I lived in Oregon for a time," he said instead. "I miss the moisture."

"And the oxygen?" she asked.

"Yeah, I've gotta say, even coming from Cheyenne is a change here. I notice it every time."

"And how often do you come to Jackson?"

She'd tried to make it a friendly question, but she could tell by the way his eyebrow twitched up that she'd gone too far toward flirtation. The wine had blurred her boundary between politeness and leering, apparently. Oh, well. If there was a chance he didn't know who she was, she had to be less hostile. She went all in and smiled.

"It depends on the court schedule," he finally said. "Most of us are based out of Cheyenne, since places like Jackson and Mammoth don't need a full-time marshal. Sometimes I'm out here once a month. Sometimes once a quarter. But this time I'm getting my fill."

He sounded sincere. Believable. He had good reason to be here, and he wasn't even new to town. So maybe everything he'd said had been the truth from the start. A rush of near painful relief rolled over her at the mere chance that he wasn't here for her.

Isabelle sat back in her chair and watched as he and Jill talked. He had a nice smile and a deep, rough laugh that made her feel bad she'd been rude to him for no reason. It was a bit of guilt, yes, and maybe a little affection for his looks, but mostly she regretted drawing attention by being suspiciously hostile. That had been dumb. But she'd been caught by surprise, and it wasn't as if she'd been trained by the witness protection program in how to avoid discovery.

She'd tried her best to erase her identity, yes. But they'd been basic choices. She'd gone to Seattle first, smart enough to use cash and not credit cards only because she'd been exposed to cop talk at the dinner table. But everything else had been one terrifying blind choice after another. She'd never even lived on her own before. She'd never had to choose an apartment or buy a car, much less make contacts to buy a new name and social security number.

First there'd been Seattle, then a smaller town a year later. And finally she'd moved to Jackson.

That had been it. No one asked questions. No one even noticed her. She was average in almost every way. Average height, average build, average brown hair color, mildly average face. Aside from that, the only noticeable things about her were her size D breasts and odd career. She'd found it fairly easy to keep those under wraps.

She'd made friends with Jill right away. It had been impossible not to. Not only was Jill irresistibly friendly, but she also always brought *food*. Isabelle had been hanging out at her place within days.

Aside from a few brief affairs and a few more one-night stands, meals with Jill had been the extent of Isabelle's social life for years. She had a PO box in town, so the mail carrier never bothered her. She couldn't get pizza delivered, so there were no wild pizza-boy scenarios acted out. And the only other neighbors were separated from her and Jill by the deep, shadowed forests of ponderosa pines and aspen.

She liked it that way. She reveled in it. She felt almost safe. But things had changed last year. After dozens of trips to the library over the years to pick up inter-library loans of rare, specialized anatomy books, one of the librarians had started a conversation. An interesting conversation. And Isabelle's bubble of isolation had finally popped.

Lauren Foster was a good friend now. And Sophie Heyer, another librarian. Those two women had pulled

Isabelle further out of her comfort zone by insisting on girls' nights out every other Sunday.

But there hadn't been much room for men. Not enough room. Her lies wouldn't accommodate a long-term relationship, and neither would her heart. So she'd had a man for a week or a month at a time here and there, but never more than that.

Maybe that explained why she found herself watching Tom as he spoke, wondering if those lips would taste as good as they looked. Or if those shoulders were as wide as they seemed.

She shook her head. She needed more wine. Or less. Or she just needed to get laid. But definitely not by a US marshal.

But it didn't matter tonight. Tonight she was full of wonderful food and less afraid of why he'd shown up on her doorstep. There was more wine, dessert was waiting and nobody was asking anything about her father. She'd be able to paint tomorrow. She could feel it.

As if the universe was offering a reward for her new good mood, Tom unbuttoned the left sleeve of his shirt and began to roll it up as he told Jill a story about a fugitive who'd fallen into an icy creek.

"The thing was, he wouldn't come out." His wrist was exposed first. The same tan color as the back of his hand, dark against the white cotton of his shirt. "His lips were turning blue. He couldn't stop shaking. He couldn't even speak anymore. But he refused to come out."

Now the start of his forearm, slim but much harder than hers, muscles visible even at rest.

"None of us wanted to go in after him. It was probably twenty-five degrees in the sun, and the creek was solid ice around the banks. We just stared at each other across the water, waiting for someone to break. I mean, this guy was going to die, and the office kind of frowns on that."

Now the thickest part of his forearm, the rolled cuff starting to tighten up around it. He was just as tan here, but the light from the wrought-iron chandelier skimmed his skin and caught on the hair of his arms, glinting golden and bright.

"So what happened?" Jill asked.

He grinned. "I broke. I had to do it. I was the senior officer. And holy shit, it was cold. So cold it felt like fire at first. The numbness set in pretty quickly, but that was only the skin. Deeper, in the muscles and joints, it *hurt*. And then when I hit a deeper pool of water…" He shook his head and turned the sleeve up one more roll. "I don't want to talk about it."

Jill nodded solemnly. "Can you still have children?"

"I doubt it. Then again, they do freeze sperm, right?"

After she stopped laughing, Jill pointed at Tom. "A hero like you deserves dessert. I hope you like cherry pie. It's Isabelle's favorite."

Isabelle laughed. "You make me sound like a bad '80s sex joke. But I do love cherry pie. Almost as much as Jill does."

A faint wash of pink appeared on Tom's cheeks. Was he blushing? That was cute as hell. Maybe he wasn't used to women joking about sex. But Isabelle had discovered that freedom was the best thing about getting older.

She'd felt a touch of it when she'd turned thirty. She'd suddenly felt less like a big kid blindly feeling her way through the world and more like an adult. Then at thirty-five she'd realized she was at that age when so many women really started to worry. That they were too old now. That they hadn't married or had children. That this was their *last chance* to really live.

Isabelle didn't feel as though this was her last chance. She felt as though she was finally free. Capable. Happy with herself. Comfortable with her body. And allowed to say anything she wanted to out loud, even if it made a grown man blush. Maybe especially if it did.

She loved it. She couldn't wait to be forty. She was going to own that shit. And then at fifty, when strangers would stop hinting that it was time to settle down and have some babies, and just start looking at her with pity? That would be glorious.

So she grinned at Tom Duncan and took an extra-large piece of pie and didn't bother stifling her moan of pleasure at the taste. Tonight she was almost sure she was safe, her mouth was sweet and tart with juicy red cherries, and tomorrow she would paint. She had every reason to moan.

ISABELLE WEST WASN'T only a mystery. She was also a distraction. First, there was that threadbare shirt, pale blue but marred with paint, and stretched too tight across her breasts whenever she reached for her glass. The shirt looked old enough to be turned into rags, and he'd been very afraid that one of those buttons was going to give way at any moment. So afraid that he'd constantly found himself checking to be sure it was still closed.

Then there was her glare, suspicious and narrow and almost as distracting as the smile she'd finally settled into toward the end of the meal. The cool smile was as interesting as the glare, as if she had a secret to go with every emotion.

Curiosity paced inside his brain like a caged lion.

Who was she? Instincts weren't everything, but Tom had learned to trust his own, and he would've bet quite a bit of money that she wasn't a criminal. But she wasn't innocent, either. Innocent women didn't press themselves into a corner to hide and listen the way she'd done at Jill's house.

"I'd better get going," she said drowsily from the couch. She was curled up with the last of the wine and didn't look as if she wanted to leave. "I'll be painting for hours tomorrow."

"At least it's not summer," Jill said. "You can sleep until eight and still get the morning light."

"So true. And I'm going to sleep like a baby tonight. A drunk baby."

Tom stood. "All right, drunk baby, come on. I'll walk you home."

Her languidness vanished in an instant. "I don't need you to walk me home," she snapped. "I've walked home a hundred times in the dark."

"I'm sure you have. But this time, there might be an armed fugitive hiding in the woods. And I'm leaving anyway. I can either walk you or I can follow behind you. Your choice."

"Walk her home," Jill cut in. "Isabelle, put your prickliness away and be nice. Maybe you'll like the feeling."

"I doubt it," Isabelle answered, but she shrugged. "And he already asked to walk me home. Apparently, he likes his girls mean and feral."

"All the more reason to walk home with him, then."

Isabelle huffed out a laugh at that then winked in his direction, completely confusing him. His mental state wasn't helped when she reached to shrug on her coat and her blouse threatened to split in two and reveal the pink bra peeking out underneath.

He spun and walked toward the entryway where he'd left his own coat, but there was no relief there. Isabelle followed close behind to tug on her tall snow boots, leaning over so that her shirt gaped to show the generous rise of her breasts. Tom just shook his head and made himself look elsewhere until she'd finished her task. He, in fact, didn't like his girls mean and feral. She was not the girl for him.

Then again, he still wasn't sure he had a read on Isabelle West yet. He wouldn't say she was mean, exactly. But as for feral…well, there was something a little wild about her. Something unfiltered. She said what she meant and wasn't coy about her moods.

Jill, waving away Tom's praise for her food, sent them out the door with warnings about ice on the steps. The woman was truly an amazing cook, not to mention a damn good pastry chef. He'd have to find one of her cookbooks and have Jill sign it for his sister. Wendy adored cooking. And she was terrible at it. But Tom liked to make her happy, so he went to her place once a month for a pleasant, polite evening with Mom and Dad and Wendy's husband and kids, and he ate her awful dinners without complaint. Cookbooks hadn't helped in the past, but maybe Jill's would be the right fit.

"You've got Jill wrapped around your finger," Isabelle said, the words warm instead of accusing.

"You have that turned around. I'd die for that woman."

Isabelle's laugh rang loud and pure into the night as they walked down the driveway to the road. "She's easy to love."

"But she likes living alone?"

Isabelle shrugged. "Maybe nobody is worthy of her. Or maybe love isn't all that great."

He shot her a look, but she was staring straight ahead, her small smile lit by the snow. "And which one is it for you?" he asked.

"Oh, me? I love living alone. And love definitely isn't all that great."

He'd heard that kind of sentiment before, but never with such good cheer. "I'd say that's cynical, but you sound happy about it."

She finally looked at him. "You're not wearing a wedding ring. Do you live alone?"

"Yes."

"No wife or kids? Are you depressed about it? Are you pining away?"

His lips twitched at the idea of sitting in the window of his apartment, staring yearningly into the night, like a sappy scene from a bad movie. "No. But I travel quite a bit."

"A woman in every port?"

"Not quite," he said with a grin. "But you make Mammoth and Casper and Cheyenne sound more promising than they are."

"Exotic locales. Exciting adventures. Femme fatales."

"I see you've been spying on me."

She nodded, still more reserved with him than she was with Jill. "Well, I don't travel, but I'm not lonely. I have my work, my friends and my home. And internet porn. Life is good."

Tom tripped over a snowdrift and nearly fell flat on his face. Isabelle laughed as he dusted snow off his knee.

So much for her reserve. "If you said that to shock me, it worked," he said.

"I said it because it's true." She grinned over her shoulder as she kept moving. "Try to keep up."

He had a feeling she didn't mean walking, but he hurried to catch up all the same. Silence fell over them as Tom tried to come up with a question that wasn't "So what kind of porn do you like?" but his brain was stuck on the topic, so he kept his mouth shut.

Still, the silence was nice on a night like this. Their boots crunched in the dry snow, and there was the occasional thump of snow falling off tree branches, but other than that, it was only the black sky and white stars and their breath turning the air pale around them. And this very odd woman smiling at her own thoughts.

When they reached her driveway, her smile disappeared, and she shot him an arch look.

"I'll walk you up," he said in answer to her irritation.

She shook her head but didn't argue when he started up the driveway with her.

"This is a gorgeous place," he said. "I keep thinking I'd love to live outside town, but I'm not sure I want to deal with commuting in winter."

"We get snowed in a few times a year, so I'm lucky I never have to be anywhere. And Jill always has food. I have had to strap on snowshoes on occasion to make it to her place, but it's worth the trouble."

"Clearly. She should open a restaurant."

"I think she likes the solitude more than she lets on. She sold her last restaurant for a bundle, and her cookbooks sell nicely. People still love cookbooks, apparently, even in this age of ebooks and internet recipes. It's the pictures, I think."

"And you? You must be a pretty great artist. Jackson is hardly a cheap place to live."

"I do all right." She didn't elaborate. She was clearly

more comfortable telling him about Jill than speaking about herself.

"I read some stories about the judge," she said as they trudged up the steepest part of her drive. "Do you really think he's in danger?"

"Obviously, we take any threats seriously, but these guys associate with some groups that have strong feelings about the federal government. And they already killed two troopers."

"I know."

"Better safe than sorry. And the judge is isolated out here. You should be careful. I mean it."

She nodded and stopped at the foot of her steps. "Okay. I guess I should thank you for walking me home, then."

"You should, but I'm not sure you will."

"Aren't you supposed to say something gracious like 'Just doing my job, ma'am'?"

"I would, but you didn't actually thank me yet," he reminded her.

"I guess I didn't." She smiled before she jogged up the porch steps. "Have a nice walk home, Marshal."

Tom rolled his eyes when she opened her door. "You didn't lock the door?"

"Oh." She paused halfway in and winced. "I meant to, but I'm not in the habit."

Tom shook his head. "Listen, I don't want to piss you off, but could I take a quick look around before I leave?"

"Is this a ploy to come in for a nightcap?"

"No."

"Peek at my etchings?"

He kept his mouth flat.

"Find out more about that internet porn?"

"Now you're definitely doing it on purpose."

She shrugged. "Maybe. Are you complaining?"

He hadn't been complaining, exactly. It wasn't that he *minded* her talking about sex. He just wanted to be prepared for it so he could act like a seasoned and stoic officer of the law instead of a blushing teenager.

"I'm not letting you in my house," she finally said. She was haloed by the entryway light, and she wasn't smiling anymore.

"Please?" he tried.

"I might have left my laptop open," she said drily.

Okay. So she didn't want to be alone in her house at night with a strange man. He could certainly understand that. "You could wait here. Watch from the doorway."

Her head tilted as if she were confused by the suggestion. "Oh," she finally said. Her forehead creased. "Look—"

Whatever she'd been about to say, it was cut off by a loud thud from somewhere behind her. Her eyes went wide, and Tom put his hand on the gun at his hip. "Step outside, please, Ms. West."

She actually did as he'd asked, her hostility forgotten in the fear of the moment.

"There's no one else staying here?"

"No," she whispered.

Tom drew his gun and stepped slowly in, switching off the light to make himself less visible from the dark rooms deeper inside the house. "Stay out of the doorway," he said to Isabelle, relieved when her shadow disappeared and left a clean rectangle of moonlight on the wall.

He was reaching for his cell to call for backup when something shot from the darkness and moved toward him. Before he could aim, it was past his feet and still moving.

Isabelle shrieked when the shadow flew out the doorway. He spun and ran toward her.

"Oh, my God," she gasped. "It was just Bear."

"A bear?" He scanned the porch and driveway.

"My cat, Bear."

Tension fell from his shoulders like a weight tumbling off. "Your cat."

"You scared him. He doesn't like people."

"Big surprise. But we don't know that he made that noise. Wait here."

She didn't object. The strange man you knew was better than the one you didn't, apparently, so she let him move past her back into the house.

Enough light came through the front window to let him navigate the living room. It didn't take him long to discover a framed photograph lying facedown on the carpet. It appeared to have fallen from an end table that held a small plate with half a sandwich on it. He picked up the metal frame. It was heavy enough to have made the sound they'd heard.

Tom switched on the light and saw that some of the meat had been pulled from under the bread. He put the gun away. "I think I discovered the crime. You didn't finish your lunch, and your cat was cleaning up for you."

She poked her head around the door frame. "Oh. Sounds about right."

She switched on the overhead light, revealing the rest of the room. It was simpler than he'd expected for an artist. A couch and chairs and a flat-screen TV along with a bookshelf stuffed full of paperbacks. And the laptop sitting dark and seemingly harmless on a desk that was crammed into a corner.

He looked at the photo in his hand, hoping for a little

more insight into this woman. It was a picture of her with two other women, their arms around each other. Sisters or friends, maybe.

He glanced around for more photos, but only found two paintings on the walls.

One was a man, turned away, his eyes focused somewhere distant. His hair curled over his ear, and wind blew his shirt tight to his back. Pine trees rose up in front of him.

If not for the signature across the bottom corner, Tom would've thought it was a photograph at first glance; it was that stark and crisp.

The other painting was a completely different style. It was a watercolor of a golden field with shadows of mountains rising far away and storm clouds rolling closer.

"Is one of them yours?"

"Yes, the portrait. I suck at landscapes. And watercolor."

"The portrait is striking. Really spectacular."

"Thank you," she said simply, not offering any protest. She knew she was good, and he liked that. He was about to ask who the man was, but Isabelle's mouth tightened as if she was waiting for just that question— and resenting that he'd ask it—so Tom tipped his head toward the dark doorway on the other side of the room. "May I please check the rest of the house? Just to be sure?"

Her eyes narrowed. She watched him for a long moment then looked around the room, as if trying to see what he was seeing. "If you really think it's necessary. Watch out for the laundry when you get to my bedroom. I haven't quite kept up with it this…week."

"Got it." He flipped on the hallway light and moved

to the right toward two open doors. The first was a small bedroom with no piles of laundry and no intruder. He checked the closet and moved on.

The second door was clearly her bedroom. A king-size bed was piled high with silver-and-blue pillows on top of a rumpled gray comforter. Despite the massive size of the thing, it looked as though she used the whole big mattress. There wasn't a smooth spot of blanket on it. Or she'd had a guest sometime recently. He couldn't rule that out.

Other than that, the bedroom was fairly unremarkable aside from the pile of laundry at the foot of her bed. There were also a few clean clothes stacked neatly on top of a dresser as if she'd gotten distracted before putting them away.

Tom moved toward a door in the far wall and found a large bathroom, empty aside from a can of turpentine on the counter and a smaller pile of laundry. He checked the closet, surprised there were still clean clothes remaining in there, then shut off the lights and headed for the other side of the house.

It was quick work. There was one more bedroom that seemed to be used for storage, and past it, a laundry room with a door that creaked in protest at being opened after so long. The last door led to the garage, which was empty aside from an SUV and a few very large canvases wrapped in plastic.

He found Isabelle in the kitchen, pouring a glass of water and not the least bit concerned about the security of her home. He shook his head. "I guess I should've asked you to wait in the living room until I'd cleared this area."

She shrugged. "I would've yelled if I found someone."

"Is that the last room?" he asked, tipping his chin toward the double doors.

"Yep, it's my studio."

He hesitated a moment. He'd never been in the home of a real working artist before. "I won't be invading your privacy if I look inside?"

"You're invading it right now, but I think I'll survive."

He opened the doors to cool air and a strong smell of paint. Even before he reached for the light he could make out easels highlighted by the moonlight that streamed through tall windows. Their shadows stretched across the wood floor, the long shapes making his neck prickle with alarm. Anyone could be standing there. He'd unbuttoned his gun strap, but he hadn't drawn it. The likelihood that anyone was actually here was minuscule, but he still put his hand on the butt of his gun as he swept the wall with his fingers.

They finally found the switch, and the darkest shadows vanished in the sudden onslaught of light.

Her studio was a large room, and the scattered canvases blocked a lot of the view, but Tom could see practically every corner when he dropped down to peer past the forest of easel legs. It looked clear. He blew out a sigh, but his relief lasted for only the two seconds it took him to stand and refocus his eyes on the nearest canvas.

This time his breath left him on a rush, and he stepped back in alarm.

What the *hell*?

His gaze skipped off that painting and moved to the next one, trying to escape the sight or just make sense of it, but the second one was no better. Just a mess of blood and sinew and flayed skin and glistening muscles.

Narrowing his eyes, he forced himself to step closer

to the first easel, but that only made it worse. Her painting was of a human abdomen, except that this person's skin had been peeled off to reveal the connective tissue beneath it. It was so incredibly detailed that he could make out the smallest capillaries on the underside of the peeled skin.

Even worse than the paintings were the photos taped to the sides of the canvas frames. These were actual pictures of bodies stripped of their skin and humanity. They were corpses. And she was *re-creating* them.

"You don't like them?" she asked from only a few feet away. Tom jumped, spinning toward her, his hand tightening on his gun. He didn't draw it, though. He had that much sense left.

"What the hell kind of art is this?" Was she a provocateur or just some sort of sicko?

She grinned at him, and he changed "sicko" to "serial killer" in his mind. Clearly, she was sociopathic. "I'm an anatomical painter."

"Yeah, I damn well see that."

Now she was actually laughing. "You should see your face." She wiped a tear from her eye. She was laughing so hard she was crying.

"What is this?" he barked.

"Just what I said it is. I work on commission for textbooks and medical art companies."

He blinked and forced his tension down a notch, but it wasn't easy. He hated seeing dead bodies. Really hated it. "Textbooks?" he managed to ask more calmly.

"Yes. Biology. Anatomy. Some surgical instruction. Photos don't really work well. There's not enough definition and contrast, usually. And digital art sucks. Don't tell anyone I said that. Ninety percent of work is digital now. 3-D rendering has its uses, I suppose. But my niche is oil. Not very common these days. It's specialty work."

He looked at the nearest painting again then turned back to her. He could feel the horrified confusion etched into his face, and he could see it in the laughter that still swam in her eyes.

"I also do posters for doctors' offices. You know, the 'This is your knee joint' kind of thing."

"This is—" he shook his head "—awful."

"Really?" She shrugged, as if she couldn't fathom his reaction. "You probably don't want to see the comparison ones, then. A small child winding up for a softball pitch on one side, and the same small child as a skeleton in the next. They're a little morbid, but the kids love them."

"The *kids*?" he gasped, looking over his shoulder again. His eyes focused on the next easel and a photo taped there. It was a thigh, half the flesh removed, the other half still intact, a tattoo of a dragon livid against the pale skin. He felt the blood leaving his head and took a deep breath to try to steady himself. "Jesus, Isabelle. How can you do this?"

Her smile finally faded. "What do you mean? It's my job. Medical students need to learn about the body. So do high school kids. Would you rather schoolkids had to work with cadavers?"

The word *cadaver* was almost too much for him. The memory of his brother's pale, stiff body flashed into his head, but he forced it back. He could control it. It was the same every time he had to deal with death, and death was part of his job. But this...

"This is your home," he said. "Where you sleep at night."

"I work here, too. It's no big deal."

No big deal. Right. Here he'd been warming to her, and the woman was a freak. A freak who looked at pictures of dead people all day. In her secluded cabin. In the dark woods. "Well," he managed to say, "the house is all clear. You're safe."

"Thank you. Want to sit down and stay awhile?" she teased.

"No, thanks," he muttered as he brushed by her. Her laughter followed him to the front door. "Have a good night," he called over his shoulder. "And lock the door."

Or bar it. From the outside.

Maybe this woman's secret was more dangerous than he'd suspected.

CHAPTER THREE

It was 11:00 P.M., and Tom was staring at the computer instead of sleeping. He'd planned to get right back to Judge Chandler's basement and do some research into Isabelle West, but instead he'd walked in to find his second-in-command, Mary Jones, yelling at their tactical commander over the phone.

Mary, the senior deputy marshal whenever Tom was out of the room, had rightly made the decision to move the judge's twenty-six-year-old daughter into his home for the trial. Veronica Chandler lived alone in an apartment just off Jackson town square, and Mary had decided that the woman would be safer in her father's home, where the security detail could keep an eye on her, as well.

Chris Hannity, the tactical command specialist, had bristled at being cut out of the decision, especially as he'd already scouted Veronica's place and had made schedules to patrol her block.

An acute case of male pride, as far as Tom was concerned, and he'd quickly dismissed the issue with a few curt words for Hannity.

"He's still pissed about that disciplinary hearing," Mary said from behind him, her Southern drawl ruining the hard edge of the words. She set a plate of cookies at his elbow. "The cookies are courtesy of Veronica Chandler."

"Thanks. And he'll get over it."

"You think? It's been a year. I told you not to report it."

Tom grabbed a cookie and shot Mary a look, noticing that she was chewing on her thumbnail. She did that only when she was tired enough to forget. "He called you a dyke. In front of me."

"It's not the worst I've heard."

"Then he chose the wrong place to say it. And you're chewing your nail again."

"Shit," she muttered, clenching her hand into a fist and forcing it to her side.

"He'll get over it," Tom repeated. "And he won't disrespect you or anyone else on the team again."

Mary was forty-five, but she looked a lot younger. Couple that with her small frame, curly blond hair and heart-shaped face, and she sometimes had trouble commanding respect. Actually, that wasn't true. She commanded respect. Her men followed her orders to a T. But there were always a few holdouts on other teams who considered her authority an insult to their testicles.

She made it a policy never to show weakness in front of those assholes, and she hated giving away that she might be stressed.

"I already read the day's report," he said as he polished off a second cookie. "Everything's in place for the trial?"

"Yes. You still think we'll hear from the brother again?"

"I hope not," Tom said, rolling his shoulders to release some of the tension. "But I've got a bad feeling. And the judge? How is he handling the detail?"

Mary shrugged. "He seems entirely comfortable with an entourage. Like he was born to it."

Tom snorted. That was no big surprise. The judge was a blowhard and pretty damn impressed with his position in the community.

"He actually calls Wes his 'driver.'"

Tom guffawed at how much that must chap Wes's hide. "I've got to see that myself."

Mary grinned. "It's pretty awesome."

They both turned toward the stairway when the door to the first floor opened, expecting Wes to head down, but these footsteps were soft and light.

A young woman Tom recognized as Veronica Chandler stuck her head past the wall, her blond hair swinging. "I just wanted to check and see if you needed anything before I turn in."

Tom stood. "No, we're all set up down here. Thank you for the cookies."

"You're welcome."

"Do you know Jill Washington up the road? She's an amazing baker."

The woman smiled. "No, my father only bought this house two years ago, and I was living in New York then. And these cookies went straight from the tube to the oven."

"The perfect recipe," Mary said.

"I'll see you in the morning," Veronica called as she headed back upstairs. She looked happy enough to be here. Tom suspected she was relieved. She'd spent two of the past three evenings here already. What was the point in driving home in the dark to sleep?

It was the same reason Tom was in the basement, after all.

"I'm heading out," Mary said.

"You can take the cot, if you want. I'll sleep here. It's a fold-out couch."

"Thanks, but no thanks. If I wanted to wake up to obnoxious men, I'd change my dating habits."

"Are you calling me obnoxious?"

"No comment." She eased her feet into the heels she wore on duty to add a couple more inches to her height.

Tom cleared his throat. "So what's your age range?"

"For what?"

"Dating."

She frowned at him and grabbed her coat. "That's a weird question."

"I'm just making conversation."

"Bullshit. You know somebody? Is it that new girl in Intake? She's only twenty-one. You should be ashamed of yourself."

"It's no one," he said. "Forget I said anything."

"Stop trying to take care of me. I'm not one of your lost causes." She tugged a knit hat over her blond curls and glared at him for a moment before heading toward the staircase. "Ten years on either side," she tossed back without slowing down.

"Good to know," Tom responded, not bothering to hide his smile.

But as soon as Mary's footsteps hit the first floor and the door closed behind her, Tom was left alone with his thoughts. And those thoughts were not on Jill anymore; they were on her freaky-ass neighbor. What the hell was up with Isabelle West?

He closed his email program and opened his browser to try her name again, but there were still no good clues, so he searched for anatomical art instead. He clicked around for a good half an hour, learning what he could about it. What he saw was pretty on par with what he'd glimpsed at her house. He didn't like one bit of it.

He could handle seeing dead bodies on the job. It

was rarely a complete surprise. He usually had the chance to brace himself against the sight so he wasn't snapped back to that long-ago moment when he'd found his brother. But tonight had sneaked up on him.

He took a deep breath and cleared the search window then tried a new one for "medical paintings" and her name. He got back garbage. That was weird. She obviously did well for herself. She must have a legitimate career. So why was she missing online?

Tom sat back in his chair and tapped a pen to his chin for a minute then thought of the other painting he'd seen in her home. The vivid realism of it. The beauty. And the very short signature in the corner.

He typed in "I. West" and "anatomical painting" and hit the mother lode.

"Bingo," he breathed. Here was her career. She'd been telling the truth.

There wasn't much to get from the search results, other than that confirmation. Her work wasn't meant for private buyers. The hits were all sites where posters and textbooks could be purchased. There was no author biography anywhere. No pictures or stories about her.

Still, the morbidity of the whole thing niggled at his brain. Combined with her initial hostility, Tom decided he couldn't ignore that prickling he'd felt on the back of his neck earlier.

He signed in to the National Crime Information Center to do a quick check on her background. Two hours later, he was even more confused. Isabelle West didn't seem to be a criminal. There were no warrants, no arrests, not even a traffic ticket as far as he could tell. So she wasn't a criminal. But she also hadn't existed before 2002.

CHAPTER FOUR

"GOOD GOD, ISABELLE, you have got to be kidding me!"

Isabelle stared in confusion at her friend. Lauren was standing on the front porch, wearing a tight red dress and heels, and she was glaring daggers.

"What?" Isabelle asked.

"It's Sunday! I texted you this morning!"

"It's Sunday?"

"Yes!"

"Are you sure you sent a text?" She swiped the back of her hand across her forehead, trying to angle the paintbrush in her fingers so that she didn't get cadmium green in her hair. "I didn't get it."

Lauren sighed. "Have you been anywhere near your phone today? Is it charged?"

Isabelle rolled her eyes. "I don't know. I'm working. I guess you may as well come in."

"Nope. We're going out. It's girls' night."

"I'll have to cancel—"

"No, you won't. You canceled last Sunday, remember? Let's go."

Now it was Isabelle's turn to glare. "I'm not going anywhere. I look like shit."

Lauren nodded and made a shooing motion. "Wash your face and put your hair up. If you don't have any clean jeans then put on a dress. Surely those don't have paint on them."

Well, some of them did. But it was too cold for a dress anyway. Then again, Lauren was wearing one, along with high-heeled boots. Isabelle had cute boots that Jill had helped her pick out. She supposed she could throw something together.

She looked over her shoulder toward her studio, but Lauren pushed past her and pointed to the bedroom. "Do it. Sophie's not here to protect you anymore. It's just me and my cruel demands."

"I think I read a book like that recently," Isabelle muttered.

"Yeah, well… Wear something pretty for me or you'll be punished."

"Does this mean I'm not allowed to wear panties?"

"Whatever it takes."

"Fine. Let me get rid of the brush first." As much as she resented having to stop painting, she still smiled as she ditched the brush and hurried to clean up. She'd gotten in almost ten hours of work, after all. Even she could be satisfied with that.

So she did exactly as Lauren instructed. She washed her face and pulled her hair up into a neater knot than usual, and she even put on makeup. Then she stared into her closet for five minutes before finally deciding that she just wasn't into dresses right now.

She settled on her favorite pair of skinny jeans and a gold top she'd worn only once before. It was sleeveless and low-cut and too sparkly, but what the hell. Tonight was girls' night out. Plus, she'd found her last pair of clean underwear, and that was something to celebrate. Of course, that meant she'd have to do laundry tomorrow. Or just go commando. Probably the latter.

"I'm ready!" she called out as she walked back into

the living room, but her smile transformed into an O of surprise when she saw Tom standing there with Lauren.

Isabelle fought down her alarm. She'd almost decided he wasn't onto her the night before. But then he'd asked to search her house, and she was fighting that fear again.

"Hello," she finally said.

"Hi." His eyes swept down to her cleavage then back up so quickly she could've imagined it. But she hadn't. Maybe he really had been interested in her internet porn.

She relaxed enough to smirk. "Braving the house of horrors? This must be important." She met Lauren's questioning look. "He saw my work. He's not a fan."

Lauren huffed, but he shook his head.

"It's not that you're not talented. I just…" His gaze slid toward the kitchen and the double doors beyond. "Wasn't expecting that."

"Want another look?" she asked.

"No!"

Isabelle laughed so hard that she snorted. "It's funny because he's a big strong US marshal," she explained to Lauren.

"Oh, that is funny!"

They both grinned at him for a long moment while Tom frowned back. "I was just stopping by to check on you."

"Hey," Lauren said, "are you here working on Judge Chandler's case?"

"Yes."

"I saw his daughter today at the library! She said she's staying at her dad's place for a while. It's right around the corner, isn't it? We should invite her over for a girls' night in. We have to replace Sophie."

Isabelle's smile fell. "We do?"

Lauren nodded, and her voice went quiet. "I talked to her last night. She was tiptoeing around it, but I think she's finally going to turn in her notice at the library. She's living her dream." Lauren nudged Tom. "Which is riding around the country on a motorcycle with a big tattooed guy. Isabelle, she'll be back for a week on Tuesday. Don't forget!"

Tom cleared his throat. "I'd better let you get to your evening."

Isabelle remembered her wariness. "Did you need something?" she asked.

"Not really. I was making the rounds of the area and decided to stop by."

Her paranoia made her want to snap at him, but she forced it back. She'd decided she didn't need to worry about him. If he were really on a stakeout, looking for her father, he'd never have walked right up and introduced himself. Isabelle had overreacted. There was nothing to fear.

She shrugged. "Everything is good. Aside from the horrifying carnage in my studio, I mean."

"Right. Well. I hope you're taking this seriously now. Lock your door. Be careful when you get home tonight."

"I will," she said. "Scout's honor."

As soon as he closed the front door behind him, she winked at Lauren. "I was never a Girl Scout."

"Yeah, he could probably tell by the way you held up two fingers instead of three."

"Oops." Isabelle cringed. "Oh, well. He's too polite to call me on it."

"Polite, huh? I was going to say 'fucking sexy,' but I guess that's just me."

"I wouldn't say it's *just* you."

"Oh, really? Honey, I'm gonna need all of these details."

Isabelle laughed off Lauren's curiosity, but she could feel her cheeks warming. He really was sexy. And if she could keep him focused on her paintings instead of her past, he wouldn't be a threat to her. "There aren't any details."

"Then I need reasons why. You've been whining about your sex drought for the past year, and now the gods have dropped a hot US marshal on your doorstep, and you haven't devoured him yet? You've got some 'splaining to do, missy. Over drinks."

"Fine. But only over drinks." Isabelle excused herself to grab her purse, feeling strangely discomfited around her friend. Tom being there had reminded her that she wasn't lying to only him; she was lying to everyone.

Somehow it hadn't felt that way with her girlfriends, at least not since those first few conversations. They knew who she was. Who she really was *now*. But having Tom around reminded her that her whole life was a lie.

No. Not her whole life. Just her past. Everything she was doing now was real and genuine, and she was not going to let one US marshal ruin that.

She grabbed her little clutch purse. "Ready?" she called out as she headed back to the living room.

Lauren waved toward the front door. "This girls' night has officially begun. Let's do this."

From the cover of the trees on the far side of the road, Tom watched the taillights of the car move slowly away. He felt guilty standing in the dark, watching, but he was in the woods only because he was heading back to the judge's on a trail he'd already cut through the snow. He wasn't spying. Much.

The problem was that he hadn't had a good reason to stop by Isabelle's tonight. He hadn't really needed to check on her. Everything had gone quiet in anticipation of the start of the trial tomorrow. They hadn't heard one word from the defendant's brother or any of his other supporters. Of course, that silence had Tom on edge, too, but not as much as his suspicions about Isabelle.

Or whatever her real name was. That name was a lie. He was sure of it. She wasn't from Washington, she wasn't Isabelle West and she wasn't an innocent isolationist suspicious of the feds.

"Or you're overreacting," he muttered.

If he used a little creativity, he could imagine that she was a girl from rural Washington State who'd been raised by parents from Cincinnati, who'd kept her off the grid until she was in her twenties. That might explain the slight accent that had nothing to do with the West Coast and the fact that there were no property, tax or motor-vehicle records for anyone named Isabelle West before 2002.

That slim possibility aside, he had no idea who she could be. A criminal, certainly. Or maybe just a woman escaping a bad past. If she'd been a victim of domestic violence, judges had the leeway in almost every state to issue an off-the-record name change. Or maybe she was just a girl who'd gotten herself into a bad situation and had been forced to make a run for it.

"Shit," he muttered, finally turning back to make his way through the woods. He had a problem. He knew he did. A compulsion to help people whether they wanted it or not. *Especially* those who didn't want it.

A problem, maybe, but it wasn't an unreasonable one. Often the people in the worst trouble were the least likely to ask for help. He knew that firsthand. And Isabelle showed all the symptoms of someone like that. She was prickly and proud and smart and self-contained. She hadn't even wanted him to check her place for an intruder. How would she ever reach out about something weightier?

He took a deep breath and tried to lose himself in the walk. The moon was almost full, and it glowed from every snowy surface, so he had no trouble making his way. But the beauty surrounding him wasn't as peaceful as it had been when he'd walked Isabelle home.

He'd gone back tonight hoping to discover more of who she was. He hadn't paid close enough attention the night before. At least he knew who was in the picture with her now. Her girlfriends. And it must mean something that she hadn't had one other framed photograph in the house. No family. No kids. No history.

Maybe he should just let it go. Mary joked all the time about his determination to fix things that were none of his business. He knew it was about his parents and their tendency to stick their heads in the sand and hope for the best. He loved them, and he'd never say it, but his brother would've had a hell of a better shot at survival if they'd stepped up and interfered.

His cell phone rang, destroying the silence of the forest and startling him from his thoughts. He was surprised to get a call out here. Service was spotty even when he wasn't in the trees.

"Duncan," he answered.

"We got another letter," Mary said without preamble. "Where are you?"

"About one minute out from the Chandler house. Where are you?"

"Just pulling up," she said as lights swept over the trees far ahead of him. "Security guards finally decided to go through the Saturday mail delivery at the courthouse."

Tom cursed. "Didn't we ask them to bring any mail to us?"

"I guess the weekend shift didn't get the news."

"Hold on," he said, picking up his pace along the packed trail of snow. "I'll be right there."

The lights from the judge's cabin blazed through the trees. Another car pulled up as he got there. Hannity got out. "A threat to the judge's family," he said immediately, falling into place next to Tom as he jogged up the stairs.

"Mary already moved Veronica here," Tom said pointedly, "so that'll make this easier to address. What else?"

"He mentioned a bomb."

"Shit. We're gonna need another team—"

"Already on it."

"Anderson?"

"Yes. He says he can have a K-9 unit here in three hours."

"Have a plan drawn up before he gets here," Tom ordered. "We'll sweep the area around the house for footprints and evacuate the judge's home if we find anything. If not, let's focus on the courthouse."

Mary was waiting for him with a copy of the letter. He grabbed it and started through the four pages of single-spaced ranting. Things were about to get a whole lot busier around here.

CHAPTER FIVE

ISABELLE SLIPPED ON her sunglasses, but she still squinted against the bright morning light as she walked through town. Well…afternoon light, maybe. Sunlight was brutal at this altitude and even more brutal when it was shining off the snow piled along the narrow sidewalks of Jackson like a punishment handed down by the cruel god of hangovers.

Halfway through their night out, she and Lauren had decided to throw caution to the wind and get unapologetically drunk. That had meant no ride home for Isabelle and a very cold midnight walk from the bar to Lauren's house, but it had been worth it. Lauren didn't have to work today, and Isabelle had needed to shake off the last of the fear Tom Duncan had delivered to her doorstep.

She'd shaken off the fear but had acquired a headache, though she'd managed to sleep off most of the alcohol.

Still, the crisp air helped eliminate the last of her lethargy, and she walked a little taller and unbuttoned her coat to feel more of the sun. She wasn't worried that she was wearing the same clothes she'd worn the night before. If anyone noticed and thought she was taking an extended walk of shame, she'd be happy for the gossip. Her "creepy hermit artist" reputation wasn't getting her any dates. Maybe "creepy party-girl artist" would help.

She smiled at the next person she passed and put a little more swing in her step. Maybe she should wear her heeled boots every time she ran errands. It certainly made walking to the post office feel less like a chore and more like the possibility of adventure.

And funny enough, when she turned the corner, adventure was waiting right there for her. Unfortunately, it wasn't the sexy kind. It was the kind that came with a heavy police presence and a scrum of reporters. She'd accidentally stumbled onto the property of the tiny federal courthouse of Jackson, Wyoming.

For a moment, she just stood there, hand tightening on her little clutch purse and heart ratcheting up her fight-or-flight response.

Funny that she hadn't thought about this at all. She hadn't considered what Tom's job really meant and how much it had in common with her past. She'd been too worried that he was actually here to scout her out.

Her father's case had never gone to trial; he'd skipped town long before that. But he had been indicted, and there had been hearings and other cases to process, and it had all looked like this, only instead of two satellite trucks, there'd been ten. All the Chicago outlets and a few national ones, as well.

This was an entirely different scene, she tried to tell herself. Nothing like what had happened to her father. Here there were only fifty or so spectators and another twenty press people, and the federal courthouse in Jackson didn't look much different from the post office. It was a one-story, ugly '60s structure that evoked none of the gravitas or Greek dignity of the courthouses of Chicago.

So yes, it was a very different scene, but she was still standing there panting as if she were the one in danger.

As if that pack of reporters was about to chase her life down and devour it in front of her. Again.

She took a deep breath. Then another.

This had nothing to do with her. It didn't have anything to do with people she knew. Except Tom.

The threats against the judge really were a big deal. She'd read a few things online, but she hadn't understood the scope of it. These news trucks had come all the way from Cheyenne, six hours away. They might even be sending coverage to a national feed.

She could no longer feel the fingers gripping her bag, but she'd calmed down a little, so she moved her clutch to the other hand and took a moment to look for Tom. He was likely inside the courthouse, running the show there, but she had a strange urge to see him in his element. She had a feeling that that much authority would look sexy as hell on him, especially when she'd been raised to find that kind of thing manly.

But her interest fled when a car pulled up to the courthouse walkway, and the reporters suddenly surged forward. She didn't recognize the man who emerged, but everyone else seemed to. Small town or not, these reporters behaved the same way Chicago reporters did, shouting at their crew, yelling out questions, rushing forward like hungry animals.

Isabelle took two steps back and spun to make her getaway, practically running to the next cross street so she could detour around the courthouse to get to her postal box. She never wanted to see that kind of thing again. She never wanted any part of a trial or a scandal or people who shouted hateful things.

Once she was out of sight of the crowd, Isabelle slowed down, but she had to force it. She wanted to run. If she'd had her car, she'd probably have sprinted straight for it and left rubber on the road as she sped out of town. But she didn't have her car. She was meeting Lauren in thirty minutes so they could have lunch before Lauren drove her home.

She put one foot in front of the other and skirted the rear of the courthouse and then worked back around to the post office.

After giving a wan smile to the clerk, who was ready with a wave, Isabelle got her mail and took it to the recycling box to ditch the junk mail. It was all junk mail. Even the one piece that caught her eye and made her hands start to tremble.

Her name and address were typed, and it looked like any other piece of marketing, except that there was a stamp in place of printed postage. And there was no return address.

She turned the envelope over. It shook in her hand. The return address was printed on the back, but with no name or company logo.

Though she meant to throw it away, her shaking hand reached for the flap of the envelope and slowly worked it open. She pushed up her shades as she pulled out the single piece of paper and unfolded it.

At first, she couldn't quite see the words. She couldn't focus. Then she started reading and still couldn't decipher them. It took her three attempts to read through the half page of text before she realized that it wasn't from her father. It was only a marketing letter from a Realtor who was fishing for seasonal rentals.

The soft sound that came from her own throat frightened her. Isabelle carefully tore the letter into long strips and dropped each of them into the trash can next to the recycling box. The letter had done nothing to her, but she wanted it gone, not recycled into something else.

She'd always told everyone that her father had never contacted her after he'd run. That he'd never been in touch. She'd sworn that was the truth to every federal officer who'd questioned her and every shady Chicago cop who'd shown up at her place with a creepy smile and assurances that they were there to help. But it hadn't been the truth.

From the moment he'd disappeared, he'd sent letters. A week of peace would go by. Maybe two. And then she'd get another letter disguised as junk mail in case anyone was watching the mailbox.

He'd pretend to be apologizing or explaining or just sending his love, but he'd always asked for money. Always. She'd sent a little, but after the fourth or fifth letter that she'd refused to reply to, he'd become less apologetic and more aggressive. *How can you do this? I'm sorry about everything, but I'm still your father. I need help. You owe me that.*

She hadn't owed him anything. After twenty-two years of being his daughter, she hadn't even known who he was. She'd thought he was a hero, but he'd killed at least one fellow officer, stolen money from countless others, and he'd brought dangerous people into Isabelle's life. Isabelle had hated him.

But none of this had to do with today. He wasn't back. He hadn't found her. And her immediate terror was pissing her off.

She sorted through the rest of her mail to be sure it was all junk, then tossed it in the trash. This was ridiculous. She wasn't a scared girl. She'd left all that behind. She'd walked away from it. She'd made a damn decision, and she'd pulled it off.

"Screw it all," she muttered. Then she slipped her shades back on and stepped back out into the day. She forced herself to walk toward the courthouse instead of avoiding it. She put the swing back in her step, and she didn't shy away from the news trucks as she made her way through the crowd.

And she was glad she didn't, because that was the moment she spotted Tom.

In action, he was just as hot as she thought he'd be. His dark gray suit showed off strong shoulders and a slim waist. He wore shades against the bright sun, too, and some sort of earpiece. Leaning in to speak to a man dressed in similar fashion, Tom looked like Secret Service or FBI or something way more urbane than a US marshal.

Damn it. He was sexy.

She saw the moment he noticed her, despite the dark shades hiding his eyes. His head cocked. One expressive eyebrow rose. His lips stopped moving. But for only a moment. He resumed talking, but his head followed Isabelle's movement down the sidewalk. She raised her chin. Better to think about him watching her than to consider the chaos surrounding both of them.

She'd recognized his attractiveness even when she'd been suspicious of him, but after talking with Lauren about him last night, her awareness had sharpened. She liked the way he looked and moved. She liked his voice. She even liked the way he smelled. His profession was a drawback, but it had somehow ceased to be a deal breaker. In fact, maybe it was a turn-on. The danger. Tempting fate. It was stupid, but she suddenly felt alive.

Hell, she'd been complaining for months that she wanted a hot fantasy man to show up on her doorstep and show her a good time. This man had literally shown up on her doorstep, and she'd be an idiot not to at least entertain the idea. Or so Lauren had told her.

Her mouth refused to hold back a smile when Isabelle remembered Lauren's assessment of his ass. Something about it being truly bitable.

Isabelle tipped her head toward him just as he turned to gesture toward the courthouse. His suit jacket tightened against his backside with the movement.

She let her smile widen. His ass did look bitable. It was taut and just round enough to make her want to squeeze it. God, she did love a nice male ass. And it had been so long since she'd dug her nails into one.

She walked on, grinning at the sidewalk in front of her and hoping he had a good view of her own ass from where he was working.

"Isabelle," he called.

Telling herself not to look too pleased, she turned to see him walking toward her.

"I figured you were too busy to talk," she said.

"I am, but there's been a delay in the defense counsel getting here, so we're in a holding pattern. A cattle truck jackknifed on the highway."

She raised her eyebrows. "Sounds like a setup to me."

He smiled, and the way the shades hid his eyes made him look dangerous. "Believe me, if it was the prosecutor's car, I'd be on my way out there with lights flashing. But the defense is on their own."

"Cruel. And the cows?"

"I gather they're fine. Regardless, we don't have the manpower to offer them protection."

His head rose, and he seemed to give a quick scan to the area before smiling down at her again, his attention tipping a little lower this time. This was a different Tom. He was…almost flirty. And totally confident. "I hope you locked up before you left last night."

Ah. So he'd noticed she was wearing the same thing.

Good. Let him wonder if she'd gone home with someone. Let him wonder what she was like in bed. "I locked the door. I'll let you know if there's any trouble when I get home."

"All right."

"I'd better let you get back to work," she said, stepping away with a little wave. "Nice suit, by the way."

He looked down, brows twitching up in surprise. "Thanks."

She couldn't resist drawing it out a little more. She'd fought off her panic, and now she felt powerful. Maybe a little reckless. "Are you going to stop by tonight and check on me?"

He'd been sweeping the area again, but his face tipped back to her. "If you'd like me to."

She shrugged. "You're probably busy," she said casually before walking on. "Good luck with this circus."

He didn't reply, but she could feel his gaze on her as she left. Isabelle barely even noticed the loud drone of the crowd around her as she moved through them. She was too busy swinging her ass.

"K-9 says the parking lot is clean."

Tom wiped the frown from his face and immediately spun to follow Mary as she moved through the crowd. She parted groups of people with just a look.

"They're stationed at the door?" he asked.

She nodded. The K-9 unit had cleared the judge's home first as a precaution, and they'd been working over the entire courthouse since six this morning, the two dogs taking turns so they weren't overwhelmed.

"Forensics?" Tom asked.

"Fingerprints confirm it's him."

Saul Stevenson hadn't bothered disguising his handwriting or keeping his prints off the paper last time, either. He wanted them to know who he was.

Mary glanced over her shoulder as they neared the building. "Postmark is Helena, three days ago."

They both flashed their badges at the security team, despite that they knew every member. It was important that no one get lax.

Tom had gone over the schedule for the day four times already. He trusted his team, and he'd briefed local law enforcement himself. There wasn't much to do now except watch and wait. The threat was likely just a scare tactic. If Saul Stevenson meant to actually plant a bomb, he'd be stupid to give them a heads-up. Then again, maybe he *was* stupid.

But it was more likely that the bomb threat was a diversion, meant to draw attention away from his true intentions. "Hannity is sweeping rooftops now?" he asked Mary as they entered the meeting room.

"He's almost done."

"A sniper shot would be a hell of a lot simpler for him to pull off than a bomb."

"Maybe he wants the drama of an explosion, though."

Tom nodded, but the buzz of his phone in his pocket cut off his next words. His thoughts immediately flashed on Isabelle, her smile teasing and her clothes advertising that she hadn't bothered going home last night. Not to her place, anyway. She'd slept somewhere else.

But when he drew his phone from his pocket, there was no incoming call from the mysterious Isabelle West. It was only his sister. He winced and put it away.

"What is it?" Mary asked.

"My sister."

He thought that was the end of it, but it wasn't. Mary

had been invited to dinner at his sister's place too many times.

"Why are you avoiding Wendy?"

"I'm not avoiding her," he answered. "I'm busy."

"Maybe she needs something."

He glanced up to find Mary leaning against the wall, arms crossed in that stubborn way that said she wasn't going anywhere. "Aren't you always telling me not to worry about my family? If she needs something, she'll call back."

"I'm also always telling you that one dinner a month is not enough time with your family."

Tom rolled his shoulders. "I need to send a few emails," he muttered.

She didn't move.

"Okay, I'll text her," he grumbled, getting his phone back out to let Wendy know he'd call her in a couple of days.

Once he'd hit Send, Mary gave up her stance and sat down at her own computer. He felt bad shutting her out, but he didn't want to talk about it.

It was his brother's birthday, and Wendy always called. He always avoided the call. His sister was like his parents. She considered Michael's death a sad accident. Tom considered it a tragedy that could've been averted if anyone had done *anything* to try to stop it. If they'd even acknowledged his addiction just *once*, maybe his brother would be alive.

He couldn't talk to Wendy about how sad it all was, because he wasn't sad. He was pissed. At Michael. At his parents. Even at Wendy when she wanted to call and reminisce. And he loved his family too much to tell them how angry it still made him.

His parents had done the best they knew how. Tom

understood that. He'd even told them that. But he couldn't say it on Michael's birthday. Not on this day. So he'd call Wendy tomorrow, and today he'd think about something else.

He meant to turn his mind to Saul Stevenson, retreating into his work as he always did, but for once it was no escape. Isabelle West kept intruding, her ass swaying as she glanced over her shoulder.

Tom smiled at the memory and figured that was as good an escape as any.

CHAPTER SIX

ISABELLE SLIPPED ON FLIP-FLOPS, tugged on her gloves and glared menacingly at her messy kitchen. "It is *on*," she growled, trying to pump herself up as she held the yellow latex gloves high in the air like a surgeon prepping for an operation.

She paused and frowned. "Music," she muttered, looking around. She needed music first. Slipping off the gloves, she went in search of her phone and the stereo connector.

Thirty minutes later, she'd finally gotten the music hooked up, tracked down the gloves she'd set down somewhere during the search for the auxiliary cable, and she was poised in front of her kitchen again. "Let's do this."

Lauren had called with the news that afternoon. Sophie had just ridden into town and girls' night in was a go for the next day. It was time to catch up and get drunk, not necessarily in that order. But drinking or not, no one wanted to look at the week-old macaroni noodles stuck to her stove burner. Isabelle didn't want to look at them, either, which was why she'd been ignoring them this whole week.

But the loud music got her dancing and singing and sipping beer as she worked, and before long the kitchen was gleaming.

She moved on to the living room, tossing out magazines she'd been hoarding for months and scaring Bear out of the corner, making him hiss in fury before he disappeared into a back room. "You're the one leaving fur everywhere!" she yelled after him. He didn't deign to reply.

It was a good thing he'd taken off, though. She had to vacuum the rug, and if she dared to do that near him, he'd disappear for a week. They were too much alike, she and Bear.

She was feeling good tonight, though. Really good. That chaotic scene at the courthouse had actually soothed her fears. This whole thing with the judge truly was a big deal. Tom hadn't lied about why he was sneaking around the neighborhood and knocking on doors. This had nothing to do with her, and her relief was bubbling over into giddiness. She danced around with the vacuum, singing along to Elvis Costello at the top of her lungs.

It took her only a few minutes to vacuum, but after she brought in wood from the porch and piled it next to the fireplace, she had to vacuum again. Before she was done with the second pass, Bear was screeching. Loudly. She glanced over to see him stretched up on his tiptoes, clawing at the front door. She shook her head. He kept clawing.

"Stop that!" she yelled over the vacuum. He ignored her then yowled louder when she switched off the vacuum.

"You know it's dangerous out there," she scolded. "There are coyotes. Mountain lions. Foxes."

He shot her a nasty look. Yeah. He could probably take a fox. And maybe a coyote.

"There are cars sometimes," she tried. He didn't relent. "All right, Bear, but please come home. Don't get lost. Okay?"

He paced in front of the door until she opened it, then shot through the narrow space, his massive body forcing its way through. "Rude," she snapped then lunged back in shock when she saw the dark shadow looming above her.

"God!" she screamed, reaching toward the door to push it closed again.

"YOU'RE SUPPOSED TO ask who it is before you answer," Tom said as she caught the door at the last minute and glared at him.

The terror on Isabelle's face quickly narrowed into irritation. "Yeah, no shit!" She snapped on the outside light. "I didn't know you were there."

"Sorry. I knocked."

She waved weakly toward the living room. "I had a lot of stuff going on."

"I noticed." He'd noticed when he'd pulled up and seen her dancing in the living room window, both with the vacuum and without it. Between the warm light shining around her in the dark and the tight orange tank top clinging to her breasts, she'd been a fucking vision. He'd watched for only a minute, though. Then he'd started to feel like a creep.

By the time he'd gotten to the porch, there'd been shouting and feline howling, plus the loud music, and all of it roaring over the vacuum.

"Elvis Costello," he said as she closed the door behind him. "Nice."

"He's great to clean to. You want a beer?"

"Not today. Too much going on."

"Well, I need something cold. I'm hot as hell."

Yeah, he'd noticed that, too. Her cheeks were pink, and there was the faintest hint of moisture glinting off her cleavage when she moved. Jesus. He tried to look away, but then she raised her arms to pull her hair off her neck and twist it up. Her breasts rose with the movement. His eyes didn't.

"Come on," she said, turning away and breaking the spell. She grabbed something metal off a table as they passed and stuck it into the knot she'd made of her hair.

"The place looks nice," he said, following the sway of her hips to the kitchen and trying to keep his mind off her curves and on the real reason he'd come.

"Thanks. I'm having a little girls' party tomorrow."

"I heard."

Her head popped up over the open fridge door. "Did Jill invite you?" She didn't sound exactly pleased.

"To girls' night? No. But we got word from Veronica Chandler that she'd like to come."

"Oh, that's right. Lauren told me she was going to invite her. Are you okay with it?"

He nodded. He was more than okay with it, because it would give him an excuse to poke around this place some more. To solve this mystery. The longer he knew her, the more he thought she was hiding from something, and the more he wanted to help. "We'll have to send a couple of agents along with her, though. We'll try to stay out of your way."

Her eyes narrowed a little. "I don't want strangers in my house."

"I'll do it myself, if you're more comfortable. And my second-in-command is a woman. I could bring her."

She shrugged one shoulder and opened a beer. "I suppose that would be all right. Veronica probably needs to get out of the house if she has a bunch of you people underfoot all the time." Isabelle took a long draw of the beer then shivered a little as she wiped the bottle over her brow. Her nipples tightened. He watched, despite that his brain was screaming at him to look away. Look away! But God, they were…perfect.

"Are you staring at my breasts, Marshal Duncan?"

He jumped as if he'd been touched with a live wire. He couldn't deny it, and he couldn't excuse it. "Shit. Um. I'm sorry."

She shrugged again, and to his complete shock, she smiled. "It's all right. If you were standing there in workout shorts, I'd stare at your ass. I guarantee it. Your thighs, too." Her gaze slid down his body to the afore-mentioned area, and Tom's face flamed. He hoped to God the enthusiasm he could feel swelling his dick wasn't enough to be noticeable.

"Plus…" Her gaze rose slowly back up until it met his. "I've got nice tits."

Her eyes didn't waver. She didn't look coyly away. She watched him as though she wasn't even flirting; she was only letting him know because it was true.

But she *was* flirting. Clearly. And Tom fucking liked it. He liked it more than he'd liked anything in a long while.

Isabelle wasn't beautiful in some striking way, but there was something gorgeous about the way she held herself, the way she moved. As if she didn't give a damn what anyone else thought. You could accept her or you could move on, but either way, she'd still be here, in her place. This was where she belonged. Tom was the in-terloper, and it felt like an honor to be let in.

He looked at her hazel eyes, tight at the corners with amusement, and her too-strong nose, and that wide mouth, tipping up just a little at the edges. She was daring him. Tom knew he shouldn't; he had a hundred reasons not to, but he still stepped forward and slowly raised a hand to her jaw. His fingers slid along her warm skin, tracing her, feeling the way her head tipped ever so slightly into his touch.

She rose to meet his mouth, and though he meant to keep it careful, she wasn't interested in care. Her lips immediately softened against his, parting slightly, teasing him with her hot breath. Her tongue touched his mouth, one little lick of fire.

He couldn't help his sound of surprise. Not surprise that she'd licked him, but that the heat of it shot through his body. Isabelle smiled against his mouth, and then she laughed. That was how he kissed her, taking a taste, touching his tongue against hers until her laugh turned to a groan, and she kissed him back.

Whoever she'd gone home with the night before hadn't satisfied her, because she pushed up to take more of his mouth, more of his tongue. Her hand, cold from the beer, sneaked up his neck and into his hair, as if she'd hold him in place if he wanted to leave.

He wasn't going anywhere.

Slanting his mouth over hers, he gave her what she wanted with a deep, slow kiss. Their tongues slid against each other with a rhythm that had him rock hard in no time flat. He must have moved closer, because she eased back until her hips were caught by the kitchen counter.

He held her there, his hands sliding over those sexy hips, feeling the fascinating curve of her body from ass to waist. That primal geometry told his hands and cock and brain that this was right and good. Yes, they urged him, this was the best part of life. This curve and heat and her mouth open and taking him.

Only a minute ago he'd been mortified that she might notice her physical effect on him. Now he wanted her to feel it. He wanted to press his hips to hers and ease some of the ache in his cock. He wanted her to know what he needed, what she'd done.

But fuck... He lifted his head. "Fuck," he murmured, hands still clutching her hips.

Her throaty laugh chased over his jaw. "Yeah. I agree. That was very nice."

His laugh was a little more pained than hers. Then again, it'd been longer than a day since he'd done this. More like eight months. Not that he was counting.

She pressed a kiss to his cheek then his chin, and then her teeth closed gently over his bottom lip. "Mmm," she murmured before letting him go. "Let's do it again."

"I can't," he said, but he kissed her anyway. He could control himself, no question. It was just that he didn't want to. Not when she'd tugged him a little closer, so that those gorgeous breasts were pressed against him, and her mouth drew him deeper, and if he just pressed his hips a little tighter...

He groaned into the kiss as he eased away. "I can't get distracted right now. I'm sorry."

"Oh. Am I distracting you?" Her smile told him she knew the answer, even before she pulled his hips into hers.

"You know you are."

"Well, I wasn't sure until just now." She pressed snug against him.

Tom laughed, loving her boldness and the challenge in her eyes. "Thank God you're not still uncertain."

"No," she said, pressing her hips tighter. "Not at all." She raised one hand to slide it up his stomach to his chest, watching her hand explore until it disappeared beneath his suit jacket. "You feel really good."

It had been a slow build before, starting with the sight of her, then her teasing, her taste, her curves. But this…this frank appreciation for *his body*? His heart thundered in his chest, and his cock was suddenly painfully hard. He wanted that hand of hers to slide lower. He wanted it to unzip his pants and curl around him and *tighten*. And he wanted her telling him how good it all was. So damn good.

"Isabelle," he said, and just that, just her name, reminded him that he shouldn't do this. "Stop trying to make me crazy."

That husky laugh burst from her, and she gave him a friendly shove. "Fine. But only because you're being cute."

He didn't feel cute. He felt bereft and a little betrayed that she wasn't keeping his cock warm anymore. But that was what he'd requested, wasn't it?

"As you can see," she said as if normal conversation wasn't difficult after that kiss, "everything around here is fine. You can get back to work."

He frowned and looked around in confusion for a moment, not quite recalling what he'd meant to do. "I know how you are about your privacy, but if Veronica is going to be here for a few hours, would you let me take a closer look? Windows, doors, that sort of thing? There was a threat against the family. In fact—" he rubbed a hand over his face "—maybe it'd be better if you disinvited her."

"No way," Isabelle said immediately. "That girl needs a night out. Look at whatever you need to." Her eyes narrowed just a little. "I don't have anything to hide, Marshal."

Damned if she didn't lie almost as well as she kissed.

CHAPTER SEVEN

HE STILL SEEMED slightly out of sorts. She liked that look on him. The big, tall lawman confused by a simple little kiss.

Okay, so it hadn't been little. Or simple. She'd been turned on before he'd even pressed his mouth to hers. And judging by the lovely size of his cock, he'd been pretty excited, too.

She'd found him attractive before, but now she knew how firm that stomach was and how his hard chest curved up so nicely into his shoulders. She looked him up and down, and her mouth watered.

"Stop it," he muttered, taking another step back.

God, he really was adorable. "You don't have to stand here and let me ogle you. Go on. Look around."

He glanced past her toward the studio doors. "I'd rather you come with me."

"You're not seriously scared of my paintings, are you?"

"No, I'm scared of the photographs."

It took her a moment to recognize the dry humor in his voice. "I'll protect you. Try to think of them as part of a case file."

"I want you to come with me because I know your privacy is important to you."

She drew back a little in surprise that he even cared. "Okay," she agreed and followed him back to the living room, where he spent a lot of time checking her window locks.

"Living here alone, you might want to invest in some pin locks. They slide into the frame of the window."

"I'm too isolated to worry much about that. Anyone who wants in can just break the glass. Even Jill wouldn't hear that."

He grunted, not looking pleased. "You've got a dead bolt on the door, at least."

"It was here when I moved in."

"Any weapons?" he asked.

She hesitated long enough for him to stop his inspection of the door and look at her. "Yes. I've got a 9 millimeter."

"Legal?" he asked, clearly wondering if that was why she'd hesitated.

"Yes." But the Luger wasn't. Tom didn't need to know anything about that. Her father had given it to her. She didn't even have ammunition for it. Still, she assumed it was illegal in more ways than one.

"Well," he finally said, "don't shoot any of my people if you see them poking around on girls' night."

"Deal."

His eyes swept over the living room one more time before he moved on to the garage and laundry room and finally the kitchen.

"You don't have any family?" he asked as he did a quick check of the window above her kitchen sink. She hesitated again. She could feel herself doing it and couldn't stop it.

"I don't see any photos," he added.

"They're all gone," she said, and that was true enough. Her father was gone for good, whether he was alive or not.

"No pictures, even though they're gone? I guess you weren't close?"

"It's complicated."

"Yeah?" he pressed.

"Yeah."

"So you don't want to talk about your family."

She set her jaw, preparing to lie or tell him off for prying or…something. She should never have kissed him. This was not a man whose curiosity could be easily brushed aside. But while she was chastising herself, he became distracted, staring down the double doors to her studio as if he were steeling himself.

"Come on," she said. "The easel lights are off. It's not so bad."

He rolled his eyes as if he hadn't been watching the doors as if they'd burst open and zombies would come shuffling out. She noticed he waited for her to open them.

"Don't you have nightmares?" he asked as soon as he stepped in.

"Of course not." Not because of her work, anyway.

He took a breath and moved quickly past the first few easels to the two-story wall of windows. "This is the weakest point in your security," he said, testing the lock on the French doors that led out to a small deck. "But at least you have a slide lock here."

He engaged the lock at the top of the door, pushing it into the frame. "Where does this lead?" he asked, flipping the light switch next to the door. Nothing happened.

"Sorry. It's burnt out."

"Could you replace the bulb tomorrow?"

"Sure. There's a deck out there."

He pressed his hand to the glass to see past the lights of the room. "Stairs?"

"Yes."

"If it's—" Something slammed against the glass. Before Isabelle could even yelp, Tom had shoved her behind his back and drawn his weapon. "Out of the room!"

"It's just Bear!" she cried.

Tom was backing up and forcing her toward the door. "What?"

"It's the cat."

Bear batted at the glass slightly more gently this time. His big paw pressed against the window, the pink pads splaying out on the glass.

"Oh, Jesus Christ," Tom barked. "That goddamn cat."

"He just wants in."

"Well, let him in."

Isabelle rolled her shoulders, trying to release the tension that had latched in like claws. "He won't come in here. He doesn't like this room."

"I'm not surprised!"

"It's the smell of the paint, not the carnage. You should see what he can do to a rabbit."

Bear hit the door harder this time, and Tom jumped even as he put the gun away. "Why is he banging on the glass if he won't come in?"

"Because he wants me to open the door so he can stare at me while I get exasperated. Haven't you ever had a cat?"

"I've missed out on that joy," he said drily.

"They have their benefits."

"Like?"

She smiled. "He's really warm on a cold night when I'm alone."

He slanted her a look as he ran a hand over a windowsill. "How often are you alone?"

"Marshal Duncan, that's a very forward question."

He sneaked another look over his shoulder. "That was a very forward kiss."

She couldn't stop her grin. "I'm not attached to anyone, if that's what you're asking."

"That's what I'm asking."

"Why?" she asked slyly. "Are you going to kiss me again?"

He looked gratifyingly pained by the question. "I can't. I need to get back to my assignment. Plus, we barely know each other."

She realized her laughter was a little impolite, but she couldn't help it. "And we're not going to get to know each other. You live on the other side of the state. But we can still kiss."

He finished checking the windows and turned to her, his mouth flat. "Come on. Cheyenne isn't that far away. Tell me something about yourself."

"You know plenty about me already. It's your turn. Do you have family?"

"Yes. Mom and Dad, and a sister who has a family of her own."

"Are they all in Wyoming?"

"Yes," he answered as he led the way out of the room.

"Do you get along with them?"

"We get along fine," he said, as if that meant anything at all. Before she could press, he asked her a question. "How did you end up here?"

"I came through on a road trip, and I liked it." Another truth. She was getting almost comfortable with it. "Why aren't you married?"

He didn't hesitate. "I travel too much."

"Oh? So US Marshals don't get married?"

"Fine. I never met the right woman. I don't want kids, so that complicates things, or so I've been told." He didn't look to see if she was following him toward her bedroom.

"Now we're getting interesting. Why don't you want kids?"

"Why don't you? You're, what...midthirties? Why aren't you married?"

Ha. She could answer that. "I'm thirty-six. And I'm too mean."

He stopped and turned toward her. "You're not mean."

"Oh, really? Am I nice?"

His head cocked, and he studied her for a moment. "You're not nice, exactly."

She laughed so hard she had to press a hand to her stomach to try to control it. "I like your honesty," she managed to say past her gasps. "You're pretty cool."

"Now, that's something I haven't heard in a really long time."

"Then we're even."

They stared at each other for a long moment before Tom shook his head. "Shit, I want to kiss you."

"Do it," she dared him, her insides already tightening at the idea.

But his gaze slid to her bed, and he shook his head. "I can't."

"Afraid I'll lure you into my bed and steal your virtue?"

"If you can find my virtue, you can have it. And if that's a euphemism, even better. But what I'm afraid of is having to leave in twenty minutes. Not very memorable. And..." He held up a hand as if reminding himself. "I really shouldn't get involved when I'm in your house on official business. Now tell me why you're not married."

"Tell me why you don't want kids."

That shut him up, and Isabelle was free to watch him work for the next five minutes until he left with a warning about locking the door. And with no goodbye kiss.

But that was okay. She could wait. He'd give in before long. And in the meantime, she could fantasize about exactly how it would happen.

DAMN. TOM WAS in deep trouble. He hadn't meant to kiss her. It would've been a bad idea even without the extra complication that he was looking into her on the side. He had Veronica Chandler to protect, and he couldn't mess around with Isabelle when he was on duty.

More than that was the trouble of Isabelle herself. Tom had been thirty-one before he'd realized he couldn't trust himself with women. Not because he had a roaming eye or a callous heart or a cruel streak, but because he didn't. He'd been a sucker for the damsel in distress. The soft girl who couldn't quite figure life out. He'd been smart enough not to fall for any hard cases, but that had only made it worse. When a girl was hot and helpless and nice, it was really hard to break things off when you finally realized you needed to.

Isabelle wasn't like that, of course. He'd finally aged out of those immature attractions. Isabelle was capable and tough and smart as hell. But she was still in some sort of trouble. He couldn't add sex to the mix, especially when he could tell just how good it was going to be. He couldn't do that when he was still checking into her past.

"Damn it," he growled as he drove carefully down her snow-packed driveway and eased onto the road.

All he wanted to do was turn around, bang on her door and spend the next few hours in her bed. But he couldn't.

Despite his misgivings, he might not have had the willpower to make it out of there, but then she'd said she liked his honesty. When the only reason he'd asked her to stay close in her house was so he could probe her about her past.

He should drop it, but he couldn't. What if she was in danger? Worse yet, what if she was a criminal and he didn't do his job because he would rather have sex with her?

He shook his head. Dropping it wasn't an option. He couldn't ignore his gut at this point. The most he could do was keep his suspicions quiet until he found out the truth.

You didn't just ignore trouble. He'd learned that the hard way at a young age. Those were the kind of lessons you got when your older brother was a drug addict. When the choice came down to honesty or tricking someone into getting help, you dropped honesty every time.

If Isabelle needed help, she'd never admit it. And if she'd done something wrong, he couldn't ignore it.

Simple enough, but he felt like biting someone's head off by the time he got out of the car and stalked toward the judge's house. He wanted to slam the door open and yell at everyone in sight, but it wasn't his home, and his people hadn't done anything wrong.

Mary was waiting for him as soon as he hit the basement stairs. "Did you really approve this night out for Veronica?" she snapped.

"Yes."

"Why?" Her tone suggested he'd lost his mind, and she was about to help him find it.

"Veronica didn't have to come here. We can't keep her prisoner. And it's not like she wants to go to the state fair. It's a private residence within shouting distance of our base. It shouldn't be difficult."

Mary was about to argue with him. He could see that as clearly as if she'd said it, but eventually she closed her mouth and nodded. "Okay. Fine. Who are you sending over?"

"You."

"Me?" she screeched.

"I'm going, too."

"What the hell, Tom? We've got twelve additional people here now, and this is a job for a first-year deputy."

He couldn't tell her that the real reason was that he wanted to spy on Isabelle. He also couldn't tell Mary that he wanted her to meet Jill. She'd dig in her heels and tell him to mind his own business. She was always telling him to mind his own business; he never did. "Those guys need all their attention on the courthouse. We know how to pace ourselves. You can sleep in the next day if you need to."

"I don't need to sleep in!" she growled before stomping up the stairs. That was the end of the discussion. Good.

They'd debriefed in the meeting room after court had adjourned, but that didn't mean there weren't twenty emails waiting for him. So far there'd been no activity at the judge's place, and Stevenson hadn't been spotted in Jackson or Boise or anywhere in between.

Tom wrote an update for his chief, laying out his plan

to feed only the smallest bits of information to the press so as not to inspire any of the defendant's sympathizers. Then he sent an email to his team with a few more specifics about tomorrow's detail, requested an expedited review of the letter from the consulting psychiatrist and was finally ready to turn in at eleven.

But he had something else to look into.

He'd considered taking a long-range photo of Isabelle and feeding it into a reverse image search, but if she'd kept a low profile for the past fourteen years, it probably wouldn't pan out. No point stepping that far over the line into invading her privacy. He'd also considered that he could've lifted some small piece of garbage from her trash to get her fingerprints, but that felt even more wrong. He really wanted to leave a moral pathway open to sleeping with her.

At this point, the best he could do without compromising his own convoluted sense of integrity was to do it the hard way. He knew she was thirty-six and that she was maybe from Cincinnati, but probably from Chicago if his ear was right, and it usually was. If there was news or an event or an arrest, it would be pre-2002. That was it, really. He cracked his knuckles and got to work.

He searched missing persons in Cincinnati first, but considering that was the location she'd given, he didn't trust it. When he found nothing related to Isabelle, he moved on to the Chicago area. There weren't any missing women in her age group that looked like Isabelle there, either. Next up were the fugitive lists. It didn't take long to get through the FBI list, but the local Chicago lists were extensive and broken down by district. An hour later, his eyes swimming from all the scrolling he'd done, he sat back in his chair with a sigh.

She wasn't a fugitive, as far as he could tell. Which

meant, as a marshal, he should just drop it. But he'd never been very good at dropping things. And he had more than a professional interest now.

If she wasn't a wanted fugitive, then she was running from something else. She had a gun, a fake identity, a Chicago accent and no pictures of her family, who she'd implied were dead.

Trying to ignore the clock screaming 12:15 at him, he searched for murders in the Chicago area for the five years previous to when Isabelle West's name had appeared on the record. There were a lot of murders. He started filtering out the least likely scenarios, but by 1:00 a.m., he realized it was useless. There was too much crime in a place like Chicago, and he still couldn't be sure he had the city right. Could be Milwaukee. Cleveland. Or any place in between.

He needed to sleep. And he needed not to care. And he really needed to drop this.

He fell asleep ten minutes later with theories about Isabelle West still spinning through his brain, but when he dreamed, it was all about that kiss.

CHAPTER EIGHT

IT WAS TURNING out to be a truly glorious day.

Isabelle had awoken to a warm band of sunlight snaking across her bed and turning January into pure heat. No matter how cold it was outside, the sun at this altitude was scorching, so she'd kicked off her covers and stretched out naked in the warmth, feeling like a self-satisfied cat.

Self-satisfied, indeed, because thoughts of Tom had turned her slick and tight, and Isabelle had touched herself. Slowly. Lazily. Thinking of his subtle tongue and hard cock and the very good things she'd like from both of them.

He was dangerous. Maybe not to anyone else, but definitely to her. He could destroy everything she'd worked hard to build. Yet something about him drew her in. Maybe that very thing. The danger. Or maybe just that even though she didn't trust cops anymore, even though she wanted nothing to do with any of them... She'd spent her whole life around cops. She knew how they moved and spoke and thought.

She loved the wariness in his eyes each time he entered a darkened room. The way his hand went to his gun when he was on alert. The way he studied her face when she spoke, trying to figure her out.

That was the problem right there. That he looked at her and *saw* her. But just the thought of it turned her on, so she imagined that. Imagined him watching as she touched herself in lazy strokes. He didn't say anything. Didn't order her around and ask to be touched. He just watched, took her in, devoured her with his eyes. Then he reached down and unzipped his pants and tugged down his underwear, and Isabelle whispered, "Yes."

Yes, she'd said, fingering herself, stroking her clit, her other hand sliding up to pinch her nipple hard. Yes, she wanted him just like that. Standing above her. Watching her fingers slide deeper. Wanted him stroking his cock. That beautiful jaw of his would get so tense. His lush mouth would flatten. The sun would glint off his chest hair, and it would shine on the wetness of her pussy and—

"God," she choked out as everything inside her coiled tight. "God, yes." She came saying his name and picturing him coming right along with her.

Just that long, shuddering orgasm would have been enough to make the day special, but she'd followed it up with a spectacular day of painting, putting the final touches on one piece before starting on a clean canvas that was the very last work of the contract.

And now...now she was in the mood to party.

Jill, well aware that Isabelle's domestic skills consisted of occasional grilled cheese construction and charring a perfect steak, arrived early with little puff pastries to be thrown in the oven. "Cheddar and jalapeño," she said.

"Jesus, can I eat one raw?"

"No, but I made some guacamole, too. With more minced peppers, just the way you like."

"Give it," Isabelle said, managing to growl out a quick thank-you before she stuffed a chip into her mouth. She groaned her approval as the creamy goodness melted over her tongue. Yes, this was the perfect, perfect day.

"I'm going to paint another picture for you this spring," she promised Jill. "Though I'd have to paint ten a year to repay you for all the food."

"If I didn't make food for you, I'd make it for myself, and I'd gain twenty pounds every winter instead of five."

"Okay. Just get those puff pastries in the oven and we'll call it even."

"All right, greedy. But first I'll grab the pies out of the car." She headed toward the front door, and Isabelle rushed after her, her skin actually flushing with excitement.

"Pie? You brought pie? You really are the perfect woman."

Jill winked over her shoulder as she opened the front door. "I normally don't hear that until after sex."

"Vixen," Isabelle said before realizing there was a petite blonde stranger standing in the open doorway, her frown answering their laughter.

"Oh, hello," Jill said brightly, as if the woman wore a decidedly more friendly expression.

The woman's scowl deepened. "I'm Deputy Marshal Jones."

"Isabelle," Jill said slyly, "you're under arrest again."

"It figures." Thank God Tom had warned her he was sending another deputy over or she'd be fighting off a panic attack. Isabelle craned her neck to see past the porch to the driveway beyond. "Is Tom coming?" she asked. "He said he was coming over to keep an eye on Veronica Chandler."

Jill gasped. "Tom's coming? I'm going to spoil him like he's the only boy at a girls' night party."

Isabelle poked her shoulder. "You're the worst lesbian ever, and a terrible feminist to boot. Focus on feeding us and forget about the boy. He wasn't even invited."

Marshal Jones watched them with a wariness that suggested she wouldn't be surprised if they both pulled out revolvers and started whooping their way down the porch steps, shooting pistols in the air.

"I'm sorry, Marshal Jones," Isabelle said. "But we are in the mood for a party. Did you want to come inside?"

"No, I'm only here to take a quick look around the property before it's full dark. *Tom* will be over soon with Ms. Chandler." She stepped quickly off the porch and headed for the side of the house.

Oh, shit. *Tom*, Marshal Jones had said with a little sneer in her voice. As if she didn't approve. As if she had reason not to.

He'd said something about his second-in-command coming by, which meant that he spent a lot of time with this woman. Time on the road, at restaurants, in hotel rooms. An occasional night of mutual stress relief would be totally normal, but those situations rarely played out with equal levels of feeling on both sides. This was going to be awkward. No wonder Tom hadn't stayed for a quickie last night.

"That woman needs some good food," Jill said, climbing back up the steps with a pie in each hand.

Isabelle quickly grabbed one and backed into the house. "I guess she's tired after a full day at the courthouse. Crap, I didn't even check the news. Is everything okay?"

"It seemed quiet. Some motion was filed by the defense, and everything ended around 3:00 p.m. Aside from the lawyers and reporters blathering on for endless interviews, of course. They received another letter this weekend. Did you hear?"

Isabelle frowned. "Maybe?" She couldn't quite remember, but she did recall how tired Tom had looked the night before. She sifted through her constantly crowded brain, trying to tuck away all the useless bits of anatomical details and medical facts that were currently crowding the way. "Right. A threat against the judge's family. I talked to Tom about it last night."

"Oh, you *did*? Now, that is something I hadn't heard."

Isabelle shrugged. "He comes to see you, too."

"Yes, but I'm luring him with food. What are you luring him with?"

"My tits. And my sparkling personality, I'm sure."

"No, it's your tits. They're gorgeous."

Isabelle actually felt her cheeks go pink. "Shut up," she said halfheartedly.

"Did you show him that painting?"

"He doesn't like my work."

Jill snorted. "He'll like *that*. Now get out of my way so I can finish the pastries."

Isabelle moved quickly to her bedroom to put on her party clothes, waving at Marshal Jones through the window before shutting the blinds. Thank God she didn't have any neighbors. She could rarely be bothered with closing curtains, and she often ran around in nothing but panties and bedhead. It was only her, after all, and half her day was spent remembering something she'd left in the other room or forgotten to do. Sometimes it took her two hours to finish getting dressed.

But not today. Today was easy, since she'd already laid out her clothes, mostly because she'd just taken them from the dryer. Black leggings, a long sage-green tank top that covered her ass and swooped low over her breasts, heeled boots and her nicest black cardigan. The cardigan would come off once the sangria kicked in.

She smiled as she wrapped a long silver chain around her neck three times. The longest loop dipped to touch the rise of her breasts. She hoped Tom would notice. She hoped he'd look at that warm metal touching her skin, and he'd want to touch it himself.

Thank God Tom's story had turned out to be true, or she'd never have let herself feel attracted to him. Not that sex with Tom was a sure thing at this point, but it was nice to have the interest. To look at a live, in-the-flesh man and feel her body say, *Yes.* The last time had been over a year ago and that had been more of a *Sure—why not?*

She hadn't been this casual about sex in her youth, but she'd been a very different girl then. As the only daughter of an overprotective, anxiety-ridden mother and a father who was a cop, Isabelle had walked the straight and narrow.

She'd done well in high school. Really well. She'd spread her wings a little in college, taking all the pre-med classes she'd meant to, but using all her elective hours on art. She'd saved her virginity for a boy she'd fallen in love with during her sophomore year of college. She hadn't quite waited until they'd gotten engaged, but that had come soon after. Her world had been knitting together into beautiful conformity, the way the bones of a child's skull slowly grew into the perfect protection.

During her junior year, she'd come to a realization that she could combine her love of painting with her love of medicine, but it had terrified her. She'd always known that she would be a doctor. Her parents had always known. Her fiancé, by then an up-and-coming attorney working for the state prosecutor, had considered marriage to a doctor a perfect match.

She hadn't wanted to let him down. She'd been afraid to shake things up.

Yes, that had summed her up nicely back then. Afraid to shake things up. And then an earthquake had hit her life and shaken everything to pieces.

Isabelle traced a hand down her collarbone then onto the warming silver and down to the tops of her breasts. Yes, she'd changed after that, thank God. She'd had her first orgasm, and it had been with a drunken one-night stand, of all things. She'd needed a man to show her what her body could do. A *stranger*. That had horrified her. She'd been so passive her whole life that she'd waited for someone else to reveal her own body to her.

That had been the end of passivity. It had been the end of a lot of things, and the beginning of so much more.

She knew it was a bad idea to sleep with Tom Duncan. It was a bad idea to even draw his attention. But she resented her fear and caution. She wanted to kick and scream and push against it. She wanted *him*.

After a quick brush of her hair, she pulled it up in a French twist that she hoped would hide any pigment she might've gotten on the ends during today's marathon painting session. Shampoo wasn't exactly effective on oil paint.

By the time she came out of the bedroom, the smell of butter and cheese had bloomed through the house. Isabelle turned on the stereo, got the first pitcher of sangria from the fridge and smiled at the sound of a car door slamming. A woman's laugh preceded the knock at the door, and Isabelle was laughing in response before she even opened it.

Girls' night was here.

SOPHIE LOOKED THE SAME. Somehow Isabelle had expected her to return looking like Sandy at the end of *Grease*: leathered and eyelinered and big-haired. But she still looked like a postwar librarian, her red hair curled under in an elegant chignon and her little black glasses doing their best to hide her naughty thoughts.

"Where's your bike?" Isabelle asked after giving Sophie a third hug and pressing a glass of sangria into her hand.

"We left the bikes in Texas for now. Alex has a quick contract in Alaska, and I decided winter in the Alaskan oil fields was not the adventure I'm looking for right now."

Lauren dropped onto the couch beside them. "Does that mean you're home for a while?"

Sophie winced. "For a little while."

"Shit," Isabelle groaned. "Just spill it."

Sophie cleared her throat. "I'm turning in my resignation," she said softly, reaching out for Lauren's hand. They worked together at the library, or they had before Sophie had taken a leave of absence four months before.

"You're really leaving," Isabelle whispered.

"I'm leaving. Finally."

"Okay," Isabelle said. "That's good." Neither of them wanted to lose Sophie, but she'd lived her entire life in Jackson, and it was time for her to see the world. On a motorcycle. With her delicious new man.

Isabelle touched her glass to Sophie's. "I'm proud of you."

Lauren sniffed a little, but she smiled. "Me, too. As

long as you promise to ride through here every year and see us."

"Oh, come on!" Sophie cried out, her eyes watery. "My dad is here. I'll be back all the time. A lifetime of crippling family dynamics can't be magically overcome with the power of one penis. Not even Alex's."

"Are you sure?" Lauren drawled. "What about when you throw in the tattoos and the bike?"

"Okay, it's close."

Isabelle nudged her a little less than gently. "Shut up already. Everyone in this room except me has access to a penis."

Jill barked out a laugh from the doorway. "Bite your tongue, woman. None of you *need* one anyway. You can order high-quality substitutes from the comfort of your own home."

Sighing, Isabelle sank back into the oversize couch, letting the first flush of sangria wash over her. "I know, but there's nothing like the real thing. Warm skin and that velvety texture and the smell of a man's body. God."

Silence fell, and Isabelle knew why even before she leaned forward and looked toward the front door. "Hi, Tom."

"Sorry to interrupt," he said, his voice as neutral as a court stenographer's.

Isabelle hopped up with a grin. "Nonsense. Your arrival was utterly apropos." Once she was standing, she saw the young woman behind him. "Veronica? I'm Isabelle. Welcome!"

"Thank you so much for inviting me!" When the woman pasted a smile on her face and stepped forward with an outstretched hand, she looked a little less young and uncertain, but only a little. Her short blond bob swung forward against round cheeks that gave her a sweet, youthful look. The pretty blue eyes didn't hurt much, either, though they were darkened with smoky gray shadow and black eyeliner.

Lauren sprang up from the couch. "You're here!" she called out, rushing forward to give Veronica Chandler a hug. "Everyone, this is Veronica. Of the infamous *Dear Veronica* page."

Sophie gasped. "Oh, my God, I was in your column! You wrote about me!"

The blonde's eyes widened. Isabelle could imagine the stories flashing through her brain. She'd been writing the advice column for only a year, but there'd been some doozies.

Isabelle tried to keep the grin off her face. "Sophie is the one who had a fling with her stepbrother."

Sophie howled with laughter. "That's a lie. I was the man-eating whore who corrupted that poor woman's son with free sex."

"Oh," Veronica said. Then, "Oh!" more brightly. Her surprise slowly faded into a small frown of worry. "I hope I didn't say anything terrible about you."

"No, you were great," Sophie said with a wave of her hand. "I was cheering you on."

A small smile turned the girl's mouth up. "So was it true?"

"That I corrupted him with free sex? Absolutely. Every chance I got. Damn, that man is gorgeous."

"I'm glad it worked out."

Sophie's gaze slid to Tom, and her eyebrows rose in question. Isabelle touched his shoulder. "This is Deputy Marshal Duncan. He's here to watch over Veronica."

Veronica cringed. "It's not that big a deal."

"It's a pretty big deal," Sophie said, looking Tom up and down. "And definitely the most adventurous girls' night *in* we've ever had. Marshal, did you bring your pj's?"

"I did not," he said drily, but Isabelle could see red high on his cheeks. He could pretend to be all "Just doing my job, ma'am," but he was paying attention to everything.

Isabelle leaned a little closer and spoke low. "Can I interest you in a sangria? It's going to be a long night without it, in case you can't already tell."

"No, thanks. I'm just going to head out and talk with Mary for a minute. One of us will be back."

Judging by the deepening red of his face, it would be *Mary*. Tom probably wasn't used to a roomful of drunk women willing to talk about *anything*. Too bad for him. He was going to miss all the fun.

CHAPTER NINE

TOM SPOKE BEFORE he got even halfway to Mary's car. "We have to trade places. You go inside."

"What?" she bit out. "What are we even doing here? Veronica's request to come to this party should've been turned down flat. Or hell, the most she needs is an escort to the door. Nobody is coming to invade the sorority house, Tom."

Tom was a bit taken aback by her anger. "It's not a sorority house. Did you meet the women? Jill's really nice and—"

"Did you assign me to this bullshit protection because I'm female?"

Tom blinked and shook his head. "What are you talking about? *I'm* here."

"Yes, you are." She crossed her arms and looked him up and down. "And that makes even less sense. Are you fucking her?"

"What?" His face flamed. "Who?"

"That Isabelle. She called you *Tom.* Well, so did the other one, but I don't think you're her type."

"I'm not fucking anyone," he snapped.

"Then what the hell are we doing here? The truth!"

Tom took a deep breath and let it out slowly, hoping to expel some of his frustration and guilt, too. He glanced back toward the house, but no one was listening. In fact, the music leaking from inside was louder than it had been earlier.

"Shit," he muttered, turning back to find Mary watching him through narrowed eyes. "I need discretion here, Mary. This isn't official."

"*What* isn't official?"

He spared one more look for the cabin, hearing the snow squeak and crunch under his feet when he shifted. "When I first showed up, Isabelle West seemed...not nervous, exactly. Hostile. Jaded. Enough so that I looked into it."

Mary's eyebrows flew up. "A fugitive?"

"No. I've checked. It's not that. There's nothing there, honestly, but I've got a hunch, and I figure they'll be talking tonight."

"Are you sure you're not just confused? She likes you."

"You've always trusted my hunches."

"Yes, but I also know how you are about playing savior. She doesn't seem like a person who wants or needs help."

"Look, I just wanted the chance to follow up." He shrugged the tension from his shoulders. "And it's possible I don't mind that she might like me."

"Oh," she said, looking a little more open now. She glanced toward the cabin with curiosity instead of resentment. "Well, then." She smiled toward the sound of the women laughing. "Tom Duncan has a crush."

"That's not what this is about."

She didn't look convinced.

"I mean, I was checking her out before I was interested in her. And I can't move on either way until I'm sure about her."

Mary nodded solemnly. "Well, you'd better get in there, then."

He cleared his throat. "I thought, um... It's girls' night. I thought maybe you could be the one..."

"Me? Hang out with a bunch of drunk mountain women I've never met? No way. This is all you. I've got nothing in common with any of them."

He wanted to say "But I thought you might like Jill," but he was evolved enough to know that *She's a lesbian, too!* wasn't a reasonable introduction. Still, he really *liked* Jill. And Mary had spent all of last year caught up in a drama-filled relationship with a thirty-year-old who'd jerked her around. She needed someone nicer. More stable. Someone kind and open enough to see past Mary's formidable defenses.

But that would go over almost as well as *She's a lesbian, too*, so Tom kept his mouth shut. Plus, girls' night intimidation aside, he really should be the one listening in. Still...they were already talking about sex.

Then again, they were already talking about sex.

"Fine," he conceded. "I'll take it."

"Good. I already made the rounds. No tracks anywhere. I'll take a drive up the road to those summer cabins, just to scope it out, and let you know when I'm back so you don't shoot me through a window."

"I'll do my best not to." Tom squared his shoulders and faced Isabelle's cabin. The curtains had been drawn at his insistence, but he could still see the shadows of the women as they moved around the room. One of them was dancing to the faint thump of the music, and he suspected it was Isabelle.

His initial impression of her had been of a guarded person. Reserved. But that had been so wrong. Distrustful of strangers, maybe, and of law enforcement definitely, but she wasn't reserved. She was…free. Bold. And honest about everything except her past.

And judging by what she'd been saying when he walked in, she was also fond of penises. He really couldn't overlook such an important aspect of her personality.

Tom was a guy who normally walked the straight and narrow, even if he had to fight his baser impulses to do it. He knew how important that was. Knew what the risks of giving in to a mistake were.

But what if giving in to the attraction meant that he could help Isabelle? What if he could get her to trust him? Still…baser impulses had a way of convincing people they were doing the right thing when they weren't. He'd have to proceed with caution.

That in itself was problematic, because Isabelle didn't seem to know much about caution. Look at the way she'd leaned into his kiss. The way she'd teased him. The way she'd dared him to do it again.

The woman was dangerous. Like a drug that could get into his veins and pull him deep under. A drug that smelled good and tasted even better.

Damn. He wanted it. Wanted her. Bad.

No. Tonight he needed to concentrate less on her cleavage and more on eavesdropping when her guard was down.

A good plan. But when he stepped inside the cabin again, Isabelle was slipping off the sweater that had kept her mostly hidden, and now it wasn't only cleavage. It was her arms, pale and so much softer than his. Her shoulders, strong from so many hours holding a brush at delicate angles. And her neck, naked and bare with the way she'd pulled her hair up again.

That was another thing he liked about her: the careless way she twisted her hair off her neck, exposing her vulnerable spine to his gaze. He liked looking at the careful steps of the bones as they descended to her back.

Tonight she wore a necklace that wound around before dipping all the way down to the rise of her breasts, resting just where he wanted to press his mouth.

Damn it.

"I thought you were supposed to be watching Veronica," Jill said from his side.

"She seems fine," he said without looking at her, but when Jill held a tray of little pastries out to him, he turned to face her before taking one. "She likes being out here in the woods," he said. "Isabelle."

"She's comfortable with solitude."

"Is that what it is?"

Jill studied him for a moment before walking away to set the pastries on the living room table. The other women pounced on the food, but Jill returned to his side. He fought the urge to shift under her direct gaze. "What do you think it is?" she finally asked.

"I think she doesn't trust people."

"True. But people aren't very trustworthy, are they?"

He didn't flinch at that, but he wanted to. "I'm the wrong guy to ask. I encounter a lot of bad people, so I'd definitely say no. But is there something more specific? Something I should know?"

Her surprise seemed genuine. "About Isabelle? You'd have to ask her."

"You never have?"

Jill shook her head. "Life is hard. I'm a black gay woman who was born in the South a long time ago. I've been hurt by more people in my life than I've been helped. By people I *loved*. If I had to guess, I'd say the people Isabelle loved hurt her, too."

Tom nodded and glanced toward the window, wanting to look away, but the curtains closed him off from distraction. "It's always the people you love, isn't it? Otherwise it wouldn't hurt."

She touched his arm. "Ask her if you want. But if she won't tell you, leave it be. She didn't come to the mountains to be poked at."

He nodded, and she smiled.

"I mean, I'm not saying that a little poking wouldn't be nice, but that's another thing you'd have to ask her about."

His face went hot immediately, and when Jill laughed in delight, it only got hotter.

"You're cute, Tom. You know that?"

"Yeah, I heard that earlier," he muttered.

"Jill!" Isabelle called out. "What are you doing to our friendly neighborhood marshal? He's beet red."

"I was telling him how cute his ass is. Isn't it cute?"

Tom did his best to ignore the roar of hoots and catcalls that filled the room. Amazing that so few women could make so much noise. He tried not to turn his back on them as he edged toward the kitchen. "I'll just give the perimeter another check," he muttered.

"I'll check your perimeter," Isabelle offered.

He shook his head and escaped to the kitchen. Jill followed and pushed a bowl of guacamole toward him. "Are you sure you don't want some sangria? You look like you need it."

"It's my first girls' night," he said, regretfully waving off the pitcher of sangria.

"You're not going to hide in here all night, are you?"

He would, but the information he wanted was all in the other room with Isabelle. "I'm just doing a sweep."

"Mmm-hmm."

He made it quick, though, giving the women just enough time to start relaxing into their booze, checking the same places he'd checked the day before, lingering for a moment in Isabelle's bedroom, just in case he'd missed a photo or a letter or memento. He wouldn't dig through her dresser, but if she'd left out a picture of her parents or a postcard from somewhere far away... Yeah, it didn't matter. He still felt like shit as he switched off the light and headed back out to the main area of the cabin.

When he hesitated at the doors to her studio, he told himself it was because he didn't want to switch on the lights and illuminate the entire wall of windows to anyone who could be watching outside. Except that was no real reason to hesitate. It was simple enough to not turn on the lights. The full moon and the snow on the ground meant he had plenty of visibility; it was only that he wanted the comfort of the lights.

But there was one advantage to stepping into the room when it was still dark. The paintings were only vague impressions of lines and darkness, and the photographs weren't visible at all.

Tom pretended the easels were landscape paintings and walked toward the silver shapes of the windows. He flipped on the porch light and frowned. Nothing. She'd forgotten to replace the bulb. Or someone had unscrewed it. Tom scanned the moonlit porch and stairway, waiting a moment before he opened the door. The bulb was screwed in tight and was dark with burnt dust. He retrieved it and ducked back inside.

"Isabelle," he said when he reached the living room. She heard him over the music and looked up, her mouth pursed around a strawberry. He held up the bulb.

"Oh, shit," she said, swallowing the fruit, which left

behind a delicious sheen of wetness on her mouth. "I forgot."

"You?" Lauren drawled. "Forget something? That seems unlikely."

"Shut up. I have things on my mind."

"You're an *artist*!" Lauren shouted, and the women collapsed into laughter as if they'd said it a hundred times.

"That's right," Isabelle said, standing up and looking tall in her boots and tight leggings, her neck stretching up to that upswept hair. "Veronica understands, don't you? She and I have bigger things on our minds than lightbulbs. Or dinner reservations. Or bills."

"I just write an advice column," Veronica said.

Isabelle stepped over her legs and headed for Tom. "Nonsense. You're a wordsmith. And a painter of the human soul."

Veronica's mouth fell open in shock. She shook her head. But when the other two women collapsed against her, laughing, she forced a smile. "If you say so."

"I do," Isabelle said with a wink.

Veronica had seemed nervous on the way over, and Tom had assumed it was about the threats in the latest letter, but she hadn't relaxed since. She was still very much on guard. He caught her eye and mouthed "Okay?"

She immediately nodded and took another sip of sangria, so Tom felt okay leaving her alone. He followed Isabelle into the kitchen. She grabbed a new bulb while Jill checked something in the oven.

"Should be ready in fifteen minutes," Jill said.

Isabelle held up the lightbulb. "Well, hopefully we'll be back before then."

"Not if you show him that painting."

Isabelle smiled in his direction. "I told you he hates my paintings."

"Not this one."

Aware he was being left out of the joke, Tom frowned as he followed Isabelle into the dark room. "What was that about?"

"Jill is trying to get me into trouble. Or, actually..." She paused in the darkness and turned to look at him. "Maybe she's trying to get *you* into trouble."

"How so?"

She shrugged and headed straight toward the French doors, not hesitating for a second in the dimness.

"Let me," he said, hurrying behind her to check the deck area before she opened the door.

"I'm perfectly capable of replacing a light."

"Just not in a timely manner?"

"Definitely not in a timely manner." She opened the door, letting cold air pour in as she leaned outside. "But we can't all be by-the-book lawmen, can we? Some of us are free spirits."

She was only joking, but Tom wanted to say *yes*. Yes, because of her laugh and the way her shoulders curved into a smooth slide of skin all the way down to plump breasts, and he was standing over her, behind her, and he could see down her shirt to the roundness of her from this angle. The softness.

And the easy way she moved through this house in the woods that was hers alone. And the way a lock of her hair had escaped its knot to trace over the skin of her neck just where he wanted to kiss her.

She was his opposite in every way. Pale and soft and curved. Amused by everything. Unconcerned by things she couldn't control. Happy to take what she wanted, whether it was him or a glass of wine or a moment to dance around the living room.

The bulb blinked on as she turned it.

He kissed her neck.

"Oh," she said softly, her hand falling away from the light. He'd thought it was a sound of shock, but her head immediately tipped forward, giving him more of her neck, and he realized the sound was pleasure. So he gave her more, kissing her again, opening his mouth against the side of her neck, scraping his teeth over her skin until her small hum became a soft groan.

The scent of her skin was already so familiar. It chased the smell of paints and thinners from the room. Lust shot through his gut.

Living in Judge Chandler's basement meant he hadn't had enough privacy to relieve the nagging stress from the last time he'd kissed her, so he was right there again, completely aroused and wanting more. He slid his hands over her shoulders, wanting to feel her soft skin again.

Isabelle reached one hand up and slipped her fingers into his hair to pull him more tightly to her neck. He sucked her flesh. Just a little. He couldn't risk leaving even the faintest mark, but damn, he wanted to press his teeth harder to her when she groaned and arched into him.

Winter air swept over them. Her nipples were rock hard and pressed to the thin fabric of her top. He wanted to touch them. Wanted to make her shiver under his mouth.

He raised his head, already breathing hard. "I'm sorry," he managed to say.

Isabelle laughed and turned in his arms. "Are you?"

"Yes," he said, half meaning it. He reached past her to switch off the light and shut the door so they wouldn't be so exposed, but those brief seconds of trying to distract himself were ruined by his awareness that her hands were sliding around his waist. They were all twisted up with each other, a loose twine of limbs that felt strangely natural with someone he'd known for only a few days.

"I like that you're having trouble resisting," she murmured, leaning back a little to look up at him.

He glanced down. "Your necklace is distracting."

"Oh, it's my necklace, is it?"

"Yes," he said, an out-and-out lie. He proved just how false it was by very carefully touching a finger to a silver coil and then letting it slide down. The edge of his finger grazed over the skin above the fabric of her shirt. He traced it again.

Isabelle shivered. "Mmm. Come here."

Expecting to be tugged closer, he was surprised when she slipped past him and grabbed his hand. "What?"

"My etchings."

"No, no, no," he said, but he let her drag him to the far side of the room.

"I'm a good artist," she said.

"I know. I can see that. It's just not to my taste and I'm not exactly—"

An easel light flicked on, and for a moment, all his brain processed was the pale flash of her arm moving away from the lamp, but then there were more parts of her illuminated. He blinked, confused and fascinated at the same time. So much of her, pale and exposed and…naked.

This painting was another anatomy painting in a way, but it wasn't medical. It was…erotic. Or just real and honest.

It was Isabelle from chin to hip, naked and completely unadorned but for a white flower she held in one hand.

Her face dipped slightly to the left, showing just the curve of her bottom lip, tipped in that secret, small smile. There was her pale neck. And her strong shoulders and delicate collarbones.

Her breasts, full and round and lovely, and just beginning to get a little heavier with age. Her nipples were dark and drawn tight, pebbled at the edges of her areolae, as if she were chilled.

There were so many details to take in, as if it were a photograph instead of a painting. She'd hidden nothing, even capturing the faint paleness of a few stretch marks at the fullest arc of her right breast. Then the lines of her abdomen curving out into full hips. And just at the bottom of the painting, the shadowed edge of her pubic hair, dark and curled.

"It's me," she said, the words calm and simple.

"Yes," he breathed. Then, "It's amazing."

"Thank you."

He tore his eyes away from her nudity for a moment to glance at her face. She looked pleased with what she'd done.

"Why are you showing me this?" he asked hoarsely.

She smiled, not looking away from the painting. "To make you a little crazy."

He laughed at her audacity, and though he tried to keep looking at her, his eyes were drawn back to the canvas. "Jesus, Isabelle. It's beautiful."

"Well, either it will drive you crazy—which will be nice for both of us—or it won't. And if it won't, then there's no point wasting any energy on this, is there?"

His synapses were a little confused. He wanted to reach out and shape her nakedness with his fingertips, but she was standing right next to him with real curves and heat and daring. His gaze bounced to her and back to the painting again.

"I'd better get back to the party," she said, turning away from the easel. She dragged one hand over his shoulder, setting his nerves on fire. "But you should think about me tonight when you go to bed."

"What?" he asked, forcing his eyes off her painted nipples and onto her retreating back.

She flashed an indulgent smile over her shoulder. "I know you're on duty tonight. I'll try not to bother you. But later, when you're alone, think about me."

His eyes flew to the open doors and the kitchen beyond, and he kept his voice low. "You're trying to shock me again."

She shrugged. "Not really. I'll think about you, too. I already have."

The meaning of her words slapped into him as if he'd landed flat on the surface of a pool. He'd never talked about this with a woman, never had a woman *ask* him to masturbate to her. And he'd certainly never been told that she'd already done the same for him.

"Don't forget to lock that door," she drawled, her hips swaying as she walked away with that confidence that drove him mad. "Wouldn't want a bad guy getting in."

Goddamn it. She *was* driving him mad. He was here to do a job—two jobs, actually—and neither of those involved getting into her bed. Not necessarily.

Tom winced at that cruel thought. No. He wouldn't sleep with her for information. But he couldn't shake the truth that she might be more willing to open up to him if they were intimate.

"No," he growled to himself. He couldn't have sex with her just to find out more. Those two things were separate. He wanted to sleep with her, and he also needed information. If those two things intersected, so be it.

The skin on his arms prickled, but he ignored it. If someone needed help, you took care of that whether they liked it or not. Isabelle didn't want help. She didn't want interference. But he'd give it anyway.

She reminded him a little of Michael, actually, before his brother had lost the greatness of his personality. Bold and brave and wild, and looking at the whole world with chin held high.

And like Michael, she'd never ask for help, even if she was drowning. Her pride scared him. And it turned him on like crazy.

He shut off the light illuminating her nude portrait, set his face in its best impassive expression and went out to join girls' night.

ISABELLE WATCHED AS SOPHIE, Lauren and Veronica slammed down their shots of vodka and grinned at each other. "I hope some of you are spending the night," she said before downing her own shot.

Sophie and Lauren raised their hands.

"I have a chauffeur," Veronica said with a wobbly smile. She was definitely starting to loosen up.

The oven timer buzzed, and for once, Jill didn't jump up. Instead, she poked her toe into Isabelle's thigh. An empty sangria glass dangled from her fingers. "Quiche is ready. Where's the salad?"

Isabelle winced. "Oops. I forgot about the salad."

"Isabelle!" Jill yelled.

"I'm sorry! I got busy and… Look!" She held up her own glass. "It doesn't matter. We have sangria fruit! That's the best kind of salad."

Lauren nodded. "She's got a point, Jill."

Jill didn't look appeased. "I just want all of you to know that I brought Isabelle's favorites, and this isn't a menu I'd normally create. Or at least there'd be vegetables!"

Isabelle jumped up to head for the kitchen. "There's spinach in the quiche. I'll get it out of the oven."

"Try not to forget between here and there," Jill mumbled.

But all seemed forgiven when Isabelle brought her another sangria and the first plate of quiche. The fact that Jill had let Isabelle do the plating—okay, the triangle of quiche was a little lopsided—showed just how relaxed she was after that drink. Or she was exhausted. Isabelle gave her a kiss on the cheek. "You okay?"

"A little regretful, but that's to be expected."

They both looked up to see the other women watching curiously. "Marguerite and I finally ended it," Jill explained and was greeted with moans of sympathy.

By the time Isabelle got quiche to the other women, everyone was telling breakup stories. Isabelle hurried back for two more plates, one for her and one for Tom, who'd just come in the front door.

"Everything okay?" she asked.

"Everything's good. I'll take this to the kitchen."

"You can stay," she said.

"No, I don't want to be in the way."

She bit back a sigh as he walked away. She'd been trying to drive him mad, but now she was the one suffering. She wanted to touch him. Wanted to kiss him. Wanted to suck his fingers into her mouth and make him moan. But she was apparently having a sleepover with friends. Damn it.

So all she could do was eat her delicious quiche and

drink another sangria and offer horrified laughter at the other women's stories.

"Speaking of exes," Lauren drawled. "I finally saw Steve over the holidays."

Sophie squealed. "Please tell me you were with Jake."

"I was. And Steve has lost more hair."

"Perfect," Sophie said. Lauren's ex-husband had sneered about her new relationship with his old friend, laughing that it wouldn't last long. Not with a bitch like Lauren.

Lauren grinned. "He tried to act cool about it, offering Jake a beer like they were still good friends, but after that bitch comment, Jake doesn't want much to do with him."

They all toasted to that.

"Isabelle," Lauren sang, "I bet you've got a good breakup story."

"Nope."

"Come on. You weren't born a confirmed bachelorette. Who's this guy?" She pointed behind her at the painting.

Isabelle smiled. That one she could talk about. It wasn't Patrick. It wasn't anyone who'd broken her heart. She glanced toward the kitchen and lowered her voice. "He replaced my roof a few years ago."

The women howled and catcalled.

"Oh, my God!" Sophie yelled. "Was there porn music playing when he showed up with his big roofing hammer?"

"No, but there was porn music playing later."

Poor Veronica spit out part of an orange, and Sophie patted her back before she pointed at Isabelle. "You're a naughty girl."

"Maybe, but only on occasion. It's not easy to lure men all the way up here."

Jill was the first one to look toward the kitchen, but eventually all the women glanced that way before turning their grins on Isabelle. She just shrugged and smiled back.

"Veronica," she finally said to change the subject. "You must have some good stories. Didn't you live in New York City? Was it just like *Sex and the City*?"

Veronica coughed again, shaking her head. "It was okay. I mean, don't get me wrong—I had a lot of fun, but I ruined all my street cred by moving back to my hometown at twenty-five."

"Are you kidding?" Isabelle asked. "I didn't even go away for college. I lived at home the whole time. You're doing great."

"Oh, where'd you go to college?"

Isabelle realized she'd walked right into a question she didn't want to answer. Panic flooded her veins, but she kept her face calm. "You're not getting out of it that easily. Tell us a New York story."

"I don't have any big breakup stories. It was mostly a lot of dating. A couple of dumps by text, that sort of thing."

"That's something I've avoided," Lauren chimed in. "There's a distinct advantage to dating Wyoming men in their forties. They don't text much. I am trying to introduce Jake to the joys of sexting, though. He's at the firehouse quite a few evenings. Sometimes I need a little jerk material." She nudged Veronica. "Maybe I'll write to you to ask how I can convince him to do it. He's worried he'll send a text to one of his guys."

Veronica nodded. "Now, *that* would be a good letter. Make sure he writes to me if that happens."

"Dear Veronica," Lauren intoned in a deep voice, "I'm the captain of a small-town fire department..."

Isabelle continued. "And I never thought something like this would happen to me."

Veronica looked a little confused by the *Penthouse* reference, but she was the youngest of the group. Jill, on the other hand, guffawed and slapped the arm of her chair.

Lauren held up the fork she'd been using to spear fruit from her sangria. "We should all start sending Veronica fake letters asking for advice and see if she can ferret them out."

"Please don't," Veronica said. "It's hard enough to try to filter out the fictional ones."

"How do you do it?" Lauren asked.

"Well, mostly I have to take them at face value. Because in all honesty, the ones I think are probably fake are often the ones that get the most follow-ups from real people. Sometimes from the letter-writers themselves, and sometimes from readers saying, 'It meant a lot to know someone else has gone through this.' People have crazy lives."

Sophie shook her head. "Tell me about it. My mom disappeared when I was five, and that was just the start of that screwed-up story."

The sangria was making Isabelle too sensitive. She knew it was. But she still reached out and wrapped her arm around Sophie. "I'm so sorry."

She couldn't imagine what that must have been like for a little girl. To live without a mom, wondering if she'd just walked away from her family. She'd lost her own father like that but as an adult, and it had still been devastating. Isabelle couldn't say that, so she swallowed her tears and said, "My mom died in a car crash when

I was sixteen. With how hard that was, I can't imagine being five and not even knowing what happened."

Sophie squeezed her back. "I'm so sorry. As a teenage girl, that must have been awful."

"It was. I missed her so much. We were a lot alike. Back then, anyway. And I needed her."

Sophie hugged her hard and then pushed her away. "Shit, Isabelle, don't make me cry."

"You made me cry first."

Jill stood up. "Nope. It is too early in the night to get maudlin. You women are supposed to be cheering me up. So let's get off this subject and party. Turn up the music. I'll get the pie."

CHAPTER TEN

TOM SHRUGGED ON his coat as his breath turned into a cloud in the cold. The temperatures were dropping like crazy tonight. Mary's boots squeaked against the dry snow. "They're starting to wrap up," he said, tipping his head toward the cabin porch.

"Thank God. I'm ready for bed."

"If you want to walk Jill home, I can drive Veronica back and then swing by and pick you up. Jill can come back for her car tomorrow."

Mary's scornful look said it all. "Why would I want to walk Jill home?"

He shrugged. "Fine. I wanted you to meet her. She's kick-ass and single."

"From what I heard from the porch, she's on the rebound."

"We're not in our twenties anymore, Mary. You're capable of negotiating a rebound."

She rolled her eyes. "I tell you what. We'll both drive Veronica home and drop Jill off on the way."

"Right," he said. "Okay." But he didn't move.

"Or you could stay here and chitchat with Isabelle and leave later. Isn't that what you're here for anyway?"

Yes. It was. Beyond that, he liked listening to her talk with her friends. He hated to admit it, but he didn't want to leave just because Jill and Veronica were dead tired. It was only ten thirty. "Deal. I'd rather walk anyway. It clears my head."

"Mmm-hmm. Just be careful, Tom."

He met her eyes and nodded. He'd be careful. He had to be. "Call me if anything comes up."

He walked Jill down the stairs and promised to load all the plates and pans into her car for the morning. "I could just drive it over now," he offered for the second time, but she shook her head.

"I've had that car for twenty years. I won't have some man sliding it off into the trees for me. You're no mountain man, Tom. It'll wait until morning."

"I'm seriously offended."

"I don't care."

He helped Veronica into the front seat and waved them away. Tom should be heading back to answer emails. He knew that. But Isabelle had loosened up enough to mention her mother. And there was no mistaking her Chicago accent at this point. It wasn't strong, but it was definitely there.

If he got her to talk for a few more minutes, maybe this would no longer be sneaking around. Maybe she'd just tell him, and then he could forget his suspicions and concentrate on her.

The living room was empty when he walked back in, but he could hear the women talking in one of the bedrooms. Tom started picking up dishes and carrying them to the kitchen to load into the dishwasher. Their laughter echoed down the hallway and made him smile as he took off his gun and set it on the counter.

So her mother had died in a car crash twenty years before. He felt like shit for being thankful for a detail that would be easy to research. He should just be feeling sorry for Isabelle. Sympathetic. He shouldn't be sitting here waiting to mine her for more details.

He should let this go. Or let her go. One or the other.

But then she walked into the kitchen, wide mouth smiling, and he couldn't do either.

"What are you doing?" she asked.

He rinsed off a plate and slid it into the dishwasher rack. "Getting ready to leave."

"By washing dishes? You are fucking dreamy, you know that?" She leaned against the counter and looked him up and down. "And you look good with your crisp little dress shirt rolled up at the sleeves."

She was going to make him blush again. Tom cleared his throat and grabbed a serving tray. "Thanks."

"I like your hands."

He washed those hands and dried them off, trying to buy a little relief from the heat in his face. "Where are your friends?"

"In bed."

"It's not even eleven."

"I know! Can you believe it? Lightweights. You want a drink now? I think you've earned it."

He glanced at the last pitcher. "It was a pretty trying night."

She pulled a clean glass from the cupboard. "The first girls' night isn't easy for anyone. It's a lot to take in."

He laughed and poured himself a glass then refilled hers when she held it out. When she walked toward the living room, he followed. "I have to admit, it was a lot more fun than any night out with the guys. I'm not sure my brain will recover from all the new things I learned, though. You girls are filthy. Like, really filthy."

"I know. It's because we have to save it up. We can't

be honest about stuff in front of men because so many of them are creeps. When it's just us and we don't have to be on guard against men bothering us… God. It's so much fun."

"Should I be insulted that I don't count as a man?"

"No." She dropped onto the couch and patted the seat beside her. "You should be flattered that all of us felt comfortable around you."

He smiled. "I honestly am. I deal with a lot of creeps. I'm thrilled not to be counted among them."

"So you won't use anything I said tonight against me?"

Tom felt punched in the gut. He couldn't even hide the way her words went through him, so he had no choice but to roll with it. "I overheard what you said about your mother. I'm sorry."

"Oh." She glanced down at her drink for a few seconds before she looked at him again. "That was a long time ago."

"I know, but—"

"I don't want to talk about it."

All right. That was as clear as it got. "You'd rather talk about the roofer?"

She giggled and covered her eyes. "You heard that?"

"I tried not to."

She laughed, looking only the tiniest bit chagrined. "It was a long time ago," she said. Then added, "Too long."

His heart skipped at that, partly because of her implication and partly because she was looking him dead in the eyes when she said it. "You were out all night this weekend," he said carefully.

"At Lauren's," she returned. "What about you? Do you and Mary still have a thing going?"

"Mary?" He felt his eyes go comically wide but couldn't stop them.

"She didn't seem pleased that you and I were friendly."

"Mary and I have never had a thing. And there are no feelings on either side, I promise."

"Okay." Isabelle's gaze drifted down to his mouth. "Maybe she was just being protective, then."

"Maybe," he agreed. "But she was irritated earlier. She thought I chose her for this assignment because it was a girls' night."

"Did you?"

He shook his head. She was still looking at his mouth, and he didn't want to distract her. And now he was thinking about the painting. About the peaks of her dark nipples. The curve of her hips.

"I should go," he said, meaning it. He should go. Yes. But her eyes flicked up to his, and she smiled. And God, that smile got him like it always did. Small and secret and downright mischievous.

"You should go," she agreed, but she leaned a little closer. Her hand sneaked to his knee, his thigh. His nerves sent thousands of excited messages to his brain. "Go home and think about me."

"Is that what you want?" he asked.

"Yes," she said immediately, her fingers stroking up his thigh. "I want you to do that."

"I can't."

"Why?" Her hand stroked higher, grazing over his hard cock. Tom had to bite back a groan. She made a sympathetic noise. "It feels like you're completely capable."

He had to stifle another groan when her fingers stroked down to his thigh again. "There's no privacy there," he explained, focusing his mind to see if he could make her do it again. Touch him again.

"And no privacy here," she said sadly. She touched him again, finally. Yes. He wanted more. Her fingers stroked up, and his cock strained, trying to get closer.

He needed to leave. He needed to get up and walk away and not do this, not yet, but instead of doing the right thing, he eased back a little in the couch, hoping she'd keep touching him if he made it easier.

Her chuckle told him she'd noticed, and her hand told him she didn't mind. She stroked up and down his cock. Slowly.

"Are you trying to drive me crazy again?" he asked past clenched teeth.

"No. I'm trying to touch your cock."

All thoughts of leaving fled his mind. He reached for her as she dragged her nails over the thin fabric of his pants, tormenting him with a dull feeling that should have been much sharper.

He pulled her down to him, wanting her kiss, but refusing to give up her touch. She was laughing against his mouth again, just like the first time they'd kissed. He loved it. Loved that she was delighted by it all. He tasted her until she stopped laughing and gave him her mouth.

Her tongue slid against his as her hand tried to curl around his shaft. There were too many clothes in the way, but it felt good all the same. It felt even better when she stroked him again. But God, just imagining what it would feel like if she unfastened his pants and slid her hand in and touched his bare flesh… Now her touch was torture. He wanted to torture her, too.

Tom slid his hand along her bare shoulder then traced that necklace down just like he'd done earlier. But this time his fingers found the soft fabric of her shirt and he slipped his hand over the curve of her breast.

Isabelle arched into his hand, wanting more, just as much as he did. He slid his thumb over her nipple and she kissed him harder, so he did it again. He meant to torment her. Meant to give her just enough pleasure that she'd need more, more, but he only circled her nipple once with his thumb, and then he forgot his intent and slipped his hand underneath her bra.

Her skin was so hot, and her hard nipple so eager against his touch. He caught it between his fingers and stroked lightly at first, but she arched impatiently into him, so he tightened his hold, squeezing her until she moaned in pleasure and thrust her tongue deeper into his mouth.

He wanted to see her. Wanted to pull her shirt down and her bra off and see how dark and hard her nipples were for him. He wanted to taste her, lick her, bite her. But he couldn't. Not here.

But maybe just a little.

He raised his head and angled his hand so that her clothing was pushed farther to the side, and he could watch as he rolled her between his fingers. And then she was right there, still leaning toward him, her fingers squeezing his cock now, squeezing harder, and he *needed* to taste her.

He ducked his head and closed his mouth over her nipple.

"Oh, fuck," she gasped.

When he sucked, her hand gave up its hold on him and went to his head to pull him tighter to her. Now he was the one chuckling, feeling pure joy at the soft sounds that vibrated through her throat as he worked her nipple with his tongue. But he still wrapped his fingers into hers and moved her hand back down to his cock.

"Yes," she said, stroking him again, her left hand still clutching his head. "Yes," she gasped when he pressed his teeth into her.

Her fingers fumbled, leaving him for a moment, and then he realized she was sliding his zipper down.

Oh, God. He needed that so much. Their current state of undress was nothing a quick flick of his hand couldn't correct, but if it proceeded any further, they wouldn't have time to recover at the sound of approaching footsteps.

Her hand would feel so good, though. Squeezing him. Pumping him. And they probably wouldn't get caught. Unless one of her friends needed to use the bathroom. Or wanted a drink of water. Or remembered she'd left her purse by the table.

Isabelle's fingertips slid along his open zipper, stroking him through just his underwear now. His hips pushed toward the feeling. She hummed her pleasure. His cock throbbed.

And Tom did the impossible. He took her hand off his dick and raised it back up to his neck.

"Tom," she whispered.

"We can't," he growled against her wet nipple. "Not here."

"My bedroom," she urged.

That hadn't been what he'd meant. He'd meant not here in her house tonight, with people only a few feet away, but now that she'd mentioned her bedroom, it seemed absurd to say no. Cruel and stupid and absurd.

He shook his head, but then he sat back and got a look at her, and she was stunning. Eyes dark with lust. Cheeks flushed. Lips parted to let her breath free. And her top pushed to one side to expose part of one breast, her nipple wet and tight and wanting.

"Your bedroom," he said, and he was lost.

ISABELLE LIKED THE way he looked when he was aroused. There was none of the helpful law-enforcement officer left in his expression. He looked dangerous and beautiful.

"We shouldn't be doing this," he said as she hit the button lock on her bedroom door. But when she whipped her top off, he started unbuttoning his shirt.

"We'll be quiet," she assured him.

He nodded, but still looked a little troubled as he reached the third button. She stopped him with a hand on his wrist. Even though the motion seemed to pain him, he nodded and dropped his hands. Silly boy. He thought she was telling him to stop, but she only wanted to do it herself.

His lips parted when she reached for the next button of his shirt, as if he meant to say something, but his objection died when she slipped the button free and smoothed her hands down to the next one. He stayed silent and watched as she tugged the tail of his shirt from his pants and finished unbuttoning.

His flat stomach was the first thing she saw when she parted the cotton. Then the sprinkling of hair over his chest. Then the muscles of his pecs and his flat nipples, and oh, she wanted to touch all of it. She pushed the shirt all the way down his arms and pressed her mouth to his shoulder.

She tasted his skin, licked it, put her teeth to the taut muscle. His hands were at her back, and she felt her bra loosen and let it fall to the floor.

Not bothering to turn off the light, she backed toward

the bed, pulling him along with her. She wanted to see him. Wanted to be seen. No hiding behind darkness tonight. If she had to be quiet, she didn't want to be blind.

Under her fingers, his belt slipped free with a satisfying sound. His hands hovered for a minute, as if he were unused to giving up control, but in the end, he stood with his hands at his sides, letting her undress him. Watching. So she took her time, smoothing her hands down his belly, feeling the muscles jump at her touch.

She sat down on her bed, and now her mouth was even with his navel. She kissed his stomach, letting him feel the heat of her tongue as she reached for the button of his pants.

When she inhaled, the scent of his skin filled her. It was all she could taste and smell. She liked being filled with him, so she breathed in again and lowered the zipper he'd so hurriedly pulled up only minutes before. She tugged down his briefs, and then he was free. And big. And hard. Now the scent of him was stronger, and her mouth watered, some animal part of her let loose as sure as she'd freed his cock.

When she wrapped her fist around him, he grunted as if he were shocked. And God, he felt nice. Thick and solid. His skin sliding over his shaft as she stroked him. She wanted that inside her. Needed it.

"Jesus, Isabelle," he murmured. "That feels so good."

"Mmm," she hummed, not taking her eyes off him. His skin was dark against her hand, the head of his cock flushed with blood. She stroked him, watching as his thighs grew tense, as his hips thrust forward. When she squeezed more firmly, a clear drop of fluid gathered at the tip. When she smeared it with her thumb, Tom hissed.

"Isabelle." His voice was a low rumble. "Tell me you have condoms."

Still circling him with her thumb, she smiled. "And here I thought you were the kind to always be prepared."

"I…wasn't expecting…"

She laughed. "Of course I have condoms. The drawer next to my bed."

"Thank God. I need to fuck you."

Those words went through her like a shot. She wanted everything from his body; she wanted to lick him and suck him and stroke him, but mostly she wanted *that*.

Tom shucked the rest of his clothes then reached for her pants. He had those stripped off in moments. Isabelle lay back and stretched her arm up to the bedside table to fumble in the drawer. She finally found a condom box wedged between her vibrators and handed it to him as he knelt on the bed next to her.

She liked looking up at him this way, his lean body so strong above her and his cock so proud and thick. She was already spreading her thighs for him, but Tom lay down at her side instead of sliding between her legs.

Poised above her on his elbow, he cupped one of her breasts before catching her nipple between his thumb and finger. "Look at you. Just as perfect as that painting."

Before she could respond, he ducked his head and sucked her nipple into his mouth. Isabelle bit back a cry. His hand plucked at her other nipple for a moment, making her back arch as she bit her lip. But then his hand slid down. Slowly. Down her ribs to her navel before shaping one hip. Then back up to the curve of her belly and into the curls between her legs.

His cock pushed against her thigh.

She waited, holding her breath, but he only cupped

her for a moment, his big hand cradling her pussy, adding his warmth to hers. Then his middle finger slipped over her wetness, sliding into the seam of her body. Isabelle gasped, her hips jumping.

"You feel so sweet," he whispered. "So wet and warm."

"Yes," she breathed. Yes, she felt perfect. Her body the exact opposite of his. Soft and yielding to his fingers as she parted for him.

His fingertips grazed her clit, and she gasped again.

"Shh," he cautioned, stroking her now. She bit her lip, trying to hold back a cry of pleasure. But when he circled her clit and bit down on her nipple at the same time, she cried out.

"Shh," he repeated, his breath cold where he'd sucked at her.

She nodded and pressed her mouth tightly closed, not wanting her friends to hear, if only because it would be awkward for them. But she rocked her hips up to meet the short strokes of his fingers. Yes. Yes. It felt so good. So unexpected after the familiarity of her own hands. Not as firm or sure as her touch, but new and teasing and— "Fuck," she groaned, pressing up into his hand.

His fingers stroked a little faster, a little harder, but it wasn't enough. She wanted more. "Fuck me," she begged, pulling his hair so he'd look up at her. When he raised his head, she kissed him. "Fuck me, Tom," she said against his lips. "Please. Now."

A low growl was his only response, but he was kneeling between her legs, thank God, and tearing open a condom wrapper within seconds. She watched greedily as he rolled the condom on, watched it stretch over that perfect cock, and she ached inside, hollowed out with need.

He fisted himself and eased between her thighs, and the first stroke of his broad head against her was a torturous promise. He stroked against her again, and she dug her fingers into his shoulders to urge him on. She wanted everything.

He notched against her and pushed in, just a few inches, but that was enough to make her moan.

"Shh," he murmured, then "Shh" again as he slowly sank another inch deeper.

"Oh, God," she whispered as her body stretched for him, and the ache spread out. Finally, he paused, his hips flush against hers. Both of them were breathing hard. His back was slick with sweat under her clutching hands. And she was full. As full as she could be. Then he drew back and thrust.

"Ah!" she cried, unable to hold back at the nearly painful pleasure. She tried to swallow the sound, but when he sank deep again, she couldn't help it.

"We have to be quiet," he breathed.

"It feels so good," she said, eyes squeezed shut, trying to hold it all in.

"I know." He pushed more slowly this time, and she squirmed with lust. "I know. Can you be quiet?"

Isabelle shook her head. She couldn't. If it felt this good at the start, there was no way. "Please don't stop," she begged. "Please."

"Shh." His hips hardly moved now, his cock just barely sliding in and out in short, slow, careful strokes.

No. She *needed* this. She opened her eyes to find his face stark and drawn, his gaze on her face. "Please fuck me," she moaned. "Hard. Deep."

He cursed, his head dropping for a moment, his forehead brushing her cheek. "Yes," he finally answered, raising his head to meet her gaze. He lifted a hand and laid it over her mouth, moving slowly, studying her the whole time. Isabelle felt her own eyes go a little wide as his palm settled over her lips. He waited a moment, holding his breath. And then he thrust hard.

Isabelle cried out against his hand. It pressed more firmly to her mouth as his cock sank as deep as it could. Electricity shot through her, sparkling through her body as she felt the weight of him everywhere. Between her legs, against her hips, deep in her pussy, along her belly and then all the way up to her mouth where he held her down.

He found a rhythm and fucked her with deep, sure strokes, and it was perfect. Perfect and raw and tight, and Isabelle wanted to come like this. With his cock inside her and his hand catching her cries.

She dragged a cruel hand down his back, scratching her fingernails hard against him. Tom arched up, his hips slapping into her, and Isabelle worked her hand down along her belly.

When he realized what she needed, Tom eased up onto his knees, wedging them on either side of her hips and resting his weight on his left hand to give her space. His right hand stayed tight on her mouth, though, and it was a good thing, because when she touched her clit, she couldn't hold back a desperate, hoarse cry.

She groaned into his hand as her nerves went wild with the bright pleasure of her tight clit and the duller, deeper pressure of his cock as it stretched her open with every thrust. She felt invaded by him, over and over. Owned by his cock and filled so tight she felt she might burst.

He fucked her faster, and her muffled cries became rhythmic as everything inside her coiled up into one hot pulse. Her thighs shook. His hand pressed harder to her mouth and she exploded, rocking up into his thrusts and screaming against his hard grip. She spasmed around his cock, her body trying to bring him with her, wanting his come, needing it. She was still shaking when he finally went stiff above her, swallowing a low moan of pleasure as he pulsed inside her.

He stayed still for a long time, breathing hard, head bent and eyes shut. Finally, he lifted his hand from her face. "I'm sorry," he whispered.

Isabelle blinked dazedly. She licked her lips. "For what?"

He opened his eyes, his pupils wide and black as he stroked his thumb over her jaw. "I didn't want to be rough like that. I just…"

She smiled and let her eyes fall shut. "It was everything I wanted."

He sighed with what sounded like relief then eased from her body and bed. He returned a minute later and lay down beside her, one arm slung over his eyes. "Jesus," he said.

"Yeah," she agreed. Her hips protested as she straightened her legs and stretched before curling into his side with a little purr of satisfaction. Her muscles felt liquid and warm, and she must have dozed for a few minutes. She opened her heavy eyes to find him staring at the ceiling, not looking the least bit sleepy.

"Hey, it's okay," she whispered. "You can go."

He jerked up a little in surprise. "What?"

"You can go. You don't have to worry about how to slip away without pissing me off."

His brow drew into that deep frown she'd become familiar with. "It's not that I want to go," he protested.

"But you need to, don't you?"

"Shit." He dropped his head back to the pillow. "I'm really sorry."

"It's okay, Tom. This isn't love. It wasn't even a date."

His frown didn't budge. "Okay."

Isabelle sat up and looked at him. Despite the frown, his eyes immediately went to her breasts. Men were so easy about some things. "Why do you look unhappy?" she asked. "I don't think I could frown right now if I wanted to. Were you faking it? Be honest."

That finally nudged his frown away. His mouth actually tipped up at the edges. "If I'd come any harder, we would've been heading to the pharmacy for a backup plan."

Isabelle collapsed back onto the bed, laughing too hard to keep her exhausted body upright. "Don't worry. I've got an IUD. So you just always look miserable after sex? Please tell me you're not one of those guys who needs the girl to be in love or it's dirty. Because then I'll have to remind you that you thoroughly enjoyed it all."

"That's definitely not it. And I hope you haven't met any guys like that."

"We've all met guys like that."

Isabelle felt his hand touch hers, and he weaved their fingers loosely together. She hadn't realized she'd managed to accumulate tension in the past minute, but it slipped away when he touched her. "My first boyfriend," she said, surprising herself. "My first everything, actually."

He turned toward her. She felt the mattress dip and felt his chest against her arm, but she kept her eyes closed.

"He was an ass?"

She smiled at that, but she wished the lights were off now. "In retrospect, yes. He was an incredible ass. He liked that I was a virgin. Liked that I *waited* for him. He talked shit about other girls who put out, and it made me feel special. So I suppose I was an ass, too."

"Well, that's understandable. You wanted it to be special with him."

"Exactly. It wasn't until later that I started examining the mystery of why those girls before me were sluts and he was a good guy. It's a mystery of millennia."

"I wouldn't know. I was always just pleased."

She finally opened her eyes. He was smiling at her now, looking much more like a guy who'd just had great sex. "Are you pleased now?"

"You have no idea how much." He kissed her.

A chaste kiss, really. A touch of their lips, but he was smiling and sweet, and something inside her tried to open up. She desperately shoved it closed again.

"So stop frowning," she said.

He nodded. "I'm sorry. It's just…I shouldn't be here."

"Oh." She was feeling sorry now. She took his face between her hands and kissed him again. "You're the boss. I get it. You probably don't want to be caught screwing the crazy neighbor during an assignment. Whereas for me, it really bolsters my quirky artistic vibe."

He shook his head, but she gave his chest a little shove. "Go on. Get out of here before one of your men checks in and finds you with your pants down. For God's sake, you don't even have your gun on, Marshal."

"Safety first," he said, but he got out of bed.

She watched as he looked for his pants. "I like your ass."

He smiled. "Thanks."

"You look really good for your age."

"Hey! For my age? How old do you think I am?"

"Forty-two?"

"Shit," he muttered. "Did you look at my license?"

"No. And I was only teasing. You look good for any age. You'll have to let me touch you more later."

He glanced over his shoulder as he pulled his pants on. "Later?"

"I mean, assuming you want to. But I was hoping for at least one more round. Not to reveal my hand, but you're really good at that."

"At what?" he asked, but she could see the edges of his pleased smile.

"At fucking."

Now his cheek was practically creased from a grin. "Yeah?"

"Yeah. But if you want to hear more about it, you'll have to come back again."

He chuckled as he slipped on his wrinkled dress shirt. "I promise I won't need luring."

"You didn't seem quite sure earlier."

He seemed to be buttoning slowly, and when he turned to face her, he wasn't smiling anymore. "I'm sorry, Isabelle. This isn't how I'd want to do this. It's… complicated."

Her heart fell a little, but she nodded and told her heart to stay the hell out of it. "It's just the job? You'd be honest if it were another commitment?" She wasn't sure why she'd asked. Someone who would lie about a girlfriend would lie about the cover-up, but she wouldn't be able to face herself later if she didn't press him. She could at least go to the effort of making a liar lie.

But he looked so chagrined by the question, she couldn't help but believe him a little. "It's just the job," he promised. "I swear."

"All right. Then come over again sometime, if you can get away."

He sat next to her and smoothed a hand down her neck to her collarbone. Then he gently cupped one of her breasts. "You're kind of amazing," he said, his eye on what his hand was doing.

"Just kind of?"

"Well. A guy can't be too eager. I think I'm supposed to wait two days to call you. Play it cool. I can't tell you I'd rather stay and do this again in an hour." His finger circled her nipple, making it peak again.

"An hour, huh?" She slid her hand over his lap and felt his cock starting to swell.

Tom chuckled and bent to press another of those sweet kisses to her mouth. "Okay. It's possible I have a weakness for your breasts."

"I told you they were nice."

"Nice," he repeated, grinning down at her. "Yes. Perfectly pleasant." He sneaked down for a quick kiss on one of her nipples and then stood up.

"Tease," she whispered.

"I have to go!"

"All right. Try not to wake Sophie and Lauren, and lock the door behind you."

"Not a chance. Get up and lock the dead bolt."

Isabelle stretched, loving the way his gaze followed her body down. "You're cruel. I should've known it when you held your hand over my mouth and fucked me."

His face turned immediately red, and Isabelle had to cover her mouth again to hide her laughter. When she finally got control of herself, she rolled her eyes at his embarrassment.

"This is gonna be fun," she said.

He only shook his head and watched her grab a robe. Isabelle stretched again, just to watch him look, and then she belted the robe and finally let him escape, telling herself she didn't care if he stayed.

He couldn't sleep.

After fourteen hours of work, one insanely good orgasm and the eight urgent emails he'd had to return, he should've been fast asleep by now. It was 1:00 a.m., and he had to be up at six. Nothing he hadn't faced before, but it was more than work stressing him out now.

He should not have had sex with Isabelle. He really, really shouldn't have. But even now, hours later, he couldn't wrap his mind around how he would have stopped. It had felt so right, even with all the wrongness swimming through his head. Every way they'd touched and kissed, every sound of arousal she'd made.

God, the sounds. Tom actually sighed at the thought of them. She was fucking glorious. But he'd had to get her quiet.

His cock thickened at the memory of pressing his hand to her mouth. That had felt wrong on every level. He barely knew her. He'd never touched her before. He didn't know her needs or kinks. And he'd never restrained a woman that way. Never thought he would.

It had been wrong. And all the wrongness of it had gathered up inside him and pulsed like throbbing lust through his body. Feeling her breath against his hand, her teeth against his fingers, her screams rising through his bones. It had felt *good.*

"Shit." Tom sat up on the cot and put his feet on the floor.

It didn't matter how good it had felt. He was deceiving her. She wouldn't have let him do that if she'd known he was digging through her past.

He had to stop.

Except tonight, before the sex, he'd gotten that one detail that was niggling at the back of his brain and was keeping him awake. Her mother had died, and he had a specific year and cause of death. His search had just narrowed significantly.

Somehow he'd forced himself to ignore that and pretend he could leave it until tomorrow. He couldn't.

Tom grabbed his laptop and fired it up. He needed to end this. He'd look up her mother's death, find out the likely boring truth and never deceive her again. He'd be honest from now on. And he could see her without any guilt. They could date. It would be good. She'd never know that he'd violated her privacy and lied about it.

Fighting a sense of déjà vu, he began searching Chicago crimes again. But this time, the outcome was very, very different.

CHAPTER ELEVEN

TOM WAS AT his most focused the next day. He had to be. If he let one stray thought about Isabelle in, he'd lose his hold on the hundred other things going on.

Saul Stevenson had been spotted by a cop in Cody the night before, but the patrolman hadn't realized immediately why the man had looked familiar. He'd noticed him at a truck-stop diner, made a mental note and only checked into it a few hours later. So Stevenson's brother was on the move and coming closer to Jackson. He could be in Jackson now.

Tom's whole team was on high alert, and there were members of both the Teton County Sheriff's Department and the state police who were part of the extended team now, too. Tom couldn't afford to think about Isabelle. Or the fact that her name wasn't really Isabelle.

He shook his head and got back to the new shift schedule that Mary had written up. He added one more pass of the K-9 units through the parking lot just before court was scheduled to dismiss. Stevenson might not be going for a big statement like a courthouse explosion. He might just be targeting the single car of someone on the prosecution team.

He sent the schedule to his team leaders and answered his ringing cell phone.

"Marshal Tom Duncan?" The man's voice was unfamiliar.

"Yes," he said impatiently.

"This is Agent Gates with the FBI."

"Good," Tom said. "I know we don't have proof that they've transported explosives across state lines, but I appreciate that you're willing to weigh in. Your team deals with terroristic threats a lot more often than—"

"I'm sorry. I'm not clear on what you're talking about."

Tom frowned and grabbed a pen and a pad of paper. "I'm sorry. Did you say Agent Gates?"

"Yes, I'm with the Chicago office."

The pen pressed into the paper and left a dark blot of ink that looked startlingly blue to Tom's eyes. "Chicago?"

"I got a hit that you accessed information about Malcolm Pozniak, and I was wondering why a US marshal stationed in Wyoming would access an old Chicago case."

Tom hesitated. There'd been a flag on the Pozniak file that information was not to be shared with any nonfederal agencies, with extra caution to be exercised with the Chicago PD. Apparently, the FBI was still taking that seriously. Tom was, too. And something about this call bothered him.

"Pozniak is a fugitive in a federal case," Tom said carefully. "He falls under the purview of the marshal service."

"He does," Agent Gates said. He waited, likely trying to give Tom the chance to say more. Tom declined. Gates finally gave in. "Do you have any information about Malcolm Pozniak or his whereabouts?"

"I do not." That was an honest answer, so he invested all his conviction in those words, hoping the lies that followed wouldn't be noticeable. "I'm sorry to raise any excitement. My territory covers a lot of isolated places.

The kinds of places where fugitives like to hole up and stay. If you could access my online activities, you'd find I scan a lot of old cases, just to keep faces in the forefront. I never know which bar or feed store I'll walk into and find myself face-to-face with an old felon."

A long silence followed. There was no way for Gates to dispute this. He didn't have access to Tom's online activity, and they both knew it. "So you haven't seen someone who fits Pozniak's description?"

"Seventy-year-old white male who looks like he's seen too much life? We got a lot of those in Wyoming. But I'm afraid I can't help you with this one."

Another pause. "All right. What about the daughter?"

"The daughter?"

"Beth Pozniak."

His heart thumped loudly, echoing in his ears. "I didn't see her on the list of federal fugitives. She's only a person of interest, if I recall."

"You accessed her file."

Tom forced an impatient laugh. "I may have followed a link. I looked at a few cases last night. That one seemed unlikely to be resolved. Guy's probably dead by now."

"Yeah." The agent went quiet for another moment before he sighed. "Well, shit. It would've been nice if you'd spotted him. This damn case has been on my desk for a dozen years now. I inherited it from a guy who keeled over in his office chair, and I'm thinking I'll carry it to my grave, too."

"I'm impressed you're still working it so hard."

"Pozniak killed a fellow cop. You know these cop-killer files are never really closed. Listen…" The guy paused as if he were thinking, but Tom recognized it as a ploy to establish intimacy. "There hasn't been a blip from Pozniak in over ten years. Like you said, he's probably dead. Seventy years old, and he ate a typical Chicago cop's diet for thirty-five of those. Heart attack. Stroke. Something got him."

Tom nodded and made a noncommittal sound.

"I'd like this off my desk, Marshal. And bringing in a guy like this wouldn't be bad for you, either."

"Hey, I wouldn't object," Tom said, trying to sound casual instead of tense. "I'm happy to help any way I can."

"All right. But listen. There's a flag on the account. The problems with the Chicago PD are obvious, but there were some…let's just call them internal problems here at the bureau. So if there's anything going on in Wyoming, anything at all…" He waited again. Tom waited, too.

"I see you're working this judge's case," Gates finally said. "Maybe Pozniak hooked up with that antigovernment outfit. Maybe that's something you don't want to share yet. Maybe you haven't confirmed it. But if you find anything at all, get in touch with me. I'll check it out personally."

"I'll help in any way I can," Tom repeated before hanging up. He meant it, but Agent Gates wasn't the one Tom wanted to help.

Beth Pozniak was Isabelle West now, and apparently, Tom was the only person who knew that. He'd just lied to a fellow federal officer, at least by omission, and it didn't feel right. But Tom was so fucked up about Isabelle that he didn't know if it was the lying that had felt wrong or something else. He needed time to think, and he didn't have time right now. Not for this.

But thoughts of Isabelle followed him out of the make-shift marshal's office and into the entryway of the courthouse. She followed him as he checked in with Hannity and then with Mary and the guards stationed at the front doors. Court was in session, and he wouldn't disturb it, but Isabelle followed him as he checked that the side doors were still securely bolted.

She'd lied to him about everything. And she needed help. The question was, what would he do to help her?

Things would be simpler if he hadn't become personally invested. Things would be *way* simpler if he hadn't had sex with her. But things weren't simple now.

He couldn't do the right thing and inform his chief, put a call in to the FBI and bring her in for questioning. He wasn't willing to just cross his fingers and let the wheels of justice turn. Isabelle hadn't been a criminal when she'd run, so he needed to find out what she'd been running from before he threw her back into it.

But it was more than that. Way more than just finding out the truth. He'd started hoping his attraction to her had led his instincts astray. That there was no past, no mystery, no problem to solve. Because he wanted to keep seeing her, damn it. He wanted to accept her invitation to come over again and then persuade her to issue another and another. He *liked* her. And he wanted her. And that was a rare enough combination that he'd needed there to be no story here.

But now that there was, he had to do more than find out the truth. He had to help her, get her free of this mess and do it with enough skill that she'd forgive his dishonesty.

Tom knew that you had to help people in trouble even if they wound up hating you for it. But Isabelle hating him would be a damn high price to bear.

CHAPTER TWELVE

SHE HADN'T LOVED a man since Patrick Kerrigan.

She'd loved their bodies. And their laughter. And sometimes their voices or their minds or just the way they moved. At the very least, she'd liked a couple of them very much. But she hadn't loved them, really, the way you might show all of yourself to someone else and pray it could be enough. She hadn't been able to.

She didn't love Tom, either. She hadn't known him long enough to love him, and it was impossible anyway. But there was something there. Some comfort and maybe even trust.

She'd gone to sleep perfectly happy the night before. More than happy. Deeply satisfied and physically spent and smiling stupidly into the darkness.

But Isabelle's mind had worked while she'd slept, and she'd awoken feeling as if she weighed a thousand pounds. She was afraid.

There was the easy fear of him being a marshal, of course, but that wasn't what was sitting on her chest when she opened her eyes. It was the terrible gravity of realizing that she could love him.

He was smart, and cute, and he laughed at himself and worried about other people and worked hard at his job. He treated women like equals, a rare quality among the law-enforcement men she'd known. He made her laugh. He held his own.

All of those were lovely traits, and all relatively harmless. Until you factored in the way he kissed and fucked and tasted.

She wanted more of that. Much more. And that was what scared her. The deep, greedy joy of that.

If he wasn't a marshal, it might have been okay. He lived six hours away. They could get close enough to have a relationship, but not so close that he'd start pressing about her past. He could see her when he was in town. She could go to Cheyenne anytime she missed him.

She could have someone. Someone to notice when she was down. Someone to tell her that her new haircut was pretty. Someone to touch her when she felt lonely.

Isabelle rubbed a hand over her face, trying to wipe away the thoughts. She didn't need any of that. She couldn't *have* any of that. Not with Tom Duncan.

By the time Isabelle got out of bed, Sophie and Lauren were long gone. They were both used to rising at a scheduled hour. Isabelle woke when she wanted to. Sometimes early to catch the light. Sometimes late when her commissions were in and she could stay up until 2:00 a.m. painting what she wanted.

Today she went through the motions, making a big pot of coffee and nibbling on a piece of cherry pie for breakfast and trying to pretend her heart was as hard as it had always been.

But even that was a lie. Her heart had once been as soft as jelly and about that smart, too. She'd loved Patrick and trusted him implicitly, and he'd waited until her lowest moment and then dealt the killing blow.

She'd been so stunned by her father's arrest and the initial wave of charges that she hadn't quite noticed Patrick pulling away. She'd been too consumed with panic.

A month later, he'd still been awkward and distant, but that had been her fault, hadn't it? She was the one with the criminal father. Worse yet was that her father's captain was Patrick's dad, and now Captain Kerrigan was under scrutiny, too.

She'd felt so awful about that. Captain Kerrigan hadn't even been her father's direct supervisor, but her engagement to Patrick Kerrigan had likely drawn the attention of the FBI. That was what Patrick had claimed, anyway. That was what he'd yelled at her one night when she'd complained that he was being cold.

If she'd been the woman she was today, she would have told him to stuff it. She'd have told him she was the one living this nightmare, not him.

But she'd still been that stupid girl, so she'd felt guilty and tried to make it up to him any way she could. She'd stuffed down her own grief and terror to sneak into his apartment for sex. Still, he'd always made her leave in the middle of the night. "You don't want the press reporting on this, do you?" he'd asked.

She'd acquiesced every time, when all she'd really wanted was to stay and feel safe and know that someone was there while she slept.

He'd finally told her the truth, four months later. That her family name was going to affect his career. That he hated her for dragging him down. That he'd waited this long to end it only because his dad had asked him to keep an eye on her after her father had skipped town. Patrick had dumped her, and she'd still loved him. He'd had to push her away in disgust when she'd tried to hug him.

The two men in her life who were supposed to protect her, her father and her future husband... They'd both walked away.

Isabelle protected herself now. She'd done a good job of it, yet somehow her defenses were slipping.

She opened the doors to her studio and let the smell of paint wash over her. The weight that had settled over her lifted a little. It wanted to lift, because it wasn't really fear. It was hope.

Useless hope. Tom Duncan was a US marshal, and if she trusted him with her heart and body on some primal level she couldn't understand, it meant nothing because she couldn't trust him with the truth.

Isabelle tried to shake off her sorry thoughts and get to work. She could normally lose herself easily in painting, but she kept thinking of Tom. She created the latissimus dorsi on the white canvas, building it out of reds and creams and blues and yellows, drawing out each individual muscle fiber until it became a human back. But then it was Tom's back, stretching and moving as he held his weight off her body and fucked her.

Most people would find that morbid. Tom would find it morbid. That she could perfectly picture the way the naked muscles of his back would contract and relax as he made love to her. But she thought it was beautiful. She wanted to trace those muscles, follow the muted lines of them along his skin, knowing exactly what they looked like beneath it. How could they not be beautiful when they'd let him do what he'd done to her?

She stepped a few feet away to get a better look at the picture, realizing that she'd painted way more than she'd planned. A glance at the clock made her chin jerk back in surprise. It was nearly 4:00 p.m. She'd been painting for over five hours.

Maybe Tom was good for her. She smiled at the thought, surprising herself so much that she pressed a hand to her mouth to hide it.

She couldn't love him. For so many reasons. Or maybe she could love him a little despite them. Maybe she could trust herself to know another person now, to see who he really was. Maybe she could trust herself to recklessly love him just a tiny bit, even if she couldn't ask him to stay. And maybe she'd have to sleep with him again to find out.

This time when she smiled, she didn't cover it. Instead, she started on the left gluteus maximus and pictured Tom's ass tightening.

CHAPTER THIRTEEN

Tom stared at the text from Isabelle, willing it to go away so he could practice some self-control. He'd hoped she wouldn't get in touch. The sex had been casual. She'd made that clear.

But then she'd texted him, asking if he planned to stop by, and the push-pull of it had nearly snapped him in two.

His body was shouting yes. Screaming it, really. *Yes, stop by. Drop everything and go over now. Tell this judge and this trial to fuck off. What you really need is that again.*

If he'd been eighteen years old, he might have imitated the Road Runner in his eagerness to indulge in a second round. A dust cloud would have poofed up around his feet.

But he had a little more control now. The bigger problem was that his brain was telling him to hightail it over there, too. To press her a little. See where she was tender. Find out if he could discover that weak point in her defenses and get her to let him in.

His body agreed, because his body still had all the nuance of that eighteen-year-old boy.

But his conscience…that was a trickier beast. His conscience told him he was an asshole. That he never should have touched her in the first place, not while he was checking up on her.

Despite that, he hadn't had the strength to say no. So he'd given her an out instead.

I'd like to, but I'm not sure when I'll get out of here. It could be late.

She'd say no. Or blow him off. That was what he'd told himself. She was a beautiful woman who liked to be alone; she didn't need a half-assed offer of sex from a guy who'd leave town in a week. He was nothing to her. Last night had meant nothing.

But then she wrote back.

Late is fine with me. Just let me know if you're up for company.

Oh, shit. Even two hours later, he could still feel the way his baser instincts had surged to life with a rough jolt.

If *you're up for company,* she'd said. *If.* Which was how he found himself in his car at 8:00 p.m. staring at her texts and unsuccessfully trying to curb his need.

He opened the text box.

Just wrapped up the last meeting. Are you still up?

"Please don't be up," he said out loud, even as every nerve in his body prayed for the opposite.

He waited for a few moments, aware that his was the last car in the courthouse lot and pretending that meant he was good at his job. He *was* good, after all. Everything was in place for the protective duty tonight. The morning schedule was set up, starting with a 6:00 a.m. sweep of the courthouse and the highway leading to it.

He was done. Even the boss needed dinner and sleep. Or something better.

His phone chimed. He cursed. His heart raced as he dared to look.

It's 8:00 p.m. Of course I'm still up, silly. Come check my perimeter?

"Damn it," he said, the words rough with strained laughter.

She wasn't who she said she was, but she was exactly who he'd suspected. She wasn't a criminal. Not really. She was a woman on the run from trouble.

He could just tell her the truth. He could confess. Beg for her forgiveness and tell her he was here to help.

But she'd run not just from bad guys, but from the cops, as well. The FBI had tagged her as a person of interest. She'd probably helped her father hide. And if she'd been paying taxes this whole time, then she'd stolen someone else's identity to do it.

Even with all that playing through his head, he started his car and hit the highway toward her place.

He needed time to review the details. He needed time to think. He wouldn't be able to think when he was near her. But in the end, he drove straight past the turnoff to the judge's and headed to Isabelle's place because she'd asked him to.

She answered the door with a big smile that would've been marred by the streak of green paint along her cheek if he hadn't found the paint adorable.

"You've been plying your ghastly trade, I see," he said.

She looked down at the spatter of white paint on her black sweater. "I have. But no cadavers were harmed in the process, I promise." She'd been premed in college before she'd dropped out after her father had fled prosecution during her senior year. These were things he should have found out during casual conversation. Instead, he'd found them in the FBI file.

Tom ducked his head and stepped past her.

"Did you have dinner?" she asked.

"I didn't, but I'm fine."

"Listen, I'm no Jill, but I can make a mean grilled cheese sandwich. Assuming you like them made with American cheese and slightly stale bread. I promise you can't even tell once it's fried in butter."

"Sounds perfect," he said, happy to hear her laugh as he followed her toward the kitchen.

She got him a glass of ice water when he said he couldn't have wine, then set a pan on the stove. "Thanks for last night," she said, as if that were normal conversation.

Tom managed to swallow the water in his mouth with only a minimal amount of sputtering. "You're welcome," he rasped. "I mean, thank you, too."

"It was nice," she said, with a glance that swept down his whole body.

"Yes." He was trying to think of a polite way to say, "I also really enjoyed fucking you," but she changed the subject before he could manage it.

"Did you have a long day? You look stressed."

"Yeah. New stuff came up."

"That guy is pretty crazy, huh? The survivalist? And his brother, I suppose."

"They definitely have some issues, even aside from being murderers." That was all he was going to say, but as he watched her smear butter over the cheese sandwiches and drop them into the sizzling pan, he realized this was an in. "They didn't have much of a chance, I guess. By all accounts their dad was a bad guy. Mom died at home, giving birth to Saul in their cabin. They were raised alone by their father, and he was a crazy son of a bitch who got in trouble with the law a lot."

"Mmm." She stared into the pan and didn't respond.

"He obviously had a big effect on their lives."

"Families are funny that way," she muttered.

He watched her flip the sandwiches and tried to think of some other way to open her up. He knew it wouldn't be easy. She couldn't trust him because he was a marshal. He had to find a way to show her he would sympathize. That he understood that the world was more complicated than the law allowed.

His neck prickled as an idea occurred to him.

"Do you want something else with this?" she asked. "You probably need more than a grilled cheese to fill you up."

"No, that's good." Suddenly nervous, he eased past her to get two plates from the cupboard. She checked the bottoms of the sandwiches then slipped them onto the plates before carrying them to her small table.

He brought their glasses and took a seat after she did. "My family…" he started, before pausing to wet his dry throat. "My family seemed perfect, I think. We had a good life. Stable. A house and a backyard and two parents. The American dream. But my brother had problems."

She frowned as she chewed, looking confused. "I thought you only had a sister."

"I do now. My brother died."

"I'm sorry," she said quickly, her voice alarmed, as if it had just happened.

"He was five years older than me. The firstborn. Popular. Confident. Star football player. I don't know what happened. He made the wrong friends at some point. Partied a little too hard. Then he was tackled in a game, and his leg was screwed up pretty badly. He wasn't the star running back anymore. He got bored and partied a little harder."

Isabelle nodded.

"None of us realized it at the time, though. He was charming and outgoing and so confident through all of it. He graduated and went to college. I was thirteen, and he was still my hero."

He stared at the grilled cheese in his hands for a moment before he set it down. He realized Isabelle had set hers down, too, but she still said nothing. He'd hoped that he would need to tell only a little bit. Let her know that he understood the kind of darkness family could pull you into. But he hadn't said that word yet. Any of those words. *Heroin. Junkie. Overdose.* The words his parents would never say, even now.

"I don't know when he started using, but he didn't make it through his freshman year of college. He was a full-blown junkie by February."

"Heroin?" she whispered.

"Yes. We didn't know it at first. All I knew was he was back home and living in his old room in the basement, and I was happy about that. Can you believe it? He had free time to spend with me. I thought it was great."

She nodded. "Of course you did."

"But that didn't last long. By the time I was fourteen, I knew he was shooting up. At fifteen, I was the only one in the house who would talk about it. My sister was older, but she was busy with school and not the type to confront anyone. And my parents were just…"

He waved a hand. "They couldn't accept it. They refused to admit he had a problem. They said he had a lot of pain with his knee and ankle and he'd bounce back."

Tom took a bite of his sandwich, surprised that it tasted good. He was halfway through it in a few bites, but Isabelle didn't say a word. Why wouldn't she talk? Why wouldn't she offer him something in return?

"He overdosed?" she finally asked.

He'd told most of the story. He might as well tell the rest. "Yes. When I was sixteen. I found him in his room the next day."

"Oh, Tom," she said. Her hand came into his vision and curled around his wrist. "I'm so sorry."

He nodded and forced a shrug. "I try not to let my colleagues know about my...phobia, but I really don't like seeing corpses."

"Shit," she whispered. "I'm sorry I teased you."

"You didn't know. I'm sorry I overreacted. We all have our secrets. It's not easy to talk about them."

This was it. Now she'd tell him a secret, too. Reward him for opening up. For trusting her. But instead, she asked for more about him.

"Is that how you ended up in law enforcement?"

He couldn't give her any more, so he shrugged. "Probably. How did you end up doing this? Were your parents artists?"

She drew her hand back. "No."

"Doctors?" he pressed.

"No, I'm just an oddball."

Tom felt suddenly furious. He wanted to help her, and he didn't know how, and she wouldn't give him *anything*. Did she think he told that story to everyone?

Just as quickly, his fury washed away on a wave of self-loathing. He had no right to be angry. She hadn't asked for his story, and for all he knew, she wanted nothing more than to usher him out the door and tell him to take his emotional baggage with him. And if he was realizing now that it had felt good to share his secrets with her, that wasn't her fault. If there was closeness between them, maybe it was one-sided.

All he really needed to do was tell her the truth. *I know you're Beth Pozniak, and I want to help.* But then he'd have to admit that he'd lied. She wouldn't trust him at all. She might even run again, and then he'd have to get the FBI involved. Even if she didn't run, if she shut him down, he'd have to take her in and turn her over, and there was something *wrong* about it all. He could feel it.

He just wanted to get her story first, so he could decide what to do. Had she helped her father escape? Had she helped conceal evidence? Did she know where he was now?

One more day, and then he'd tell her. He just needed more information first. He had to figure out what he was missing.

He barely registered when Isabelle swept his plate away.

Her father had been a good cop, by all standards. Steady, but not ambitious. Almost anyone could've made sergeant after fifteen years. He hadn't gotten there until nineteen, and he'd never bothered with a detective rank. So, unremarkable, but a decent, steady, average guy. Until he'd shot a fellow police officer to cover up a ring of cops who'd been skimming drugs and money from busts for years.

Quite a fall from grace. A jettison from grace, really, once the extent of the corruption had been revealed.

Still, it all would've been just another Hollywood

movie script about crooked cops. Standard Chicago stuff, even if the public would be shocked to hear that. Tom had tracked down ex-cop fugitives before. There were bad cops all over the place, and in Chicago it was practically tradition.

The corruption ring would've carried on for another twenty years if some young idealist with a new badge hadn't become suspicious about cocaine missing from the evidence locker.

It had been her bust. She'd been protective. She'd asked a few questions. Fine. But she hadn't been willing to be waved off. She'd dug in. Pushed the wrong guy. Followed the wrong cop. She'd seen things she shouldn't have seen, and it had all exploded.

The hit on her had gone wrong. It was supposed to have looked as if she'd stumbled onto a drug deal in public housing while checking an outstanding warrant. But she'd been only wounded before managing to escape from the apartment complex onto a crowded street. She would've gotten away and ID'd the cop who'd shot her, so she was chased down.

The eyewitnesses to the second gunshot had given chaotic descriptions of exactly how many cops had been there and what had gone down, but in the end, Sergeant Malcolm Pozniak had been arrested for the murder of a fellow police officer. And then he'd talked. Just a little. Just enough to make everyone nervous before he lawyered up.

A few weeks later, he'd run.

Isabelle slid a plate of pie in front of Tom and sat next to him at the table.

"Aren't you having pie?" he asked. "I heard it's your favorite."

"It is. I had a piece for breakfast. And lunch. This one is yours. You look like you need it."

"I don't want to eat your pie," he said then smiled stupidly at her when she laughed.

"Well, that's kind of disappointing, Marshal Duncan."

"Too easy." He held up the spoon when she started to speak. "I meant the joke, not you."

"Then you don't know me very well," she countered.

"We'll share the pie." He took a bite and offered her the spoon. "No forks?"

"I got distracted halfway through loading the dishwasher this afternoon. It happens."

"A lot?" he asked.

"Maybe. I bet you never forget to run the dishwasher. I bet you clean the kitchen every night before bed."

He shrugged. "Only when I'm home."

They laughed their way through the piece of pie, and by the end of it, Tom had almost forgotten why he was there, the same problem he had every time he came to her place, only now the stakes had gotten higher.

Now he was lying to his boss, lying to the FBI, lying to her. He parted his lips, drawing in a long breath while he braced himself to speak words that would blow apart the safe world she'd made for herself.

And then she kissed him.

She tasted of the same cherries that he'd eaten, but they were somehow sweeter on her tongue. Richer. Or maybe that was just her body and what it meant to him now, because the very first taste of her reminded him of pure pleasure and how much he wanted more.

He slanted his mouth over hers, taking her tongue deeper as he slid his hands up her thighs. She was wearing leggings under her black sweater, and he could feel every curve of her leg, and he wanted those curves on him. She seemed to have the same idea, because she slipped her thigh over his and shifted until she was straddling him. He was hard in an instant.

He slipped his hands down her back and realized that this sweater held a secret. She was naked underneath. His hands slid along her curves, feeling nothing beneath the thin material. He feathered his thumbs over her ribs. She stretched up, as if trying to draw his hands higher.

Following her movement up, his hands found the undersides of her breasts. So soft and warm and irresistible. He cupped her, memorizing the weight of her as she eased away from his kiss and lowered her eyes to watch.

The neckline of her sweater had dipped tantalizingly low. He pressed a kiss to the bare skin there and then another. Her breathing quickened at that soft touch then caught in her throat when he found her nipples through the sweater and squeezed.

He'd meant to tease her for a while, but why tease her when he could be looking at her bare breasts? Teasing was for people who had time. They didn't have time. A few nights, at best.

He dragged her sweater up, and Isabelle helped pull it over her head. God, she was beautiful. Not perfect and so beautiful for that, for being proud and easy with her body.

She leaned back against the edge of the table, letting him look at her, *wanting* him to look.

He slid his hands back up her ribs, this time watching as her skin went rough with goose bumps under his touch. Her nipples got harder, drawing tight before he even cupped her breasts. When he did, when he held her in his hands, his breath left him.

"God, you're gorgeous," he breathed, as he dragged his thumbs over her nipples. She sighed in response. He loved how rosy brown her nipples were against her pale skin. How they were so sweet and dark they made his mouth water.

He circled one with a light fingertip, loving the way she shuddered. He didn't want to tear his eyes away from the lovely sight, but he managed to do it so he could see her face as he circled her one more time.

Her head was tipped down, her eyes watching her own breast as he teased it. Her lips parted on a breath. When he pinched her nipple, her teeth pressed into her lower lip. He kissed the spot on her lip she'd just bitten, his hands sliding down to wrap around her waist.

As much as he wanted to scoot her hips forward so he could press her against his erection, he lifted her up instead.

She stood before him, smiling slightly as he stripped down the tight layer of her pants, taking her panties with them. "I like this," she said as she stepped out of her clothes and kicked them aside.

"What?" he asked, distracted by the pretty sight of the dark triangle of curls covering her pussy.

"I like you in your suit. You look so severe. And me…I'm so naked." She scooted onto the table then hooked her feet behind his knees to pull him against her. "Your clothes feel wicked against my skin."

He obliged her by leaning down, pressing her to the table, sliding his hand along her naked thigh and hip as he pressed his cock against her. "You look wicked," he growled.

"Good." She was still smiling. Still slightly removed and enjoying the tease.

His anger surged back, surprising him. It was all

mixed up with his lust for her. He wanted her to *give* him something. To give something real. He'd shown her something vulnerable, and she still held everything back.

He slid a hand between her legs, found slick heat and pressed two fingers deep inside her.

Her neck arched as a cry tore from her throat. She wasn't removed anymore. She was stretched out and naked and tipping her hips up for more. He slid his fingers inside her, moving slowly, watching the way she met his rhythm. She was looking at his face now, her lips parted, her gaze steady and unashamed of what she wanted. His thumb touched her clit, and she inhaled so sharply that air hissed past her teeth.

Tom smiled and slipped his fingers free. "Don't move," he murmured as he shrugged off his suit jacket and took off his tie. He set his gun and harness on top of a chair and threw his jacket over it then rolled up his sleeves, aware of Isabelle's eyes on his hands.

He put those hands on her thighs, easing her legs farther open before he went to his knees before her.

The taste of her flooded his tongue as he put his mouth over her pussy and sucked gently at her clit. Her cry filled his ears. When he felt the bud of her clit get harder, he worked his tongue against her. Lightly at first then with more pressure and speed as she groaned her approval. Her fingers clutched at his skull, and when he reached a hand up to pinch one of her nipples, she bucked against him.

"Oh, fuck, you're good at that," she gasped, making him smile against her.

He lifted his head. "Should I keep going?" he teased.

"Mmm." She wrapped her legs around his back and tugged him closer. "Only until I come."

He laughed, but that urge was back. To make her give him some secret part of herself. He didn't want her capable of speech, much less joking.

He pinched her nipple again and licked more lazily at her pussy, memorizing the taste and feel and smell of it so he could jerk off to her for years. He waited until she was squirming for more, and then he slid his hand back down her belly and pushed those two fingers into her again.

Her hips jerked against his mouth, but he didn't let her get away. He fucked her hard with his fingers and flicked her clit with his tongue, and she wasn't talking anymore. She was gasping and moaning and twisting up for more. This was what he wanted. Her heels digging into his back and her pussy dripping wet and her cries echoing against the walls. He eased his tongue off her until it was barely brushing her clit.

"Please," she panted. "Please. Tom."

Yes, he thought, *beg me. Give me that, at least.*

"Please," she groaned. Her nails dug into his scalp. "I need it."

He curled his fingers up, pressing against her as he gave her more of his tongue, and she broke, screaming, her hips spasming as she came against his mouth, the muscles of her pussy squeezing his fingers.

When she finally went quiet, Tom stood, wincing at how much his cock ached. He'd bought condoms at the gas station, and he meant to reach for one, but before he could, he was caught by the sight of her. She was spread over the table like a decadent treat, her beautiful, lush body gone rosy with pleasure. He wished he could take a picture, to show her later. Maybe she'd paint it for him.

She was watching him past heavy eyes, happy to let

him look as she stretched. But just as he reached for his belt, she sat up. "Let me do that," she purred.

He backed up when she scooted off the table. "The bedroom?" he asked.

"Oh, I don't think that's necessary." With that familiar secret smile he loved, she backed him up until he was against the kitchen cabinets then unbuckled his belt. "We can do this right here," she teased. His blood went thick and heavy when she slowly lowered her body until she was kneeling at his feet. She tugged his zipper down and then his underwear, and then her heavenly fist was around him.

She made a noise of approval and glanced up at him. "You've got a nice cock," she said, sliding her hand along it.

Tom couldn't speak. If he'd thought he was going to get more from her than he gave, he was wrong, because at that moment, he would've begged if she'd asked him to. But she didn't ask.

Still smiling, she pressed a small, nearly chaste kiss to the head of his cock. Then a more lingering one, just her pursed lips, brushing gently against him. He held his breath. Another picture he'd like to take, this one for himself, so he'd never forget the sight of her soft lips parting for him.

And then her tongue licked at him, sliding beneath the crown of his cock and stealing the air from his lungs. He managed not to gasp, but just barely.

Her hold on the base of his shaft tightened, and she stroked up and then back down as she swirled her tongue around him. It was torture. Perfect, delicious torture. His hips shifted forward of their own accord, and Isabelle chuckled.

"Greedy," she murmured just before she slid her mouth over him.

Oh, shit. Yes, he was greedy. He wanted her mouth like this a hundred times. A thousand. Because she was pure heat and wetness as she closed her lips around him. And then she sucked, and his world turned to pleasure.

She worked her way slowly down his cock, each draw of her mouth making a promise that there would be more soon. A half an inch more, and then another, until she was halfway down his cock, and he was panting. He couldn't get enough air to feed his thundering pulse, but somehow he didn't feel weak from the airlessness. He felt solid and strong and feral.

She drew away from him with a slow, maddening slide of her mouth. "God, you're delicious," she whispered. "I like you on my tongue."

He said her name, a crazed sound of need that was begging even if he didn't form the words. Because she liked him on her tongue. Because he loved everything about that. Because he needed someone just like her, and there was already too much between them.

But she didn't know any of that. She just took him into her mouth again. Deeper this time, and all at once, and Tom couldn't stop the tortured groan that tore from his throat.

She used her fist then, sliding up and down in time with her mouth, sending waves of sensation through his whole body. His knees shook a little. His heart shook a lot.

He reached back and curled his hands over the edge of the counter, squeezing hard.

She'd made him vulnerable again, but this time it was good, as if she were kissing all of him at once. He watched her sucking his cock, and he let himself fall completely under her spell. It didn't matter who was lying to whom. This was so fucking good.

"Isabelle," he growled. She quickened her strokes in response, and it felt as if every nerve in his body had congregated right there. Right where her mouth sucked and her hand squeezed and his balls tightened.

He managed to mutter something about coming, a warning, but she didn't stop. Thank God she didn't stop, because he wanted to come like this, engulfed by her. He wanted her to want it. And she did.

The orgasm slammed through him, the release so great he groaned in relief as he pulsed into her mouth over and over again. She slowed. Her touch gentled. His arms shook from the tight hold he had on the counter, and he was damn relieved that his knees didn't buckle.

Isabelle sat back on her legs and looked up at him.

"You're fucking amazing," he rasped. She sat there, naked and wet-mouthed, and she laughed up at him, and Tom fell a little further into her.

HE COULDN'T STAY. He knew he couldn't. But they still collapsed onto the couch together. He'd fastened his pants, and Isabelle had pulled on her sweater to keep the chill off, and now they were cuddled close in the darkness of her living room.

Her ex-lover hovered over them. At least the man was turned away.

Tom smoothed a hand over her hair and tried one last time to get her to talk. "I'm glad you didn't stay with that guy who made you feel bad about sex."

"Me, too. We were engaged, but I can't imagine things would've worked out in the long run. In two years with him, he never made me come."

That shocked the hell out of him. "And you still wanted to marry him?"

"I was young and stupid. And I didn't know my worth."

"Clearly. Because you're worth a lot."

He felt her cheek tighten against his shoulder when she smiled. "Must've been a good blow job."

"It was, but it's not even about that. You just seem really…comfortable. With sex. With yourself. It's attractive."

"Yeah?" She went quiet for a long moment, and he was afraid he'd insulted her just when she was beginning to open up. But she finally spoke. "It's really hard for a woman to like sex."

"Because guys are terrible at it?"

"No," she laughed. "Even aside from that. We're taught from day one that we're supposed to resist it. That we'll eventually be talked into it. That we don't want it as much, and we definitely don't need it. Not like boys do. I believed that. So much so that I wasn't the least concerned that I'd never had an orgasm. Because lots of women don't."

He nodded.

"Can you imagine that? I mean *really*. Think about that. What if you had sex your whole life and never came?"

Tom frowned. "That's awful."

"It is awful!" she shouted, laughing again. "And that was almost my life! But then when I figured out how much I liked sex and exactly how I liked it… Jesus, that's even more confusing. To be a woman and like sex. To want things just as much as the man does and still be treated as if you've given in and given something away. It's no wonder women hit their sexual peak later in life. It takes decades to find the confidence to have good sex."

Tom was frowning harder now. "How so?"

She shook her head. "Some men can make it hard to feel good about it afterward, no matter how much you liked it. Men say things like 'I got some' or 'She put out,' or whatever that dialogue is. Girls are stupid cows giving the milk away for free. And suddenly you feel like you were conquered."

"Oh." Tom had never heard anything like that before.

"It takes a lot of self-possession to know that a man's attitude doesn't change what you wanted. It doesn't change what you got out of it."

He rubbed a hand against the back of his neck. Hadn't he had those thoughts when he was younger? That sex was a game, and he was the winner if he could get some?

And just tonight, he'd been wanting her to give in. He'd wanted to take. The difference being that she'd taken, too.

"How did it end with him?" he asked, thinking he knew but wanting her to say it.

She didn't, of course, but she didn't go rigid in his arms, either. "We broke up over something else. A few weeks later, I got drunk and slept with a stranger. And it was great."

Tom smiled at her laughter. "And a new you was born?"

"You know what? It kind of was. I'd spent my whole life doing what I was told, and it took waking up in a stranger's bed to realize I could do whatever I wanted. I could be who I wanted to be, instead of—" She cut herself off. "Anyway, it all worked out. And here we are."

"Yes," he said, "I'm glad." He was glad. He wanted

her to know that. He was glad she'd run, and he could help her. "Was your mom strong like you?" he asked.

She let out a long breath but didn't push away. Didn't get up. Eventually, she answered. "No. My mom was timid and quiet. She deferred to my dad. I loved her, but I wish she'd been stronger."

"And your dad?"

She shrugged. "He left one day. That's all."

"Isabelle—" he started, but she interrupted him by stroking a hand over his chest.

"You're pretty great, you know," she said. "You make me comfortable. It's easy to trust you."

The pleasure that had melted through his body turned cool. She trusted him. Obviously. She'd let him into her home and her body. Hell, he'd encouraged her to trust him so she'd open up.

She must've felt him stiffen. "Hey, don't freak out. A girl in every port, right?"

"No," he said. His phone buzzed, and he was embarrassed to feel relieved, because it wasn't that he wanted an excuse to leave; he just couldn't stay and lie to her anymore.

She kissed his cheek and moved off him, letting him sit up. "I'm glad you came by again."

"Not as glad as I am."

"Are you sure?" she asked, eyebrows raised.

"After what you said tonight, no. Were you using me?"

"Absolutely." She was giving him an out. Keeping it light so he could retreat with grace. The worst part was that he was about to take full advantage of that and get the hell out of her house as if he really wanted away from her.

He cleared his throat and headed back to her kitchen

for the rest of his clothes. She followed and started doing dishes as if she were totally comfortable wearing nothing but a sweater that fell just short of covering her bare ass.

Fuck, she was cute.

He strapped on his gun and shrugged on his jacket, feeling guilty as hell. "When I'm done with all this, I'd love to do this right."

"If what we just did was wrong…"

Right. Keep it light. "I meant we could go out. Dinner or a movie or skiing."

She stopped washing dishes and turned to look at him. He tried to keep his eyes above her waist, but failed several times. "I'm not much of a skier," she said. "I love the part where you get to the top of the mountain, and it's so quiet and solitary. But all the lift lines and the crowds at the bottom… That's not for me."

"Rock climbing is more my thing," he admitted.

"Oh! I'd love to try that! Would you teach me?" She shook her head before he could speak. "Not in the winter, I guess."

"No, but in the summer, I'd love to." He ignored the awkward pause. "Anyway, I wish I had more time right now."

"It's okay. That was fun."

It had been fun, but he wanted to stay. Wanted to wake up in the morning and slide his hand over her naked body, and find out if she was a morning person. He was pretty sure she wasn't, but that didn't mean she wouldn't be horny.

"Keep your curtains drawn," he said. "And be careful. Things are getting tense."

She nodded, and even as he wondered if he should, Tom walked over and gave her a kiss goodbye. She kissed him back, stroking a hand down his jaw with a murmur of pleasure. When she kissed him again, Tom cupped her ass in his hands and pulled her tightly against him, surprised to realize he was getting hard again already.

"Damn, you're sexy," he whispered.

She dropped back to flat feet and smiled. "Really?"

"Yes, really."

"Good."

She smiled so sweetly up at him that he couldn't resist one more kiss, because it might be the only time she looked so sweet for him. It might even be the last kiss. Every lie they told each other made it more likely.

He pulled reluctantly away, lingering over the taste, but once he got to the front door, he put it from his mind completely.

He had to do his job, whether he wanted to or not. And then the call came through.

CHAPTER FOURTEEN

ISABELLE WAS GLAD she'd had trouble sleeping that morning when she saw the black sedan climb up her driveway. Glad, because she'd decided to get out of bed early and go for a snowshoe hike through the trees, and she wasn't inside to answer the door when the man knocked.

She'd ducked behind a tree when she saw the unfamiliar vehicle, thanks to instincts honed from years of avoiding strangers. But as soon as the man stepped out, she knew he was one of Tom's guys. There was no mistaking the dark suit and the flash of a shoulder holster when he reached up to shield his eyes from the sun.

Isabelle watched as he knocked on her door. He was impatient and obviously on a long shift. This wasn't the first time he'd run his hand through his short hair. It stuck up in odd angles. But whatever assignment Tom had given the guy, she wasn't going to help out. He could keep on canvassing the area without her input. She didn't want to interact with more law enforcement than she needed to. She was being stupid enough with Tom as it was.

She frowned when the man cupped his hands around his eyes and tried to look into her window. She considered shouting at him and telling him to get the fuck off her porch, but he gave up quickly and headed back to his car.

"Dick," she muttered, before turning to trudge into

the fresh snow. She might let Mary into her house and Tom into her bed, but that was the end of her cooperation with the feds. If that Stevenson guy had been spotted in the area, Tom would've called her himself.

She stopped for a moment when her heart tripped over itself, wondering if she was actually in danger. She held her breath and listened to the forest around her. It was as still as ever. But not quiet. Not if you really listened.

Birds called to each other. Pine boughs shushed in the wind. Branches creaked. Water trickled into tiny streams beneath the snow. Everything was normal.

And the guy hadn't looked worried about her or even alarmed. He'd just looked irritated.

Still, when her phone rang, Isabelle jumped. The fronts of her snowshoes sank into the snow, and she pinwheeled her arms, desperately trying to keep upright. She'd done this before, and she didn't relish falling face-first in the deep snow; it always took a remarkably long time to get upright again.

She finally shifted her weight backward and breathed a sigh of relief before digging her phone out of the pocket of her jacket.

"Hey," she said when she saw it was Lauren.

"Oh, my God, your new boyfriend is so sexy!"

"Yes," she agreed immediately, before realizing she shouldn't. "I mean, what?"

Lauren laughed. "I knew it. Anyway, congratulations on boning a hero."

"What?" she asked with genuine surprise. "What are you talking about?"

"You are so disconnected," Lauren groaned. "Have you seriously not heard?"

"Tell me!" Isabelle shrieked, suddenly alarmed about

what that guy in the suit might have wanted. "Is he okay?"

"He's fine. But he raided a motel in Jackson this morning and caught one of those survivalist guys."

Isabelle almost fell over again and had to sit down on her butt to stop from teetering. "Really?"

"Yes, really!"

"God," she breathed, "that is sexy." She imagined him kicking down a door with his gun drawn and actually sighed with lust. An awfully sick reaction considering her own ambiguous legal status and hatred of cops. But some things soaked into you from birth.

"Is he really your boyfriend?" Lauren asked in a lower tone.

"No." She heard the note of regret in her voice and shook it off. "Definitely not my boyfriend."

"Uh-huh. So just a boy toy? God, you get the best deliveries."

Isabelle laughed and tried to push up to her feet. "So he caught the guy?"

"Not *the* guy. Someone from their group, I guess. But Ephraim's brother is still out there."

That must have been what that marshal was spreading the word about earlier.

"Be careful," Lauren said. "Really. Maybe you should come stay with me."

"And leave Jill alone up here? No way. Anyway, he's after the judge, not me. And I have Bear."

"Are you locking your doors?"

"Tom insists."

"Oh, *Tom*," Lauren said with a laugh.

Isabelle finally pushed to her feet and smiled at the way her stomach fluttered. It was nice to feel that after so many years. "You're sure he's okay, right?"

"You can read it yourself on the paper's website. The story is only three paragraphs long at this point, but it specifically says that no shots were fired, and the guy was taken into custody."

"I guess he's going to have a busy day," Isabelle said, already thinking selfishly of the night to come and whether he'd have time to stop by. Probably not.

"Why don't you come down and have lunch with me and Sophie? You can tell us more about Marshal Tom."

Isabelle snorted. "You've both met him. What is there to tell?"

"You know what we want to hear."

"Pervert," she said on a laugh. "But I can't. Too much work." That wasn't exactly true, but Lauren probably understood that Isabelle had reached her limit of socializing for the week. She needed time to not speak to anyone for a while. Except Tom. That she could handle, but only because it led to other forms of relaxation.

They said goodbye, and Isabelle tucked her phone away.

If he'd raided a motel at 6:00 a.m., he'd probably been up nearly all night getting ready for it. And he had a full day at the courthouse. There was no way he'd come by tonight.

"That's fine," she said aloud. It was casual. He'd be gone in a few days. Better not to get used to seeing him every day. What if she was lonely when he left?

A strange thought.

Not that she'd never been lonely in her little cabin, but it had only been isolation, never actually missing a specific man. Normally, she was relieved to get back to her routine and forget about the whole world once a fling was done. But her day felt a little emptier now that she knew she wouldn't see Tom at the end of it. Even this snowshoe hike through the forest felt muted now, but she trudged on.

The sound of a car carried through the trees from the east. The car wasn't visible, but the distant sound of the engine meant that young deputy had headed farther down their road. Clearly a guy assigned a mindless task, because there were only summer cabins up that way. Maybe he'd get stuck.

Nothing she could do about that. He could hike out just as easily as she could get to him. Plus, she didn't give a damn. Isabelle took a path heading a little farther west and walked on, trying to recapture her earlier excitement and wishing she could have last night all over again.

CHAPTER FIFTEEN

"I've got a stack of paperwork to catch up on," Tom said, rubbing a hand over his eyes to try to clear the exhaustion from them. "You get some sleep."

"It's 6:00 p.m.," Mary said, even as her jaw cracked with a yawn.

"Yeah, and neither of us slept last night." He tipped his head toward the window that looked out on the courthouse grass. "Your room is only two blocks away. Go crash. I won't be in bed until midnight, but I'll call then if I need you up and alert. If not, hopefully we can both get a whole night's sleep."

She nodded. "All right. Shit, it was a good day, at least."

"It was a good day," he said. Not great. Great would have meant getting Saul Stevenson off the streets. But that shithead hiding in the motel room had clearly been here in a supporting role. He'd had three assault rifles, one sniper rifle and boxes of ammunition for additional firearms he wasn't carrying. With a felony conviction under his belt, Butch Abrams wasn't allowed to have any of it.

The tip had come from a motel employee who claimed not to have seen anyone else with Abrams when he'd checked in or anytime since. Abrams himself claimed he'd come to town only to check out the trial and offer

Stevenson his support, though he hadn't actually gone to the courthouse once.

Saul Stevenson was out there. He was close. The tactics team had taken the judge home, and the entire prosecution team was under guard by the state police. Now that Stevenson had lost whatever support Abrams had meant to provide, Tom hoped he was on his own and less of a danger.

Still. Half the tactics team had gone ahead to survey the area around the judge's home.

An hour later, Tom had wrapped up the urgent work and was hit by a sudden wave of exhaustion. Or hunger. He couldn't tell anymore, but he had hours more work to do.

Stupidly, he wished he could see Isabelle. It wouldn't make any difference. He'd still be exhausted and starving and stressed. And he still hadn't come up with a plan.

"Damn it," he muttered, scrubbing his hands hard over his face. Any decision would have to wait until the trial was over. He couldn't concentrate on Isabelle's problem long enough to sort it out and come up with an idea.

He'd managed to read a few newspaper articles about her father's case in the past twenty-four hours. Beth Pozniak had disappeared three months after her father had skipped town. There'd been weeks of speculation. Assertions that she had joined her dad in some hidey-hole overseas. Theories that she'd been killed by the people her father had betrayed.

After a few weeks, the stories had slipped away. The whole thing had slipped away. A few cops had been charged with conspiracy and bribery, and they'd served a few months. But no one had ever been convicted of the murder, and only six other low-level officers had been kicked off the force.

But there was more to it. There had to be. There was a reason the FBI had flagged the file and warned against sharing any information with the Chicago Police Department. Something was very wrong with that case. He suspected Isabelle knew exactly what that was. There hadn't been another reason to run, as far as he could tell.

He'd ask her as soon as the trial was over. And he'd try to avoid her until then. Easier said than done, when all he wanted was to fall into bed with her and sleep for twelve hours. After fucking her until neither of them could walk.

Shit, he needed food and more coffee.

Tom was just closing his laptop when his phone rang, and Hannity's name popped up on the screen. "Everything secure?" Tom asked.

"The judge is tucked in safe and sound, but my guys found some tire tracks that we're checking out now."

"Where?"

"On White Ridge Road."

Tom froze. "That's a public road. People live there."

"Yes, but the tracks go all the way up to an unoccupied cabin a mile past the last house."

A mile past Isabelle's place.

"We're checking it out now," Hannity said. "Figured you wouldn't want to wait until morning."

"No. I'll be there in thirty." Tom hung up and immediately called Isabelle. His racing pulse slowed a little when she answered.

"I heard about all the excitement," she said. "You're okay?"

"I'm good, just dead on my feet."

"I'm truly sorry to hear that," she said, and despite everything, Tom smiled.

"It's worse than that," he said. "I'm still working."

"All right. I guess I'll have to get off without you to-night. Desperate times and all."

He chuckled as he grabbed his bag and left the office, drawing the attention of one of the guards, but the guy just tipped his chin in greeting as Tom passed. "Listen," he said once he was out of earshot. "Have you seen anyone around today?"

"Just one of your men. Why?"

"We're on pretty high alert here after that arrest. Be careful, all right?"

"It's supposed to start snowing soon. I'm not going anywhere."

"Good. You're all locked up?"

"Yes, sir," she said with a little purr that nearly made him groan.

"All right. I'm sorry I can't keep you company."

"It's okay," she said. "I'll make good use of you in my imagination. If you feel your ears burning, that's me sucking your cock."

Thank God Tom had made it out of the courthouse, because he burst into laughter, though it was slightly edged with pain. "You're out of control."

"I know. That's my appeal."

"It might be a little of it," he conceded, still smiling, even as he scanned the area around his car before getting in. "But definitely not all of it."

"You're sweet," she said, her voice going a little more quiet.

"No, I'm—" He'd been about to say "honest," but his throat choked off the word. He wasn't honest. He couldn't say that to her. "It's the truth," he said instead.

"I'll miss you tonight." After a pause, she added, "I hope that's not weird to say."

"I feel the same way, weird or not."

"I guess we both needed this."

"Yeah," he said, sitting in the quiet of the car for a moment. "I guess we did."

"Be safe tonight, Tom. And get some sleep."

"I will. And try to ignore our guys driving around. We're doing extra patrols. Will you let Jill know?"

He hung up and headed out, relieved about Isabelle's safety and knowing that his primary reaction should have been continued stress for the judge. But shit, the judge had nearly a whole US Marshals office watching his ass. Isabelle had only Tom and one weird cat. And a gun. And a kick-ass ballsiness that was sexy as hell.

Plus, she'd implied that she was going to masturbate tonight while fantasizing about going down on him. That was a woman worth protecting through hell or high water.

She'd been right about the weather. Snow began hitting his windshield just as he turned off the main freeway onto the winding road that led up into the trees. He hit the gas, needing to get to those tracks before they were covered by new snow. Not that he was some expert tracker, but he wanted to see them for himself.

He drove past Isabelle's place ten minutes later, slowing to take a look at her softly glowing windows. She'd pulled all the shades and curtains, he was happy to see. She was taking the threat more seriously than she had in the past. Or she was simply annoyed by the cop cars that had been going by in the darkness.

The road past her drive was usually untouched aside from deer tracks, but today his headlights caught the straight slashes of crisscrossing tire marks.

This was exactly why he'd walked this road on his first day here. It was almost a straight shot through the woods from Isabelle's house to the judge's. From her place, the road curved around ridges and dropped down hills until it reached a few seasonal cabins. The first cabin was quite a drive on this rutted road, but no farther from the judge's place on foot than Isabelle's was. He'd worried it could be used as a hideout by someone who needed cover for a night or two.

Two SUVs were parked about fifty yards from the first cabin. Tom pulled behind them and cut the engine then tugged up the hood of his parka and jumped out to meet Hannity in the middle of the road.

"One set of tire tracks," Hannity said. "Wes followed them out here and drove on past to check the other cabins, but the tracks in the driveway of this one aren't his."

The snow started coming down harder, so Tom hurried to take a look. There were more than tire tracks here. "So someone parked here and went inside?"

"I don't think so. Looks like someone just went up the steps and knocked. The tracks end there, aside from a few steps over to the front window. Then the prints head back to the vehicle. That's it."

"You're sure it wasn't one of our guys?"

"Definitely not. I took a look around back, and I found an old trail of bootprints leading up to the cabin, but I'm hoping they're yours."

"I was up here a few days ago, but I'll check them out to be sure." Tom shone his flashlight on the steps. "Place is still locked tight?"

"Yep. And no sign of any tracks at the other cabins."

"Have you been able to reach the owner of this one? Any chance they were up here checking on their place?"

"We're looking at property records now."

The south side of the cabin was visible from the road, so Tom hiked through the deeper snow on the north side, just to be sure the cabin was still secure. He found the old tracks and was reasonably certain they were his, judging by the wear from melt and wind. Even if someone else had come through, Tom's prints would've still been visible. They had to be his.

If there was no one in the cabin, there wasn't much to be done. "I don't like it," he said to Hannity when he rejoined him in the front, "but it could've been anyone. The homeowner. A lost tourist. Hell, it could've even been a reporter looking for a good vantage for a photo of the judge's house."

Hannity agreed and promised to get back to Tom once the owners had been tracked down.

Tom held back a yawn. "I'll take another hike around early tomorrow. With this snow moving in, I'll know if anyone else has been out and about. Have the team keep careful track of their movements tonight so I can eliminate them."

"Got it."

Tom drove on a ways, but there was only the one set of tracks leading in and out, and there were no bootprints anywhere that he could see. He'd check again in daylight, but the snow was coming in a steady, gentle drift now. It looked like nothing, but he knew from experience it could end up being two feet of powder by sunrise.

At least adrenaline had kept him going for a while. The exhaustion didn't return until he slowed in front of Isabelle's house again. Her driveway was already smoothing out, the new snow hiding the jagged ridges of the evidence of her girls' night.

He slowed at Jill's, too, happy to see that even she had

pulled her blinds. Isabelle must have called her, because normally her windows were a riot of light and glass sculptures and hanging plants. He wistfully considered knocking to beg for another frozen packet of food, but he drove on to the judge's and all the work that waited there. He had an early morning tomorrow that would start well before he needed to leave for the courthouse. And if Hannity found anything else, Tom would be up all night again.

For once, he hoped that Stevenson would stay hidden for a little while longer. Tom wanted to be lying in bed waiting for his ears to burn.

ISABELLE TIPTOED UP the front steps of Jill's house and tapped softly on her door. She didn't know why she was being quiet. No one on the road would be able to see or hear her past the shifting sheets of snow. But she felt guilty after promising Tom she'd stay in.

She'd meant it when she'd said it, but then she'd decided to call Jill and talk to her about Tom, and Jill wasn't answering her phone.

Isabelle tapped on the door again, telling herself it was really the responsible thing to do, coming over to check on Jill. After all, there was a bad guy on the loose. But really, she just wanted to talk to someone else who knew Tom.

The blinds of the front window finally parted, and Isabelle sighed with relief, but that response was short-lived. Jill opened her door only a few inches.

"What are you doing out here?" Jill demanded in a low voice. "You left me a message saying Tom was worried!"

"Oh, please. If there's a weird survivalist out here, he's hiding out from the snow like everyone else." Isabelle stomped the snow from her boots. "Come on. Let me in."

"You're supposed to be at home!" Jill grouched, but she opened the door anyway.

"I was bored."

"You're never bored. And since when do you want company? Just put on a bad movie and do a puzzle like you always do."

"God, you're grumpy." Isabelle toed off her boots, but then she stopped and narrowed her eyes at Jill. "What's going on with you? Why's your hair all squashed?"

"I was already in bed."

Isabelle looked suspiciously around. "And why are we speaking so softly?"

Jill didn't answer that, and a spike of fear suddenly pierced Isabelle's self-absorption. "Are you okay?"

"I'm fine."

Isabelle lowered her voice to a whisper and leaned close. "Is there someone here? Give me a signal and I'll make an excuse to leave. Tom is—"

"No, it's fine." Jill's shoulders slumped. "Everything is fine."

A distinctive creak sounded from the other side of the house. Isabelle felt her eyes widen until they hurt. "Then why did I just hear your bedroom door open?" she whispered, reaching for Jill's hand to tug her toward the door, bare feet or not.

But before she could get Jill to move, a woman stepped into the living room. A very young woman. Wearing a T-shirt and tiny black underwear.

"Oh, hi," the woman said, pushing her long brown hair off her face. "Jill, do you have a charger I can borrow? I need it for my phone if I'm going to stay the night."

"Sure," Jill said, her voice slightly strained at the edges. "It's on the kitchen counter. See if it's the right kind."

"Thanks." She walked by, her perky ass half exposed by the panties. A moment later, she retraced her route. The door to the bedroom closed. The pipes whooshed as the shower started.

Isabelle forced her lids to blink before her eyeballs fell out and rolled across the floor. "Oh. My. God."

"Shut up," Jill said.

"Please tell me she's over eighteen."

"She's twenty-two."

Isabelle turned her gaze on Jill. She closed her jaw, but it fell open again. "Oh. My. God."

"Stop saying that." The tips of her ears turned red.

"*That's* why you weren't answering your phone? That girl is young enough to be your daughter!"

Jill shrugged and crossed her arms. "I was about to give in and call Marguerite. I needed to distract myself."

"So you called 1-800-HOT-COED?"

"Stop embarrassing me! There are…apps. Ways to meet people with the same…interests. You should try it yourself."

Isabelle clapped a hand over her mouth to stop a laugh.

Jill glared at her.

"I'm sorry! You know I understand! I just didn't know you dated hot young things, that's all."

Jill stalked past her, heading for the kitchen, but Isabelle followed. "I don't, all right? I just needed to do something crazy."

"Good. I'm glad." She put her hands up in defense when Jill shot her another glare. "I'm serious. I know how much you've missed Marguerite."

Jill's eyes filled with tears. "I know it's stupid," she rasped.

"It's not!" Isabelle rushed forward and squeezed Jill tight. "It's not stupid."

"It is! Breaking up hasn't even made anything different. She's still not here, just like always. We're still not talking. I still haven't seen her for eight months. But I'm so much more lonely, knowing I can't reach out. I can't even let myself *want* her."

Isabelle squeezed her tighter. "I know."

"I've been so mad at her for so long, but there was always the *possibility*."

"There still is. You're just taking a break."

"No, we're not. Not if I have any self-esteem left. It's over. I have to let her go. And I just wanted to find a way to forget."

Her voice had calmed a little, so Isabelle leaned back to look at Jill. She used her own sleeve to swipe at the tears on Jill's face. "So did it work?"

Jill shrugged. "For a couple of hours. Yes." The silence of the shower turning off surrounded them.

They both looked toward the bedroom before turning slowly back to each other. "And maybe for a couple more hours?" Isabelle asked.

Jill shrugged again, but her mouth relaxed into a half smile. "Maybe."

"Good. I mean it. I'm really sorry I barged in on you."

"It's okay. At least now I can talk to you about it tomorrow. She wasn't going to spend the night, but…"

"But you're that good?" Isabelle asked.

"I'm pretty good."

Isabelle had to slap a hand over her mouth to stop

her laughter again. This time Jill joined her, relaxing for the first time since Isabelle had arrived.

Jill filled a glass with ice water and sucked it down as if she'd been working out. "So what was so gosh-darn urgent you had to interrupt my night of illicit love?"

"Nothing. I wanted to talk about Tom."

"Why?"

"A night of illicit love."

Jill set the glass down hard. "I knew it! You two were throwing off sparks from day one."

"There's a little chemistry."

"So what is there to talk about? Was it weird?"

"No, it wasn't *weird*!"

Jill arched an eyebrow as she refilled her glass and poured one for Isabelle, too. "I don't know what you people are into."

Isabelle was laughing again, half at Jill and half in delight because she was talking about Tom. That was a sad state to be in. "The problem is that there's actually a lot of chemistry. And it wasn't weird at all. And I just wanted…some confirmation, maybe? Some reassurance. You like him, right?" Before Jill could answer, Isabelle held up her hands. "Oh, God," she groaned. "I don't even know why I'm asking. It's only temporary." What was she thinking? That Tom could be her boyfriend? That it would be safe because she'd see him only once a month so he'd never find out more about her?

Jill ignored her outburst. "I like Tom a lot. He's a good guy. I can tell."

"Maybe he just makes a good first impression."

"Maybe. But I've met a lot of people in my life, and I've got good instincts. I grew up black and poor. Cops are not my favorite people in the world, but I liked him right away. Unlike, say, that asshole FBI guy who came knocking today."

Isabelle's body went numb. She almost dropped her glass of water. "The FBI?"

"Didn't he come by your house? I saw him head over there."

"No. He… I went snowshoeing today. He must have missed me." She pictured him trying to look through her window, and her pulse picked up. "Why would the FBI be here?"

"Same reason everyone's here, I guess. He was asking a lot of questions about who lives around here, and he was interested in the summer cabins. Frankly, I got the idea he was checking on Tom's work. I guess those two agencies don't like each other."

Isabelle nodded, hoping her face wasn't as pale as it felt. "So he wasn't asking anything odd?"

"Odd?" Jill frowned at her, but she shook her head. "Not really. Asked how long I'd known the neighbors and all that. He asked me about an older man. Maybe it was someone related to the guy arrested this morning."

"Right." A man. Could have been any man.

"He asked about a woman, too. I hadn't heard there were any women involved, but I guess they must be married and have families, after all. It makes sense."

A woman. Sweat prickled her brow. "What was the FBI agent's name?"

"I don't remember. You should ask Tom. Why?"

Shit. Why, indeed? "I'm just…worried he was rude to you. You said you didn't like him."

Jill clicked her tongue. "No, he was only smarmy. Glad-handing me, pretending we were friends. I don't trust that."

"All right. I'll keep that in mind." Isabelle briefly

considered running back home and packing a bag just in case this was about her. But that made no sense, did it? How would the FBI have found her after all this time?

But she knew, of course. Tom. Or one of his team. Mary, maybe. But that didn't make sense, either. They were US Marshals. If they knew who she was, they'd simply take her in. She was being paranoid.

"I'll leave you alone," Isabelle said, spinning to rush toward the door. "I'm sorry I interrupted."

"We can talk more about Tom tomorrow, if you want," Jill offered.

Isabelle was actually confused for a moment, forgetting why she'd come here in the first place. "No big deal," she finally said. "I was just being neurotic. It's a casual thing with him."

"If you say so."

She'd tugged on her boots and was out the door in ten seconds flat. Jill turned on the porch light, startling Isabelle, and she suddenly felt far more vulnerable than she had on the walk over.

Practically leaping down the stairs, she rushed into the deep snow, trying to escape the reach of the lightbulb. Someone might be watching. Not an unknown survivalist, but an FBI agent who knew exactly who she was.

Instead of marching straight across the rocky field that separated their houses, Isabelle moved toward the back of Jill's house and ducked into the trees just behind it. She stopped there, back pressed to a tree, eyes closed, trying to catch her breath.

What if Tom had realized who she was? No. Tom wouldn't have lied to her this whole time. He couldn't have.

Except that he could have. Everyone was capable

of deception. She'd learned that from her own father. And she was hardly an exception. Her entire identity was a lie.

She had to be logical, so Isabelle ignored the pain that twisted through her stomach and considered the possibility that Tom knew. He would've contacted the FBI, and they could've told him to back off. They wanted her father, after all. They might want to watch and wait, set up another sting to see if Malcolm Pozniak got in touch. Or maybe they suspected he was living somewhere nearby, leaning on his daughter as his contact with the world.

As if she would've done that. Her dad had confessed to her. That he'd done lots of bad things. That he'd shot that officer.

She might have forgiven him eventually. Even though he'd been her hero, and everything about that had been a terrible, world-shifting lie, maybe she could have forgiven him and loved him and gone to prison to visit on holidays.

Maybe. If he hadn't run and left her to face the very men he'd been afraid of.

They'd started visiting right away. Men she'd known her whole life; men who'd patted her on the head and called her *sweetie*. They'd pretended to be checking on her at first, but that hadn't lasted long. Soon enough they'd started pressuring her, and then threatening, and finally she'd come home from class to find that the house she'd grown up in had been ransacked.

She hadn't called 911. She'd been too scared to. Instead, she'd called her fiancé's father. She'd trusted him to take care of her.

What a helpless idiot she'd been.

Isabelle opened her eyes. All she could see was falling snow and three or four trees in front of her. Which meant that was all anyone else could see. She was being stupid again. Panicked. She was right back to that fear she'd felt fourteen years before.

"Fuck this," she whispered, glad no one else could hear how pitiful it sounded.

She was a grown woman now. A woman who'd stood alone and made her own life. A woman who'd walked away from everything she'd ever known.

She could take care of this problem, too. She'd figure out what was going on, and she'd fucking deal with it.

Isabelle set off through the snow, determined not to be afraid of her own house or the night that surrounded it. If the FBI had found her, then she'd face the consequences of what she'd done. Maybe it would be a relief.

She'd spent many sleepless nights wishing she could go back and make a different choice. Turn over the evidence her dad had asked her to hide, tell the truth and *then* disappear.

But she hadn't known whom to trust. What if she'd taken the gun to the wrong person? What if she'd told her story to yet another dirty cop and found herself dead for her troubles?

No, running hadn't been the wrong choice, but she wouldn't do it the same way again.

At least the snow was a comfort tonight. She stopped a few dozen feet from her front steps and looked around. No one had been here since this afternoon. No one was hiding on her dark porch, waiting for her to approach.

She was alone. Exactly the way she needed to be. And if she wanted Tom here so much that it brought tears to her eyes, that was nothing but the aftermath of shock and fear.

CHAPTER SIXTEEN

TOM NOTICED THE fed in the suit right away. The guy was standing a few feet from the meeting room door, a visitor's pass clipped to his expensive suit jacket. Not the normal FBI agent uniform, and Tom might have mistaken him for an attorney, but he'd looked up Agent Gates's record, and Tom recognized the face.

Tom wrapped up his phone call with Mary as he walked past Gates to unlock the door, trying to buy himself a minute to process this. It wasn't good. It wasn't good at all.

He felt the FBI agent come up behind him, but Tom didn't turn around.

"Agent Gates," he said as he opened the door and walked in. He had to acknowledge the guy, but he didn't have to be polite, which was a good thing, because right now Tom wanted to grab him by his expensive suit and throw him against the wall.

"Pleasure to meet you, Marshal Duncan," Gates said, following Tom to the conference table.

Judging from the guy's ingratiating tone, he was holding out a hand and expecting Tom to turn and welcome him at any second. Tom didn't look at him.

Instead, he busied himself with unpacking files from his case and getting out his laptop. He was angry and alarmed. He couldn't let a hint of that show.

But irritation? He could show all of that he wanted.

"Please tell me you didn't fly all the way to Wyoming just because I glanced at a case."

"I did," Gates said.

Tom finally looked up. Gates looked to be in his late thirties, but he was still lean and in good shape. His brown hair was clipped short and styled to hide the fact that it was starting to thin on top. His eyebrows were suspiciously neat. Waxed, probably. Tom didn't like anything about him. "I told you it was nothing," Tom said.

"Well, I decided to poke around anyway."

"And I assume you've found nothing, since there's nothing to find. You've wasted your time, Agent, not to mention a lot of money. But by all means, have a seat."

Gates smiled and eased smoothly into a chair. "I like to see things for myself. Get a feel for a place. You know how it is."

"Sure," Tom said, taking a chair on the opposite side of the table. "But I'm a little too busy with an actual case to show you around town."

Gates waved a hand. "I've shown myself around. Talked to a few people."

"Good for you."

"There's one woman I haven't managed to track down yet. Up near where you're stationed at the judge's place. She's the right age and description for Pozniak's daughter."

Tom leaned forward, steepling his hands and letting irritation show on his face instead of alarm. "The daughter?" Tom frowned. "If I remember correctly, she was a white brunette who'd be in her thirties now? That covers a hell of a lot of women in Wyoming. Good luck."

"She's got a wide mouth. Kind of a big nose. Not bad-looking, though."

Tom shot the guy an impatient look. "I assume you showed a picture around and didn't get a hit?" He held his breath, waiting for an answer.

Gates leaned back and eyed Tom carefully. "Not yet. If they're here, I don't want to alert them. These people know how to disappear. I'm not going to give anyone a chance to give them a signal. I pretended I was after someone associated with the Stevensons. Hope you don't mind. It seemed a natural cover."

Thank God. Isabelle wasn't exactly active on the Jackson social scene, but in a town this size, someone was bound to recognize her. "If you want to go on a wild-goose chase, there's nothing I can do to stop you, but I don't have time for this shit. I've got real work to do, and now you're getting in the middle of it."

"You mean babysitting a judge?"

"Yeah, it's nothing like the exciting search for a long-lost woman who isn't here and never even committed a crime."

"You don't know that," Agent Gates countered.

But Tom did. She hadn't killed anyone. She wasn't hiding anyone. The worst she'd likely done was not rat out her own father.

He sat back in his chair. "We're on the hunt for an armed and dangerous man here, Agent Gates. You go knocking on strange doors or poking around property that doesn't belong to you, and you're likely to get shot, either by Saul Stevenson or one of my team or a nervous property owner. So why don't you just get out of my hair?"

Gates shrugged. "I've got a job to do, too. No reason for that to interfere."

"Really? You were the one who drove up to the summer cabins on White Ridge Road, I assume? My men and I wasted two hours checking out your tracks and following up with the property owners. I'll be letting your boss know."

"You think he gives a shit that a deputy marshal has a bug up his ass? Look..." Gates smiled and shot Tom a wink, as if they were old friends. "I'm sorry I stepped on your toes. There have been a lot of shady dealings around this case. You tripped a wire, and I had to come out and take a look around."

"I told you that was happenstance."

"Then you won't mind if I hang around today and get a good look at the folks in the courthouse, right? I mean, a survivalist compound in the middle of nowhere would be a great place for a fugitive to hide."

Tom held the man's gaze, trying not to let his relief show. Gates suspected that Tom had seen someone associated with Pozniak. But he didn't know where. Around the judge's home or at the courthouse or just at a restaurant in town. And here in town would be a target-rich environment. "If you think I'm lying to you, then be my guest. Waste all the time you want."

"It's not that I think you're lying," Gates said with a smile. "But I don't know you, do I?" His smile only got friendlier. Tom didn't like this asshole at all. The problem was he couldn't actually call the guy's boss and complain. Not if it would later come out that Tom had recognized and protected Beth Pozniak.

He stood, forcing Gates to stand, too. Tom waved him to the door, trying to look only mildly annoyed. But as soon as Gates crossed the room and closed the door, Tom grabbed his phone and texted Isabelle.

You might want to avoid the courthouse area today. We've really got it locked down around here and traffic is a mess.

A few seconds dragged into the eternity of a few minutes before she finally responded.

No problem. I'm painting all day.

He hesitated a moment.

Can I come by tonight? Maybe bring dinner?

It took her even longer to reply this time. What if she'd already made plans? What if she was going out with her friends and she ran into Gates? Tom couldn't let that happen. He'd have to tell her the truth.

But his phone finally buzzed.

Yes. Let me know when you're on your way.

Tom threw himself into the morning with a vengeance. He sent new alerts about Saul Stevenson to every sheriff's office and police department in the state. He sent a press release to every media outlet. He had one of his men stop at every motel and open campsite in Jackson Hole. He sent another guy to check on each closed campsite he could get to.

Tom had to get this case under control so he could fix this thing with Isabelle. And something was bound to go down with Stevenson soon. The prosecution had just rested. Ephraim Stevenson's defense would likely be done in three or four days, and then the case would go to the jury.

There wasn't a lot of question about the conviction. The evidence was substantial, and Saul was smart enough to know that. He wasn't going to hang back and hope for acquittal.

Of course, there was always the chance that Saul Stevenson would act after a conviction, trying to grab his brother during the transfer to prison, but Tom wanted to get the guy before he got anywhere near innocent civilians.

A few random leads came in before lunch and a few more around noon, but they were scattered. Stevenson couldn't have been sighted near Gillette at the same time he'd been spotted near Laramie. The leads were shit. And Tom was pushing this too hard. Concentrating on tracking down Stevenson, when he should have kept his focus on protecting the judge. He was trying to force it because of a personal distraction.

At two o'clock, just as he was deciding he was being irresponsible, Tom got a real lead. A forest ranger had followed some vehicle tracks in the snow to a high-altitude campground that was closed for winter. Someone had spent the night there, and it had been someone with enough skill to hunt and kill and cook a rabbit in the middle of a snowstorm.

The site was only sixty miles outside Jackson. It was a possibility. But only a possibility. Maybe just a poacher. Or a modern-day mountain man. Or maybe a guy trying to stay off the main roads while he worked his way toward the Jackson federal courthouse.

Tom didn't want to spread the team too thin, so he tempered his excitement and sat down with a list of the personnel at his disposal. His first priority was the judge and the judge's family then the prosecution team.

The courthouse itself had bailiffs as protection, though he'd hardly leave it vulnerable.

"What do you want to do?" Mary asked.

Tom looked up to see her standing in the doorway, arms crossed and a frown in place that looked more angry than thoughtful. He'd been texting her updates. "I want to go after this bastard," he said.

"Then let's do it."

"I'm working out the numbers now."

"You got a hunch?"

"I do," he muttered.

"Then fuck the numbers. Court just adjourned for the day."

Tom looked up from the paper. "Seriously?"

"Yep. The defense made a motion, and the judge wants time to research. He can do his thinking at home. Let's get him settled and hit the road."

"Fucking A," Tom said, folding the paper in half and stuffing it in the shredder. But he narrowed his eyes at Mary. "Why don't you look happy?"

She shrugged. "I'm pissed at you for interfering with my life again."

"What the hell did I do?"

"You remember that little rebound relationship you assured me I was old enough to navigate?"

"I did not use the word *old*," he clarified, "but yes."

"Fine. I admit that you got me thinking about it. That alone pisses me off. You know I hate letting you in my head. But while I was out this morning, I drove by her place, thinking maybe I'd give her a heads-up about what was going on."

Tom knew he shouldn't smile, but he couldn't help it. "Oh? You went to see Jill?"

"You can stop looking so pleased with yourself.

Some young piece of ass was leaving her house when I pulled up."

Tom shook his head, unable to pair Jill with a young piece of ass. "A woman? Must have been a niece or something."

"Unless she gives her niece goodbye kisses on the mouth, I doubt it."

"Oh," Tom said. "I see."

"Yeah, well. At least Jill looked embarrassed when she spotted me driving by."

He cleared his throat. "So she went on a date. That doesn't mean you shouldn't ask her out."

"Tom. Be serious. You'd date someone who lives six hours away and sleeps with younger men? You'd compete with that?"

He thought of the painting above Isabelle's couch. "Yes."

She shook her head and left, muttering something about men under her breath that he couldn't hear.

"I think I'm being reasonable!" he called, but she didn't return to the doorway.

On any other day, he probably would have followed her and tried to talk sense, but not today. Today he had a good lead, and now he had the time to follow up on it. Tom pulled out a map of the entire Jackson Hole valley and marked an *X* on the National Forest campground.

The park rangers had followed the tracks to a dirt road that serviced an active logging area, so the tracks had been lost there. The ranger Tom had spoken to had guessed the guy was driving a large truck outfitted with studded tires, based on the tracks that had been left. There were plenty of forest roads and unnamed country roads around here, but only a few that would be passable in winter, even with a well-outfitted vehicle. And the thing was, there weren't very many ways to approach Jackson itself at this time of year.

Saul had to come by the highway, and if he was coming from the north, he had to catch the highway somewhere above Moran. There weren't any other options.

If it was Stevenson, he could be in Jackson already, but the ranger had said when he found the fire, it had been smothered by snow, but still warm at the bottom of the pit. It hadn't been put out at 6:00 a.m. More like noon. Only a couple of hours ago.

Ten minutes later, Tom hung up on his contact at the sheriff's office and grabbed his jacket. He stepped into the hallway just as Hannity and Mary were assembling their teams. "Hannity," Tom called, "you've got transport under control?"

Hannity gave him a thumbs-up.

Tom spotted Agent Gates leaning against a wall and ignored him. "Mary, want to take a ride?" With another car from his team on their tail and the promise of more backup from the sheriff's office, they were on their way.

"I decided to go with my hunch," he said to Mary as they pulled onto the road out of town. "I don't think he would have shown his face the first few days. We'd be too alert. He's waiting for our guard to drop."

"It'd be the smart thing to do," she said stiffly.

"Yeah, this guy might not have gone to school past eighth grade, but he's wily as hell."

"Yeah," Mary said.

Tom shot her a puzzled look as they drove past the elk refuge on the outskirts of town, but she didn't look back. She stared out the window at the large herd of elk gathered around a pile of hay.

"Hey, I'm sorry about Jill," he tried.

"It's not that."

"Is Hannity giving you shit again? I know you don't like the way I handled that, but this is my team and—"

"I spoke to that FBI agent."

Tom's fingers tightened on the steering wheel until they went numb, but he managed to keep his face blank. "Yeah?"

"I wanted to know why the hell he was hanging around being useless."

"He's keeping an eye out for another suspect," Tom said carefully.

"Tom. He showed me photos. Asked me to keep it quiet. He wanted to know if anyone looked familiar."

Fuck. Of course he had. He'd probably asked Hannity, too, but Tom couldn't recall any time Isabelle would've interacted with Hannity. With Mary, on the other hand... "I've got it under control," Tom said.

"Yeah? Then maybe you could clue me in on why you're lying to the FBI about a person of interest in a police shooting."

"She didn't do anything wrong."

"Her father shot a cop, and she may have helped him get away," Mary said, sounding pissed now and still not looking at him.

"Something isn't right with this case, Mary," he said. "You trust my hunches. You always have. I was right that Isabelle was hiding, and I'm right that—"

"Beth," she interrupted, finally turning to look at him. "You mean Beth."

Tom held her gaze for a moment before looking back to the road. She looked pissed but not furious. She was willing to listen. "Fine," he agreed. "Beth Pozniak left everything behind and ran fourteen years ago. She's not with her father. She doesn't have any other family. She's hiding."

"You're *involved* with her, Tom."

He thought of denying it for a moment, but if he wanted Mary's help, he'd need honesty. "I got involved before I knew." He held up a hand when she started to speak. "Yes, I had suspicions, but I thought they'd pan out to be nothing. You know that. By the time I realized who she was…"

He saw from the corner of his eye that she was staring at him. "So you did sleep with her."

It wasn't a question, so he didn't bother answering.

"This Gates guy is asking around. Showing her picture. He's going to find someone who knows her."

"No. He doesn't want to alert her. He only showed you the photos because you're with me."

"He'll get to that eventually."

"I'm hoping he'll give up before then. The only reason he's here is because I stumbled onto a flagged file. That's it."

"So he's got good instincts, too," Mary said darkly.

Shit, she was right. Tom didn't like the guy, but Gates wasn't an idiot. "You didn't tell him," he said quietly.

She turned to look out at the hills again for a long moment. Finally, she sighed and shook her head. "He's a smarmy asshole, and you're not, so I figured I'd give you the benefit of the doubt."

"I'm honored," he said, going for sarcastic, even though he really meant it.

"If you aren't being honest with Agent Gates, you have a good reason. I've known you too long not to trust that."

"Thank you."

"Plus, you're my boss, and I didn't want to be fired."

He managed to huff out a laugh. "All right. Just give

me twenty-four hours. I want to get her side of it. I've
been hoping she'd open up, but..."

"You might not have twenty-four hours, but I won't
be the one to say anything."

"Thank you."

Mary shrugged. "She'd better not be hiding a whole
gang of fugitives in her basement, because I'll throw
you under the bus and take your job. Now, tell me what
we're planning once we get to Moran."

He told her. And he hoped to God that Gates had
given up on White Ridge Road.

CHAPTER SEVENTEEN

SHE'D PAINTED ALL NIGHT. Not because she'd been inspired, but because she was worried she'd need money for lawyers soon, and she wanted to get this commission done before she was taken to jail. Of course, the FBI might not even let her have the money when they found out she'd been working under a false social security number. But she'd made sure to pay her taxes. She'd overpaid, really, just to be sure she'd never be audited.

Her entire career was courtesy of a sympathetic art professor who'd had no reason to help her. Professor Cervaz had spent two of Isabelle's college years trying to steer her away from premed and into medical illustration. She'd loved the work, but she'd resisted him out of fear of what others would think. Her father, because he'd been so exuberantly proud of his daughter being on the path to becoming a doctor. And her fiancé, who'd said so many times what a dynamic team their marriage would be. A district attorney and a doctor, both of them children of Chicago cops. They would have been a dream couple in the political circles he'd been so fond of.

But a medical illustrator? What the hell was that? Nothing to be proud of. It was something weird and obscure and a little creepy.

So she'd resisted. But when she'd been thinking of running away from everything, she'd gone to her professor and asked if he might have any work. Anything he could farm out to her, even if he wanted to claim it as his own. She needed money, she'd confessed, and he'd understood right away. It wasn't as if her family's situation was a secret. Everyone knew.

It had been risky, but the only alternative would have been working at low-paying jobs her whole life. She didn't have any other skills, and her fake identity wouldn't have withstood a background check.

Her professor had sent her anonymous work for a year. And when she'd finally given him a new name— Isabelle West—and asked him for some introductions, he'd obliged.

He'd been the only connection to her old life. She might have suspected he'd been the one to turn her in this week, but he'd died three years before.

She still felt guilty about the relief she'd felt when she'd seen the news on one of the tight-knit artist forums. The man had been so good to her. So absolutely kind. It had been so wrong to feel relief, but she hadn't been able to lie to herself about that. He'd made her life what it was, and she'd been relieved when he died.

Maybe that made her too much like her father, happy that someone else's death could make her life easier. She looked at the picture of the flayed thigh attached to her easel. Hell, maybe that philosophy was her entire career.

Isabelle set down her paintbrush and stretched hard. It was 7:00 p.m., and she still hadn't heard from Tom. She'd napped from noon to three, but she was still exhausted, and she hoped he wouldn't be too much longer.

Lauren had called, hoping they could have dinner in the next two days before Sophie left, but Isabelle hadn't known what to say. She didn't know if she'd still be in Jackson herself.

She checked her phone one more time, feeling like a desperate teenage girl, but it was more than just wanting to hear from the boy she liked. The torture of wondering if she'd be found out was so acute that she was half inclined to confess.

What if he already knew? What if he'd just found out who she was from the FBI agent and that was the reason for his lateness? What if he came over and got a call from the feds while he was here, and she had to look at his face while he learned the truth?

What if this was all just paranoia?

She took a deep breath, trying to calm her fear, but it wasn't just fear now. It hadn't occurred to her to worry about Tom, but if it came out and he hadn't known, he was going to look like a fool. He could even be in trouble. She should have thought of that before she'd gotten involved with him. She should have thought of a million things.

Her deep breath had turned into another and another, and now she was close to panting. She closed her eyes and told herself to calm down.

The FBI agent had asked about an old man and a woman. That was all. He could be searching for anyone. And the simplest explanation was that it had something to do with the ongoing Stevenson case. Of course it did.

But Isabelle jumped at every sound. She cringed when her phone buzzed. She watched from darkened rooms whenever a truck drove slowly past, searching for fugitives or for her.

The FBI guy hadn't come back, and wasn't that a good sign? He'd only been canvassing the neighborhood, doing a boring job, and now he was done.

But just in case, she put the last touches on the last painting and went to get her packing supplies. The final two paintings would need to dry overnight, but she could box up the others, get them labeled and get them into her truck for the morning.

Her good intentions flew out the window when her phone rang. She dived for it then tried not to weep with disappointment when she saw Jill's name. Still, if Jill was calling with gossip about her ill-advised night, Isabelle would listen. She wasn't that far gone.

"They got him!" Jill yelled.

"Who? What?"

"They caught Saul Stevenson! I just saw it online!"

"Really?" Isabelle breathed.

"Got him up near Moran around four today. He had a rocket launcher!"

"Holy shit." That was why Tom was late. That was why he hadn't called. It had nothing to do with her.

"I'm sure glad they finally found him," Jill went on. "A rocket launcher. No team of marshals could've stopped that. Poor Tom."

"Is he okay?" she gasped.

"Yes! I just don't like thinking about what could have happened."

"Me, either," Isabelle said, her throat thicker with emotion than it should have been. "Wow." When her phone beeped, her heart skipped. "I think Tom's calling. I'd better go. Thank you so much for telling me."

As soon as she clicked over, Tom said, "I'm sorry I'm late."

"I just heard!" she squealed. "You did it!"

"We did it," he said, sounding deeply pleased.

"God, Tom. I'm so happy for you. You're okay? Everyone is okay?"

"We're fine. I've got about another hour of processing ahead, and then I'm sending my whole team to bed."

"Including yourself?"

"Yes," he said, his voice softer.

Her heart fell a little. "You must be really tired."

"I am. Will you take me in?"

She sighed, letting go of the disappointed breath she'd held inside her. "Yes."

Yes, she'd let him in. To her house. Her body. Maybe even her confidence.

She shook her head at her own thoughts. No. She couldn't do that. It didn't matter that she'd been fantasizing about a relationship with him. She couldn't let it matter.

"I'll see you soon," he promised.

Isabelle hurried through packing the first few paintings, but her heart was no longer in it. She got the first box into her SUV and then rushed to her bedroom. She'd already showered and pulled up her hair, but she suddenly wanted to look nicer.

He'd caught Stevenson. He'd be moving on soon, and she couldn't follow. A few more nights with him, and that would be it. A few more really good nights, and she would let him go.

It had been stupid to ever engage him. Stupid and dangerous, and she never should have done it, but God... She couldn't quite regret it.

She'd told herself she was never lonely, but maybe she had been. Lonely for that deep, primal connection that wasn't exactly sex. It was a profound demand to be wanted and seen and desperately needed. Something she'd never had and so hadn't known she was missing.

This was that thing that kept a woman connected to a man she couldn't have. The thing that kept a man with a lover he could barely stand. Some animal vibration that hit all of your chords with the exact right note. She barely knew him, but her body craved him already.

Maybe it hadn't been stupidity that had led her to get involved with a man so likely to learn her secrets. Maybe she'd wanted him to see her. Everything about her. Maybe she was tired of the lie.

That was too bad. Tired or not, now that she was looking exposure right in the face, she wanted to gather all her secrets tight to her and hold on to them forever. If the FBI didn't know about her, that was the end of her risk taking. She had to end it with Tom. Just not tonight.

She tugged on jeans and quickly painted her toenails bright red. Then she put on a blue shirt that looked deceptively modest, but she loved the way the loose, draped lines parted occasionally to reveal a deep, narrow neckline that dipped low between her breasts. She didn't bother with a bra. He loved her breasts, and she wanted him thinking about them.

She added a little color to her cheeks and her lips, and hoped that would be enough to make her look younger, prettier, more rested…whatever it was she was going for. She just wanted him to *need* her. To take one look and remember the taste of her on his tongue. That was all. Just the kind of need that would make him remember that taste forever.

She finally heard the low rumble of an engine and the grind of tires against snow. Not inclined to be reckless, she watched carefully through the blinds as headlights approached up her driveway. She'd never gotten around to plowing, unwilling to help that FBI guy get to her any faster, but the SUV approached steadily, if slowly, over the mounds of snow.

It pulled close to the walk, but it was still too dark to see inside. She moved to turn on the porch light, but then hesitated. If it was that FBI agent, she'd pretend she wasn't home. Turning on the porch light would give her away.

After what seemed like an eternity, the interior light of the SUV finally came on, and Isabelle watched as Mary got out of the passenger side and came around the back just as Tom opened the driver's-side door.

Isabelle laughed as she shoved her feet into boots, turned on the porch light and rushed outside. "Congratulations!"

They both looked strangely subdued when they turned toward her. "Thank you," Tom said, but Mary just stared. Isabelle still wasn't sure what Mary's feelings were, but if Tom said they'd never been intimate, she'd have to take him at his word.

"You two had a damn good day," Isabelle said.

Tom finally smiled. "That we did."

"Is it over?"

"Nothing is certain, but there's no evidence that there was a backup plan."

Isabelle crossed her arms as the wind caught her. "A rocket launcher, huh?"

Tom laughed. "That's a new one."

"Well, it was a productive day all around, then. I didn't catch even one domestic terrorist, but I did finish my last painting. The commission is done."

Tom's eyebrows rose. "If I'm happy for you, that doesn't mean I have to look, does it?"

Isabelle was laughing when another voice rang in the dark. "Good thing I brought champagne!" Jill called. "Sounds like we have a lot to celebrate."

Isabelle was so chagrined at having company that she almost missed the way Mary's eyes went wide. "It's just Jill," she said in reassurance, but Mary didn't seem less disturbed. And when Jill came around the side of the SUV, her eyes went wide, too. She froze in the act of holding up a bottle of champagne in one hand and a cake pan in the other.

Well, that was interesting. And there was cake.

"I'm sorry," Jill said, frozen in the glow of the truck's headlights. "I just wanted to say congratulations to Tom. And to you, of c-course," she stammered.

Very interesting. Jill never stammered.

"Come in," Isabelle said, waving everyone toward the stairs before the wind froze her solid.

"I've got to go," Mary said flatly.

"Me, too," said Jill.

"Oh, come on," Tom scoffed. He reached past Mary to turn off the truck. "Jill, you brought champagne, and Mary, you earned it. Get inside."

Jill headed up the steps with Isabelle. Mary cleared her throat and didn't move until Tom closed the truck door. She followed him up the walk.

"I'll get glasses," Isabelle said quickly, hoping to move it along. She had only wineglasses, but no one complained as Jill popped open the bottle and began to pour. No one said anything at all, in fact. Jill set the bottle down, muttered something about plates and rushed toward the kitchen before Isabelle could get there.

"What's going on with you?" Isabelle whispered as soon as she caught up.

"She drove by my house this morning," Jill answered.

"So?"

"So, my guest was leaving."

"Oh." Isabelle cringed. "It's okay. You'll never see her again once she leaves the judge's house. What's the big deal?"

Jill groaned. "I think she's cute. And it was the worst possible moment I could've seen her."

"Oh," Isabelle said. Then, "Oh!" Tom's absolute conviction about Mary's feelings made sense now. "Well…" Isabelle said, trying to spin it. "Now you seem like a hot commodity. So it's good."

Jill's look said she wasn't buying a word of it, so Isabelle didn't try again. She knew how embarrassed her friend was about the whole thing, but maybe grumpy-pants out in the living room wasn't the best fit anyway. "Come on," Isabelle said as she grabbed forks and a knife. "Cake fixes everything."

"No, but the champagne might help," Jill muttered.

A boomingly awkward silence fell over the living room as they took seats and Jill sliced the Bundt cake.

"Is it lemon?" Isabelle asked, trying to break the quiet, but Jill only nodded.

Tom tried next. "Jill's an amazing baker," he said to Mary. "That's not usual for a chef, is it, Jill?"

"I suppose not, but my mother was a baker, so I learned how to bake before I could read."

"Where are you from?" he asked.

"Outside Birmingham."

"Really? Your Alabama drawl isn't that strong."

She grinned and seemed to finally relax a little. "I left home at sixteen and moved to California for a good long while. I suppose I didn't want to sound country once I got there."

Now that the conversation was going, Isabelle accidentally interrupted it with a loud moan. Three pairs of eyes locked on her. "Sorry," she said past a mouthful of cake. "This is so good. It's still warm."

Tom took a big bite and made embarrassing pleased

noises, too. "So good," he agreed. "Thank you. You really are the best."

"Well, thank you," Jill said, raising her glass. "I'm gonna sleep a lot better to…night." The last word dragged through her throat as if she'd tried to put the brakes on.

Tom was the only one who didn't notice. He simply raised his glass with another "Thank you" and took a big drink. Isabelle and Mary stared at Jill for a moment before sipping from their glasses. Jill drained hers.

That must have helped, because she relaxed and told a few stories about Alabama. Then it came out that Mary was from a place in Georgia only two hours from Birmingham and they knew a lot of the same landmarks and history.

As the two women began to talk, Isabelle and Tom raised their eyebrows at each other, and each had another piece of cake.

"So," Jill eventually asked, "are you two almost done here? There aren't any more bad guys to catch."

Isabelle thought Mary's head jerked up at that, but when she looked, she didn't catch Mary watching.

Tom shook his head. "Some of the team will probably leave, but our core group will stay until the end of the trial. The Stevensons are a small clan, but we can't be sure how small."

"All right," Jill said. "Well… Before you leave, you should all come over for dinner at my place. I'll do it up right. Try out a new menu."

"Deal," Tom said immediately. "You should really take up catering. You'd be the go-to caterer for every event."

She slapped his arm, but her face glowed with pleasure. "Then I'd have to keep some kind of schedule. I like what I've got going on here."

"I like it, too," he said as Mary stood. "But that's totally selfish on my part."

Jill stood, too, and started for the door, but Tom held up a hand as he started to get up. "I'll take you home."

"I'll drive her," Mary said tersely.

Tom hesitated then sat slowly back down. "Okay."

The two women left without another word. Isabelle looked at Tom next to her on the couch. "Is that a thing?" she asked in confusion.

"I don't know. But I was kind of hoping it might be."

"Really?"

"Yeah, but this morning—" He cut himself off and shot her a glance.

She nodded. "Jill was really, really embarrassed."

Tom winced. "Well, maybe those two crazy kids will work something out on the drive home."

She grinned. "It's a pretty short drive."

"Yeah, but you women on Spinster Row work crazy fast."

Laughing, she let her body lean into him just the way it wanted to. Tom's arm fit around her shoulders as if it belonged there. She melted into him and sighed with pleasure.

"Are you as tired as I am?" he asked.

"Yes."

"Want to go to bed?"

"Yes." And it was that simple. Despite everything hanging over her, despite the fear of the past twenty-four hours, she forgot everything and just said yes.

CHAPTER EIGHTEEN

THIS WAS SOMETHING NEW, Isabelle realized. The first time they were undressing and simply getting in bed together like civilized adults. But there was no reason to be too civilized about it. Isabelle stripped down to her panties, but she left her shirt on just because she wanted to feel him taking it off her.

Tom seemed to notice what she'd done and left his briefs on before he slid under the covers. That was fine with her. She wanted him to feel her hands dragging those off.

She took down her hair and got beneath the covers, too. Before she was even settled, Tom was on his elbow leaning above her, his bare chest and shoulders filling her vision. She reached for him without thinking, her hand seeking out the muscles of his chest.

"You look so beautiful," he said, smoothing out her hair on the pillow.

"Maybe you're tired."

"No," he said simply. "I'm just really happy I'm here tonight."

"Me, too." She traced a finger around his nipple, and he shivered.

"Jesus, you turn me on," he said.

She laughed in delight as she felt his hand trail up her arm.

"This shirt turns me on, too." His fingers dipped all

the way down the narrow front opening. "Did you know it would? Did you wear it for me?"

She only gave a coy smile as his hand kept moving down, skimming over her abdomen and pushing the blanket out of the way. He touched her hip and then her thigh, his hand still light and slow. This was exactly what she'd wanted. Time and touch. Long moments of exploring, just this one chance for that.

His knuckles brushed the little pink panties she'd worn for him, and Isabelle shivered. She slid a foot up, bending her knee, but Tom had already moved on, curving over her belly.

He'd been watching the slow path his hand traveled. The only light in the room this time was from her bathroom, but it was more than enough to light her body and his hand and his gorgeous profile as he ducked his head to kiss her breast. He found her nipple through the thin fabric of her shirt and caught it with his teeth.

Her breath hitched, and she set a hand to his neck, despite that she was trying to hold on to her patience. She'd wanted it slow, and Tom was willing to give it to her.

The heat of his mouth teased her, and his teeth scraped over the slippery fabric, tormenting her. She felt his hand edge beneath the bottom of her shirt, and she tried not to squirm. He felt good against her stomach. She wanted to enjoy just that, and not anticipate what it would feel like when he cupped her breast and pressed his teeth into her nipple until she cried out.

But then her nails were against his neck, and her other hand was shaping the tight muscles of his shoulder, and she was arching into his mouth. His arms flexed as he shifted above her, and Isabelle slid a hand down to feel his biceps. He wasn't bulky; he was lean and hard, and he felt so strong. "God," she breathed, "you're gorgeous."

His hand spread over her breast, cupping her for a brief moment before he pushed her shirt up. Yes. She wanted his mouth on bare flesh now. She was already done with teasing. But Tom wasn't.

She let go of him to get her shirt off, but he was still poised above her instead of pouncing on top of her. "I could look at you forever," he said. She shook her head, but he didn't notice because he was tracing a fingertip around her tightening areola.

He licked his fingers then spread the moisture over her nipple, making her groan in frustration. Tom smiled, but she knew how to get him back.

Isabelle wrapped her hand around his and dragged it up her chest to her neck and then her jaw. When his fingers touched her mouth, she opened for him and sucked one finger inside.

"Oh, fuck," he breathed as she drew at his finger. "I love your mouth."

She slid his finger slowly out. "I love your fingers," she said, licking the next one until he pushed it into her mouth. He watched as though it was the most important thing he'd ever seen. She rubbed her tongue firmly against the pad of his finger, and his eyelids fluttered. When she bit his knuckle, his eyes were wide-awake again.

She pulled his wet finger free with a pop and chuckled. "You've got nice hands," she said, licking at the space between his fingers. "But your arms are spectacular."

"My arms?" he asked a little vaguely.

"Yes." She pulled his arm higher and licked the underside of his wrist. "They're so different from mine.

You're so hairy and lean, and I can see the muscles work beneath your skin." She turned his arm over and rubbed her mouth lightly against the golden hair there.

He swallowed hard. "That's why your arms are nicer," he breathed. "They're soft and smooth…"

"No. No, this is better." She bit at the bulge of muscle in the middle of his forearm. "So much better."

He jerked when she pressed her teeth too hard, so she soothed the mark with her tongue and then licked all the way up to the inside of his elbow. She sucked there, and his breath hissed in.

He'd finally had enough, and he pushed up on his hands to lean over her. He kissed her then, filling her with the taste of him, pressing his whole, gorgeous body against hers. She could tell he was trying to keep his weight off her, but she pulled him down, wanting it all. She wanted taste, smell, touch, sound, weight, heat, everything that was Tom Duncan.

His cock was pressed to her now, and she rocked against him as he kissed her, rubbing her clit over the length of him. Such sweet pleasure, and so dull compared to what she wanted.

But it felt good, making out like teenagers, soft fabric separating them from each other as the head of his cock pressed between her legs, and she swallowed his moan. He pressed harder against her, and she knew she'd soaked through her underwear and into his, but he couldn't get any deeper. Still, she clutched his ass in her hands and pulled him harder to her clit. Harder. Yes.

He broke free of the kiss. "God, Isabelle. Please."

"Please, what?" she asked.

"This," he growled, rising to his knees to grab her panties and yank them down. She brought her legs up so he could slide her underwear off her feet.

She grabbed a condom, but when he reached for it, she shook her head. "Let me," she said as she reached for his underwear.

His fingers wrapped around hers. "Wait. I want to taste you."

Isabelle ignored him and cupped her hand over the shape of his cock. "No. I want to get fucked."

His hand tightened for a moment, a small spasm of need before he let her go. She tugged down his briefs, and his cock sprang free of the fabric.

"Oh, God, Tom. You're so fucking big for me." His breath grew harsher as she wrapped her hand around him. She felt a little crazed, too. "I love it. I want it inside me."

He didn't say "Yes" or "Hurry" or even nod his head. He just watched as she squeezed hard and moved her hand slowly up his shaft until a drop of precome formed at the tip.

"So nice," she murmured.

"Put the condom on," he ordered, his voice harsher than she'd heard before.

Isabelle smiled up at him, but he didn't look amused. "Right now?" she asked.

"Yes," he growled. "Now."

She opened the condom and rolled it slowly onto his cock. So slowly. Until he was pressing forward, trying to hurry her along. "Now fuck me," she said, still smiling.

She'd been playing at control, but he wasn't playing anymore. He grabbed one of her legs and pressed her knee up and over until she was on her belly. Isabelle's pulse quickened, pushing blood into her tight clit.

He wasn't careful this time. His hips were between

her spread legs, and his cock caught at the notch of her pussy, and he pushed into her. Hard.

The breath was shoved out of her with his thrust. His next thrust was even harder.

"Is this what you want?"

"Yes," she gasped. This was what she wanted. To be fucked as if he'd die if he didn't get deeper.

His hands grabbed her hips and pulled her up on her knees, his fingers digging in hard as he thrust again. Isabelle put her face into her pillow and moaned. He'd given her too much, too soon, and the pleasure bordered on pain. She loved it.

He held himself still inside her for a long moment, letting her feel the way her body was trying to stretch to ease his way. She heard him let out a long breath as if he were gathering himself before he began to move inside her.

He started with a slow, hard rhythm that made her fists curl into the sheets. "Yes," she gasped into the pillow. "Yes, like that."

"I love fucking you," he rasped.

"Yes," she said again. She wanted him to love it. She wanted to be the best he'd ever had. She wanted him still thinking about it ten years from now when he was settled down with someone nicer, someone more stable, someone whose entire life wasn't a lie that kept her from the world. If this was all the love she'd get from him, then she wanted him to love fucking her more than he'd ever love it with anyone else.

She forced her fingers to unclench from the sheets and slipped a hand down her stomach.

"Yes," he said. "Touch yourself. It's so fucking hot when you do that."

Not as hot as it was for her. Her clit was hard under

her hands, her pussy slick. She rubbed herself and arched into his next thrust, trying to take him deeper, deeper. So deep it would hurt.

He held her still and fucked her as she touched herself, her cries getting louder as her pleasure built. She loved his hands so tight on her. His cock so big. The sound of his hips slapping into her ass. The way her clit got tighter and tighter with every stroke.

She loved the way he was polite and reserved, and then he fucked her just the way she needed. Just like she— "Yes," she cried out as the orgasm built into impossible tightness inside her.

She keened as the pressure crested, and then suddenly it was upon her, taking her under.

She felt the cry in her own throat, but she couldn't hear it past the rushing pleasure, and she couldn't feel anything of his body anymore, only hers. It was nearly violent, as if she'd break apart in joy, but finally the waves ebbed and she could hear again, could feel his fingers on her hips and his cock so tight inside her.

She was shaking, gasping for breath, and he was so strong and still behind her. She was wondering if he'd already come, too, but then he moved within her, a slow, long stroke. His hand left her hip and smoothed over the small of her back, tilting her hips up even more as he fucked her. Her thighs shook, but she didn't give in to the weakness. She stayed on her knees for him, because that was what he wanted.

His strokes quickened as his breath got ragged, and she expected him to crash into her with his orgasm, but in the end, he held himself still. So still. His hips hard against hers as he buried himself deep. She felt his cock pulse inside her as he came, but his hips didn't move.

She'd never felt a man come like that. As if he wanted to feel every cell in his body as he climaxed.

His breath left him on a long sigh, and he finally pulled free of her. Isabelle collapsed, facedown. She couldn't quite breathe, and she didn't quite care. She was exhausted, in every way possible.

She heard Tom return to the bed. She felt the sheets settle over her naked body and then the comforting weight of the blankets. Even better, he slid in next to her, and his heat soaked through her sweat-cooled back.

"Is it all right if I stay?" he murmured near her ear.

Isabelle thought she nodded, but she wasn't sure. She just moved back until her ass was pressed tight to him, and she fell asleep.

CHAPTER NINETEEN

Tom woke to the smell of frying bacon, and he floated there for a long minute, warm beneath the covers of his childhood bed while his mom made Sunday breakfast. It was a strange feeling. Half contentment and half a niggling awareness that he'd have to get up soon and go to church for two excruciatingly boring hours.

He frowned. No, the worry was something darker than that. His mind touched on his brother before it shied away in horror. That was when his eyes opened, and he looked around in a panic, wondering where he was and if his brother was still dead.

His brain finally recognized that he was in Isabelle's bedroom. And yes, his brother was still dead.

But there the darkness was, hovering above him. Not grief for Michael, but something more urgent.

He had to help Isabelle. Keep Gates away from her. Or deliver Isabelle to him, if that was the wisest option.

But he didn't think it was.

Tom glanced around, looking for his phone. It was in his pants, probably, somewhere on the floor. But at least he found a clock. It was only 6:15. If he jumped in the shower right now, he could be at the judge's in twenty minutes. Thirty if he stayed for bacon.

Then Tom would take care of his team, get the judge to the courthouse and take an hour of calm to look into Isabelle's situation.

He knew the bare bones of it. He knew what her father had been charged with and the further crimes he'd been suspected of. But the supporting cast was a sticky, tangled, dangerous mess of unnamed cops and shady figures.

The FBI had known that people high up in the Chicago PD were, at best, protecting some of the players. At worst, they'd been in charge of the whole racket.

But...

Tom stretched hard, noting the various sore muscles in his body and wishing he had time to enjoy the memory of what had caused them. But he couldn't. Because there was that one big question hanging over him as he headed naked for Isabelle's small shower and turned on the tap.

The FBI wouldn't have put a flag on a federal file because of the activity of the Chicago PD. It wouldn't have attached a warning about leaking information to Chicago. Unless it had already been done.

Someone in the FBI was working with those bigwigs in Chicago, or had been.

Tom had gotten only a quick look at the federal files before Gates had called. He knew Gates hadn't been the head agent on the case back then, but what if he'd been associated? What if he'd been the leak?

A long shot, but Gates was suspiciously invested. If he hadn't been the leak then, that didn't mean he hadn't been bought off since.

Tom needed another look at that file. And shit, Gates was already here. Tom didn't need to worry about drawing more attention if he looked again.

Determined now, he cleaned up and got out of the shower in record time. He was pulling on his wrinkled suit pants when Isabelle walked in.

"Hello," she said, her mysterious smile in place as she looked over his bare chest. "Sleep well?"

"I don't remember a thing after I passed out. I hope I didn't snore."

She moved closer and kissed his chest. Tom closed his arms around her without even thinking about it. Fuck, she felt good against him. He recognized the blue shirt she'd been wearing the night before, and he wanted to strip it off her. Again.

"I didn't hear you snore," she said against his skin. "But are you saying you don't remember that second round?"

His mind flashed on warm skin and dark pleasure. "Damn. I do remember that. I half thought it was a dream."

"A wet dream," she murmured. "Want breakfast?"

"Hell, yes," he said, not realizing he'd decided to stay until he spoke.

He followed her to the kitchen, buttoning his shirt as he walked.

"It's not much," she explained. "Bacon and scrambled eggs. Leftover lemon cake."

"Sounds perfect."

It was. Nothing had ever tasted so good. Or he was really hungry and finally remembering the night before, when Isabelle had come so beautifully around his cock. She was beautiful. And as soon as he left her house, this spell would be broken.

"I'm sorry," he said, stopping her as she moved to pour him another cup of coffee. "I have to run. It's not very romantic…"

"I'm not very romantic," she said with a smile. But it wavered. "And you're not my boyfriend. We both have a lot of work to do."

Right. He wasn't her boyfriend. He couldn't be, and he knew why. Or maybe he didn't. Maybe she didn't like him that much, and sex was always this good for her.

But if it was only her past between them, maybe they could work it out. Maybe she wouldn't panic and lash out and hate him. Shit.

"Isabelle—" he started, but she shook her head.

"Go to work. Maybe I'll see you again tonight. But it's no big deal if you can't."

It was a big deal to him. And he thought it might be a big deal to her, too. She had to say it didn't mean much, because what choice did she have? He was a US marshal.

He opened his mouth, one more attempt to tell her the truth. He'd hoped to come up with a plan sometime between midnight and morning, but it seemed more impossible than ever. He needed Mary's advice. He couldn't just wing this, or he'd screw it up and lose Isabelle for good.

"I'll see you later, then," he said as he shrugged on his coat and pulled his gun off the shelf he'd left it on the night before.

She gave him a kiss on the cheek, a gesture so innocent that it made him smile. Once he had everything together, he pulled on the boots he'd left on the porch and headed down the steps, trying to think of ways to mitigate the reaction she'd have to the truth. He wanted to keep seeing her. It wasn't just sex, at least not for him.

He didn't hear the car approaching until after Isabelle had closed the door behind him. Not that it mattered in that first moment, when he assumed it must be Mary. He even had a fleeting thought that she'd spent the night at Jill's and was swinging around to pick him up.

But then the car appeared, easing up Isabelle's driveway in the muted light of sunrise. Tom froze on the last step and thanked God that Isabelle wasn't here. Because the driver wasn't Mary. It was Gates.

His heart filled so quickly with fear that Gates could have seen Isabelle in the doorway that Tom was halfway down the walk before he realized he himself shouldn't be here. It was before seven in the morning. The FBI agent was already suspicious. And Tom was walking out of this woman's house, unshaven and in wrinkled clothes. He almost stopped dead at the realization, but bluffing was all he had at this point.

He met Gates halfway down the driveway and glared as the man rolled down his window. "Can I help you with something, Agent Gates?"

One look at his face, and Tom's heart fell. Shit. The guy looked smug. "Help me?" Gates asked. "You're the one who seems to be lost."

"Not lost at all. This is my jurisdiction. You, on the other hand..."

Gates looked past Tom toward the cabin. "Yeah. I wasn't sure what your motive was here, but now I get it."

"Motive?"

"In protecting a certain Isabelle West." Agent Gates offered that smarmy, helpful smile as he pulled a square of paper from his jacket pocket and unfolded it.

Tom caught the flash of the Wyoming state seal, and his blood froze even before he saw Isabelle's picture on the driver's-license photo.

Gates smiled wider. "I'll inform your supervisor as soon as I've brought her in."

"She's not a fugitive," Tom snapped.

"So why lie to me?"

Tom looked him straight in the eye. "I don't like you. And I don't trust you, either."

Gates put up his hands. "Come on, Duncan. We're on the same side. Well…" He inclined his head toward the cabin. "Maybe not quite the same side. But that hardly matters now." Gates put the car in gear.

"Wait," Tom barked, gripping the window frame as if he could stop the vehicle with his hand. "You want her father."

Gates frowned. "Her father is dead."

"Yet you're asking around about him."

He put the truck back in Park and tapped his fingers on the steering wheel. "Are you telling me you know he's not?"

Tom almost lied. He needed to buy time. But he knew he could buy it with manipulation instead of an outright lie. "I don't know. She hasn't opened up much about him yet."

He felt filthy just saying that to this guy, discussing Isabelle and her private life, but there was going to be a whole lot more of it in the future. He just wanted to get her alone and explain what was happening. He could help if only she'd let him.

Tom leaned down, bracing his forearm against the top of the truck. "Let me work on her. If I can get her to talk about her father, maybe you can have him."

"Bullshit. He's not here."

"He's not here," Tom agreed, "but maybe she knows where he is. She has a life here. She won't want to blow it up."

Gates shrugged. "She already did it once, my friend. She gave up Chicago for that fucking killer."

My friend. Tom wanted to punch him in the face. She hadn't left Chicago; she'd left *everything*, and she hadn't done it for her dad.

Then again, she hadn't come straight to Wyoming.

She'd been somewhere else for a while. And that was what really pissed Tom off, because maybe she'd done exactly what Gates suspected.

Agent Gates eased back a little to look up at Tom. "You planning to help her run again?"

"Jesus Christ," Tom barked. "I'm a fucking marshal. You think I'm gonna throw away a twenty-year career for a woman I met a week ago?"

"You're here, aren't you? Just doing reconnaissance?"

Tom's hand squeezed into a fist. He ignored it and kept his voice calm. "Give me a few hours. That's all I'm asking."

"She'll run."

"Where's she going to go? This is her place, her land, her life. Christ, let me help you find the guy you really want. You won't even be able to hold her for more than twenty-four hours."

"Oh, I'd bet she's got a few felonies piled up by now."

Shit. Gates was probably right. She was living under an assumed name. There was no way that had been accomplished legally.

But Gates seemed to have thought it over. "An hour," he said. "I'll be at the bottom of the hill."

He backed down the driveway while Tom's mind spun. Relief tangled up with anxiety until he thought his head would explode. He had to tell her. Now.

Tom moved numbly up her driveway. He couldn't feel his feet as he walked to her porch and stepped up, but he knew he was moving. Her door opened before he could reach it. He looked at her pale face and wished this wasn't happening.

"Why was he here?" she asked.

He stopped at the threshold.

"He's FBI," she said, surprising Tom.

"Yes."

"He's not part of your team. What was he doing here?"

He couldn't answer. He couldn't tell her. But her face crumpled as he stared at her.

"Tom." Her voice cracked. *"Why was he here?"*

He took a deep breath and tried to pretend this was any other case. "He's here about your father," he said.

Isabelle slammed the door in his face.

SHE BACKED UP until she felt the wall behind her. The doorknob jiggled.

"Isabelle," he said through the wood. "Please open the door."

She pressed both hands to her mouth and flattened herself against the wall. This couldn't be happening. He knew.

How long had he known?

"Isabelle, let me help you. Please." His hand slapped the wood. *"Beth."*

"Don't call me that," she whispered as fear swept through her body. When it hit her heart, it turned to rage. *"Don't call me that!"* She leaped for the door and wrenched it open. "How long have you known?"

Instead of answering her, he pushed past her. It didn't matter that she tried to hold him back; he just walked in as if she weren't even there.

"Get out of my house!" she yelled.

"I'm trying to help you."

"How? By fucking me?"

"Isabelle." He actually had the nerve to reach for her.

She heard the growling noise coming from her own throat, and she couldn't stop it. She didn't want to. She slapped his hands away, and then she kept on slapping, hitting his arms, his face, trying to scratch him and make him bleed. Trying to make him hurt for what he'd done.

He caught her wrists before she was satisfied. "Stop it."

"Why didn't you take me in, huh? Were you waiting to see if my dad showed up? Or were you just holding out for a few more blow jobs?"

"It wasn't like that, damn it!" He looked furious, as if he was the one who had a right to be mad.

She tried to jerk her arms away, and when that didn't work, she kneed him in the balls. Or she tried to. He blocked her knee with his thigh and twisted her arms around until she was facing away from him.

"Stop," he said close to her ear, his arms wrapped around her in a parody of intimacy. She screamed and struggled, but she knew it was hopeless. All those muscles she'd admired so much weren't just for show, and she was just a stupid, useless artist who couldn't fight or hide or protect herself. Her screams turned to sobs.

"Isabelle. I'm sorry. I'm so sorry. I didn't know how to tell you."

"How long have you known?" she managed to say past her thick throat. Her voice sounded like a stranger's.

"Shit," he muttered, and she knew. He'd known from the start.

"You knew before. Before you even got here."

"No. It wasn't like that. You acted so suspicious of me when I first showed up that I started checking into you. That's all. That's all it was."

She slumped, giving up on fighting. She'd given herself away, just as she'd feared, and now it was all over. "Just take me in," she rasped. "I don't want to talk to you anymore. Ever."

"I'm not taking you in. Stand up."

She eyed him warily, suspicious about what he wanted from her now. But when his arms loosened, she found the strength to stand on her own two feet, though she put one hand on the wall as he let her go, just in case.

"Do you know where your father is?"

She laughed. "No."

"Are you helping him?"

"I haven't heard from him since I left Chicago. He doesn't know where I am or what my name is. All right? Is that all you wanted?"

He sighed. "Can we sit down?"

"Sure. Maybe I can serve coffee and cake. We can pretend we're fuck buddies again."

"Just sit!"

Isabelle shrugged. She'd gotten her composure, finally, but her legs still trembled as she moved carefully to the living room. She took the chair so he couldn't sit near her.

He collapsed onto the couch. "I didn't know who you were the first time we... After your party... I didn't know until the next day when I had a chance to look up your mom and her accident."

Her heart twisted so hard it hurt. "You were spying on my personal conversations. And trying to get me to talk about myself... I thought you were actually interested in me. Jesus."

"I *was*. I'd realized how much I liked you and, I swear to God, at that point I was trying to disprove my own suspicions so I could let it go and get to know you."

She concentrated on the one mark she'd managed to leave on his face. The scratch was already fading. It wouldn't hurt him for more than a few more minutes, if he'd even felt it at all. "We slept together," she said, "and you kept checking into me."

He looked away from her. "Yes."

"And you thought that was okay?"

He met her gaze again and set his jaw. "I thought you might have needed help. And I was right."

"How were you right? I didn't need any help. I was fine until you called the FBI."

"I didn't call them. When I finally realized who you were, I checked the federal file on your dad. The account was flagged. Agent Gates called me a few minutes later. I denied having seen you or your father. Told him I was only conducting some routine research on federal fugitives. He didn't believe it."

"Agent Gates?" She frowned. That name sounded familiar.

"Do you know him?"

"I don't know. Maybe. There were a lot of people involved in my father's case. A lot of bad people. And you've led them to my door."

"What happened?" he asked.

She shook her head. It was hopeless. There'd never been anything terrible enough to put a stop to any of it. There'd been late-night visits and veiled threats and anything she'd told a federal investigator had gotten to all of her father's associates within hours.

Once her father had vanished, the visits had increased, the cops constantly asking if her father had left anything or asked her to hide anything or if she'd seen him leaving with a package. Some of them had been the good guys, maybe. Some of them hadn't. And the only one her father had warned her about had been the one she'd refused to believe was involved. She'd needed him not to be.

"Why did you run, Isabelle?"

"Because I was afraid I'd end up dead if I didn't."

"Someone threatened you?"

She laughed again, an ugly sound. "No one out and out said they would kill me, but there was a lot of 'If you don't help us, there's nothing we can do to protect you.' And that was true. My own father didn't protect me. He left. So did my fiancé. I ran because I was on my own, and I didn't know any other way to save myself."

"Why were they threatening you?"

"At first they wanted to know where my father was. Everyone wanted to know."

"Were you helping him?"

She shrugged. "Barely. He was moving place to place, asking for money. I obliged a few times in those first weeks and then told him to fuck off. I have no idea where he went after that. Out of the country, I assume. You want to arrest me now for aiding and abetting?"

"No," he said simply, and then he watched, waiting for her to continue.

"That's all there is to it, Marshal. That's the worst I did. When I wouldn't give up my father, it was all about evidence. The FBI, the police department, the district attorneys. They all wanted to know if he'd left anything or taken anything. The house was ransacked one night. The threats started in earnest. I left."

"And was there any evidence?"

She looked him dead in the eyes and lied like she had a hundred times before. He was one of them now. It made no difference. "No."

Tom blew out a long breath and then pulled out his phone. "Gates gave me an hour," he muttered as he typed a text. "Mary will have to take care of the team."

"What? An hour for what?"

He sent the message and glanced up. "We've got an hour before he takes you in."

She shook her head. "No. I'm not going with him. I'll run."

"Isabelle. I'm a US marshal. You're not going anywhere."

"You don't understand. He'll take me back to Chicago. I won't be safe."

"It's been a long time. The people who were after you—"

"You think it's safe now?" She stood and started for her bedroom. "He flew all the way out here after you told him I wasn't here! Why is he so invested?"

Tom was right on her heels. "I don't know. I was hoping you could tell me."

"They're all fucking crooked, that's why."

"Come on. That's not reasonable."

She rounded on him with a sneer. "It's not? Do you really think that gang of crooked cops just all happened to be below the rank of lieutenant? They'd been shaking people down for fifteen years, and none of them were ever promoted higher than that? They couldn't have survived that long without their bosses taking a cut of the action and covering their tracks. Yet the investigation stopped there at the DA's office. It never rose higher in the ranks. And somebody in the FBI made sure the police knew exactly what was going on with every move."

She crossed her arms tightly, holding on to herself before she realized how weak that gesture was and made her fingers let go. "Anytime I had a meeting scheduled with an investigator, there was someone knocking on my door the night before, talking about my dad and loyalty and how many good men could be hurt by all of this if it got out of control. How the hell did they know when I'd be talking to the FBI?"

"Shit, Isabelle," he murmured.

She poked him hard in the chest, but he didn't even raise a hand to stop her. "Why didn't you turn me in as soon as you realized who I was?"

"It didn't smell right," he admitted.

"No. Because it's not right. And I'm not going with Agent Gates. If you won't let me run, then take me in yourself." She grabbed her jeans from the floor and jerked them on. She'd already jumped in the shower and brushed her teeth before Tom had awoken. But she couldn't think about him in her bed now. She couldn't think about the way he'd reached for her in the night and made love to her in darkness, both of them half-asleep and murmuring sweet words of pleasure. It hadn't been sweet, after all.

"You're not a federal fugitive," he said.

"Arrest me for contempt or something. I'm sure I missed a subpoena or two."

"Isabelle—"

"I can't go with him," she growled.

"If you really feel you're in danger, let me talk to my boss about the protection program."

She burst into bitter laughter. "Are you kidding? They're going to spend thousands of dollars to protect me from the *feeling* I'm in danger? I'm not even a witness in a trial. I'm just a stupid, naive girl who got caught in the middle."

"Shit." He rubbed a hand over his face.

"You did this! You lied to me. You fucked me. You led them to me!"

"Goddamn it, you were lying, too. You lied about

everything, and that didn't stop you from fucking me, did it?"

"No," she said, hating the way tears filled her eyes. "I did it, too."

"Jesus, just give me a minute, all right? I need to think about what to do."

She wasn't sure what she'd expected, but pacing help-lessly around wasn't his style, apparently. He got his laptop from its case and sat down in her living room. "Don't sneak out the back door," he said. "You'll be easy to track in the snow."

"Fuck you," she tossed back, then went to pack a bag. She had cash. She always kept cash, just in case. If she couldn't leave right now, she'd leave as soon as she could.

Bear jumped into her suitcase and stared at her as if she'd already done something wrong. God. She'd have to ask Jill to take him in. Bear wouldn't like that at all. Then again, Jill would feed him table scraps. Maybe he'd be happier there with all he could eat and no more oil paint in his fur.

Isabelle started to cry, but she scrubbed furiously at the tears until they stopped. That was all she'd done for weeks in Chicago. Hidden in her house being scared and weepy. She didn't even like to think about that girl; she definitely wasn't going to *be* her again.

She picked Bear up out of her suitcase. "You can't come with me," she said sternly, and then she held him tightly to her, burying her face in his fur. But Bear wasn't big on self-pity, either, and he stiffened up and yowled within a few seconds. When she let him go, he ran off to hide. They were just alike, she and Bear.

Now that she'd had a moment alone, she realized she was being weak again, asking Tom for help. He was only the latest in a long line of supposedly honorable men who'd spent every moment lying to her.

She couldn't trust him.

He was suddenly in the doorway of the bedroom, the lines around his eyes far deeper than they had been the night before. "Gates was one of the original guys assigned to the case. Fairly low down on the totem pole back then, but…"

She stared Tom dead in the eyes, trying not to gloat over such a sad victory.

"Maybe…" he ventured, "that's why he's still so dogged. It's an important case to him."

"You know that's not it," she said. "I'm leaving."

"Wait. I have an idea. Do you think you could trust me?"

She laughed. "Why the hell would I do that?"

"Because you're right. I made this happen, and I don't trust Gates, and I'm going to take care of you."

"Ha!" The bitter sound turned into honest laughter. She had to stop and catch her breath. "Are you kidding me? You're not going to take care of me. Let me tell you exactly what you're going to do. You're going to make promises. You're going to say pretty things. And then as soon as it gets rough, you'll walk away, and I'll be worse off than I was before."

"That's not how I work," he growled.

"That's how everyone works. My own father taught me that. The man who loved me from the moment I was born. My fucking hero. So no, Tom, I can't trust you."

"I'm going to bring you in," he said as if she hadn't just laughed in his face. "You have information about a federal fugitive, and I'm going to bring you in for questioning."

"I don't have any information, and you're not taking me anywhere."

"Isabelle," he said darkly. Then he started toward her.

She backed away. "No. We still have thirty minutes. Just leave and give me a head start. You owe me that."

"I'm bringing you in. It'll at least buy us twenty-four hours."

She meant to fight him. She had every intention of getting away. But he reached out and grabbed her wrist, and one quick flick later, she was on the bed with both her hands clasped in one of his. "No," she said, trying to scream the word, but it came out as a whimper. "Please don't."

"This is for your own good," he answered. "I'm not letting you run anymore. You deserve better."

"No!" she said more loudly. "No, Tom, please!" But she heard the handcuffs click into place, and panic flooded her blood. "Let me go. I can take care of myself. I'll disappear, and I'll be out of your hair. *Please.*"

"Ms. Pozniak, you're under arrest for aiding and abetting a federal fugitive."

"Let me go!" she shrieked, struggling against him as he took her arms and pulled her to her feet. She broke free for a moment, falling back to the mattress, but he didn't even stop talking as he grabbed her again.

"You have the right to an attorney. If you—"

"I fucking hate you, Tom Duncan," she said as he swung her around. "You're a lying bastard, and I wish I'd never touched you."

He didn't even flinch. He just kept on reading her her rights.

She really wished she hadn't started to fall a little in love with him. She knew now that it was the very last time she'd let that happen.

CHAPTER TWENTY

HE DIDN'T KNOW what to do with her.

If he'd been in Cheyenne, it would have been fine. A locked interrogation room, a meeting with his boss, he would have had this under control. But Tom was in Jackson, and the federal courthouse didn't have an interrogation room, and the holding cell was being used for the trial.

He damn sure wasn't going to drop her off at the county jail and leave her there. In the end, he took her to the meeting room he'd been using as an office, handcuffed her to the table and stepped outside to call Mary.

He was met by a very angry Agent Gates, who'd seen them pass by on the road and must have scrambled to follow.

"What the hell do you think you're doing, Duncan?" the man asked past clenched teeth.

"I brought her in for questioning. I thought that was what you wanted."

"This is my fucking case," Gates growled.

"Yeah, well, Pozniak is my fugitive, isn't he? I mean, if you were up for finding him, you would have done it by now, right?"

"You're so fucked," Gates said, that infuriating smile in place again. "You won't have a damn pension when I'm done with you, much less a job."

"Do your worst. Just get out of my fucking courthouse before I have one of these fine officers assist you."

Gates glanced back and seemed surprised to find a couple of uniforms standing right behind him. "Christ, Duncan. I hope that pussy was worth it."

"Get the hell out," Tom growled.

Gates left, pulling his cell phone from his pocket in a deliberate movement as he headed for the front doors of the courthouse, making clear he was going to follow through on his threat to get Tom in trouble.

Tom had notified Mary just before he'd cuffed Isabelle, and while they'd waited for a ride, Tom had called his chief to ask for a little leeway on a case. "She's a witness in a federal fugitive case, and the FBI agent in charge of the case isn't going to like this, but I don't like him." His chief had seemed unconcerned. Tom had a damn near perfect record, and he and his superior had shared more than a few late-night beers together. But once the wheels of the FBI started rolling over them, Tom wasn't sure just how much leeway he would get.

Gates was right about one thing. Tom's job was on the line, but he wasn't walking away from Isabelle no matter what she thought.

Mary frowned as she approached across the lobby. "How's your savior complex coming?"

"You're funny."

"You do have a tendency to date women who are a…bit of a mess."

"That was a long time ago, and Isabelle isn't a mess," he said. "She needs help."

"Semantics."

He stiffened. "You don't have to be involved in this if you don't want to be."

"That's not what I said. Has she told you anything?"

"She's not speaking to me."

Mary raised one eyebrow. "What exactly is this going to accomplish, then?"

"It keeps Gates away from her for another day."

"And then?"

"Then I help her get away," he said.

"Jesus, Tom," she breathed. "Have you considered that she might just be delusional?"

"The whole damn case is about dirty cops, and along comes Agent Gates, asshole extraordinaire. You really think he's the one good guy in the scenario?"

"Well, shit. When you put it that way…"

Tom rolled his tense shoulders, but they felt only tighter after. "The judge is settled?"

"Everything is under control," Mary said. "Proceedings begin in forty-five."

"Do you have a minute to take a look at the Pozniak file? I'd love your take."

"I'm on it," she said, already moving away.

Tom stepped back into the meeting room, half expecting to find the heavy conference table overturned and the window open, but no. Isabelle was there, staring straight ahead, hands flat on the table.

"I'll take the cuffs off if you promise not to run."

"Do whatever you want," she said, refusing to look at him.

"I'm trying to help you, Isabelle."

She shrugged.

He reached for the cuffs, cringing when her hands jerked away from him, but when she stilled, he held one wrist in his hand and unlocked the cuff. It felt strange to touch her, as though he was violating her even though they'd touched so intimately only a few hours before.

He unlocked the other cuff and watched as she rubbed her wrists.

"He's going to ask for a search warrant," Tom said.

Her eyes flew up to meet his, finally. They went wide with fear.

"Is he going to find something?"

"I have money," she said. "Cash. I need it."

"Is it yours?"

"Of course it's mine! Who do you think I am?"

Tom sat down across from her. "I'm not sure. You've never actually told me."

She bared her teeth in a smile. "I lied about my name. You lied about everything else."

"Not everything," he said, but moved on quickly. "They obviously want something from you. Maybe it's something you don't even know you know. Something your dad said once. Or maybe he gave you something that seemed meaningless at the time. A piece of jewelry. A picture."

"There's nothing," she said, the words clipped.

"Then why are they so sure of it?"

"They're not sure. They're desperate. My dad obviously knew something important."

"Like what?"

She shrugged, but she was more nervous now. Her fingers plucked at the sleeves of her shirt. The same shirt he'd taken off her the night before. "He told me not to trust anyone."

"He didn't give you names?"

"No. He just said 'Don't trust anyone. Not the police. Not the FBI. Not even family.'"

Tom leaned forward. "Family?"

"Yes, but we didn't have any family left."

That couldn't be right. And she was frowning hard at her hands. "He must have meant something, Isabelle."

"I was engaged. My fiancé worked in the DA's office, but he'd only been there a year."

"But it had to have been him. There weren't any cousins or uncles?"

She cleared her throat. He'd never seen her nervous before. Hostile, yes. Pissed. Even scared. But not this. "My fiancé's father," she started, then swallowed hard. "It was how I met him. Patrick, I mean. His father was my dad's captain."

Tom sat back, the air leaving his lungs. "It was him."

"I don't know," she said, but he could see she didn't mean it. "I thought he was trying to help at first. He came around a lot after my dad left. To take care of me, he said. They were the only family I had left. I actually tried to talk my fiancé into eloping in the middle of all of it, just because I needed them to be my family.

"But I noticed Patrick's father kept telling me not to report things, or that I was only imagining the danger. I made the mistake of telling my fiancé that I was feeling nervous about it. It was stupid, and I was scared. But I asked if his dad might be involved. That was the end of the help."

"What do you mean?"

"My fiancé broke it off. They cut me off entirely. Defense attorneys started bad-mouthing me to the press. Saying I'd helped my father escape."

"They didn't want you credible anymore."

"Yes. They wanted to destroy me just in case I asked that question of someone else."

"But they didn't destroy you."

Her hands stilled, and her gaze focused on him. "No. They didn't."

HER HANDS SHOOK when she didn't keep them pressed to the table. She finally gave up and put them in her lap.

Tom had excused himself after she'd given him Captain Kerrigan's name, but a uniformed member of his team had been standing next to the door before it closed. Funny that he'd excused himself as if she were his guest instead of his collar.

That had been unexpectedly humiliating. Tom had made sure her coat had covered her cuffs, but it hadn't mattered. *She'd* known. She'd known that the man she'd just had sex with had forced her into handcuffs and walked her into a waiting US marshal vehicle.

And he wanted her to trust him.

She might have laughed, but she was afraid she'd start crying.

When the door opened, she hated that she jumped, but she was expecting Agent Gates to burst in at any moment, an armed team at his back. Not that he'd need one. She was humiliatingly easy to overcome.

But it wasn't Agent Gates; it was Mary, her face set in yet another glower. Isabelle glared back. Mary was the one who'd driven her here, after all.

"I read your file," Mary said.

"Was it a cliff-hanger?" Isabelle snapped.

"I understand that you're angry." Her voice was a calm contrast to her tight face. "But you can trust us."

"If you'd paid attention to my file, you wouldn't say something that ridiculous to me. I met you a week ago. You're yet another cop. That's all I know about you."

"But that's not all you know about Tom."

She clenched her hands into fists. "Isn't it?"

Mary's hand sounded like a shot when it hit the table. "No, it's not. He's going to let you leave. Did you know that? He's going to help you leave, and if he does that, he'll be fired. Over nineteen years as a marshal down the drain. For some woman he met a week ago."

For one quick beat, Isabelle's heart softened toward him. But Mary could say anything; that didn't make it true.

"I'm not even sure that part matters," Mary said. "He's already in big trouble. He kept you a secret, and he got personally involved with you, a woman who's neck deep in a murder investigation." She leaned forward until she was halfway across the table, her eyes blazing now. "So when I say you can trust us, I mean that Tom Duncan, a good man and my very good friend, will probably lose his lifelong career because he wanted to help you. Do you hear what I'm saying?"

She leaned back and took a seat in one of the chairs, but her eyes never left Isabelle.

Isabelle blinked, shocked into silence. Had he willingly put his career in danger? Or was this another ploy? Why would he take those kinds of chances? It made no sense. "I didn't ask for help," she finally said.

"Right. I know you didn't. But doesn't it mean something that you didn't have to ask?"

The door opened again, and it was Tom. Isabelle felt a little numb watching him. A little removed. Her whole world was foggy and confused.

He collapsed into the chair next to Mary and started filling her in, but Isabelle didn't hear much of what he said. He wasn't looking at her now, so she could watch him. He didn't look sincere or convincing or earnest. He didn't look as if he was trying to talk anyone into anything, and God, she'd seen that look a hundred times on the faces of a hundred cops.

Tom looked tired. Worried. He looked like a man who was trying to solve a problem. The problem of her.

She hated him. She really did. But she'd trusted him from the start. Either her instincts were good or she was completely broken, in which case, what did any of this matter?

And she didn't want to run anymore. She wanted this over. She wanted to be done with it for good. Maybe she could trust him. And if she couldn't, there'd never be anyone to trust. Ever.

She licked her lips, but her mouth was so dry it didn't work, so she swallowed hard and licked her lips one more time so she could speak. "He gave me a gun," she said.

Tom stopped talking, and they both turned to her. "What did you say?" he asked.

Isabelle wasn't sure she could speak the words again. She never thought she'd say them even once. But she looked into his green eyes, so new and so familiar, and she said it one more time. "My dad. He gave me a gun. He told me to get rid of it and never tell anyone. I hid it instead."

"This was after the shooting?" Tom asked, his body straining closer, face intense.

"Yes. Just before he ran."

"You still have it?" he asked.

"Yes. At first I thought it was his, but then I realized they already had the gun he'd used in the shooting. Why would this one be so important? Why was everyone looking for it?"

"Isabelle—" he started, but she couldn't stop talking now.

"Who was I supposed to give it to?" she rushed on before Tom could interrupt. "Who could I trust? If I chose the wrong person and the gun disappeared, I'd be the last one who knew it had ever existed. I'd be a loose end."

She gulped in a breath, embarrassed at the strained, high sound of it.

His hand curved around hers and squeezed. "Listen. Isabelle. If you give me the gun, you won't be the only one who knows. I'll know. Mary will know. My boss will know. My whole team. You can tell your friends, too, and you won't be alone."

She nodded, and when she spoke again, she couldn't produce more than a whisper. "I think it's the gun used to fire the first shot. I think it belongs to whoever wanted that cop dead in the first place."

Tom nodded. He was squeezing her hand too hard, hurting her fingers, but when she looked down, she realized it was her hand wrapped around his. Her knuckles were white.

"We were the same age, you know. Me and that girl my father killed. It was one of her first big busts, and she was protective. That's all. That's why she noticed the drugs missing from holding. She was trying to do her job, and she didn't know yet that she wasn't supposed to."

She let go of Tom's hand and wrapped her own fingers together to hold tight. "He still treated me like his little girl, like I was still too precious and innocent to take on the world, and he shot that girl in the back while she was running for her life. My dad did that."

"I'm so sorry," Tom murmured.

She nodded. "I just want it over. I don't care anymore. Just keep them away from me."

"Is it at your cabin?" he asked.

"Yes."

"Mary," Tom said softly. "Can you handle things here while I drive Isabelle home?"

She heard them discussing something quietly, but Isabelle didn't pay any attention. She couldn't be bothered. Nothing mattered except getting this over with.

She'd known the gun was key to everything, but it had also been the thing keeping her alive. If she had the gun, or even if she only knew where her father was *with* the gun, then she was both dangerous and valuable. Without it, she was nothing. Just a possible link that would be safer to eliminate than ignore.

Making her disappear would've been the easiest thing in the world. A few people would've suggested to the press that she'd run away to live with her fugitive father, and no one would've even looked for her body. That was what her dad had left her with. No protection. No security. No love.

She realized Tom was speaking to her and looked up. "What?"

"I won't put the cuffs back on you, but we're probably going to pass Gates, so wear your coat loose and hold your hands together."

She nodded and shrugged on her coat. There were no marks on her wrists. The cuffs had been loose enough that she probably could have slipped out of them if she'd been willing to hurt herself. But she could still feel them there, the cool steel of them on her flesh. She clasped her hands together and let Tom take her arm.

She heard Gates yell something at Tom as soon as they hit the parking lot. The FBI agent popped out of a parked car with his cell phone to his ear.

Tom's hand on her arm kept her moving, but she stared at Gates as he strode across the lot, trying to discern some evil on his face, but he looked like anyone else. Maybe he hadn't been bought out. Maybe he was only a dedicated federal agent. If so, she didn't have to feel the least bit guilty. He'd be thrilled to have the case solved.

When he was almost on them, his foot slipped on an icy patch of slush, and Isabelle looked down to his shiny brown dress shoes. They weren't practical here. They weren't practical in Chicago at this time of year. And they looked very, very expensive.

Tom opened the back door of the SUV, and she slipped in without looking at Gates again. He kept yelling at Tom, asking where the hell Tom thought he was taking her. Tom remained calm. "I'm booking her into the county jail. You can see her in a few hours, I'm sure, once she's out of processing."

Gates shouted about making sure Tom lost his job, but Tom just got in the SUV and pulled away.

Isabelle bit her lip. Maybe he really was going to lose his job.

His phone rang, but he only glanced at it. "My boss," he murmured.

"Does he know what you're doing?"

"I'll call him as soon as I have the gun."

She didn't want to ask, but she did. "Will that be okay?"

"It'll be fine," he said. She didn't press for the truth.

She stared out the window at the mountains she passed every day and still felt humbled by. It was cloudy today, and she was thankful for that. The typical azure Jackson sky would've been too much to take when she felt like a mass of open gray wounds.

"Why did you sleep with me?" she asked, her breath fogging the window. "After you found out who I was."

He didn't answer. After a dozen heartbeats of silence, she looked up to see him watching her in the rearview mirror.

"Why did *you* sleep with *me*?" he asked. "When you knew I was the last person you should be around?"

She turned her head to hide the tears that sprang to her eyes. She hoped he couldn't see, because she couldn't stop them this time. She'd slept with him because it had made her so happy. His body, his mouth, his need. Because it had felt so right, and she hadn't known that he was gathering information about her with every touch.

It had felt real.

She didn't say anything else. Instead, she used the last ten minutes of the drive to numb herself again and make sure her eyes were dry by the time they pulled onto her lonely little road.

It hadn't been real.

Reaching for the door before Tom could open it for her, she got out and walked toward her porch without a word. He followed her into her house and down the hallway to her bedroom. She didn't look at the twisted covers and rumpled sheets of her bed as she moved to the bathroom and her closet beyond.

She tossed her coat on the floor and pulled the attic door down, then got the ladder secured just as Tom was reaching to help. She didn't need help; she just needed him to do his job. "There's not enough room for both of us," she muttered before heading up the ladder. It wasn't strictly true, but there wasn't enough room to be in the tiny space without bumping into each other with every movement. She couldn't touch him that way.

She climbed up to the small finished area of the attic, but within ten steps, she was walking on beams. She passed the chimney and carefully put her foot onto one of the joists that angled up from the floor, then grabbed a rafter above her head and pulled herself up. Eight feet up, where the chimney was flush with a rafter, sat the bundle she'd put there on the day she'd moved in.

Dust clouded around her as she pulled the awkward package down. She tucked it under her arm, then reached blindly back with one foot to find the wood beneath her. Hands circled her waist. She didn't even jump in surprise. Of course he'd come up to help. He couldn't keep away from her secrets.

"Try not to step through my ceiling," she muttered as she turned and shooed him away, but her skin still tingled from his grip. How could she want him when she hated him so much?

He descended the ladder first then reached for her again. She couldn't scream at him not to, because she didn't want him to know how much it affected her, so she gritted her teeth at the way his hands framed her hips before they slid up her waist in a torturous imitation of lust. In that moment, she wanted him to push for more. She wanted him to press her to the ladder and push his cock against her ass to show that she'd made him hard. She wanted his mouth on her neck, kissing her even as she cursed and screamed for him to get his hands off her. She wanted him to ignore all her hatred and force her to do what she really wanted. Because she did want it. And she despised herself for it.

She'd never understood angry sex. She'd never been able to fathom how you could want someone you were pissed at. But she got it now, because with some people it was about the animal that lurked beneath the civilized being you showed the rest of the world.

She never wanted to speak to him again, but she'd fuck him at the drop of a hat.

His hands had left her, and she was standing with her forehead pressed to one of the rough wooden rungs of the sliding ladder. He took the package from her and set it aside.

"Isabelle? Are you okay?" She felt his body heat hovering so near. He wanted to touch her. She wanted him to.

She shook her head, feeling the wood press into her skin as a tear dropped straight from her eye and landed on her wrist. "No," she whispered.

His fingers brushed her neck. "I'm so sorry," he murmured. She tipped her head, wanting him to touch more, and then his mouth was there, warm and whispering, "I'm sorry," against her skin, and she sobbed.

"Don't cry," he said. "Please." But he didn't stop kissing her neck, and his hands were at her waist again, and this time they kept sliding up to cup her breasts as she pressed her ass to his hips.

He was hard for her and she groaned, pain and need all mixed up in her chest, the tendrils of it brushing between her legs.

"I'm sorry," he said again, but his cock didn't regret anything. His cock was thick and long and eager against her ass as she rubbed into him.

His hands slid down again, reaching for the button of her jeans, and she could feel the way his fingers trembled against the bare skin of her stomach. He whispered her name, asking for permission, maybe, but she wouldn't give it to him. She wouldn't ask for this.

In the end, he didn't wait for her word. His hand slid inside her jeans and into her panties, and she was soaked and slick beneath his fingers. "Oh, fuck, Isabelle."

She nodded as another tear dropped to her hand. She

put that hand over his and moved him lower until he could curl his fingers into her.

She didn't say yes, but she moaned and ground her ass tighter to his cock.

Tom cursed beneath his breath, and for a moment she was worried he'd stop, but he didn't stop. He drew his hand free and pulled down her jeans with two vicious tugs that left her skin feeling raw. She heard his zipper open. Heard the crumpling sound of a condom wrapper. She reached behind her and found his hip as she shifted her feet back and watched his stance spread wider behind hers. His cock rubbed against her aching pussy. Isabelle held tight to the ladder and arched back to tilt her hips higher.

He pushed slowly into her, stretching her carefully, trying not to hurt her. Didn't he know she was hurt already?

She dug her fingers into his hip and pressed her ass back hard, and he sank deep into her, setting off exactly the ache she wanted. But he was still too careful. Still trying to read her. His hand rose to her neck, fingers spreading gently up her jaw to her tear-wet face.

"I'm sorry," he said. "Isabelle, please..."

She turned her head and bit his wrist, making him hiss and jerk away from her. "I hate you," she growled as she pulled his hips back to her and sank his cock deep again. "I hate you."

"Goddamn it, Isabelle," he said, but he finally gave her what she wanted. He fucked her. Hard. No sweet words or caresses or care. He sank his cock into her over and over as her hands went tighter and tighter on the ladder.

His hands joined hers, gripping the wood just above her hands, and he pounded into her. She focused on those lovely hands, his knuckles turning white, tan skin and golden hair disappearing beneath the white cuff of his dress shirt. She watched the tendons strain beneath his skin, and she took his cock, and it was exactly what her body wanted.

The anger and lust built inside her until she couldn't take it anymore. "Come," she ordered, the power of it intoxicating. The power of making him want her past all his good intentions and morals and guilty feelings. "Come for me," she moaned.

This time he didn't hold himself still. There was nothing subtle about this. His thrusts grew short and brutal and fast, and then he grunted against her neck, his breath hot and heavy on her skin as he came.

Every muscle in her body trembled. Her pussy ached. Her forehead hurt where she'd scraped it on the wood.

His breath calmed a little. He loosened one hand from its hold and slid it down her shoulder. "Let me make you come," he whispered, his fingers trailing down her stomach.

"No," she said, straightening until his cock was free of her, one last, long slide of unexpected pleasure. "I don't want to."

"What?"

She tugged up her jeans and swiped at the tears on her face. "I don't want to come." Not with him here. Later, when she was alone, she'd think of this and get off, but she couldn't do it in front of him. Not now.

"Isabelle—" But she ducked under his arm and left him there. He followed her to the bedroom a minute later. "If you didn't want—"

"I wanted it," she said tersely. "But I don't want to come for you."

He looked hurt and confused, as if she'd slapped him

hard. She tipped her head toward the package under his arm. "You have the gun. You can go now."

"Jesus," he breathed.

"I don't want to see you again," she said.

He stared for a long moment before he seemed to snap from his shock. He stood a little straighter and wiped the confusion from his face. "We'll need statements and—"

"Then send Mary to talk to me. Or someone else. Just not you."

He looked around, his gaze jumping over the room before he shook his head. "It might not be safe for the next twenty-four hours or so. Gates won't know—"

"I'll stay with Lauren," she said. "Sophie's there, too. I'll be fine."

He opened his mouth then closed it. Finally, he took a deep breath and shook his head. "All right. If that's the way you need it to be. But this isn't what I want. All of this…" He waved a hand toward her sad, rumpled bed. "All of this was…"

"Goodbye, Tom."

His hand fell to his side. He watched her. He watched for so long that she was afraid her mask would crack and she'd lose it and let out all the tears inside her. But she held tight to her control, and he finally gave up.

"Goodbye, Isabelle," he said.

He walked out, but he didn't leave. He sat outside in his truck for nearly thirty minutes, making phone call after phone call. Finally, a marked sheriff's truck pulled up next to him. They spoke for a long moment while Isabelle watched through the window, afraid she'd made Tom so angry that he'd changed his mind and was going to have her taken to jail after all.

But then the sheriff's vehicle pulled away and parked

on the road just below her driveway, and Tom finally drove off. He'd left someone to watch over her.

Her throat thickened, but she didn't have time to cry.

An hour later, she drove from her home with all her paintings boxed for shipping, one angry Bear hiding under her seat, enough clothes to get her through a week away and $20,000 in cash. Just in case.

She stopped next to the sheriff's truck just as fat, sullen snowflakes began to fall from the sky. The deputy rolled down his window, and she was surprised to realize she recognized him as the boyfriend of Jenny, one of her favorite bartenders in town.

"Ms. West," he said politely.

"Hi. Are you here to follow me?"

He frowned. "Ma'am, I'm here to be sure no one bothers you for the next little while, so yes, I'm afraid I'll be following you to wherever you want to go."

"But that's all? Really?"

"Yes, ma'am."

"Okay, thanks. It's Nate, right?"

He relaxed and winked. "Yes. Known as Jenny's boyfriend when I'm not on official business."

"All right." She started to roll up her window then rolled it back down. "I'm sorry if this is weird."

"I'm sorry if it's weird for you," he responded.

She drove away, off to explain to her girlfriends that Isabelle West was actually a fugitive of justice who'd likely committed several felonies on her long run from the law. Shit. They'd probably love it.

CHAPTER TWENTY-ONE

Tom LEFT HIS disciplinary hearing and walked straight out of the US Marshals Service building and down the front steps. It was spring, finally—for a couple of days, at least—and he needed a walk.

A week's suspension without pay, which he'd start serving tomorrow, and a demotion that had more meaning on paper than it did in reality. Tom had been lucky. Really lucky. He could have been fired, could have lost his pension, but in the end, his "temporary lapse in judgment" had been outweighed by the corruption he'd helped expose in a case that had left a good police officer dead.

The gun hadn't been registered, of course. It had disappeared from the evidence room in a Chicago police precinct over twenty years before, and it hadn't shown up since then. But the fingerprints on it…those had been on file. And they'd belonged to Captain Kerrigan.

Fingerprints were only a small piece of evidence, of course, and the man hadn't yet been charged with any crime, much less murder, but the wheels were turning. Kerrigan had stepped down from his new position as deputy superintendent of the police department, and a special prosecutor had been brought in from Washington, DC, to head up the corruption case. This time, it wouldn't be only small-time cops going down.

Tom was relieved with how his own disciplinary

hearing had turned out. He'd been on desk duty since January, and he was ready to get back to work after the suspension. But he'd do the same thing all over again, given the choice, even the parts that had left him hollowed out and yearning inside. He'd do it for her.

Tom tipped his head up to the sun, feeling the heat on his face and trying not to think about Isabelle. An impossibility considering where he was going.

The Cheyenne office of the FBI was even less impressive than the Cheyenne marshal's office. The place looked like an accounting firm, and not a successful one, but the metal detector inside the building's entry gave away that it wasn't just another door.

Tom showed his badge and told the guard he didn't have his service revolver on him, and he was escorted to a tiny seating area while a receptionist made a call. It seemed unnecessary. Tom could hear the phone ringing in a room just a few feet away.

"Deputy Marshal Tom Duncan to see you," she said about five seconds before a young agent stepped out of that open doorway.

"Deputy," the guy said, holding out a hand. "I'm Special Agent Browning."

Man, they made Special Agents younger every year. "Nice to meet you. I hope I'm welcome here."

Browning laughed. "More than welcome. From what I hear, Chicago's pretty pleased to be rid of that Gates guy. Nobody liked him."

"I can't imagine why."

"He probably won't be charged for selling information, but he'll never be in law enforcement again."

"I guess that'll have to be good enough," Tom said.

Browning clapped a hand on his shoulder. "Come

on in. I have that box right here. I just need you to sign for it and affirm that you'll deliver it to Ms. Pozniak."

"It's West," he corrected him. "Legally now, from what I understand."

"Right." Browning sat down and slid some papers across his pristine desk. This guy was organized. No wonder he was moving up quickly. "Nice of you to take this stuff personally. I'm sure it's a difficult situation for her."

"Yeah." Difficult. Tom glanced at the cardboard box. It wasn't much of anything, from what Tom had seen on the evidence sheet. The box was sadly small. He signed all the paperwork and left with the box under his arm. He had a week to drive it out to her, but he planned to leave this afternoon.

Mary was waiting by his car when he returned to the marshal-service building. "I heard," she said. "You doing okay?"

"I'm fine, but you're the one who'll have to give up the acting-supervisor gig when I get back in a week," he said, pushing her affectionately away from the door of his SUV.

"You know I don't care about that."

"Don't pretend you haven't loved being in charge," he said.

"Well, if it had to be someone," she said with a smile, "then I'm thrilled it was me. Are you leaving tomorrow?"

"Today."

"Oh. Okay, just…"

"What?" he asked.

"Be careful. I mean, I don't know what you're hoping for, Tom, but…"

He wasn't hoping for anything. He just wanted to

make things right for Isabelle. "I'm only trying to make amends for what happened."

"You don't need to make any amends," Mary snapped. "You risked everything to help her!"

"Mary," he said. They'd had this discussion a dozen times. "She's had it a lot rougher than I have. She didn't do anything wrong, and she lost everything except her actual life, and she was damn worried about that, too."

"That wasn't your fault!"

"No. But I didn't exactly restore her trust in people, did I?"

She shrugged. "Whatever. You'll do what you want. Just say hi to Jill for me while you're out there."

"You just said hi to her two weeks ago."

Mary's cheeks flushed. "She was in Cheyenne for a meeting. She picked me up here, and we had dinner. That's all."

"Mmm-hmm."

"We're taking it slow," she protested. "Both of us."

"That's smart," he said.

"Yeah." She looked away. "But a little frustrating."

Mary walked away while he was still laughing at her. Not that he had any good reason to laugh. He knew all about frustration.

Tom drove home to change into jeans and a green button-down that Mary had once said made his eyes look nice. He grabbed the bag he'd already packed and hit the road for Jackson.

Okay, so maybe he was hoping for something, thinking Isabelle might have softened toward him a little. There'd been a lot of changes in the past three months, after all.

In February, with all the new activity on the case,

the FBI had finally requested DNA samples of a John Doe who'd died about five years before. The man had been living in Central America with a fake passport. The DNA tests proved that he'd been Malcolm Pozniak.

His remains had been long since buried in Ecuador, but the US Embassy had still had his personal possessions in a box in storage. Tom had fought hard to have everything sent to him once it was processed.

He'd also fought hard to get the charges that had been pending against Isabelle dropped. He wasn't sure how much of a difference he'd made. After all, she'd had an attorney. But all but two misdemeanors had been tossed out. She wouldn't be serving any time. She didn't deserve to.

So maybe, after all those changes and with the danger having released its hold on her life, maybe she'd changed her mind about him a little.

Or maybe she'd been so busy and stressed, she hadn't been thinking about him at all. Or maybe she hated his guts.

However it was, he couldn't leave it the way they'd said goodbye. He needed to say goodbye when she wasn't crying and so damn angry and… He still couldn't believe he'd touched her like that. He'd thought she'd needed it the way he had. As a moment of grace. Of connection. Of knowing they'd make things better. But that hadn't been it at all.

"Damn," he muttered as he pulled onto the highway out of town. Damn, indeed. It was going to be a very long drive, but he didn't have much doubt that the drive home would be even longer. It was one thing to drive toward hope, and a very different thing to know you were driving away from it.

LAUREN STOOD UP from the corner table she'd managed to snag at their favorite restaurant. "Congratulations!" she said, holding up a glass of champagne as Isabelle approached. "You're not a felon!"

"Oh, my God," Isabelle groaned. "You're the worst."

"Are you kidding me? That's a big deal!"

"Thanks." She took the glass Lauren handed her and downed a big gulp.

Yesterday she'd signed a deal in her lawyer's office that would allow her to plead down to two minor tax-fraud counts for using a fake name and social security number. All other charges, including the stickiest one of withholding evidence in a federal murder case, had been wiped away. She was a free woman, basically. And not just free, but legal. This morning a state judge had granted her a name change. She was no longer living a lie.

"Where's Veronica?" Isabelle asked. This would be Veronica's second girls' night out with them. She was a little quiet, but Isabelle had been quiet with the other women at first, too. It wasn't easy to trust people. She understood that.

"She's running late. Something about a deadline for her column. She told us to start without her."

Isabelle took another sip. "Did she think we wouldn't?"

"She's new. So how are you holding up? You look good. You stopped losing weight."

"Yeah, I felt like eating again once they told me they probably wouldn't even need my testimony. The gun has Kerrigan's fingerprints on it, and ballistic tests confirmed it shot the first bullet. I won't have to go back there and face those people."

"Good. And everything else?"

"Everything else is good. I just started a new commission. It feels great to get back to work."

"Mmm." Lauren sipped her champagne and watched Isabelle over the rim of her glass.

"What?"

She shrugged. "I heard Jill saw Tom a couple of weeks ago."

Isabelle felt her face go hot for a brief moment before it went ice-cold. She shook her head. Her ears buzzed. "I don't want to know about that." She'd known Jill might have seen Tom when she met Mary for dinner, but Jill hadn't said a thing about it.

"Isabelle," Lauren said, "you still like him."

"No, I don't," she said. "He lied to me about everything."

"You lied about everything, too."

"It's not the same."

"How is it not the same?" Lauren pressed.

"Because," she started then had to swallow the thickness from her throat. "Because..." She felt her face crumple, and there was nothing she could do to stop the sob that escaped. "Because I didn't want him to do that to me."

"Oh, sweetie," Lauren said, sounding slightly panicked. She grabbed Isabelle's hand and squeezed tight. "It's okay."

"It's not okay," Isabelle said, covering her face with her other hand. "I thought it was real and so good, and it wasn't real."

"Isabelle, shh. You don't know that."

"He was lying!"

"Well, you've been lying to me the whole time I've known you, and this is real, isn't it?"

Isabelle sniffed, but more tears just filled her head again. "Yes."

"And Jill? You've known her for more years than anyone, and you were lying to her and it was real, wasn't it?"

"It's not the same," she muttered, reaching for her napkin. She dumped the silverware and covered her face with the white square.

"How?" Lauren didn't sound very sympathetic.

"He handcuffed me, in case you don't remember! Brought the whole federal government down on my head."

"Now you're just being silly. That's a funny story you can tell about how you met."

"Shut up," she snapped, but Lauren didn't sound chastened when she spoke.

"You can say whatever you want, but you still miss him."

Two more fat tears escaped her control at that. She wouldn't admit that she missed him. She wouldn't admit that she thought about him every day and looked up news stories online to see if he might be mentioned. He never was anymore. After the initial few stories, he hadn't been named again.

She took a big sip of champagne and a very deep breath and raised her chin. "It doesn't matter. It's over."

"You could get in touch."

"No."

"You could ask Jill to ask Mary."

"No!" she cried then looked around to see if anyone was listening. "Are you crazy?"

"So you're just never going to see him again?"

Oh, shit. Tears spilled over her cheeks again, because she knew she was never going to see him again, and because she felt stupid. Stupid for still wanting to. Stupid for missing him so much when he'd been here for only a week. Stupid that she'd had to look up "how to stop thinking about someone" on the internet.

She wiped at her face and then leaned closer to Lauren. "Why would he want to see me, Lauren? I lied, too. And he still might lose his job over it. I'm supposed to call him and say, 'Hi, this is the crazy fugitive girl who's still pissed at you and may have ruined your life. Want to go out for a drink so we can rehash that terrible week?'"

"No. You're supposed to say that you're wondering how he's doing. That's all."

"And if he just tells me to fuck off?"

"What if he does? You're being a coward over *that*?"

"I'm not being a coward! We had sex a few times. What makes you think it meant anything to him?"

"Because he risked his job for you, Isabelle. For *you*."

"I'm sure he regrets it," she snapped.

"Why don't you ask him?"

"I don't want to! I'm still mad!"

Lauren rolled her eyes as though *Isabelle* was the one being unreasonable.

"Oh, hey, Veronica!" Lauren said, standing up to hug their newest friend.

Veronica waved cheerily at Isabelle, though her smile faltered when their eyes met. Isabelle imagined that her face was a blotchy mess.

"I'm so sorry I'm late. This last column was a challenge. Some guy had a question about sex, so there were a lot of substitutions to be made in his original letter. And a lot of stuff I had to look up."

"About sex?" Lauren asked, sounding surprised.

"I don't automatically know everything about sex just because I write an advice column, you know," Veronica said, color rising on her cheeks.

That made even Isabelle smile. "We've got to get you out more if the mere mention of sex makes you blush."

"I have pale skin!" she protested.

"Okay," Lauren said, "I have a hypothetical advice question for you. Say you lie about your identity to a man, and he later arrests you, but you guys really, really like each other…"

Veronica's eyes went wide as saucers. She glanced at Isabelle as if she were afraid there was going to be a fistfight. But screw it. Lauren was slowly wearing her down.

Isabelle waved a hand. "Oh, go ahead. Give your advice."

"I thought you were still furious with him," Veronica said carefully.

"I don't know what I am anymore. Horny, maybe. And he—" she poured a second glass of champagne "—was really, really good. And sweet. And funny."

"Did he get in touch?"

"No," Isabelle said firmly. "He has not gotten in touch."

Veronica looked down at the table for a long moment. Her cheeks went pink again. She looked very young when she blushed like that. "I think…" she started before she looked up at Lauren, then Isabelle. "I think that he did something that was really good for you." She raised a hand to stop Lauren from commenting. "And I don't mean sex. I mean he did the right thing for you, even though neither of you liked it. So if he's also sweet and funny and great in bed, then you're being really stupid, Isabelle."

Isabelle sucked in a breath as if she'd been slapped. "What?" She looked at Lauren, but there was no help there. Lauren looked disappointed in her. "He hasn't called me!" Isabelle said.

"You told him you never wanted to see him again," Lauren pointed out unhelpfully.

"He…he…" Isabelle heard the panic in her voice and cut off her own words. She nodded. Swallowed hard. Nodded again. "He probably doesn't want me. And I don't want to know that, you guys. I can't take that."

"Yes, you can," Lauren said.

Veronica nodded. "You need to find out."

Isabelle shook her head, but she knew they were right. The scary thing wasn't that she still wanted him; it was that he might not want her. It was that he might walk away and leave her alone. The thought turned her skin to ice. She was so cold she felt like shivering. She was a problem, and he was going to walk away from her, and she couldn't take that.

She knew she was quiet through dinner, but Veronica and Lauren kept the conversation going, trying to keep it light. Lauren picked up the tab, claiming that getting a new name deserved to be counted as a birthday celebration.

"This is your new life, Isabelle. Everything is different for you now. The world is your oyster and all that. But!" She pointed at Isabelle with a stern look. "That doesn't mean you get to leave Jackson. We already lost Sophie. I'm putting a moratorium on anyone moving."

Isabelle agreed, trying not to get teary-eyed again.

Lauren was right. This was a new life. She could travel if she wanted to. She hadn't been able to do that before. She could call attention to herself. Live in town.

No. That sounded awful.

"Are you sure you don't want another drink?" Lauren offered.

"No, I have to drive home."

"I could make Jake drive you again."

"If you make Jake drive me one more time, he's going to personally stage an intervention. He probably thinks I'm drunk every night."

"No, just on Sundays and a few special Tuesdays like today."

Isabelle gave them both sincere hugs, but when she got to her car, she breathed a sigh of relief. She needed to be alone. Maybe for a few months. She just needed to shut off the world and her feelings and paint.

April evenings weren't exactly warm, but it wasn't freezing, either, so she drove home with the window open and the fresh air on her face.

It was spring, and that was something to be thankful for. It was spring, and she had a new life and maybe that could be enough. Because it didn't matter how brave she pretended to be; she couldn't call Tom. She never would. She'd move on and pretend that she'd never really wanted him. For once, she'd make that choice, instead of being the one standing there, begging, crying.

Her hands were sore from clutching the steering wheel by the time she passed Jill's house. She noticed the black SUV in Jill's drive, but she was too upset to be curious. The evening was lovely, but her mind was a mess. She breathed a sigh of relief when she saw her house. Her hiding place.

Then she saw the box on the doorstep, just at the edge of the circle of porch light.

She hit the brakes so hard that the seat belt caught her. Just a UPS package, maybe. Except she hadn't ordered anything.

So it was probably a bomb. Great.

She got out and pulled open the garage door, pretending for a moment that the package wasn't there.

She couldn't call 911 to say that someone had left a mysterious package on her doorstep until she determined that it was mysterious, so she pulled calmly into her garage, turned off the engine and got out.

Halfway to her porch, it occurred to her that the box could be a ploy to get her to walk to her porch in the dark. She hesitated for a moment and waited, but when she heard nothing, she headed for the steps, unwilling to cower in the night. The box wasn't from UPS. There was a letter attached.

With another glance around to be sure no one was sneaking up on her, she reached slowly out to grab the edge of the envelope. It wasn't taped to the box. It didn't trigger an explosion. And no powdery substance sifted out when she opened it.

"Dear Isabelle," it started, and then she began to cry.

> I was really hoping to see you today. I'm not sure how to say this in a letter, because I meant to say it in person.
> I'm sorry...

She didn't read the rest of it. She dropped the letter and started running. The black SUV in Jill's driveway. It had to be Tom. It had to.

She'd gone to dinner only two hours before. He wouldn't have left without stopping in to see Jill.

The heels she'd worn to dinner were making running downhill treacherous, so she stopped to take them off and then kept running, hoping she didn't turn an ankle on her rough driveway.

When she hit the road, it was much smoother. She was so caught up in the triumph of that that she hardly noticed the shadow walking up the hill toward her.

Isabelle gasped and slowed her frantic run until she could stop without pitching forward onto her face. The figure was still fifty feet away.

"Isabelle?" he said.

It was Tom. And all her fear was back, twisted into a fear for her heart instead of her safety. "Hi," she whispered. He kept walking, and she was afraid he hadn't heard her. "Hi," she tried again.

"I'm sorry if I scared you. I left something for you. I saw you drive past Jill's. I didn't know…"

He stopped. He was ten feet away. She couldn't quite see him. She wanted to see him, but he didn't come closer.

"Did you just get here?" she asked.

"Yes. An hour ago."

Her only comfort was that he sounded as unnatural as she did. "For work?"

"No."

That was all he said. "Oh," she managed to say.

He stepped closer, and she could finally see him in the light of the new moon. He looked so tall and handsome, and for some reason she felt more herself. It was just Tom, after all, and she knew him.

"My feet are freezing," she said. "Do you want to come inside? Have a drink?"

He glanced down at her feet with a smile. "Yes. I'd love that."

When they reached the porch, Tom picked up the box he'd left as she unlocked the door.

"What is it?"

He shook his head.

She turned the light on and shut the door, and it felt so oddly comfortable to be inside with him that she smiled. It felt just like it had the first time she'd let him in. "It's not the gun, is it? Because I really don't want it back."

"Ha," he said. He smiled, then laughed. "No. It's not the gun."

Oh, God, he looked so handsome, and so different, wearing jeans and a button-down shirt already rolled up at the sleeves. She suddenly realized that it was a Tuesday night. And he was here. Her happiness fell away.

"Tom. Oh, my God, you weren't fired, were you?"

He laughed again, thank God. "I wasn't fired." He winked. "But I did get a few days off whether I wanted them or not. It's lucky, really, because I wanted to bring you this."

She took the box he handed to her, ready for it to be heavy, but it felt nearly empty.

Her birthday wasn't until July. She couldn't guess what else it could be. "I'm glad you weren't fired," she finally said, making him laugh again, and somehow that made her want to cry. She liked him laughing. She liked him here in her house.

"Should I open it?" she asked. "Do you want a drink?"

"A drink sounds good," he answered, and Isabelle agreed. She handed him the box and went to get a couple of beers. He was waiting on the couch when she returned.

For a moment, she wondered if she should take the

chair, but that was stupid. So stupid when she could be close to him for a moment.

He set the box on the table. "It's from Ecuador," he said, and she finally understood that this wasn't about her and Tom.

She went stiff and stared at the box. "More evidence?"

"No! Christ, Isabelle, I wouldn't do that to you. I just wanted to bring you something of your dad's. They told you he'd died, but I didn't know how much else you knew about his life."

"His life?" She shook her head in confusion. "You mean in Ecuador? Nothing."

Tom nodded and drew his keys from his pocket. "He had a small apartment." He drew the key over the tape that sealed the box. "No wife. No family. He arrived fourteen years ago and never left. He went for coffee every afternoon at 3:00 p.m. after siesta." He opened the flaps of the box and handed it to her.

"He was quiet," Tom said. "His life was quiet. He died of a heart attack five years ago. There's not much else to tell."

Isabelle looked into the box, still in shock. She lifted out the crushed paper and drew out a plastic evidence bag. There was a black wallet inside.

"I'm sorry. They took his driver's license, so there's no photo of him. But there are some old pictures inside."

"Can I open it?" she whispered. When he nodded, she drew the wallet out and spread it open, amazed that the smell of leather still wafted up. And just beneath it, the faint scent of the cheap cologne her father had always favored. "Oh," she breathed, even before she pulled the photos from the wallet.

There was one of her as a baby. A pose she recognized. Then another of her as a teenager. She'd never seen that one before. It was her, smiling and cheerful and open and waving at the camera. The last picture was of Isabelle's mother. It was a tiny square, cut from another photo. Her mother in their kitchen, a hand held up to shoo the camera away.

"It's not much," Tom said. "They kept his passport. It was a counterfeit. But his wedding ring is supposed to be in there. And a watch."

She nodded.

"He was at church when he collapsed. An ambulance took him to the hospital. He died a few hours later."

She nodded again, as if she knew, but no one had told her anything.

"That's all," he said. "I wanted to be sure you knew, and that his things got to you."

She was still staring into the mess of paper and plastic in the box when Tom stood.

Bear, disturbed from his sleep beneath the side table, hissed at Tom then took off across the room to disappear down the hall.

"The cat missed you," she said.

"He just ran away."

"He does that."

"Isabelle—"

She cut him off before he could say goodbye. "I missed you, too," she said, the words running together in her rush to force them out.

Tom was just standing there, staring at her, and now she wanted to follow Bear from the room. Isabelle had let her friends get to her, and what did they know about any of this? She was all screwed up in a million ways, and she wasn't sure about anything except that Tom must hate her. And she should hate him, shouldn't she?

She stood and backed a few steps away. "I'm sorry," she whispered. "I shouldn't have said that. Thank you for bringing my dad's things."

He shook his head. "You don't need to apologize."

"You were being nice, and I've made this weird."

"Isabelle..." He looked so confused. As if he were dealing with a crazy person, and he couldn't even grasp what she might mean. "You said you never wanted to see me again."

"I know."

"I would've called if I'd thought... I didn't want to leave it that way. I just... I didn't know we were saying goodbye. That's not the way I would've said goodbye."

She nodded, her chin bouncing up and down way too many times before she finally made herself be still. "I'm sorry. I wasn't being rational. I was trying to hurt you. Or hurt us both. So this will be better. Saying goodbye like this."

His forehead crumpled in a frown. Isabelle had no idea what her own face must look like. A little manic. A lot freaked out. She couldn't tell him how much she still wanted him. She couldn't watch him squirm and try to extricate himself from her inappropriate affections. She was a criminal. A fugitive. A liar. The kind of person he locked up every day.

"I wanted to call you," he said. "Every day. Would you have talked to me if I had?"

"Not at first. At first I hated you."

"And now?" He took a step toward her. She locked her legs so she wouldn't turn and run.

"Now I think..." She had to swallow the emotion that clogged her throat. "I think I was just terrified. And I think I wanted you to find out about me."

"What?" Another step closer.

Isabelle clasped her hands together and held tight. "You asked me why I slept with you, knowing you were a marshal. I asked myself the same question a thousand times, and the only thing that makes sense is that I wanted it over. I wanted out of the lie. And for some reason, I trusted you."

He shook his head. "But you had a life. A good life. I screwed that up."

"I know. But I wasn't really free, was I? I couldn't let myself fall in love. I couldn't trust anyone."

"And now?"

He'd gotten closer. She could reach out and touch him, but she wouldn't. Her heart raced at the thought of it, but her hands gripped tighter together. She kept them snug against her stomach, protecting herself.

"I can't trust anyone," she repeated.

"You said you could trust me."

"I don't know. I don't know you." She didn't realize she was shaking her head until Tom reached out, and his fingers gently stopped the movement.

She sighed at the touch. Tears stung her eyes. She didn't want him to see that. She ducked her head, and his hand slid to the back of her neck, and then she was pressed to his chest, his arms warm around her.

"You can trust me," he murmured.

"I don't trust anyone," she managed to say past her tears.

"I know that. Why would you? Everyone has let you down."

"You haven't," she whispered, but then she was crying too hard to speak. To say that Patrick had dumped her for his reputation, and Tom had risked his career for her. To say that her father had run to save his own life, and Tom had stayed right there and protected her. That even after she'd been cruel to him, he'd been kind. She couldn't say any of it. She could only cry harder when his arms tightened around her as if he'd never let her go.

"I missed you, too, Isabelle," he said, the words warm against her temple. "I thought about you every day. I called Jill once. I even looked up Veronica's column on the off chance that you'd written in to say, 'A man I was dating arrested me, and I can't stop thinking about him.'"

She laughed. An embarrassing, coughing sort of laugh that made her aware of how wet she'd gotten his shirt. "I actually presented her with that problem tonight. Really."

"And what did she say?"

"She said I was being really stupid. She said I should call. I told her you probably never wanted to see me again."

"Not true. I always want to see you. In fact, even if you'd kicked me out, I was going to try to buy that painting from you."

"What painting?" she asked. Then said, "Oh," when he drew back to frown down at her. "My boobs."

"Yes. Exactly."

She buried her wet face back in his shirt, and they laughed. They just laughed, as though everything was okay again. As though they could just pick up where they'd left off. As if they fit together easily and trusted each other, so everything would be fine. Why could she feel that way with him even when everything else was so scary?

"I could have mailed that box to you," he said quietly. "But I couldn't bear the thought of never seeing you again. Even if you were just going to tell me to go to hell, I wanted to see you while you did it."

"Is that all you wanted?"

"No," he said, pressing a kiss to the crown of her head. "No, I wanted to tell you how sorry I was for lying. And I wanted you to say that we might have a chance."

Her chest ached. The pain was awful. Hope hurt a lot worse than fear.

"I'm sorry for lying to you," he said.

Isabelle fisted her hands in his shirt and held on for dear life. "We might have a chance," she whispered.

She felt some of the tension leave his body, his muscles softening around her. She finally realized how good he smelled, how much she'd missed his skin. She didn't want to let him go. "You must be tired," she said. "Did you stop for dinner or anything?"

"Jill fed me."

She nodded. "Do you...do you want to stay? Here?"

He stood straight, pulling away from her. "I thought maybe we'd take it slow this time."

"Oh. Okay. Sure. Really?"

His sincere frown bloomed slowly into a smile. "No, not really."

She made a little noise of relief, and then he kissed her. She'd forgotten his taste in the past few months, but she remembered it now. Every nerve in her body woke up and asked for more. But for once, she showed a little restraint. Isabelle pulled back and looked up into his eyes.

"If you stay," she said, "it only means there's a chance. I might not be able to do it. Trust...that's not easy for me."

"I know. I'm relieved that you'd even consider it. And I have my own issues. I have trouble letting things be. I want to *fix* them. And you don't need fixing, Isabelle."

She smiled at him. "That's a generous assessment. But I'll take it."

"So I can stay? Just tonight? Just to see?"

In answer, she took his hand and led him toward her bedroom. She'd bought a new comforter and pillows, trying to turn it into a new bed, a bed he hadn't been in, but now he'd be in this one, too. And maybe he'd stay.

CHAPTER TWENTY-TWO

FOR ONCE, ISABELLE ignored the dessert that sat in front of her. She was a big fan of Jill's chocolate torte, but what was making her happy tonight wasn't the food; it was the company.

Lauren sat with her boyfriend, Jake, the very hot fire captain who was a little too good-natured to be hanging around this group. And Jill had set her hand on Mary's arm as she leaned toward her in laughter. The two women hadn't declared themselves a couple yet, but they sure looked comfortable together.

And there was Tom, of course, his hand on Isabelle's knee under the table. She was very aware every time he moved, his fingers sliding over her skin. Two months into their new start, and her breath still caught every time he touched her. She wanted him more now than ever. A frightening thought.

His thumb brushed against her thigh. "Are you okay?" he asked, leaning closer. "You're not eating your cake."

She smiled at him and picked up her fork. "I guess I'm full of wine." And sticky, scary love.

This was his third trip back to Jackson, and she'd gone to see him once for a long weekend that had somehow turned into five days. Next time she was having dinner at his sister's, though he'd warned her that his sister was an even worse cook than he was. Thank God for Jill, or they'd starve to death out here in the forest.

It was starting to feel like a real relationship. A normal relationship with a future instead of a looming end date. Still, when she looked at his hand on her leg, she wanted to paint the image a hundred times so she could remember it when he was gone.

Lauren pushed back from the table. "We'd better get going. Jake is on duty at six tomorrow."

"I'm fine," he said. "It's only 9:30."

"Well, I wasn't planning on getting dropped off with a kiss at the front door, so we need a couple hours of padding."

Jake shook his head as if he were exasperated, but there was no missing the smile on his face when he ducked his head. "Let's go, then."

While they were thanking Jill for dinner and exchanging hugs and handshakes, Isabelle tipped her head toward the door. She was ready to go, too, and Jill and Mary probably wouldn't hate some time alone.

Tom and Mary had both arrived in town only three hours before, setting up for another federal case. This one was low-key. More of a precaution; and it was only the two of them in town.

One more bite of cake and several hugs later, Isabelle and Tom were out the door and walking into the summer twilight. They walked slowly, fingers twined together, and Isabelle assumed that Tom was enjoying the cool midnight blue that settled over them just as much as she was, but when he cleared his throat, she realized his arm was tense.

"I was thinking…" he said. That was it.

Isabelle's heart dropped. She knew what was coming. He was going to go. Of course he was. They'd given it a shot, and she wasn't good at this. She nodded, pretending to agree.

"I hit retirement in a year," Tom finally said. "It's a ways off, but I was thinking that things are going pretty well."

"At work?" she asked.

"No. With us."

Her feet stopped moving for a moment, but she forced them quickly on, hoping he hadn't noticed. But he'd definitely noticed that she hadn't said a word. He glanced at her, trying to study her face, but she kept it blank.

"You've stopped giving me an out," he said.

"What do you mean?"

"You used to tell me I didn't have to stay. After sex, you'd tell me I could leave if I wanted. Or you'd tell me I don't have to stay at your place when I visit. Or that you could get a hotel room when you're in Cheyenne. You finally stopped doing that. In Cheyenne, you asked if you could stay longer."

"Oh. Was that…? Should I not have?"

"Isabelle." He stopped and turned toward her, his hand sneaking into her hair, his mouth brushing a soft kiss over hers before he pulled away. "You're so confident about everything. It kills me that you're waiting for me to leave."

Tears suddenly burned her eyes, her nose, her throat. She shook her head, trying to deny them.

"Do you want me to leave?" he asked softly.

She could barely speak. "No," she managed to whisper, terrified as she said it. If he wanted to go, she wouldn't stop him. You couldn't stop a person from leaving.

"Good. Because I love you, and I'm going to stay, and if you didn't want that, it would break me."

One tear escaped her control and slipped down her face to his thumb, but she swallowed the rest of her tears.

When she was sure she wouldn't sob, she took a deep breath. "I love you, too. I want you to stay. With me."

Everything inside her twisted up with terror that she'd said such a thing. But Tom just pressed another kiss to her mouth and smiled. He took her hand and they walked again as if she hadn't just given voice to her most terrible hope.

"I hope you don't regret saying that," he said.

She did. She regretted it, but only because it was true.

Tom cleared his throat again. "Because I was thinking that I could retire in a year and move here. I can check into work at the sheriff's department or maybe even the park service. They need a lot more law enforcement than you'd think."

"Here?" she asked. "So we'd live together?"

"I'd get my own place. You've got your work. You need space."

She did, but... It was easy with him around. Surprisingly easy. Sweet in a way she hadn't expected. In a year...anything might be possible. But she couldn't say that to him, could she? What if he didn't want to move in? What if he was hoping she wouldn't ask?

She looked at him, his face beautiful in the falling light, his eyes tight with worry when he glanced at her. What if she could just say what she wanted?

"It's just an idea," he said. "We've got a whole year to think about it." He was giving her an out. He knew she'd been mapping out escape routes for fourteen years.

She didn't want to escape from Tom. "I own quite a few acres, you know. I've always liked the idea of building a little studio."

He frowned as if he didn't understand.

"I could have my own space to paint. To be alone. But I'd only be a few feet away from the house."

"Oh."

They turned up her driveway, still strolling as if her heart hadn't gone wild with panic.

"Bear might not approve," Tom said, his tone still careful, but he was smiling now.

The panic slowly filtered from her blood, replaced with a relief that made her muscles ache. "He'll have a year to get used to the idea," she said.

"So will you."

She wasn't sure she needed a year. In fact, that seemed like an awfully long time. "I miss you when you're gone," she admitted.

"Yeah? I'm pretty lovesick when you're not around, Isabelle."

The twilight had erased the years from his face, and his smile was full of boyish chagrin. She could see what he must have looked like twenty years before. That sticky, scary love was a warm mess inside her.

"Come on," she said, tugging him up the porch steps. "I have something that might make that better."

"Oh?" The hopeful rise of his eyebrows made her laugh.

"It's not a blow job. Not yet, anyway. Just come on."

He didn't balk when she led him toward her studio, which was good progress. He'd told her more about his brother's death, about finding his body and being terrified but still unwilling to leave him alone. She warned him now when she was starting a new commission. He only needed the heads-up and he was fine, but she'd covered up her newest work, just in case.

She turned on the lights and led him to the far side of the room. "Here," she said, picking up a canvas that she'd leaned against the wall. "I want you to have it. She can keep you company for the next year."

He took her old self-portrait from her, his eyes looking over the nude lines of her body in a way that made her smile. "I can't take this, Isabelle. You said you wanted it for when you're eighty."

"I have a new one," she said, gesturing toward the very last easel.

Tom glanced up and froze. Then his head tilted a little to the side. She looked at the painting, too, wondering if he liked it. She hadn't shown his face, just the edge of his jaw angled to kiss her neck.

She was posed the same in this painting as she had been in the old one, but now Tom was pressed to her back, the straighter line of his naked hip visible just past her curves, and his beautiful arm around her, one hand splayed just below her breast.

She'd worked for days on his hand and arm, making sure to get the muscles beneath his skin just right, along with every freckle and scar and glint of hair. She loved his hands. She loved them on her.

"I hope you don't mind," she said softly. "You didn't volunteer as a model."

"Mind?" He stepped closer, reaching out a hand, but then he dropped it as if he were afraid the paint was still wet. "It's amazing."

She smiled. "You like it."

"I love it," he said. "It's the greatest thing I've ever seen."

"Really?"

He shot her an incredulous look. "Are you kidding me? I'm in a sexy nude painting. With *you*."

She laughed as he pulled her into a hug. She laughed because anything seemed possible now, here, with him.

"Are you sure I can't take the new one home?" he asked. "Not that I don't love the first one."

"No. If you want to see your hands on me, you have to come visit. That's the deal."

"It's a good deal," he murmured before he kissed her. This time his mouth lingered, tasting her for a little longer. "Thank you for trusting me with your painting."

"It's no big deal." She smiled, trying to keep it light, but when his eyes grew serious, she looked away. His touch brought her face back to him.

"Thank you for trusting me."

She took a deep breath. She wanted to say it was no big deal again. But it *was* a big deal. And he deserved more than a lie. "I love you," she whispered. "Now come to bed and put your hands on me. And stay as long as you can. Please?"

He answered with his hands and mouth and heart. And Isabelle trusted all of them.

* * * * *

FANNING *THE* FLAMES

CHAPTER ONE

FIREFIGHTERS. THE BANE of her existence.

Shaded beneath the fading awning of the Jackson Town Library, Lauren Foster watched as Fire Captain Jake Davis jogged along the other side of the street, his eyes straight ahead, brow furrowed against the bright sun. It was one of the hottest days of August so far, so he'd shucked his shirt and wore only black shorts, the Jackson Fire Department logo bunching at his hip with every stride. His shoulders and chest were tanned from months of summer running.

The noise from the firefighters annoyed her every day, but the most torturous thing about the library being attached to the fire station was this: being exposed to Jake Davis's beautiful body.

He crossed the street and moved closer, and Lauren watched a trickle of sweat slip down his skin to tangle in the salt-and-pepper hair in the middle of his chest.

God, she loved a hairy male chest. If she wanted to feel soft and smooth, she had free dibs on her own chest. No one else was using it.

Sighing, she frowned at Jake's wide, taut shoulders as he approached the building. He looked up then, of course. She imagined the picture she must make: the spinster town librarian sitting primly on a bench with a book, frowning her disapproval over a man's sweaty public nudity.

Lauren looked back to the book in her hands and frowned harder. No, she couldn't even claim the cliché of spinster. She was just an empty-nester divorcée, counting down the years to menopause. She was in the single digits now and could feel the hot flashes looming over her, strobing in the distance like approaching lightning. Every time she went to that cute little boutique in town, she was more and more attracted to the wildly painted reading glasses with the beaded chains that let them hang around your neck.

And she didn't even need reading glasses. Yet.

But a pair of new shades might do her good. Then she could truly enjoy the sight of Jake's glistening chest as he jogged toward the fire station. Sharing the building made for a nice summer view during her lunch hour, but it was bittersweet, looking at what she could never have.

Lauren didn't realize he was moving straight toward her and not the door of the fire station until he stopped right in front of her. She sat up straighter.

"Lauren," he said in that familiar gravelly voice. "You wanted to see me?"

She blinked in confusion before remembering that she'd sent him an email. "Oh. Yes, but…" *But not half-naked,* she wanted to say. As she hesitated, another little rivulet of sweat trickled down his neck and made its eager way toward his chest hair. "Uh." Jesus. Lauren gave herself a mental shake. "Your guys are playing music again."

His brow tightened with momentary irritation. "Loudly?" he asked.

His irritation fueled her own and helped her get over his glistening chest. "Yes. Loudly enough that I can hear the lyrics in the library."

"They're working out. Give 'em a break. They only—"

"Earbuds. Check into them."

Another twitch of his brow. Lauren stared him down.

"It's a library, Jake. Come on. Our whole shtick is silent contemplation. When your sirens aren't blaring, we need it to be quiet. Plus, your guys have terrible taste in music."

His face finally relaxed into something that was almost a smile. "All right. I'll give you that. Their music sucks."

"Just remind them of the library's hours, okay? They can blast music as loud as they want after closing."

He ran a hand through his short hair, and another drop of sweat slipped down his neck. This time it curved over his shoulder and disappeared down his back. "They've got earbuds, but listening to music together is bonding. It's good for team cohesion."

Lauren took a deep breath and closed her eyes for a moment, hating the stereotype she was becoming. "Do you really think I want to be the uptight middle-aged librarian asking the young guys next door to turn down that terrible rap music?"

When she opened her eyes, she thought she saw his gaze rise, as if he'd been looking at her body, but maybe that was just her own wishful thinking.

"What?" he asked.

Lauren sighed and stood. "Take pity on me and don't make me ask again, okay? I don't enjoy being the nagging house mother."

He was frowning again, but he at least offered an unenthusiastic "Sure," as she turned to open the library door.

"Thank you, Jake."

His hand appeared above hers to pull the door open, and there was no mistaking the scent of his clean sweat as the air moved around both of them. It hit her hard, drawing something tight deep in her belly, and Lauren considered it a triumph that she didn't turn and lick him before moving inside. He smelled the way a man should smell when he was in your bed and working hard for it.

The door finally whooshed shut behind her, and she breathed a sigh of relief that all she could smell now were paper and Windex.

Her thirties had been a fairly dry decade, what with her failing marriage and then her divorce. But her forties? God. Her body clearly wanted her to get busy humping any man who caught her eye before all her eggs dried up. What her body didn't seem to understand was that there were plenty of healthy-egged young twentysomethings who were attracted to men like Jake Davis, too. She couldn't compete with them. But honestly, she wouldn't mind a few hopeless tries.

Why had it taken her four decades to realize how beautiful the male body was? And how very much she wanted more of it? She'd never *once* thought about tasting a sweaty male chest in her twenties. Now she wanted to lick Jake Davis clean.

Sneering at her own absurd thoughts, she headed for the privacy of the tiny office to the side of the circulation desk. "I talked to Jake," she said, collapsing into the chair next to her best friend Sophie.

Sophie looked up from her computer. "Oh, you talked to Jake, huh?"

"He said he'd have a word with the guys."

"Yeah? Did he also say, 'Oh, Lauren, it's so hot I can't wear a shirt when I run. I hope that's okay with you'?"

Lauren's face felt as if it burst into flames. "What?"

"I saw him when I was driving back from lunch. That is one hot fire captain."

"I didn't notice!" Lauren hissed, ducking her head and opening her own laptop.

"Liar! Oh, my God, you're beet red."

"Shut up. I mean it. Having those stupid firefighters right next door is a damn work hazard."

Sophie shrugged. "They have their uses."

Lauren tried to shove her curiosity down and keep her mouth shut. She and Sophie had been friends for two years, but despite their frequent joking, Sophie rarely divulged concrete details about her own love life.

This time Lauren was going to nail her down. "Exactly how many firefighters have you used?" Sophie was the picture of modesty, always wearing knee-length skirts and button-up shirts with her sensible heels. But she wasn't as innocent as she looked. Once you got a drink in her, she could dish about blow-job techniques with the best of them.

Sophie shot her a wicked grin, but she didn't answer.

Lauren crossed her arms and refused to let the girl off the hook this time. "Spill it, chick. How many firefighters?"

"Only one."

"Jake?" Lauren asked, a stone dropping into her stomach from thin air. She didn't want to picture him with her cute friend. She couldn't deal with that.

But Sophie laughed. "No, not Jake! A guy who doesn't work there anymore, thank God. The fire station is a little too close to home for me. In a town this size..."

Lauren nodded in understanding and tried not to let out the sigh of relief pushing at her throat. It hadn't been Jake.

Sophie poked her arm. "But you need to ask him out."

"Who?" Lauren asked, her heart already speeding up to belie the question.

"Jake."

"You just said it was too close to home. And it is! If he said no, I'd have to see him every day. And if he said yes, even worse."

"Lauren, ask him out. Good God, you two have been pretending not to eye each other for at least a year."

On her part, it'd been more like two or three, but his wife had died only four years before, so he'd probably still been grieving then. Which made her a terrible person. Even more terrible than the fact that Jake and her ex-husband were good friends. "You know why I can't."

"Oh, my God, your divorce was eight years ago! As long as you don't have sex with Jake on your ex's dining room table during Christmas dinner, I think you're ethically okay."

Lauren just shrugged, but she knew it wasn't okay. That was probably why Jake had never asked her out. That or the fact that even forty-six-year-old men didn't typically date forty-three-year-old women. Stupid youth culture.

"Fine," Sophie said. She glanced over her shoulder and spoke in a lower voice. "Then just take one of the younger guys home for a discreet evening of fun. Firefighters love adventure, you know. They're risk-takers. And they stay in such good shape. Close to home is a bad idea, but there's a reason I couldn't resist. Have a little fun, Lauren."

"I'm too old for that."

"Please," Sophie snorted, then ran a careful hand along the chignon she so often pulled her pretty red hair into. "Thanks to all the talk about cougars, those guys are totally into older women. They've heard you fortysomethings are insatiable."

"We are," Lauren grumbled, but she couldn't help but smile as Sophie broke into peals of laughter. "Shut up."

"All right. But let's do a girls' night out tomorrow. Mountain-bike season is almost over. Maybe you need a quick and dirty hookup with a tourist you'll never see again. If you don't do it now, you'll have to wait for ski season."

"Maybe *you* need a quick and dirty hookup, if you think it's such a good idea!"

"It's more complicated for me. You know."

Lauren did know. Sophie's family had a history in this town, so she was extra careful about her reputation.

"Anyway," Sophie went on, "maybe I will, too. Maybe we'll pick up a whole group of guys and split the difference."

Lauren grinned at her. Sophie was awfully fun to work with, and Lauren was thankful they'd gotten so close. It had been a long time since she'd had a friend as close as Sophie, and now Isabelle, too, the one who'd come up with girls' night out six months before. "We already canceled girls' night because Isabelle isn't done with her commission."

"Isabelle won't care if we go without her. She doesn't care about anything when she's finishing up a painting. Let's go. Just us."

Lauren hesitated for one more moment before giving in. "Okay. Fine. Tomorrow."

Sophie jumped up with a squeal. "Yes! After work. Dinner and then fun. Wear a cougar dress."

"I don't even know what that means!"

Sophie shrugged. "Something that says you're putting out."

"But I'm not putting out," Lauren croaked.

"You never know." Sophie exited the room with a wink.

Lauren swallowed hard. She considered chasing Sophie down to say she'd changed her mind. She wasn't putting out. She didn't even feel fun anymore.

But she had been once. She'd been fun and sexy and childless long ago. It felt as if that had been another person's life, but now that Sawyer had left to drive across the country for college, she was childless again. And single.

Even if she wasn't young anymore, she was hornier than she'd ever been. That had to count for something. Maybe it was time to find out exactly how much she could make it count.

"ANNABELLE!" JAKE CALLED. "I'm on my way out."

His daughter popped out of the bathroom and flashed her endearingly wide smile as she waved a curling iron. "Whatever happened to twenty-four on, twenty-four off? You worked yesterday."

"I'm captain now. That's what happened."

She set the curling iron down and hurried toward him, her blond curls bouncing. He was struck, as always, by how beautiful she was. It still amazed him, even after twenty-four years. "I'm worried about you, Dad."

He scowled. Hard. This again? "I'm great." It was nice having his daughter back in the house, but she wouldn't stop with this.

"You need to have some fun."

"I do have fun. I run. I bike. I help you plan the wedding."

"You don't plan. You sit there, pretending to listen and grunting halfhearted agreements when I force you to weigh in on decorations."

He scrubbed a hand over his hair. "I like helping. I just don't have much to offer. If your mother were here…"

"Well, she's not here, and you need to start dating."

Jake managed to hide his wince. "I've dated. Not that it's any of your business."

"Have you gotten back in the saddle? Like, really in the saddle?"

"Jesus, Annabelle!" Jake grabbed his keys and backed toward the door, heat climbing up the back of his neck. "You don't need to know that. Just like I don't need to know what you and Kevin do. I assume you're waiting for the honeymoon—"

"Dad!" she laughed.

"And that you're also really careful with birth control."

Annabelle rested a hip against the counter and cocked her head. "While waiting for the honeymoon?"

"Exactly." Jake pointed at her as he backed out onto the front porch. "Condoms. Pills. Celibacy. All of it."

Her laughter followed him out to his truck. She was home for only another three months, and then she'd get married and be gone again. Overprotective as he was, Jake really liked his future son-in-law, which was a damn good thing since he worked with the guy.

Kevin Chen was as outgoing and adventurous as most young firefighters were. Jake could see why Annabelle liked him. But the reason Jake liked him was that Kevin was also deeply caring and kind. The other guys looked up to him already, even though Kevin was only twenty-seven.

Kevin had been working in Casper when he'd met Annabelle, but he'd happily agreed to move to Jackson so Annabelle could come back home. The good skiing in Jackson hadn't hurt Kevin's decision, either, according to him, but Jake suspected it was more because he was crazy about Annabelle. Even an old dog like Jake could see that they were perfect for each other.

He still gave them a hard time, though. He'd told Annabelle all her life never to date a cop or a firefighter. In retrospect, he should've kept his mouth shut so she wouldn't get any ideas.

Now she was the one giving dating advice. Jake shook his head as he pulled into the parking lot behind the station. He'd tried dating. He hadn't been able to avoid it. The whole world seemed to have a hard-on over the idea of a widower dating again. And it wasn't that he wasn't ready. His wife had died four years ago. But it all just felt…weird. He'd met his wife in college, when you wandered through parties until you ran into a woman who made your heart beat faster. This "meeting over coffee" crap was just awkward.

He'd progressed to dinner and drinks with a few of them, and he'd even gotten back in the saddle, not that he'd ever tell Annabelle that. But Jesus. What had happened to just noticing someone across the room? Feeling that surge of awareness when a pretty woman walked your way? It was all online dating and finding a computer-generated match these days.

Sometimes a guy just wanted to notice the swing of a woman's hips as she walked past his truck and headed toward the library, her ass perfectly hugged by a tight black dress that ended a few inches above her knee and—

Jake blinked and frowned toward the woman reaching for the back door of the library. His eyes rose from her nicely rounded hips to the pretty curve of her waist to the dark hair streaming straight down her back. Was that…?

"Lauren," he murmured.

Of course. Speaking of women to be noticed. He'd been noticing her for so long that he hardly registered it anymore. Lauren, whose blue eyes always met his straight-on. Who never backed down from anything. Who'd been married to one of his oldest friends.

He admired her, or that was what he'd been telling himself, but that was an easier lie when she was wearing khakis and a modest sweater and reading a book to a gang of kids.

But today she was a woman with hips. And an ass. And shiny hair that tempted a man's hands.

Jake cursed and reached to turn off his truck before realizing the engine was already silent. After making sure he'd put the damn thing in Park, he headed inside, telling himself that Lauren Foster's ass was none of his business and never would be.

CHAPTER TWO

LAUREN SHOULD'VE WORN a regular work outfit and changed at the end of her shift. Sophie had been making flirtatious comments all day, and now Lauren felt supremely self-conscious as she hid behind the closed office door and slipped off her flats to replace them with heels. But when she'd gotten out the black dress this morning, she hadn't been able to force herself into something more frumpy.

She'd bought the dress during a rare trip to Salt Lake City, telling herself that everyone needed a simple little black dress. But that had been a year ago and she hadn't gotten the chance to wear it until today.

She smoothed her hand over the skirt. It was tight enough to take off a few pounds, the material was thick enough to hide some flaws, and she loved the way it made her feel perfectly curvy.

Once the black heels were on, Lauren untied the royal-blue silk scarf she'd worn around her neck to hide her cleavage. Then she brushed her hair, powdered her nose and slid on deep pink lipstick. The sight of that new berry shade reminded her instantly of the cougars Sophie had spoken of. Lauren looked like a woman on the prowl.

Maybe that was just what she needed. One night in bed with a hot young stud who'd be thrilled to let her take the edge off these new needs. She'd use him, he'd use her and they'd both leave spent and happy.

A sharp shock of lust pulsed through her at the thought of a man above her, his shoulders slick with exertion, her nails digging into his skin as he filled her over and over.

God. She needed that. It had been more than a year, and longer than that since anyone had really made it worth her while.

Someone knocked on the door. "Ready?" Sophie called.

Lauren stood, grabbed her purse and opened the door. "I'm ready," she said and meant it.

Sophie's eyes widened. "You look perfect."

No, not perfect. She wasn't as thin and young as Sophie. And there was no competing with that pretty red hair and tiny waist. Sophie adjusted her scarlet lipstick and pulled the pin from her hair twist. "Let's go."

Lauren tried not to grin, but she couldn't help the extra swing in her step as she followed Sophie to the back door. By the time they walked outside, she was laughing for no other reason than it seemed funny to wear such high heels when the sun was still up.

She startled a little when she realized the boys from the fire station were playing basketball. But she watched idly as she nudged the door closed behind her. She'd noticed that a lot of them shaved their chests out of some misplaced vanity, wanting to show off their twenty-something muscles. Idiots. Jake's hairy chest was much hotter.

That guilty thought killed her smile entirely when she saw that Jake was leaning against the wall of the station, watching his men play. Or she assumed he had been watching them. Now his eyes were locked right on her.

"Hi," she said, the syllable half strangled by her shock.

"Lauren." His gaze slipped to Sophie and then back. "You ladies hitting the town?"

She nodded, but her throat somehow produced only a nervous laugh. Her hand rose of its own accord to cover the unusual amount of cleavage she was showing, but instead of shielding it, she only drew Jake's attention. His very brief attention. After a quick look, he blinked and his eyes locked with hers again.

"The Crooked R," Sophie volunteered. "In case you're out later."

Lauren felt her eyes go wide. Why the hell had Sophie told him that?

But Jake seemed unfazed. And uninterested. "I'm sure I'll be tucked into bed by then. It's been a long week."

"That grass fire," Lauren blurted out.

"Yeah, we put in some extra hours on that."

"Right," Lauren said. "Good."

His eyebrow rose and Lauren frowned.

"I mean, I'm glad you were there. As a firefighter. Not that I want you in danger. Just…thank you."

"You're welcome." His gaze slipped away, but not before dipping lower along her body again. Lauren glanced down and realized her modest hand had now morphed into the equivalent of a flashing neon sign. Her fingertips rested temptingly against the rise of her own breast, the perfect example of a woman trying to display her wares.

Dropping her hand, she spun toward Sophie and called, "Have a nice evening!" as she rushed away.

There was no mistaking Sophie's giggle of amusement behind her. "Lauren, my car is the other way."

"Dammit," she muttered, turning on her heel to head to the other side of the parking lot. She wasn't going to look back—she was never going to look at Jake again—so she could only hope that Sophie was following.

Lauren lunged for the car door as soon as it beeped. But when Sophie got into the driver's seat, her laughter made clear that they weren't off the subject yet. "That was totally smooth."

"Shut up. My breasts are halfway out."

"Yet somehow that didn't bother you until it was Jake looking at them."

Oh, God. Sophie was right. So horribly right. Lauren's skin was hot with awareness, not because she was showing cleavage, but because she'd shown it to Jake. The most pitiful part was that men would look at any cleavage, at any time, given any opportunity. So he'd only done what any man would do, and yet she was sadly aroused.

"I think he's got a crush on you," Sophie said as they pulled out of the parking lot. The words sent a jolt through Lauren's nerves and her pulse sped, but laughter jumped from her throat.

"Jake Davis? With a crush? That's the most ridiculous thing I've ever heard. He's so…"

"Yes, he has that strong, silent thing going, but he could barely tear his eyes away to acknowledge me."

Lauren glanced at Sophie's button-down blouse. It was sexy in an understated way, like everything Sophie wore. White and fitted and modest. She showed only the tiniest hint of cleavage. "He's a man, Sophie. Yours are covered. Mine aren't."

"Is it really so hard for you to believe a hot guy wants you?"

Lauren shook her head, not wanting to answer. It was more complicated than that with Jake. Yes, she'd been divorced for a long time, and both she and Steve had very much moved on. But Jake had known Steve longer than Lauren had. They'd gone to junior high together and been teammates on the high school wrestling team. Jake had come to Lauren's wedding. And Lauren had gone to his. But maybe it wasn't awkward loyalty to Steve making her hesitate. Maybe it was the memory of sweet Ruth.

Ruth had been the kind of wife and mother who'd always made Lauren feel inferior. She'd been sweet and patient and always smiling. She'd probably never cursed in her life. Or gotten drunk. Or considered going to a bar and picking up a younger man for a meaningless lay.

Yeah. Lauren could never live up to a woman like Ruth. And she couldn't live up to the cute young things Jake had likely dated in the past year or two.

That was the most pitiful thing of all. She'd always thought she'd had self-confidence, but at forty-three, she no longer relished the idea of getting naked in front of a new man.

Frustration tightened her next breath into a sigh. She was all about positive body image. She thought women of all sizes should be proud of their bodies and their sexuality and the years they'd put in on earth. But somehow it was just too personal when it came to her own naked body. She'd perfected the art of self-induced orgasm long ago, so why rock the boat?

Then again, boat-rocking could be fun. Lauren made herself relax as Sophie drove toward the restaurant they'd chosen for dinner.

"How's your family?" Lauren asked, hoping to keep the subject off her sex life for a while. "Has your brother gotten a job yet?"

Sophie groaned. "My brother will never get a job. He's a twenty-six-year-old man-child who helps around the ranch as little as possible and still lets me do his laundry."

"Then I'm glad you moved into town. You shouldn't be the family maid."

"It's only temporary," Sophie said immediately. "My dad still needs my help. When my great-uncle realizes he's not coming home from assisted living, he'll sell his house and I'll move back to the ranch."

"Sophie…" Lauren started, but Sophie's eyes flashed a warning. They'd had this discussion many times. "Fine," Lauren said. "But someday I'm going to write into *Dear Veronica* about you. Maybe you'll listen to her advice." The new advice column was their favorite part of the local paper, and everyone else's, judging by the way that section got crumpled and creased in the library's reading area.

"I don't need advice," Sophie countered. "You do."

"Oh, really?"

Sophie grinned. "My family might be crazy, but my sex life is just fine, thanks."

"How am I supposed to buy that when you never discuss it?"

"You'll just have to believe me," Sophie said, before chirping "We're here," as she pulled into a parking space and cut the engine. "Now, let's go find so much fun that you'll be writing into *Dear Veronica* for advice about how to juggle your many admirers."

That was so ridiculous that Lauren let out a belly laugh as she followed Sophie into the restaurant. The only thing she'd likely be juggling was her collection of vibrators, but Sophie was sweet to be so hopeful.

"So you'll be tucked into bed?" someone said from behind him.

Jake glanced over his shoulder and spotted his future son-in-law watching with a crooked grin. "What?"

"You told them you'd be tucked into bed tonight. Instead of, for example, going to meet two beautiful librarians at the bar they purposefully told you about."

Jake grunted and crossed his arms, turning back to watch the pickup game.

"Seriously, Pops, you should go to the Crooked R. No doubt."

"Why?"

"Why?" Kevin repeated, his voice rising a little. "Are you kidding?"

"No, I'm not kidding. Even if I wanted to go, which I don't, either they really didn't mean the invitation, or...you're basically saying that a man would be a fool not to jump at the chance to sleep with such a beautiful woman."

"Sure."

"So if any woman asks, a man should just jump on it?" Now he turned back to Kevin, who'd lost his smile.

"I mean... No. Only if he's single."

"So when you were single, you'd never pass up an opportunity like that, no matter how bad an idea it was?" Jake could see the "Oh, shit!" warning flashing brightly behind Kevin's eyes now. Good.

"No. No! That's not what I meant. I just meant that two pretty women who are both respectable and completely datable invited you out for a drink and I think you should join them because you've been single for a while, and Annabelle and I think..." He paused to draw a breath, but then seemed to run out of thoughts.

"It's none of your business. I told Annabelle the same."

"All right," Kevin responded with a shrug. When he exhaled, he deflated a little. "But you still need to work on your game."

"I don't have a game."

"No, you definitely do not."

Jake sighed. "Anyway, as I said, I'm gonna go tuck myself into bed."

"Watch a little *Matlock*?" Kevin countered, apparently recovered from his close call with his future father-in-law. "You're only forty-six, you know. Prime of your life."

Jake threw an affectionate punch at Kevin's shoulder. Affectionate enough that the younger man stumbled back two steps. "Remember that."

The truth was he was heading home to go for a long run, but he probably would be in bed before Lauren and Sophie made it home.

Prime or not, he couldn't quite handle four days on anymore. Not without collapsing at 9:00 p.m., anyway. But even if he'd been fully rested and dying for a beer, he wouldn't have headed to the Crooked R tonight.

First of all, Lauren hadn't been the one to ask; Sophie had. And Lauren had looked horrified at the suggestion. But better horrified than excited, because if she'd smiled at him, if she'd raised her hand from her breasts to his shoulder and teased him about going to bed early… Jesus. He probably would've met them there. And then what?

Jake pulled his keys from his pocket and headed for his truck. When he slipped on his sunglasses, he felt a little safer. He wished he'd been wearing them earlier. He'd never seen Lauren dressed like that. Her tight black dress cut lower than he'd expected, showing off the pale skin of her full breasts. Her mouth looking plumper than ever and glossy pink.

He'd noticed her mouth before, of course. How could he not? And her bold blue eyes and strong nose. And he'd definitely noticed her breasts. But now that she wanted them noticed... Hell, he was a lost cause. And she was still his friend's wife.

"Ex-wife," he said aloud.

They'd all known each other. Not that they'd had dinner every week or gone on vacations together, but they'd socialized once or twice a year, and the fact that they'd known each other as couples... The idea of dating Lauren just felt wrong. As if that would mean they'd been doing something wrong the whole time.

Better to just let it go.

Five minutes into explaining to his brain that her breasts weren't really as enticing as they looked, Jake heard a squawk from his radio. A vehicle fire near the airport. Sounded pretty harmless and the guys at the station were closer than he was. Despite his hope for a distraction tonight, Jake drove on. He'd let the guys handle this one.

But as he was pulling into his driveway a few minutes later, an update came over the radio clarifying that the vehicle on fire wasn't a car. It was a fuel tanker. Jake turned around, hit the lights and headed back toward town. There was steady traffic, but nothing like the weekend, so he made pretty good time until he got to town, and then he skirted around the town square and back out onto the highway.

Black smoke rose in the distance, and he saw the flash of the engine's lights before he got anywhere near the actual fire.

Their second company engine roared up from behind, and Jake let them pass with a wave. The guys with the gear needed to get there more than Jake did, but his hands itched with the need to be in the thick of things. He didn't have to wait long. Slipping his car behind the engine, he trailed it for the last mile as cars parted to let it through. They were always slightly more eager to get out of the way for a shiny red twenty-ton truck than his pickup.

As soon as they stopped, he knew he'd done the right thing in coming. He jumped out and raced toward his lieutenant, noting which men were on the hose and which were scrambling to extract the passenger from the overturned truck. Highway patrol worked to get the closest cars turned around and out of danger, though there was no help for the car whose hood was crushed beneath the back end of the tanker. But for a hundred yards on either side of the truck, the road was cleared of everyone except fire personnel.

"Car driver and passenger are out," his lieutenant said quickly. Jake noted the open ambulance doors and the stunned face of the woman inside it. "A little banged up, but nothing bad so far. The driver of the truck is out and fine, but his passenger is wedged inside and unresponsive."

"Foam truck?"

"En route."

Jake's eyes flew over the scene again, noting the gas leaking onto the roadway, the flames dancing off it, the hose keeping water between the flames and the body of the tanker and, most important, his men working inside the cab of the truck, trying to stabilize the passenger before pulling her out through the broken windshield.

He registered that the firefighter deepest inside the truck was Kevin. And in that moment, Jake saw the fuel that sneaked past the column of directed water and started working its way toward the cab. Flames licked over it, as if it were crouching low and stalking its prey.

"Get her out!" Jake shouted, as he broke from the

huddle and rushed toward the cab. "Everyone clear *now.*"

Kevin glanced up, met Jake's eyes and gave a quick nod, before abandoning his efforts to stabilize her and easing her free of the wreckage. If there weren't the threat of an explosion, the woman would have been carefully loaded onto a spine board. But when faced with roasting alive, they'd have to risk loss of limb or paralysis. The cervical collar Kevin had already put in place would have to do.

The rescue efforts sped up now as the men outside wedged a spreader between the pavement and the overturned truck's door. As Jake nearly dived through the open windshield to help, he saw the reason for the holdup. Her leg was pinned under debris.

"Hurry," Jake said simply, and Kevin nodded before throwing all his weight against a crowbar.

Jake pulled back out to eye that rogue stream of fuel. "McCurdy!" he called to the closest guy working the hose, then pointed. McCurdy set his mouth and cut the spray for a moment before aiming it closer to the truck. Jake knew the calculations going through the man's head. He didn't want to wet the cab yet, not while they were trying to free someone. And he didn't want to push the fuel closer to the truck.

Jake ducked back in to see the progress inside. The spreader was working, creating a space, but the woman's twisted leg was caught just below the knee.

"Almost there," Kevin said calmly.

"Kev. We're in trouble."

"Then you should back up. I've got this."

"Captain!" McCurdy shouted from outside.

"We're about to get wet," Jake said. "She might have to lose the leg."

Kevin shook his head. "Not yet, Pops." The calm in his voice told Jake that helping him get the woman out was the only option at this point, so Jake just cursed and eased closer.

"Come on, then, dammit." The smell of fuel filled the cab as he grabbed the crowbar and heaved, while Kevin worked on the woman's leg.

"Cap!" McCurdy shouted, then, "Heads up!" Water suddenly pounded the back of the cab, the sound exploding around them as spray began to rain down.

"You about ready now, Kevin?" Jake shouted over the noise.

"Just about."

Jake gave one last shove on the bar, and then Kevin said, "There," and started easing the woman's knee up. Her foot caught again.

Despite the storm of water raining over them, gas fumes stung his nose and Jake said, "Force it," just as a whoosh rolled over the back of the truck. Heat touched his calf as he and Kevin got their hands under the woman's arms and pushed her out the windshield. Other hands grabbed her as Kevin tried to ease her foot from the mangled metal, but it still caught sickeningly as they forced her free. Blood pumped from her ankle as Jake grabbed the stiff arm of Kevin's coat and hauled him toward the windshield, as well. "Go, dammit!"

"Yeah, yeah." As soon as the woman was pulled free, Kevin vaulted out, then reached back and half dragged Jake out, too. The stench of melting upholstery swelled around them until they got to their feet and hauled ass for the waiting line of emergency vehicles. The woman was already on a stretcher and being slipped into an ambulance. More hoses moved in.

"You're smoking, Pops."

"No shit," Jake said, reaching down to brush at the thick canvas of his work pants.

"You okay?"

"I'm fine."

Kevin ignored that and called a paramedic over before shoving Jake down onto the bumper of a truck. "I'm fine," Jake said again, but he gave in and rolled up the cuff of his pants before one of those bastards got itchy and cut it off. "Nothing big."

And it wasn't. A second-degree burn covering a few inches of leg. "Shit," he said, pretending it was only disappointment that his pants were charred and not a bark of pain as the paramedic cleaned the burn.

"You should be more careful," Kevin said. "I don't have a scratch."

"Jesus." Jake had to bite back a laugh. He should probably discipline Kevin. Cite him for disobeying orders, but damn if that wasn't what this job was about sometimes. And it was Jake's own fault for jumping into a flaming truck with zero protective gear. He was the one who deserved to be written up.

While the paramedic wrapped his leg, Jake watched as his men kept the flames down and waited for foam.

He let his head fall back against the truck and sighed. He'd have to get his affection for Kevin under control. Kevin had the right to do his job the same way any of the other firefighters did. Jake would have to review his own reactions tonight and decide if he'd have had the same responses to any of his other men.

On the other hand…Kevin was safe and so was Annabelle's heart. So everything had turned out fine.

Kevin slapped his shoulder. "Thanks, Pops. You deserve a beer. In fact, I'll buy you one."

"No, thanks," Jake said immediately, but he didn't feel

quite the same conviction he had earlier. A beer sounded damn good now. Adrenaline still rushed through his veins and the idea of seeing Lauren in her little black dress and heels, that full mouth wide as she laughed, her eyes bright with happiness… Yeah. Damn. He'd love to see that.

An hour later, all the reports filed, Jake headed home again. His adrenaline rush had long since faded, but that image of Lauren was stuck in his brain. He normally felt tired after that kind of energy subsided, but this time he felt a little angry.

Why shouldn't he go out? Why shouldn't he see Lauren that way? She was a beautiful woman, and he was alive, dammit.

He shook that thought off, refusing to examine it. It felt too large inside him, too significant. But that low anger remained, even as he let himself into the house and hit the shower. Even as he toweled off and dried his hair. Annabelle was out. She was probably at Kevin's apartment, waiting for him to come home so they could spend the evening together.

Jake walked out of the bathroom and stopped to stare at his bed. The same bed he'd slept in for over twenty years. It needed a new mattress. Badly. Ruth had been trying to talk him into getting a new one for years. Then she'd gotten sick. Then she'd been gone. He wouldn't have dreamed of replacing it after that.

But tonight he didn't want to get in it. He stared at the bed, at the oak posters and unmade sheets and warm comforter and crumpled pillows, and told himself to do what he always did. Make a microwave meal. Have a cold beer. Go to sleep and try not to dream and start again tomorrow.

But the sun was barely setting and the world still moved outside. The world still *moved*. It always did.

No matter who died or how lives were changed, life moved on. For the first time, Jake honestly wanted to move on, too.

CHAPTER THREE

LAUREN WAS HAVING a great time. It didn't hurt that she was slightly tipsy. It also didn't hurt that Sophie was offering hilarious commentary about the available mating options.

Lauren was losing her nervous edge and starting to get into it. "Oh, he's pretty," she said, poking Sophie's shoulder to draw her attention. "That guy by the jukebox."

Sophie's eyes slid across the room. "He's pretty, all right. So pretty he's terrible in bed."

"You've slept with him?"

"No, I can just tell."

"What?"

Sophie nodded in the face of Lauren's incredulity. "Look at that smile. Those dimples. See how cute he thinks he looks. He was the cutest guy in his high school, and he never had to do anything to get laid except show up and wait. I promise you he knows nothing about cunnilingus."

Shocked, Lauren looked him up and down. The pretty boy noticed and shot her a wink. Oh, God, Sophie was right.

Sophie nodded sagely. "What you need is someone who's just coming into his prime. Maybe he was skinny and nerdy in high school, but now he's twenty-five and really into river rafting and his muscles have filled out. He's spent a lot of time thinking about—"

"No." Lauren cut her off. "Twenty-five? I can't do that, Sophie. No way. Has a twenty-five-year-old even seen stretch marks? Or breasts that have actually fulfilled their function? No, this is not happening."

"They're breasts, Lauren! Men like them. All of them. Keep the lights low and let him play with them. Instant happiness."

Lauren forgot her fears and laughed so hard she snorted. "I can't believe the words that come out of that cute little face."

"This little face buys me a lot of leeway. Nobody suspects a thing."

A rumbling voice cut off Lauren's laugh. "Hello, ladies."

Lauren gulped and her gaze rose to the man at her side. And it kept rising.

Sophie offered a cheerful hello, but Lauren couldn't do more than stare. Jesus, he was big. And so young. Probably only a few years older than Lauren's own son. Sweat prickled her brow at the thought.

She couldn't do this.

She tried to calm herself down. She wasn't actually *doing* anything. It was a bar. No different from a party, really, and if she were introduced to this young man at a party, she'd be perfectly capable of having a conversation. A conversation with…

"I'm sorry," Lauren croaked, then cleared her throat. "What did you say your name was?"

He smiled, and he looked so young in that moment that Lauren relaxed. She wasn't taking this boy home. "I'm Gerard," he said.

Which was when she noticed his French accent.

Eyes widening in horror, she looked toward Sophie, who offered a wide grin and nodded.

Lauren shook her head and sprang to her feet, nearly knocking over the bar stool. "A pleasure to meet you. Could you excuse me for a moment, Gerard?"

She felt Sophie's hand brush her arm, but Lauren hurried toward the bathroom, clutching her purse so tightly that she could barely feel her fingers when she reached for the door and pushed into the quiet. Letting the door close behind her, she leaned against it and closed her eyes, fully aware that she was now hiding in a saloon bathroom. She wasn't even ashamed. She needed a moment. Needed to catch her breath.

She'd been dating for seven years now, but she knew she'd never really been invested in it. She'd never been hopeful. A requisite one man every year—or two—just to tell herself she was staying in the game. Three dates if he wasn't awful, then a decision about whether she'd sleep with him or not, calculated on mathematics she couldn't fully explain to herself.

But this felt different. Now she *wanted* things. She was actually tempted by that too-young man even when she didn't want to be. Her body was trying to override her mind. Her dating choices had never been based on this kind of lust and need. Never on this urge to have a man inside her, to be filled and used and satisfied.

She opened her eyes and looked in the mirror above the sink. There was nothing wrong with it, really. It was just so new that it scared her. The sharp lust that overtook her at strange hours. The fantasies she spun as she touched herself, of animal sex, raw fucking, using a man's body to get what she wanted.

And in her fantasies, she was never self-conscious or doubtful. She was turned on and hungry and taking what she needed.

She stared into her own eyes, the same eyes she'd always had, even if they had a few more wrinkles around them. She'd earned those lines. She shouldn't be so worried about them or any of the rest of her parts.

Maybe what she needed was a too-young Frenchman. Maybe not. But what she didn't need to feel was too old to be worthy of mutual pleasure. Even if she needed to turn the lights off, that was fine. It could be all scents and sounds and touch and taste.

Yes. Her body thrummed to life at the thought of being in the pitch dark, a hot body over hers, her hands clutching a back that was smooth and slick with sweat. Her heart sped at the thought, and then it multiplied, splitting into smaller hearts that lodged in her throat and wrists and between her legs.

Lauren got out her lipstick and stroked more bright color over her mouth. Then she set her shoulders and smiled. She might not do it tonight, and she might not do it with that French boy, but she was going to get laid, and soon, because she was forty-three years old and she damn well needed it.

Chin high, Lauren stepped out of the bathroom and moved toward the table with a new swing in her step. She didn't have anything to worry about. She knew what she wanted.

The big French guy had leaned close to Sophie, but he glanced up to smile at Lauren as she worked her way across the room. He wasn't going to leave this to chance. He'd flirt with both of them, apparently, and hope one of them took the bait. Or both of them.

Laughing to herself at the thought, Lauren let her eyes slide away from him. He was cute, but not so cute he shouldn't know that she was keeping her options open. She meant to give the room another quick survey, but her eyes never made it past the bar. There, tucking his wallet away as he reached for a glass of beer, was Jake. His eyes were on Lauren. His head tipped toward her and one eyebrow rose in greeting.

Lauren would've skidded to a stop, but she bumped into a chair and her confident walk came to an abrupt end. Holy shit. He'd actually shown up.

She looked at her table again, not sure what to do. Somehow, the idea of introducing Jake to Monsieur Gerard made her skin tighten with horror, but she was just as horrified at the idea of ignoring Jake to flirt with a boy nearly young enough to be her kid.

Her indecision decided it for her. Jake was already halfway across the bar and headed straight for her. She felt strangely relieved and smiled more genuinely.

"Having a good time?" he asked.

Nodding, she couldn't resist a quick scan of his body. "You look different," she said, surprised by his transformation. She hadn't seen him dressed so informally in a long time, aside from his near-naked running outfit. Tonight he wore dark jeans and a green button-down shirt. She could just see the hollow of his throat and a few enticing curls of chest hair not covered by fabric.

"So do you," he answered.

She blushed then, reminded that her breasts were pushed up and half exposed, but the blush felt good, tightening her nipples and making her skin warm.

"Can I buy you a drink?" he asked.

Her pulse quickened with alarm at the question. It was just so…not familiar. Not harmless. *Can I buy you a drink?* was something a man said to a woman when he wanted to get to know her better. More intimately. She darted another look at her table and saw that Gerard was now speaking very close to Sophie's ear, and

Sophie's smile seemed to approve. Good. Let those two kids have fun.

"Yes," Lauren finally answered. "I'd love a drink. Whiskey on the rocks, please." Jake smiled as if he approved.

"Give me a minute. I'll bring it to the table."

"No!"

His eyes darted over to Gerard.

Lauren made herself smile. "Let's sit at the bar."

He nodded, then led the way and signaled the bartender with a subtle wave, like a man who'd been ordering drinks for twenty-five years. Lauren liked that. She liked watching his hands as he drew his wallet from his jeans and slid out a few bills. His hands were wide and scarred and dark from years in the sun. She wondered how he touched a woman in bed. If he was careful or rough.

Careful, she decided, remembering Ruth's petite frame and kind eyes.

When Jake handed over the drink, she took it gratefully and tossed half of it back, feeling almost defiant. Let him see that she wasn't delicate or subtle. Better that he know. Not that he was likely to have any doubts. Most of his interactions with her in the past few years had been listening to her bitch about his men, after all.

They took the last pair of stools and settled in, both of them facing the bar instead of each other.

"It's a young crowd tonight," Jake said.

Her chuckle was more of a gasp. "I know."

"I mean, I haven't been here in years. Is it always a young crowd?"

When she didn't answer, she felt him turn slightly toward her, waiting. Was he wondering if that was her thing? If that was why she'd come here? "I think so," she finally said, meaning that she didn't know, either, but it came out a little breathless, as if she knew and didn't want to admit it. "I mean, it's my first time here in a long time, too."

Clutching her drink, she glanced at him, and Jake's serious mouth curved into a smile. He leaned a little closer, surprising her pulse into a gallop. "It's weird, isn't it?"

"The saloon?"

He shrugged. "Everything."

God. Yes. It was weird. All of it. Lauren smiled back at him. Then she found herself laughing. Hard. She cradled her forehead in her hand. Her fingers were cold from the drink, and they felt so good against her hot face. "God, yes, Jake. It's so weird."

"These girls are all my daughter's age. Or younger."

"I was just thinking that. About the boys, though. How am I supposed to flirt with them? They're babies."

"Well, I'm glad I rescued you, then. I wouldn't want you flirting with little boys."

"They're not all so little," she said without thinking, then blinked down at her drink in horror.

But Jake just laughed and picked up his beer for a sip. "Listen. Don't let me cramp your style. A cold beer sounded good, but I'll get out of your way if you want."

Did she want that? She stole another look toward the table, but Sophie and Gerard had been joined by another, even younger couple. Even though Sophie was thirty, Lauren felt as if she should hand them all condoms and pamphlets about sex education.

She turned back to find Jake watching her carefully, the lines around his eyes slightly tight. "No," she finally said. "This is nice."

He smiled again, and she noticed he had dimples, just

like that pretty young boy by the jukebox. Only Jake's dimples were camouflaged by the shadow of day-old stubble that glinted silver and black against his skin. He wasn't smooth and unlined. He was rough and prickly and so damn handsome it made her heart hurt for a few brief beats.

"Another?" he asked, gesturing toward her drink.

"I probably shouldn't," she said, but she tossed back the last sip and gestured for another glass.

Jake laughed, and when his arm brushed hers, she didn't move away. A few minutes later, as he slipped his wallet into his front pocket, his fingers touched the bare thigh she'd pressed close to his hip, and he didn't move away, either.

CHAPTER FOUR

JAKE WATCHED LAUREN return from a quick talk with Sophie. His head buzzed, and not from the beer he'd had. She smiled a little shyly as she approached. "Can I bother you for a ride home?"

Jake sat straighter. "Sophie's not taking you?"

"I want to skip out early and I hate to interrupt her fun, but I can stay if it's a big deal."

No. No, it wasn't a big deal. He'd had only one beer and he'd love to drive Lauren home, whether that meant just a drive or more. But he felt like a player as he gave her the honest answer. "It's no problem at all, but I walked. My truck is at my house, though. It's just around the corner, if you wanted to come over…"

"Sure!" she answered, grabbing her purse from the bar.

Jake pretended he wasn't surprised by this turn of events and moved quickly toward the saloon door to hold it open for her. "It's two blocks. Are you okay in heels?"

She tossed him a smile. "Oh, I can walk just fine in heels."

"I see that," he said, unable to help himself. Her curves were delicious and he could still feel the ghost of her thigh under his fingers, so damn soft and warm. And now she was coming to his house. Just so he could grab his keys and give her a ride home, though. Not for…any other kind of ride. He assumed.

But just the idea of that possibility was enough to heighten his senses. Her shoulder bumped companionably against his as they strolled and talked. She laughed up at him, her eyes so warm and happy, and Jake's heart twisted with a pain that felt sweet and right. He'd been avoiding her all these years, trying to forget how much he'd always liked her. How well they'd always gotten along as friendly acquaintances. At a Christmas party nine or ten years before, they'd spent an hour talking about horror novels and how they were nearly always ruined when made into movies. He'd forgotten that conversation, but he remembered it now. Her laugh. Her sharp mind. The way she touched him when she was making a point.

But no matter if he'd found her attractive before, he hadn't let himself think of her sexually. Still, just admitting that was a condemnation. That he'd always had to stop himself from thinking about her that way.

But tonight…tonight was a very different animal. Tonight the temptation of something forbidden transformed warm friendship into something sharp and dangerous. He'd known her as a friend. Now he wanted to know her differently. Know her body and her needs and what made her gasp. What made her *wet*.

The stunning thought of Lauren wet—wet for *him*—hit Jake square in the gut, and the shock radiated out from there. He felt his cock starting to swell, and was half horrified, feeling like a teenage boy walking a girl home and knowing her house was empty.

"This is it," he said roughly, gesturing toward his front porch. "I just need to grab my keys. Unless you'd like to come in for a drink?"

"Sure," she said again, just that easy, as if she was

letting this unfold naturally instead of torturing herself about it. Well, shit. Maybe he should try that.

It wasn't until he was opening the door that he remembered Annabelle. His arm stuttered to a stop, but the rest of his body was still moving forward, and he nearly nailed himself in the forehead with his own front door. Dammit.

Hoping he didn't look as awkward as he felt, Jake forced himself to push the door open and sighed with relief when he saw that all the rooms were still dark. Annabelle wasn't home. She always left a trail of lights on as if she were still five years old and afraid of the dark. It was nearly ten o'clock, so Annabelle was likely spending the night with Kevin. That evidence of adulthood had been hard for Jake to accept up until tonight. Tonight he was damn glad for Annabelle's relationship.

"I've got Scotch. It's nothing too fancy, but probably better than what they serve at the saloon."

As he turned on lights, Lauren wandered over to look at the old pictures of Annabelle on the living room wall. "She's getting married in a few months," he said as he handed Lauren a Scotch and sipped from his own. "To Kevin. From the station."

"I heard. Congratulations."

He waited for her to sit on the couch before following her lead. "Thanks. They grow up fast."

"Mmm. Sometimes it didn't feel all that fast to me. High school homework, Little League practice…"

Jake choked on a laugh. "You know what? You're right. Everyone says it goes fast, but some of Annabelle's teen years dragged on for a damn long time."

"I'll drink to that," she said, then made a little noise of pleasure. "That is nice Scotch. I'm glad you invited me in."

"Is that all it takes to make you happy? Midpriced Scotch?"

She laughed, but as her laughter died away, her eyes snapped with heat. "No, actually. It takes more than that to make me happy."

Her voice had gone low and warm, and regardless of worry or guilt, Jake was damn sure not going to miss that hint. "Lauren," he said, setting down his drink. "Are you drunk?"

"I'm a little buzzed."

"How buzzed?"

Her gaze slipped down to his chest. "Buzzed enough to tell you that I love watching you run without a shirt on."

"Oh." That blasted all thought from his brain and left him blank for a moment.

"You're really sexy. I shouldn't tell you that, but I'm buzzed and I really *want* to tell you."

"Lauren—"

"Because you walk around without a shirt like it's no big deal. Like you don't even know. And, Jake? It's really, really…" She reached out her hand slowly, fingers brushing over the fabric of his shirt. "Distracting."

His chest filled with a strange, hot mix of pride and arousal and embarrassment as her fingers sneaked beneath the edge of his shirt to touch the bare skin of his collarbone. Her eyes looked greedy as she watched her fingertips stroke his skin. She caught her bottom lip with her teeth, turning it even pinker and leaving a hint of moisture when she smiled. "I'm not drunk, Jake," she said, and that was all he needed.

He curved his hand around her neck and carefully drew her closer. "Then I'm going to kiss you," he murmured just before his mouth touched hers.

She sighed against him, the whisper of her breath teasing his mouth as he pressed a gentle kiss to her lips. He angled his head and her lips parted just enough so he could feel the heat of her. He tasted her. The briefest taste. Teasing. Her neck arched against his hand as she melted a little closer. One more brief taste then, loving that her tongue touched his as if she couldn't wait another moment.

But he wanted her to wait. He loved that part, so he pressed a kiss to the corner of her mouth, then her jaw, then her neck. Her long, pale, arching neck, which he'd looked at a hundred times tonight, thinking of how soft it would feel.

He opened his mouth against her skin and her breath quickened. When he sucked gently, her voice cracked over a sigh.

"I've been staring at your neck all night," he whispered. "You're so beautiful."

"Oh," she sighed, turning her head a little, even as her hands reached for the buttons of his shirt. She worked a few free and then her hand pressed to his bare chest as he groaned.

He couldn't quite believe that she wanted to touch him so much. That she thought he was *sexy*. He was just a forty-six-year-old guy with graying hair and a bad shoulder. But her hand slid along his chest as if she needed to feel him, and when he scraped his teeth against her neck she gasped and her hand rose to grip his hair.

"God, yes," she said. He wasn't sure if she pulled him down or he eased her lower on the couch, but he was over her then, kissing her, their mouths pressed hot together, her tongue demanding more, more. Her greedy hands pushed his shirt half off and, God, her touch drove him mad. The way her hands explored, alternately smoothing and clutching at him, as their tongues found a sweet rhythm.

Her knee rose to his hip, and his hand was on her pale thigh again, but this time there was nothing tentative about it. His whole palm was against her, his fingers stretching to hold as much of her as possible. Her muscles moved beneath her skin, tightening as she urged his hips closer.

She moaned as he settled tighter, and he moaned, too, at the feel of her pressed to his cock. Fuck, he hadn't been this hard this fast in so long he couldn't remember. He still felt like a damn teenager, but she seemed to approve. Her hips tipped up as if she wanted him inside her already.

Jake pushed her dress higher, reveling in the heat of her raw curves. He told himself to slow down, take his time, make sure this wasn't a mistake, but it felt like something they'd both been waiting for and had no patience to resist.

When he stroked up her hip for the third time, Lauren reached for him and guided his hand lower. His fingers slipped into her panties. "Oh, fuck," he breathed when he found her wet heat. Lauren cried out as his fingers brushed her. When he touched her clit again, she threw her head back and pushed against his hand.

Jake braced a hand next to her head and raised himself so he could slide his fingers deeper and watch as her face melted with lust. This was a new Lauren, a Lauren he'd never even imagined, and she was beautiful.

"Jake," she urged. "God, you feel good. Just…" He stroked her slowly and her hips worked in time with him. "Yes. Just like that."

He felt slightly stunned by her response. By the harsh catch in her breath and the soft whimpers that urged him on, and the sweet abandon on her face as her nails dug into his wrist. When he pushed two fingers deep into her, Lauren cried out and pressed him even tighter to her. He thought she'd come, but no. When he stroked her again, she was still needy and wild, her clit a tight bud under his fingers.

His wife had been more gentle. Nearly silent. A sweet, easy partner who'd blushed when he'd teased her about sex. But Lauren…Lauren was fighting for her pleasure, back arched and nails digging and every breath a plea for more. He'd give her more.

He lowered himself to kiss her, burying his hand in her hair to hold her still as he dragged her panties down. She kicked them the rest of the way off, and then he pushed his fingers into her again. "You're so fucking wild," he murmured as she writhed under him.

She kissed him with tongue and teeth and lips as he fucked her with his fingers, her hips meeting every thrust. God, he needed to fuck her. He needed to hear her make those noises for his cock instead of his hand. Needed her pushing up to meet his thrusts, taking him deeper, urging him to do it harder, faster, *more.*

She seemed to have the same thought. Her hands reached for his belt and scrambled to unbuckle it, but as he freed his fingers, he slid over her clit and Lauren cried out and bucked against his touch.

"Oh, fuck," she screamed, her hips working, working as she came. Jake gave her what she needed, circling her clit over and over, watching her face as she let go. She was beautiful and wild. He could watch that every day.

She shook beneath him. Her panting breath filled his ears. When she finally opened her eyes, they were dark with shock. "Jake," she said simply.

His heart thundered. The hand he'd twisted into her hair shook.

"My God," she sighed. "That was so good."

Lust and pride swelled inside him, but when he kissed her, he tried to keep it soft and careful. His attempt at calm failed when her knuckles brushed his cock and he hissed in near pain.

Lauren smiled against his mouth. "Not quite as good for you?"

"Oh, it was damn good. I'm completely satisfied."

Laughing at his lie, she cupped his erection and stroked. Despite the torturous barrier of his jeans, Jake moaned at the pleasure.

"That doesn't sound like satisfaction. Maybe we should take care of that."

She unfastened the last buttons of his shirt and pushed it open, her hands spreading over his chest and down his ribs. "God, you're gorgeous."

He said her name, shaking his head in denial, but he couldn't say more than that. His heart beat so hard that it shook his chest and made it hard to breathe. She ducked her head and licked one of his nipples, and he was shocked at the pleasure that zinged through his body. No one had ever done that before, and when her teeth pressed into him, he jerked in shock and watched her smile against him.

Her hands roamed down his sides, around to his back, up his spine, and then slid slowly down to his hips. Finally, she reached for the fly of his jeans, and Jake hung his head so he could watch her hands work the button free, then the zipper. The whole world narrowed down to the slow work of her hands. He held his breath.

Finally, she reached into his briefs and curled her fingers around his shaft, and Jake groaned.

"Oh, my," she breathed, sounding happy with him. Thank God.

He thanked God again when she stroked him. He couldn't stop from pushing his hips at her, fucking her hand as she murmured something so softly that he couldn't understand. He said her name again, still stunned that this was her beneath him, her hand around his cock, her mouth rising to his neck to make him groan again.

He needed a condom. Now. He needed inside her.

His mind was working so hard at that frustrating puzzle that he didn't register a faint clicking noise from the other side of the room until it was followed by the slamming door.

Lauren gasped and Jake froze.

"Dad?" Annabelle called.

Blocked from view by the back of the couch, Jake and Lauren stared at each other with wide, horrified eyes.

"Holy shit," Jake whispered. The sound of keys hitting the counter was like a gunshot.

He didn't realize Lauren's hand was still around his cock until she let him go and her warmth vanished with shocking speed. She pushed at his chest as his pulse sputtered with panic.

"Dad?" Annabelle said again. Then, to someone else, "Maybe he's in the shower." Fuck! Kevin was here, too?

Balancing on one hand, Jake managed to zip his jeans as Lauren shimmied her dress down from her hips while keeping her head below the back of the couch.

He couldn't button his jeans or fasten his belt from this angle, so he had no choice but to push up to his knees.

He managed only the button before Annabelle's head swung around.

"Hey!" she said with a grin. "Did you fall asleep?"

"Uh."

Kevin seemed to register the scene before Annabelle did. He closed his hand over her shoulder as his gaze jumped from Jake's chest to the couch and then back up. "Maybe we should..." he said.

Jake shrugged his shirt back onto his shoulders and started buttoning. "I was just—"

Lauren's hand pushed frantically at him, and he glanced down to see that she couldn't get her dress fully down with his knees still spreading her thighs. She was open and exposed and Jake nearly leaped off her, hoping to rectify the situation.

When he stood, Annabelle's confused smile finally faltered. Her eyes swept down, and Jake tried not to imagine what he looked like. Belt unfastened, shirt half-open, hair mussed from Lauren's grip.

He couldn't begin to come up with a lie that would cover this.

"Oh," Annabelle finally said.

Without a word, Lauren sat up.

She might have been fully dressed at this point, but she looked even more guilty than Jake did. Hair wild, cheeks flushed, mouth swollen and pink.

Annabelle blinked several times before she gasped out, "Mrs. *Foster*?"

"Hi, Annabelle!" Lauren said brightly, blinking in the light that poured from the kitchen.

"I... Hi."

"We were just—" Jake started at the same time that Kevin began to say, "Should we, maybe...?"

"Right!" Annabelle chirped. "Yes! Of course!"

Lauren stood, still sliding her dress down to cover her thighs. Everyone's eyes followed the movement. "It's pretty late," Lauren said, her voice still falsely cheerful. "I'd better go. Early day at the library tomorrow."

"Right," Jake said. "Me, too. At the station, I mean. Probably."

She picked up her heels from where they'd fallen on the floor and slipped them on, flashing another too-wide smile at Annabelle and Kevin. "Anyway, it was nice to see you again, Annabelle. It's been years. Welcome home. From college, I mean. Not from…tonight." Her words ended on something that resembled a laugh.

"Thanks, Mrs. Foster. You look really great."

Not one of them could think of anything to say after that. Lauren did look great, but she also looked as if she'd just been screwed on the couch.

Lauren suddenly nodded. "Okay, I'd better go. Have a good night." She grabbed her purse from the coffee table and gave everyone a little wave. It wasn't until the door closed behind her and plunged the room into awkward silence that Jake remembered she needed a ride home.

"Shit!" he cursed. He skirted the couch to chase after her, but his shoe caught on the carpet and he nearly stumbled. When he followed his daughter's gaze to the floor, he saw that the carpet wasn't the problem. Lauren's black panties were wrapped around the toe of his shoe.

He swooped down, moving with what he hoped was blinding speed to grab her underwear and ball it in his fist. Blood rushed to his head. His face was on fire. "I'll be back in a few minutes," he rasped before rushing for the door.

It took a moment for his eyes to adjust to the night, and he thought she'd just run off into the darkness, panty-less and disoriented. But there she was, standing frozen at the bottom of his driveway, staring down the sidewalk toward the next intersection.

"Lauren."

Turning toward his approach, she shook her head. "I can't believe that happened."

"Yeah."

"I'm so sorry. Your daughter..."

Jake cringed, but he tried to smile. "If it makes you feel better, she was telling me this morning that I needed to get out and date. So maybe I'm just good at taking advice?"

Her laugh was slightly more natural, but it definitely ended in a little hiccup of horror. He felt exactly the same himself.

"Will you still let me give you a lift home?" he asked.

"I'd better. A walk of shame is really the only thing that could make this worse."

His heart fell a little. It was terrible. Awful. Undeniably awkward. But he'd kind of hoped that Lauren would tell him it wasn't as bad as he thought.

But she looked as miserable as he felt as he unlocked the truck and opened the door for her.

When he got in, they sat quietly in the close cocoon of the truck for a moment. He didn't know what to say. Didn't know if they should forget this ever happened or vow to try it again. Hell, he didn't even know which of those he wanted at this point. He was torn between never seeing her again and asking if he could take her home and spend a naked, sweaty night in her bed.

He gave up trying to figure it out and handed Lauren her panties.

Clutching them, she stared down at her white-knuckled hand. "She called me Mrs. Foster."

"I know," he said miserably. There wasn't much to add after that.

CHAPTER FIVE

LAUREN COULDN'T BELIEVE she had to go into work. That she had to get out of her car and walk across the parking lot and into the building. The same building where Jake worked. And not just Jake, but Kevin, who'd witnessed her shame last night. And not just Kevin, but Sophie, who'd want to know every detail of the hot hookup.

Lauren groaned and let her head fall back on the headrest. Maybe she should return home and call in sick.

"I'm sorry," she said to the roof of her car. "I can't come in today, because I came all over the fire captain's hand last night, and then his daughter walked in and realized her dead mother's friend is a loose woman with no morals."

Oh, God. It was almost tragically funny. Or it would have been if everything leading up to that moment hadn't been searingly perfect. The chemistry made it that much more painful.

Jake's body had felt even better than it looked. He was all hot skin and flexing muscle and soft hair. And he smelled so damn good. Her mouth watered at the memory of the taste of him.

She wanted more. So much more. Starting with that thick cock she'd gotten her hand around for such a brief moment.

Lauren squeezed her eyes shut and moaned in sorrow. She'd be haunted by that memory for the rest of her life, because it was never going to happen again. She'd never get to see him naked or taste his cock or feel him deep inside her.

You're so fucking wild.

She was. Or she wanted to be. But not with Jake. Not with a man who was used to someone nicer. Look what she'd already done to him. Tempted him into disaster right in front of his daughter and one of his men.

She waited until the parking lot had been quiet for five minutes, then slipped out of her car to hurry for the back door of the library. She didn't make a sound today. There were no heels to clack against the asphalt and no jangling bracelets to draw attention. No, today she wore black leggings and a long sweater and the most innocent of ballet flats. Granted, it was already warm outside, but she'd be hiding in the stacks all day, deep in the shadows, where she couldn't seduce anyone. The leggings should keep her panties, carefully chosen for full granny effect, securely in place.

She should have listened to Sophie. Lauren needed to work out her newly blossomed lust with a few strangers. Get it out of her system in a way that left no evidence.

But hopefully this would stay quiet. No harm done. Just a little personal humiliation whenever she saw Jake. Or Kevin. Or Annabelle. And a devastating, soul-wrecking boost to her already racing libido.

One tiny taste of good sex and she was ravenous. She'd already gotten off to a fantasy of Jake this morning. It was the first morning of many, she imagined. And maybe it was better that way. She'd keep him close enough to feed her fantasies, but not so close that he could ruin her.

Head down, Lauren made it all the way across the lot

without spotting any firefighters, much less one who'd been witness to her indiscretion. She thought she was home free, but before the door closed behind her, her cell phone rang and she tensed for the worst.

And it was the worst. Her ex-husband.

"Karma," she muttered before answering the call.

"Hi, Steve," she said, her face already warming with guilt. There was no way he'd heard anything already.

"Lauren! How are you?"

"Good. Hold on a second." She meant to escape to the library office, but she glimpsed Sophie in there, typing away. Cell phone calls weren't allowed in the library. She had no choice but to step back outside. Steve only ever called about their son. "Is everything okay?" She'd just talked to Sawyer yesterday morning, but maybe he'd called Steve with a problem.

"Everything's good. I was just checking to see if you're going to homecoming next month."

She smiled at the thought of interfering with the football fun during Sawyer's first experience of homecoming weekend at college. "No, I know Sawyer's looking forward to the weekend with you. I don't mind. You boys have a good time."

"Are you sure?"

"I'm sure. Why?" They tried to be friendly for Sawyer's sake, but it was a little extreme of him to try to talk her into a trip.

"Oh. No reason. Just…"

She waited him out. Steve didn't like silence.

As expected, he gave in quickly. "I thought I might bring someone along, and I didn't want to make you unhappy."

"Oh, for God's sake," she snapped. "I'm not affected by you dating."

"Well, sure, but it's getting a little serious, and you know, I wouldn't want to flaunt it in your face. With your history…"

She was honestly dumbfounded. "*What* history?"

"Well, you weren't really into marriage, and you haven't managed to settle down since then."

"You weren't really into marriage, either, if you remember correctly. Neither one of us was particularly happy."

"You're right. Of course. It's just that at your age…"

Lauren gasped. "At my age? You're two years older than I am!"

"And I'm in a relationship. That's my point. I don't want to rub it in."

"What the hell?" she sputtered. "What kind of arrogant, condescending sh—"

"Lauren! I don't want to fight. I was trying to be nice. Why do you always do this?"

Lauren closed her eyes and took a deep breath before she got fired for cursing at the top of her lungs outside the library. "'Nice?'" she finally growled. "Nice enough to try to accommodate my sad, lonely life by keeping your happiness under wraps? You're a real saint, Steve."

He sighed, the weary sound letting her know that he found her as impossible and bitchy as he always had. "Fine. I'm the bad guy again. I'm sorry I upset you. I shouldn't have bothered asking. I'll see you during the holidays, I'm sure."

He hung up before she could tell him where to stick the holiday turkey. "What an unbelievable ass," she hissed, squeezing her phone until it creaked. Which was when she looked up to see Kevin hovering halfway out the back door of the fire station, a duffel bag slung over his shoulder.

"Um…" He swallowed and his eyes flicked toward the parking lot. "Good morning, Mrs. Foster. I was just grabbing a few—"

She spun on her heel and fled into the library without a word.

"I'm repairing books today," she said flatly when she walked into the office.

Sophie's eyes went wide with alarm. "You don't look happy. Why don't you look happy?"

"It's a long story."

Her friend cringed. "Is everything okay? I take it things didn't go well last night?" She lowered her voice. "With Jake?"

Lauren really didn't want to talk about it, but it wasn't fair to leave the impression that Jake had done anything wrong. "Jake was great. But I shouldn't have done it."

Sophie leaned closer. "Done what, exactly?"

"Just…" Lauren waved a hand. Sophie watched as if she expected Lauren to pantomime a specific sex act. "It was nice. Better than nice. Really. But it won't work out, and I don't want to talk about it."

"Shoot." Sophie's face crumpled.

"You were right. I should avoid local guys."

"I'm sorry, Lauren. But anytime you want to go out, I'm your girl."

Lauren put on a game smile. "It's a deal."

But her smile faded as she moved into the back room to start on the pile of broken and battered books. The truth was that she *was* impossible and bitchy. And not great at love. And terrible at being the better half. She'd never been like so many other women she knew, happy to be in a marriage with a man who held down a job and loved being a dad. She'd resented the inequalities and resisted doing what was expected of her. And God, she'd hated all of her husband's little digs.

No, she wasn't good at cooking and cleaning and selflessly assembling countless preschool crafts. She wasn't happy to contribute to the car pool or whip up a nice dish for the potluck at his office. She'd eventually decided she wasn't good at marriage, either, and what a relief that had been.

And one more way she wasn't like other women? Divorce hadn't devastated her. She'd felt awful for her son, but God, she'd felt free, and she'd hoped that a happy mom was more important for Sawyer than a married one.

Lauren set her jaw and straightened her shoulders. The chemistry she had with Jake was special. It was wonderful. But there was no relationship in the cards. He was used to a sweet, normal woman. Lauren couldn't step into the role his wife had filled. Not for him and certainly not for Annabelle. Better to nip this in the bud, and leave it at that, or a lot of hearts would be broken.

Including hers.

CHAPTER SIX

ANNABELLE HAD DISAPPEARED while Jake was dropping Lauren off at home the night before, but she'd left a note. *Spending the night at Kevin's. Love you.* Just that. No mention of the scene she'd stumbled upon. Not even a "Let's talk tomorrow." Jake was sure she'd meant to be kind, but by nine the next morning, it was just torturous.

He'd already gone for a run—wearing a shirt—and he'd showered, gotten dressed and done the dishes. Now he was sitting at the kitchen table with his third cup of coffee turning sour in his stomach.

Annabelle might have been encouraging him to date, but that didn't mean she'd been ready to see evidence of it. Certainly not such graphic evidence. And he was damn sure she hadn't expected the woman to have been a friend of her mom's. Would she think, now, that something had been going on when her mom was still alive?

On one hand, Jake knew it was none of his daughter's business whom he dated. He believed that. But on the other... The whole damn town was invested in his life.

As a first-grade teacher with twelve years of experience, Ruth had had a connection with almost every family in town. When she'd died, it had been a community tragedy. Grief counselors had been brought in to speak with the kids. The funeral had been a huge memorial service with another private family service at the gravesite. Annabelle had been in college, but everyone had treated the situation as if Jake was faced with the tragedy of raising a young girl on his own. There'd been advice. So much advice. And after a discreet six months, talk of meeting another woman as nice as Ruth.

Now the community was getting worried. It was time to move on. Maybe it was even time to start a new family. He was a healthy, steady man, after all. They were invested in his future.

So even though Jake knew it was nobody's business... It seemed to be everyone's business, and he'd resisted the casting call. Oh, he'd been tricked into plenty of dinner parties where there just happened to be a single woman in her thirties seated next to him, but other than that... He'd refused to discuss it with anyone.

He couldn't refuse anymore. Not with Annabelle.

He jumped up when the front door opened and met her at the entrance to the kitchen. "Hi, sweetie."

"Hi, Daddy." She offered a hug and then a tentative smile. "So... Did you sleep well?"

He winced.

Annabelle cleared her throat. "Well. I guess when you told me you were dating, I should've believed you."

Jake looked up at the ceiling in hopes of some insightful reply, but there was no answer there. "I'm really sorry about that. I thought you were spending the night at Kevin's and then I kind of...forgot about the whole issue for a few minutes."

She covered her face and laughed. "Yeah, I guess so."

"God, Annabelle. About Lauren..."

"Dad, it's no big deal. Mrs. Foster seems nice."

"You can call her Lauren," he insisted flatly. "And she is nice. But I want to be clear that there's never been anything between us in the past. Last night was the first time we'd seen each other that way."

"Wow. You move fast, Dad."

Now Jake was the one who wanted to cover his face. "There wasn't... We... Never mind."

She leaned against the counter and looked at him long enough to make him squirm. Which really wasn't that long in this situation. "She's pretty, Dad. And I'm glad you're seeing someone."

"It's not weird that you knew her before?"

"It's a small town. It would be weird if I hadn't known her before."

He slumped a little, the tension of the past few hours leaving him. "Your mom knew her. And I'm friends with her ex. It feels like a betrayal of...someone. I don't even know who."

"Dad." She waited until he looked up and met her gaze. "Maybe it's not a betrayal of anyone. Maybe you just really like her and you're looking for an excuse not to."

"Why would I do that?"

She shook her head as if he was being difficult. "Because you really loved Mom and it broke your heart when she died?"

Jake crossed his arms. "That sounds like something from a TV movie. Of course it broke my heart. But we're just talking about dating here. There's no reason to get maudlin."

"Stop being such a boy. We're talking about getting involved with a woman to see if you could love her. Right? Unless this was just a quick hookup?"

His face heated at just how quickly things had gone from tentative to I-need-this last night. Had it just been a hookup? "Shit, I don't know."

"You do know what a hookup is, right?"

"Jesus, Annabelle, I was in college in the '80s, not the nineteenth century."

"Really? Did people have sex back then and everything? Did you do it in black and white?"

Jake groaned. "I've raised an incorrigible brat."

She laughed because she knew it wasn't true. In fact, Jake knew he'd raised an amazing woman. She was handling this a lot better than he was. Maybe she could even help.

"In all honesty, I don't know whether it's anything at all. And after last night, I'm not sure she'll ever want to see me again."

"Come on. It'll be really funny in a few days. That was like a classic romantic-comedy scene. We'll tell that story over Christmas dinner for years to come."

He shot her a glare. "Not funny."

"Totally funny. Have you talked to her?"

"Not yet. She's working today, and God knows she probably doesn't want me coming into the library and starting rumors."

Annabelle just shook her head. "You're going to call her, right?"

Yes, he was going to call her. There was no denying the attraction between them now, and he felt stupid for having spent so long trying. Yes, Ruth had known Lauren, and worrying that there'd been a subliminal attraction before didn't honor his wife's memory. She would want him to be happy. In fact, she'd told him that close to the end. She'd smiled and told him to remember he had a whole life left to live.

Steve might be a stickier issue. He seemed to hold a small flame for his ex-wife, but who wouldn't? Jake had last seen him at the city's Fourth of July barbecue, and even so many years after the divorce, Steve had seen fit to say Lauren didn't know what she was missing. Screw that bastard if he hadn't been able to make it work with a woman like Lauren. Screw him for bragging about being free to date younger women.

After what Jake had felt with Lauren last night, he'd be a fool and a coward to lose her out of fear. He did have a whole life left, and Lauren made him feel damn ready to live it.

CHAPTER SEVEN

LAUREN PINNED HER hair up in a knot and headed for the kitchen to pour herself another glass of wine. She'd made it through the day without dying of embarrassment, and now her only plan was to soak in a hot bath and get fantastically drunk while doing it.

The day Sawyer had left for college, she'd bought herself the silkiest little black robe she could find. She loved the feel of it against her skin. She might not be taut and twenty, but she loved being herself so much more now. She loved her own hands on her skin and the way her body worked. She needed to embrace that. Not with Jake. And maybe not with a twentysomething French guy, either. But with herself… Oh, with herself, she was getting pretty darn confident.

That was something good, and a girl had to embrace what she was good at…and then leave behind all the other crap that she couldn't quite manage.

She'd almost talked herself into a good mood, but before she could get out of the kitchen with her wineglass—and the bottle—someone knocked on the front door.

Lauren froze, bottle and glass clutched in her hands, gaze sliding toward her front door. If she'd been more proactive, she could've made a break for it. She'd been meaning to frost the little window in the front door for years so that no one could see inside and she could ignore visitors at will. But she'd never gotten around to it and now the man on her front step could see straight through her tiny living room into the kitchen beyond, where she stood as though she'd turned to stone.

And because it was still light out, she could see him, too.

Jake. Of course.

He raised an eyebrow. She raised one back.

She knew he wasn't going to go away, but she gave him a few seconds just in case. As the past twenty-four hours flashed through her mind, her heart stepped up to an anxious pace. Then it scrambled from anxiety to alarm. Shit. She really didn't want to do this. Now or ever. But especially not now.

He cocked his head, and Lauren forced herself to walk toward the door. She set down the wineglass on the little table where she kept her keys, and then she unlocked the door.

Jake was holding yellow roses. Her heart stopped its flailing and fell into the pit of her stomach.

"Lauren," he said simply.

She stared at the flowers for a long time before she took them.

"I hoped we could talk."

"Sure," she breathed. But she just stood there, flowers in one hand, bottle of wine in the other, as if they were about to begin a night of sweetly meaningful debauchery.

She shook her head, trying to force her shock away, then opened the door wider. "Come in."

For a moment, everything inside her told her to throw the roses out the door. She didn't know why, but she needed to get rid of them. They weren't *right*. But she hadn't had enough wine to be that irrational, so she took the wine and the flowers to the kitchen and left them both on the counter.

"I didn't know what to say last night," Jake started.

Lauren didn't want the flowers, but she started fussing with them now, because that was better than facing him. "You didn't need to say anything."

"Everything happened so quickly."

Yes, there was that. She'd quickly pulled him down on the couch, quickly kicked off her panties and very quickly come for him. She'd been just seconds from jumping straight into quickly getting him inside her.

He'd probably been in shock, just as she was now, filled with lust that was shot through with horror. Even now, she wanted him. Badly.

Lauren cleared her throat. "I know this is awkward. We've known each other a long time. We probably should have thought of that before picking each other up at a saloon."

She heard his footsteps draw closer as she reached up to pluck a vase from a cabinet. "It seemed like a good idea at the time," he said.

"Yes."

"A really good idea."

Oh, God, his deep voice was so close now. Two more steps and he'd be pressed to her, his mouth at her neck. That was when she remembered that she was wearing a black silk robe. It came to only midthigh. He could open it with a flick of his fingers and touch all of her. He could have her just the way she wanted to be had.

Lauren spun to face him. "You shouldn't have brought flowers."

"It was no big deal. I—"

"No, I mean you *shouldn't* have brought them. I'm not…" She waved a frantic hand. "Like that."

"Like what?" He looked puzzled. Of course he was. His wife had probably been gaga over flowers. He'd probably bought them for her every week, and she'd loved them and had never forgotten to water them and had never killed them within forty-eight hours because she was ungrateful and unromantic and unfeminine and just plain *un-*.

"Jake," she sighed, "last night was a mistake. I'm really not your type."

He looked left and right as if he were trying to figure out whom she was talking about. "My type?"

"Yes. So let's nip this in the bud before we make a bigger mistake." Her gaze slipped involuntarily down his body. A bigger, harder mistake, dammit.

"Lauren, I don't know what you've heard, but I really haven't dated much, so even I don't know what my *type* might be."

"I'm thinking it's something along the lines of 'nice girl.'"

He flinched and took a step back. "What?"

"You brought me flowers!" She punched a finger toward the bouquet. "Did last night seem romantic?"

He opened his mouth and then closed it with a snap.

She pushed on, feeling as if she were kicking a puppy. But she had to say it. She couldn't fall for him. "I was looking to get laid. I got dressed up and I went out and I was looking for sex. That's the kind of girl I am. I was on the prowl. I was a *cougar*. You just got caught up in it. It was a mistake."

His jaw jumped with tension. "A cougar. So you're saying I'm too old for you."

"What? No!" Lauren looked around for her wine-glass, before remembering it was all the way across the room. Desperate, she picked up the bottle. "Excuse me for a moment." She tipped it up and took two gulps. "I'm sorry," she gasped. "Look at me. This is what I'm talking about." She jiggled the bottle.

"Lauren—"

She rushed on before she lost all her nerve. "You're a good guy, Jake. I can't do this. Not with you."

He took a deep breath, making her want to reach out and touch his broad chest. "Lauren, I have no idea what you're trying to say."

She had to be blunt. She had to just say it. He deserved that, at least. He hadn't even gotten an orgasm out of this disaster.

Lauren held up a hand and took one last swig of wine. As the warmth of the alcohol sank into her, she took a deep breath and tried to calm her pulse. "What I'm trying to say is... If I could just have sex with you and walk away, I would. Like, you have no idea how much I would. But we practically work together, and you're friends with Steve, and even if it were only a one-night stand it would be so awkward, but I *like* you, Jake."

For a moment, he still frowned. His jaw clenched again. Then he shook his head. "That's not really a problem, Lauren. I like you, too. And I liked last night. We don't need to decide everything right now. We could just date. Just see if this could be—"

"I'm nothing like Ruth!"

That brought confusion back to his face. And shock. And a little hurt. He took another step back.

Lauren wished she could take it all back. Everything. Even that first touch of his skin. Even that first kiss. Her heart was going to break a little, after all.

"What?" he finally breathed.

"I'm nothing like her, Jake. I'm not selfless or sweet."

"You're sweet—" he started, but she shook her head.

"No. I'm sure I seem nice enough. Ha! A middle-aged mom. A quiet, small-town librarian. But I'm not sweet. I'm not *good*. I was happy to get divorced. I was relieved. Do you know that? I was so tired of all the arguing and compromises. I never want to get married again. And I love my son so much, but I'll tell you a secret… Everybody else is sad when their kids go to college. You were sad, right? I'm not sad. I'm not sad, Jake! I'm thrilled to have the house to myself! I can do anything I want! I can walk around in black silk. I can have you over. I can drink straight from a bottle of wine in the kitchen!"

He only looked more dumbstruck. He probably couldn't process it. A divorcée empty nester who didn't regret her solitude? She was a goddamn unicorn of selfishness.

"You…" She pointed at him, letting one fingertip touch that chest she wanted so desperately to caress. "You are a good guy. You need a *nice* woman. And we can't just hook up. It's too much. I like you. It won't work for me. I'm sorry."

He stared at her. His eyes were dark with something she couldn't decipher. Also, the wine was really taking hold, and his chest was starting to distract her. Granted, he was wearing a shirt this time, which was helpful. But somehow her one-fingered gesture had accidentally lingered, and now she was trailing her fingertips over his muscles.

"Why does everyone think I need a nice woman?" Jake finally asked, his low words rumbling up through her hand.

"What?"

His fingers closed over hers to stop her petting. "Everyone wants to set me up with a nice woman. This whole damn *town* wants to set me up with a nice woman. Why?"

She shot him a wry look. "You know why."

"No, I don't. I don't get it."

She smiled at her greedy hand, caught by his fingers, but still pressed to his chest in an attempt to cop a feel. "They want to protect you from women like me. You don't know what we're like."

"I think I can take care of myself."

"How can you be sure? You probably think all women are kind and sweet and perfect. You—"

"Ruth wasn't perfect. She was sweet, yes. She was wonderful—"

She pushed off his chest. "Jake, she was a goddamn first-grade teacher! The kind of first-grade teacher every kid wants! Pretty and sweet and patient and generous. Do you know how much time I can spend with a dozen six-year-olds? Fifty-five minutes. I've timed it. Fifty-five minutes, and then I have to lock myself in the office and fantasize about the Scotch I'm going to down three minutes after I leave the library. I'm not like her!"

"What the hell does that matter? Yes, she was wonderful. And I loved her. I loved *her*. Not some caricature of who she was. Not some *type*."

"You don't understand. I don't bake cookies. I don't want to take care of a man. I'm bitchy. I'm demanding. I want my own space and free time, and when I'm in a bad mood, I'll tell you and I'll use bad language while I do it. Speaking of, I like to fuck." She poked his chest again. "I. Am. Not. Sweet."

He caught her hand again. "Jesus, Lauren," he said, laughing.

His chuckle irritated her, and she tried to snatch her hand back, but he held tight. "Fine. You're not sweet and patient and selfless. You're stubborn. And bold. And irritable. And you're mean enough that you're the only one who ever dares to come over and yell at me about my firefighters. They're heroes, you know. You're supposed to be generous to them."

"They're also loud and obnoxious," she grumbled.

His half smile blossomed into a grin. "They are loud. They also stink like you wouldn't believe, and they're rowdy and immature. They're like first graders, sometimes. And you're the only one who ever points it out."

"See?" she muttered, but she spread her fingers out again, wanting to feel him one last time.

"Lauren." He tugged her closer. Closer. Until his arm wrapped around her waist and her chest was pressed to his. She wanted to sigh. She did. She sighed as his mouth brushed her temple and brought sudden tears to her eyes.

"You're amazing," he whispered. "You're fiery and strong and intimidating. And you turn me on like crazy."

"Jake…" She didn't know what to say, and her throat was so tight. She could be his dangerous fling. The wild woman he dated before he settled down again. She could get what she wanted, and she wanted it so much. But to watch him fall for some sweet young thing afterward? God, that would be too hard.

"Lauren, I don't need someone to bake for me or take care of me or replace my wife. And Annabelle doesn't need a mom." He kissed her ear. "I was twenty-one when I got married, and I loved my wife like crazy. But she's gone, and I'm a grown man, not some kid in college. I'm old enough to know what's worth trying. To know what turns me on. I'm old enough to know what I *like*, and I like you. Not some type. Not someone who needs me, but someone who *wants* me. *You*, Lauren."

She drew in a shaky breath.

"And," he whispered, "I'd be so damn happy to be the guy you fuck."

His mouth was on her throat now, so hot and demanding, and Lauren groaned. He'd said all the right things and kissed all the right spots, but she was still scared. "And after?" she whispered.

"Does there have to be an after already? We haven't even started. I just want to try. To see what happens when we're by ourselves. With no one else between us."

"What about—?"

"No one," he growled, and his teeth found that spot that made her nerves shake. "Just us."

"Oh, God," she breathed. "I want to fuck you."

His pained laugh chased over her skin. "If that's supposed to scare me off, you've clearly underestimated how much I want to fuck you, too."

"Don't say that," she moaned. "I won't be able to resist."

"Thank God." His hand sneaked beneath the front of her robe and he growled when his thumb grazed her bare nipple. She wanted him to tear off her robe and do her right there on the kitchen counter, but he was wiser. "The bedroom this time," he said. "Behind a closed door."

"Good idea." After all, anyone who came to the front door could see right in. But she wouldn't have resisted if he'd picked her up and taken her right there. She was too desperate for him.

As it was, he gave her a long kiss and caressed her breast before giving in and herding her toward the hallway.

Laughing, she tugged him to her bedroom, her lust brightening into something sharp and dangerous when she saw the hard length of him beneath his jeans. She'd fantasized about him this morning, thinking she'd never get her hands on him again. Now she was starving.

He was kissing her before they even got to the bed, as if he were starving for her, too, so Lauren gave up any pretense of patience and unbuckled his belt. She didn't need to be seduced. Hell, she didn't even need foreplay these days. He slid off her robe and she let it fall to the floor. Only the bedside lamp was on, but it cast more than enough light to reveal everything. Still, she stood straight before him, letting him look his fill. She wasn't self-conscious anymore. She wanted him to look. And judging by the way his cock thickened, he liked looking.

She took him in her fist and slowly stroked him, hoping the feeling was as soul-breaking as his fingers had felt inside her last night.

His hands framed her face as he lowered his head. "Jesus," he hissed, pressing small kisses to her mouth and jaw as his breath grew rough. "Fuck, you're beautiful."

He was as thick as he'd been the night before, and so damn hard, and she loved it. She loved making his hips jerk and his breath catch.

When his thumb brushed her mouth, she licked it and his eyes narrowed to slits. He touched her again, and she sucked his thumb between her lips and rubbed her tongue against him. "Oh, God," he said, as she sucked it the way she wanted to suck his cock. As she stroked him and made him feel exactly what she wanted him to feel.

He slid his thumb free, and she loved the way it slipped warm and wet over her lips. Lauren went to her knees in front of him.

He was gorgeous. Straight and veined and so thick.

He would have made her nervous in her youth, but now... Now she went wet and weak at the sight of him. She wanted that. All of it.

She stroked his cock and watched a drop of liquid form at the tip. Jake didn't say a word. She wasn't sure he even breathed. She tasted it. Just a tiny touch of her open mouth. Then another as the salty drop melted over her tongue.

He tasted perfect. And he smelled delicious. As she opened her mouth for him, her clit felt tight and swollen. She'd forgotten how good a man could taste, how the scent of sex could take you over. But now she felt as needy as an animal. She wanted to roll around in him. Stretch out and purr her pleasure.

But he wouldn't have heard. As soon as her lips closed around him, as soon as she sucked, Jake groaned her name.

Yes, that was what she wanted. She took him deeper, letting the weight of his shaft slide over her tongue. Letting him feel how much she wanted it. She tightened her hand around the thick base of his cock and worked her mouth and fist at the same time.

He urged her on with his hips and his growls of approval. His fingers brushed her hair, and she knew he was being polite, trying not to do what he really wanted, trying not to cup his hand around the back of her skull and urge her deeper. But she wasn't a delicate flower. She wanted everything, so she reached for his wrist and pulled his hand to the back of her head.

"Oh, God," he moaned, his fingers spreading over her hair. "Oh, God, Lauren." His touch was light, but she still took him as deep as she could, loving the way he pressed against the back of her throat. His fingers tightened. He thrust deeper as she worked him, his movements rougher as his breath tore from his throat.

"Stop," he said, though his hips begged for more. "I don't want to come like this. I…"

But she didn't stop, and his hand fisted in her hair as his thrusts quickened, and then his cock jumped against her tongue and he flooded her mouth. He gasped her name as she swallowed him down. His hand trembled against her head. His body curled around her.

She'd never felt more powerful. She wanted to do this again. In an hour. In the middle of the night. In the morning. She wanted to wake up like this, shaking and strong and whole and broken all at once.

He slid free of her and she looked up at him and let him see how much she still wanted him.

"Christ," he panted. "Lauren. Just…" He sat on the bed as if his strings had been cut. Lauren pushed him the rest of the way down and pressed her body to his side.

"God, I've been thinking about doing that," she whispered.

Eyes closed, he shook his head. "Women fantasize about *that*?"

"I don't know. I do."

"Again, if you're trying to scare me away…"

Laughing, she slapped his shoulder. "I can't help it. It turns me on."

One eye popped open. "Yeah?"

"Yeah."

He rose up on his elbow as she turned to her back. "I'm not sure I believe you," he whispered, his hand trailing down to trace the curves of her breasts.

"Oh," she sighed as goose bumps spread over her skin.

He kissed her breast, his mouth a whisper against her

nipple, then a brand, so hot against her skin. He touched her as if she wasn't too old or too soft. As if she were perfect. Like he never wanted to forget the feel of her.

His hand sneaked beneath her panties and slipped into her heat. "Oh," he said, his breath tightening her wet nipple. "You did like that."

Her laugh was strangled and tortured as he brushed her hard clit.

"I love the sounds you make," he said, touching her again and drawing another noise from her throat.

Jake slipped her panties off and eased her higher on the bed, and then his mouth was on her, sucking and licking and pressing and pushing her to make more noise. She gave in gracefully, moaning for him, sighing, gasping, whimpering. It didn't take long. He was good with his tongue. Really good. He'd obviously had decades of practice, and Lauren was coming within minutes, shaking and screaming as he pushed her relentlessly higher.

As she floated back to mindfulness, her heart still thundering in her ears, she had a brief fear that they were done.

But then Jake rose to his knees and she saw that he was thick and hard for her again, thank God. "I don't know if I can come," he said, but she reached greedily for him.

"I don't care. I need you inside of me. Please."

His mouth quirked in a brief smile as he dug a condom from his jeans pocket. "Okay. Since you asked nicely."

She was so glad he took a moment to strip naked. She'd been too eager to care before, but now she wanted to see all of him, just the way he'd seen her. And she wanted his skin on hers. She wanted to *feel* him. The heat of his thighs between hers as he lowered himself. The brush of his chest over her breasts. Then his mouth on hers as he notched the wide head of his cock against her.

Her heart quickened again. She waited. Jake teased her a little, rocking just enough to let her feel the pressure, then easing back. She kissed him harder and dug her nails into his back, but when she tilted her hips up, he didn't give her more. The slide of him against her was torture. She whimpered. He teased.

"Please," she finally gasped against his mouth. "Please. I need it."

He rewarded her with a careful push of his hips. His cock stretched her, filling her by slow centimeters as she held her breath inside her tight throat and waited. He pulled back and pushed deeper.

"Oh, God," she gasped. Yes. This was what she'd been missing. For years. This feeling of being made whole. As though she'd been empty without him.

When he was as deep as he could get, he paused and breathed slowly. She felt the way his heart thundered against hers, and tears pricked her eyes at the realization that this meant just as much to him. That he'd needed this. That it was good and frightening and so *real*.

He held himself deep and still for a few more heartbeats. And then he fucked her. Carefully, at first, his eyes on her face as he moved. He watched her, as if testing her reactions, seeing what she wanted. She wanted it all. Deeper. Harder. *Yes*. But he refused to quicken his pace.

Even when she pressed her nails into the muscles of his ass, he held back. If he wanted to make her beg again, he'd be disappointed. She had her own tricks.

Lauren let go of him and slid her hand between their

bodies. Her fingers brushed the wet heat of his cock as it slid out of her, and Jake's body jerked against her. But she wasn't out for his pleasure. She was out for hers, and when she slipped her fingertips over her clit, Lauren moaned low in her throat and arched into his thrusts. She didn't need it harder now. It was all perfect as she stroked herself and took his cock inside her.

Now he was the one who needed more. He pushed up on his arms, giving her better access and deepening his thrusts. Lauren smiled in animal triumph. Not that she minded begging, exactly, but she also knew how to take what she wanted.

Jake growled at the sight of her grin, and then he fucked her so hard she almost regretted teasing him. Almost. But instead of regret, she was filled with dark pleasure that pushed her quickly toward another orgasm. She came hard, her muscles clenching around his cock with each spasm. She dug her heels into the bed and pushed up to take him deeper and she felt him stiffen, his body bowing into hers as he grunted past clenched teeth.

They stayed like that for a long moment, bodies still joined, breath tearing from their throats. When she opened her eyes, he looked beautiful above her, the tight muscles of his face relaxing into the same satisfaction she felt.

Finally, he slipped free of her body and collapsed next to her. Lauren stared at the ceiling. Did he feel as shocked as she did? As moved by what they'd done together?

She didn't want to feel unsure with him, so she broke the silence. "How old are you? Forty-six?"

She felt him nod.

"Well, then…that was pretty impressive, Captain. Twice in half an hour?"

The bed shook from his bark of laughter. "Yeah? Well, don't raise your expectations. It's been a while. I was trigger-happy."

"I wouldn't say *that*."

They laughed together, and the uncertainty that had loomed faded away. It felt good with him. Frighteningly good. Until the sweat cooled on her skin and a chill settled over her. "Do you want to get under the covers?"

He took care of the condom and met her under the comforter, and while she was still trying to decide if she should snuggle close or not, he lay snug next to her and wrapped his hand around hers, making her smile. It didn't feel awkward. Maybe she was just too old for awkwardness, but it felt more comfortable than that.

"This is nice," she whispered.

"Nice?" His head turned toward her. "Men consider that a curse, you know."

"Really? What if I said you have a truly gorgeously nice cock?"

Pink rushed to his cheeks. "Oh. I guess that would be okay."

"Because you do. And it made me very happy. As happy as your mouth and your fingers did before. And now just this… It's nice with you, Jake."

He stared at her for a long moment, studying her. "Damn, Lauren," he finally said.

"What?" She tried not to feel anxious. She tried to feel confident. If this was the part where he said it was nice, but it was just sex, and… That would be okay. It wouldn't hurt that much. Wasn't that what she'd tried to frame it as herself?

"I liked you before. And now? Now this is just dangerous."

She swallowed hard and looked away. He was right. It felt comfortable and dangerous at the same time. There were too many levels here. Too much connection. "I thought firefighters liked danger," she whispered.

He touched her chin then, and she had to meet his gaze or she'd be a coward, so Lauren pulled the covers higher and made herself turn toward him. His brown eyes were clear. Honest.

"What do you want from me, Lauren? Whatever you want, I'll try to give you. I wouldn't say I like danger, but I'm willing to run into it if it's worth the risk."

She tried to think. Tried to breathe. She touched his chest, that chest she'd spent years coveting. His heart felt steady now. It thumped slowly under her hand.

"Jake," she whispered, feeling her mouth shape his name, tasting it.

He didn't blink or look away. He watched.

She forced herself to be brave. "I've had a crush on you for a long time."

Now he blinked. "Really?"

"Yes. So if you're asking me what I'd want? What I'd choose? It's this. With you. Only with you. Whenever we want it. I just… I like you. A lot."

She didn't realize she was crying until he brushed a tear from her face.

His eyes smiled at her, even though his mouth was serious. "Are you saying you want me to be your boyfriend, Ms. Foster?"

"I don't know. I can't promise I'll be good at it. I'm not good at this. I'm not—"

"Stop telling me what you're not, Lauren. I know what you are, dammit. Right now. Here. With me."

Turning her head toward the pillow, she desperately tried to hide her tears, but Jake pulled her close and kissed them away. She hated this. It was too much. She couldn't do it. It was…

She took a deep breath. It was *nice*. So damn nice.

"Whatever you want," she said back to him. "I'm willing to try. With you."

CHAPTER EIGHT

LAUREN SLIPPED ON her sunglasses and settled onto the metal bench that sat a few feet from the back door of the library. She didn't exactly need the glasses, as the little clump of aspen at the edge of the parking lot shaded her, but she had other reasons. Other sweaty, bare-chested reasons.

Jake was out there on the basketball court again, mixing it up with the young guys. And God, he looked good doing it.

The scratch marks she'd left on his back the week before must have healed, or he'd never have taken off his shirt. The other firefighters would've razzed him for years about that. Still, Lauren couldn't manage to feel sorry at the idea. She'd liked marking him. And she liked the way he still seemed stunned that she'd want to.

Lauren pulled an apple from her lunch bag and took a bite just as Jake paused to down a bottle of water. He glanced over then, squinting against the sunlight. When he finally realized who was watching, he smiled. Lauren smiled back. Then she caught a drop of apple juice that had slipped down her chin and licked it off her finger.

Even from across the lot, she could see the way his cheeks went red at that. Hopefully he was remembering two nights ago when she'd licked him just that way. Hopefully he was thinking she'd do the same tonight.

She laughed and wiped her chin.

"Hi, Mrs. Foster."

"Oh, Jesus," Lauren yelped, jumping two inches out of her seat as her head jerked toward Annabelle. The girl had an uncanny ability to find Lauren at her least dignified and most perverted.

"Sorry!" Annabelle smiled. "I was just here to see Kevin." She gestured toward the station, seemingly unperturbed by her dad's new girlfriend mouthing obscene gestures in his direction. Hopefully all she'd seen was a woman eating an apple.

But this was the first time Lauren had seen her since two weeks before, when Sophie had caught her in flagrante. Lauren's face was on fire.

"Annabelle," she finally started, then had to swallow and try again. "I feel like I should apologize about that night. I can't imagine what you must think of me. It was…unfortunate. I'm so sorry."

"Mrs. Foster—"

Lauren cut her off, shuddering. "Call me Lauren. Please."

"Lauren," Annabelle corrected herself with a smile. "I'm pleased you're hitting it off so well with my dad."

Lauren tried not to cringe in guilt. She and Jake had been purposefully spending the night at Lauren's house, because Annabelle was still living with him, but it wasn't as if it was that discreet. Annabelle knew full well when her father wasn't home and what that meant.

Taking a deep breath, Lauren told herself they were both middle-aged adults and there was no reason to be embarrassed. But she'd been to this little girl's tenth birthday party. And watched her blow out the candles with her mom's help.

"Thank you, Annabelle," she finally said. "I'm sorry this is all so strange."

"It's not so strange," she said, shaking her head as if Lauren were being silly. "And I was hoping I'd run into you. Here." She handed Lauren an envelope. "An official invitation to the wedding. I'm sure you were going to be my dad's plus-one, but I wanted you to know that I'm looking forward to you being there."

"Oh." Lauren lowered her hand slowly, staring at the linen-textured paper in shock. "Thank you. That's so kind, but…" Jake's whole family would be there. His in-laws. Friends who'd only known him with Ruth. People who would know Lauren wasn't anything like his late wife, wasn't close to good enough.

Somehow, Lauren hadn't really considered that she might be there with him. *With* him. Being introduced as…what?

She was too old to be some man's girlfriend. And she wasn't sure she ever wanted to be a wife. She stared at Jake, back in the game now and rushing past one of his guys to toss the ball at the basket.

"He's been so happy," Annabelle said softly.

Lauren turned to see that she was watching Jake, too.

"Really happy, Lauren." She smiled toward her father. "Ever since that night he brought you home. I mean… He whistles while he's cooking. I hadn't even realized he'd stopped, but as soon as I heard it again, it was so obvious that the house had been quiet. So thank you. I mean it. And I hope I'll see you at the wedding."

She walked off with a happy wave, while Lauren still sat in stunned silence, her mouth parted and heart pounding.

It was all nice with Jake. Even what could have been an awkward relationship with his daughter was going to be nice. And in that moment, Lauren realized that she'd planned on being alone for the rest of her life. Somehow over the past few years, she'd settled on that for herself. She'd been satisfied with it. Even pleased. But it wasn't going to happen that way at all.

It didn't matter what Jake called her. It didn't matter what Lauren said or how much it scared her. Because she loved him. Already.

And she was so wrong for him.

And he was *happy*.

It was dangerous, just as he'd said, but it was a danger worth running into. And she was going to risk it all.

* * * * *

JULIE PLEC

From the creator of *The Originals*, the hit spin-off television show of *The Vampire Diaries*, come three never-before-released prequel stories featuring the Original vampire family, set in 18th century New Orleans.

Available now!   Coming March 31!   Coming May 26!

Family is power. The Original vampire family swore it to each other a thousand years ago. They pledged to remain together always and forever. But even when you're immortal, promises are hard to keep.

Pick up your copies and visit
www.TheOriginalsBooks.com
to discover more!

Discover four incredible stories from the biggest names in romance...

Pick up your copy today!

Be sure to connect with us at:

Harlequin.com/Newsletters
Facebook.com/HarlequinBooks
Twitter.com/HarlequinBooks

www.HQNBooks.com

PHMFSA947

VICTORIA DAHL

77861	LOOKING FOR TROUBLE	___ $7.99 U.S.	___ $8.99 CAN.
77789	SO TOUGH TO TAME	___ $7.99 U.S.	___ $8.99 CAN.
77746	TOO HOT TO HANDLE	___ $7.99 U.S.	___ $9.99 CAN.
77688	CLOSE ENOUGH TO TOUCH	___ $7.99 U.S.	___ $9.99 CAN.
77602	BAD BOYS DO	___ $7.99 U.S.	___ $9.99 CAN.
77595	GOOD GIRLS DON'T	___ $7.99 U.S.	___ $9.99 CAN.

(limited quantities available)

TOTAL AMOUNT	$ _____
POSTAGE & HANDLING	$ _____
($1.00 FOR 1 BOOK, 50¢ for each additional)	
APPLICABLE TAXES*	$ _____
TOTAL PAYABLE	$ _____

(check or money order—please do not send cash)

To order, complete this form and send it, along with a check or money order for the total above, payable to Harlequin HQN, to: **In the U.S.** 3010 Walden Avenue, P.O. Box 9077, Buffalo, NY 14269-9077; **In Canada:** P.O. Box 636, Fort Erie, Ontario, L2A 5X3.

Name: _____
Address: _____ City: _____
State/Prov.: _____ Zip/Postal Code: _____
Account Number (if applicable): _____

075 CSAS

*New York residents remit applicable sales taxes.
*Canadian residents remit applicable GST and provincial taxes.

HQN™

www.HQNBooks.com

PHVD0215BI